Second Chance Bird

RING OF FIRE PRESS TITLES.

Arrested Development
As Ye Have Done It Unto one of the Least
Bartley's Man
Blood in Erfurt
Essen Defiant
Essen Steel
Gloom Despair and Agony on You
Incident in Alaska Prefecture
Joseph Hanauer
Letters Home
Love and Chemistry
Medicine and Disease after the Ring of Fire
Muse of Music
No ship for Tranquebar
Second Chance Bird
Storm Signals
The Battle for Newfoundland
The Danish Scheme
The Demons of Paris
The Evening of the Day
The Heirloom
The Play's the Thing
The Society of Saint Philip of the Screwdriver
Turn Your Radio On

Second Chance Bird

By

Garrett W. Vance

Published by Eric Flint's Ring of Fire Press
Copyright © 201? by Garrett W. Vance
ISBN: 1980843074
ISBN-13: 9781980843078

All rights reserved. No part of this book may be reproduced or transmitted in any form or by any electronic or mechanical means, including photocopying, recording or by any information storage and retrieval system, without the express written permission of the copyright holder, except where permitted by law. This novel is a work of fiction. Names, characters, places and incidents are either the product of the author's imagination, or, if real, used fictitiously.

Eric Flint's Ring of Fire Press handles DRM Digital Rights Management simply: We trust in the *Honor* of our readers.

Cover Art by: Laura Givens

Author's Note: The following is revised from the version originally serialized in the Grantville Gazette

Contents

Chapter One: Dodo Story	1
Chapter Two: Personal Affairs	39
Chapter Three: Out the Door	47
Chapter Four: Out to Sea	55
Chapter Five: Getting to Know You	65
Chapter Six: Salt Tears and Sea Legs	75
Chapter Seven: Under Southern Skies	81
Chapter Eight: Sacrifice	89
Chapter Nine: *Redbird* Down	95
Chapter Ten: On the Beach	105
Chapter Eleven: The Flood May Bear Me Far	111
Chapter Twelve: *Redbird*'s Last Gifts	121
Chapter Thirteen: Crazy for Coconuts!	127
Chapter Fourteen: Keeping Busy with Bamboo	131
Chapter Fifteen: *I'm No Darwin*	135
Chapter Sixteen: Gerbald, Dinosaur Hunter	137
Chapter Seventeen: Pam's Pot o' Gold	143
Chapter Eighteen: Birdwatching	147
Chapter Nineteen: Dodo Do's and Don'ts	151
Chapter Twenty: Strangers Come to Call	165
Chapter Twenty-One: Pam Hatches a Plan	169
Chapter Twenty-Two: Harlot Dancers	175
Chapter Twenty-Three: Boarding Party	187
Chapter Twenty-Four: The Prize	197
Chapter Twenty-Five: Breakfast of Champions	201
Chapter Twenty-Six: Ups and Downs	207
Chapter Twenty-Seven: Farewells and Beginnings	217

Chapter Twenty-Eight: The Last Day Of Camp	225
Chapter Twenty-Nine: An Unexpected Promotion	229
Chapter Thirty: Galley of Celestial Delights	235
Chapter Thirty-One: One Man's Junk is Another's Treasure	241
Chapter Thirty-Two: Counting their Blessings	251
Chapter Thirty-Three: The Captain's Ball	257
Chapter Thirty-Four: Anchors Aweigh	269
Chapter Thirty-Five: Smoke on the Water	275
Chapter Thirty-Six: Contact	279
Chapter Thirty-Seven: Hair Today, Gone Tomorrow	287
Chapter Thirty-Eight: Man Down	291
Chapter Thirty-Nine: A Ruse By Any Other Name	297
Chapter Forty: All Hell Breaks Loose	307
Chapter Forty-One: Victory Lap	323
Chapter Forty-Two: There's Got To Be A Morning After	327
Chapter Forty-Three: A Kiss And Some Coffee	333
Chapter Forty-Four: A Private Consultation	339
Chapter Forty-Five: Therapy Session	347
Chapter Forty-Six : Twilight and Evening Bell	351
Chapter Forty-Seven : A Mysterious Figure	357
Chapter Forty-Eight: A Bit of Exercise	363
Chapter Forty-Nine: Looking Glass	373
Chapter Fifty: The Ones That Got Away	375
Chapter Fifty-One: Welcome to Wonderland	379
Chapter Fifty-Two: The Ships Come In	383
Chapter Fifty-Three: Time Flies	395
Chapter Fifty-Four: Precious Cargo	401
Chapter Fifty-Five: Mission Accomplished	407

∞ ∞ ∞

Second Chance Bird

Chapter One: Dodo Story

Cair Paravel, Grantville, Early Spring 1635

They were on holiday, enjoying the warmest day of the year yet on the broad back porch of the rambling old house named after a castle in Narnia. Princess Kristina's Swedish guards were invited to have a glass or two of lemonade, for which they thanked her profusely before becoming part of the backyard scenery again. It was story time; the young girl sat in rapt attention as her friend and sometimes supervisor Caroline Platzer read aloud in the comfortable twang of up-time English. The book was Lewis Carroll's *Alice's Adventures in Wonderland*, and the princess, at a most precocious nine years old, could certainly have read it for herself, but it was much more fun to listen to Caroline, especially since she used funny voices for many of the characters.

The denizens of Wonderland had just run a "caucus race" (in which everyone runs but no one wins), and Alice had finished awarding prizes to all the participants when the Mouse pointed out that Alice herself had not received one.

" 'Of course,' the Dodo,' " whom Caroline chose to characterize with a Foghorn Leghorn old-time southern drawl, "*replied very gravely. 'What else have you got in your pocket?' he went on, turning to Alice.*

"*'Only a thimble,' said Alice sadly.'*" Caroline wondered if Kristina was aware that she always tried to read the part of Alice in her best imitation of the princess herself.

"*'Hand it over here,' said the Dodo.*

"*'Then they all crowded round her once more, while the Dodo solemnly presented the thimble, saying 'We beg your acceptance of this elegant thimble'; and, when it had finished this short speech, they all cheered.'*"

Kristina laughed. "But her prize was something that already belonged to her, Caroline!"

"I think it was the spirit of the thing that mattered; finishing the ceremony correctly whether it made any sense or not."

Kristina nodded, being well aware of the importance of ceremonies, as well as their tendency to be illogical. She was required to attend many such in her capacity as princess, and usually found them to be a dreadful bore. Kristina was also aware that although Alice's adventures were written as a children's story they often contained satires of adult activities, even if she wasn't always quite sure which they referred to. Getting a prize that already belonged to you seemed quite in keeping with the general silliness she had witnessed in royal doings. Before Caroline could begin reading again, Kristina asked, "Caroline, just what *is* a dodo?"

"It was a kind of bird. Here, in the illustration." Caroline turned the book around, a hardcover that had come through the Ring of Fire, to show Kristina the original John Tenniel illustration from the now never-to-be Victorian Age.

"What a strange looking bird! Are dodos a real animal or a make believe one?"

"Actually, dodos were real, although they did look pretty weird." Caroline saw something flash in Kristina's large and liquid brown eyes.

"What do you mean 'were'?" Kristina handed the book back to Caroline with a tremendously serious look on her young face.

The princess could be very sensitive and Caroline knew the sad story of the dodo's demise would not go over well. She also knew it was much better to level with Kristina, than face the consequences of getting caught in a lie, even a white one, later. The girl was truly a prodigy, *scary* smart just like her father, the emperor.

"Well, there aren't any more dodos, Kristina. They're all extinct."

"Like the dinosaurs?"

"Yes, well, kind of. No one is completely sure how the dinosaurs died out, but we do know what happened to the dodos . . ." Caroline saw a shadow cross those great, dark eyes, so much more aware than other children her age.

Kristina pursed her lips and blew out a thin puff of disgust. "I suppose it was *people* then."

Caroline nodded solemnly. "I'm afraid so. From what I recall they lived on a small island with no dangerous animals to eat them. They had never seen humans before and didn't know that they should run away. I think hungry sailors ate them all. By my time, the dodo had become a symbol for endangered species, a reminder of our responsibility to protect animals."

"That's just not fair! They didn't even know they were in danger! Why didn't anyone try to stop those sailors from eating them all?"

"I don't know, Kristina. It was a very long time ago."

Kristina's eyebrow's arched. "*How* long ago did the last dodos die, Caroline?"

Caroline felt a brief shiver; the small town normalness of quiet backyards and shady porches during this springtime visit to Grantville tended to make her almost forget. *How long ago indeed?* She sat frozen there, with her mouth partially open while the princess' eyes narrowed, lightning-quick thought working behind them.

"The library," Kristina announced. She jumped up and ran into the house so fast she left behind a breezy wake to gently riffle the pages of *Wonderland.*

Caroline closed the book. She looked up unto the crystal clear blue of the seventeenth-century sky.

"How long ago?" Caroline whispered, caught up in the princess' excitement herself now, goose bumps forming on her arms. "Or, *when*?"

She followed Kristina into the converted sitting room that served as Cair Paravel's library, where Kristina stood on a step stool with her nose deep in an up-time encyclopedia, eyes focused in careful study. At last she looked up at Caroline, her cheeks flushed with excitement, her voice tense.

"We still have time."

Pam Miller's House, Grantville

Thorsten Engler surveyed the wide, sloping front yard from the street, wondering if there was indeed a house somewhere up there, behind all the gigantic, yellow flowers; either some strange, early-blooming up-time variety, or the product of magic. He found the narrow concrete walk, almost a tunnel, and started up it. A breeze rustled the bright green stalks that stood nearly as tall himself, the dinner-plate-sized flower heads, with their still unripe seed pod faces, and bright yellow petals, seemed to nod at him in greeting. He had never seen anything like them before, and mused that he had perhaps really wandered into one of the princess' fairy tales.

At last, he reached a funny-looking little pink house, a rectangular box with a door, a curtained picture window, and a concrete front porch. The sight of a porcelain garden gnome lurking under a bush below the window actually made him jump; he wouldn't have been surprised if it had doffed his hat to him in such odd surrounds. He pushed the tiny doorbell button and heard electric chimes sound within.

Shortly, the door opened to reveal a middle-aged woman wearing a green sweatshirt blotched with a rainbow splatter of paint, faded blue jeans, and muddy boots. Her age might have been anywhere between mid-thirties to mid-forties, it was always so hard to tell with up-timer women. In any case, she appeared to be very physically fit. She wasn't exactly pretty, but she wasn't unattractive, either. She had a broad, serious face colored in the ruddy tan of someone who spent a lot of time outdoors. Her unruly, dishwater-blonde hair was pulled back in a no-nonsense ponytail, the hairstyle showing off her best feature; steel gray eyes with flecks of a winter sky's blue. They were the eyes of a keen observer, like a soldier's eyes, and as a soldier himself Thorsten recognized their power.

"Yes?" she asked. Her alto voice was polite, but by no means filled with patience.

"Pardon me for bothering you, ma'am," Thorsten replied in the West Virginia style English he had been practicing. "Are you Miss Pam Miller?"

"That's *Ms.* Miller, and, if you're here because your church, school, barn or castle has a bat infestation, you are out of luck. I am *not* in the bat removal business, never was!" She began to close the door, so Thorsten had to talk fast.

"Please, wait! I am not here about bats, ma'am, er, Ms. Miller. I am Thorsten Engler, the, uh, Count of Narnia." How he had gone from being a simple soldier to a count was a chain of events that still amazed Thorsten, and he wasn't sure he would ever be comfortable with the title. This was made worse by the suspicious look Pam Miller regarded him with.

"The count of *what?*" Those eyes could freeze a pond in summer, if they chose to.

"The *Count of Narnia*, ma'am. The district used to be called Nutschall, but Princess Kristina had it renamed to honor her favorite children's stories. Actually, I'm here at her request, as her representative." Thorsten found himself feeling flustered, there was something formidable about this woman.

"Here at the princess' request, huh? Well, these days who knows what the hell might happen next? Come on in then, *Count of Narnia*, but if you brought any satyrs or talking hedgehogs with you, they are going to have to wait outside." She motioned for him to follow her into the house, stomping ahead of him in her muddy boots.

Thorsten entered a space that might have once been a twentieth-century living room. All that could be seen of that former role was a lumpy old sofa along one wall. The rest of the space was filled with art supplies and a hodgepodge of canvases featuring works in various stages of completion. The floor was completely covered in paint-stained drop cloths. Apparently the artist was going through a "birds" period. Thorsten thought the drawings and paintings of avian life were quite realistic. He noticed a large, hand-painted poster of a black-and-orange songbird he had never seen before. Its uneven lettering proclaimed "Don't Shoot, I'm an American!" Obviously the work of a child rather than the house's artist, but still quite well done. On an incredibly cluttered desk he saw a hand-printed manuscript titled *Birds of the USE*.

"So, it appears I have come to the right place. You must indeed be the celebrated 'Bird Lady' of Grantville!"

At this Pam Miller gave him a perfectly murderous look.

"I beg your pardon, ma'am, but you *are* the Pam Miller who is working with the school system to promote the protection of wildlife, particularly birds . . . are you not?"

The fierce-looking woman softened her gaze somewhat. "Yeah, that's me. Is the princess interested in joining our summer birdwatching and nature program?"

"Well, perhaps she would be. The princess is interested in just about everything; she is an exceptionally bright young person. Actually, she has sent me here to invite you to visit her at her Grantville residence. She has a project related to the protection of a certain bird species that she wishes to consult with you on."

"What species?"

"I am sorry, but the princess prefers to tell you herself and has instructed me rather strongly not to 'spill the beans.' "

Pam Miller's eyebrows rose. "Well, I do love a mystery. All right then, I'm game. Never thought I'd be consulted by a princess." A hint of a smile appeared on her stony face.

"I know the feeling," Thorsten confided with a cautious grin.

"Well," Pam declared, "no time like the present."

Pam asked Thorsten to wait on the porch for a moment as she gathered her bag and walking stick. She mumbled to herself as she ran a hand through escaped strands of her unruly hair.

"Meet the princess, huh?" Pam muttered to herself as she changed her top. "Sometimes down-time is like living in a magical kingdom that reeks of manure." She emerged a few minutes later with the same well-worn jeans and mud-caked boots on, but she had changed into a clean sweatshirt and denim jacket, Grantvillers being just as casual about a royal audience as they were everything else.

Thorsten, as a professional soldier, was impressed with the woman's pace as they walked quickly across town. He was pretty sure she could last all day in a forced march. They arrived at an ornately decorated old mansion, one of the town's "painted ladies," occupying a spacious, fenced garden that took up at least half a block. It had been repainted in bright blue with yellow trim, the Swedish colors, and the front gate boasted an arch with a sign proclaiming *Cair Paravel* in a fanciful, gold-inlaid script.

Pam rolled her eyes at this bit of princessy excess but secretly thought it was kind of charming, too. *Gawd, I'm going to meet a princess in Narnia. Wonder if they have a talking lion?* Pam made her face straight as they neared the gate.

There were several USE soldiers bearing shotguns standing guard, they nodded politely at her and one of them, a high school friend of her son Walt, greeted her with a hearty "Howdy, Ms. Miller! Welcome to the castle." She couldn't recall his name right then so she just said "Hi!" and gave him a friendly smile in lieu of any small talk as he unlocked the gate for her.

At the top of the stairs a woman dressed in casual up-time clothes met them. Thorsten introduced her as his fiancé, Caroline Platzer.

Caroline shook Pam's hand. "Thank you for coming, Ms. Miller. Princess Kristina is very excited about meeting you. She's recently developed a keen interest in birds."

"Well, that's good to hear. I've been promoting youth birding with the school district, perhaps she would like to join us sometime?" *THAT would be some good PR for the summer nature program . . .* Pam knew from the news that the princess had achieved great popularity in Grantville as well as throughout the odd, patchwork version of Germany they had become a part of, an impressive feat.

"I'll bet she would!" Caroline kept Pam's hand a moment longer to catch Pam's eye. "Ms. Miller, I should say that the princess has a *very* keen interest, *intense* actually. Kristina is an extremely intelligent and kindhearted girl. She is also a princess, and so can be a bit demanding at times, although we are working on that. But I assure you, she means well! I do hope that you will be understanding."

"I'll keep that in mind. I've worked with kids quite a bit lately and raised one, too. Ms Platzer, are you the princess' teacher?"

"Do call me Caroline. Well, I'm kind of her cultural adviser, but mainly I'm her friend, and temporary governess on this visit. Her regular governess, Lady Ulrike, is on vacation." Pam could infer from the weight placed on that last word that said vacation might have been well earned, and much needed. Pam blew back a wisp of hair that had come loose from her ponytail. She followed Caroline through the house to its library, thinking *Good lord, I hope this kid isn't a royal monster. What am I doing here?* She had met some royal types over the last couple of years and generally couldn't stand them.

"Princess Kristina, Pam Miller is here." Caroline announced as they entered a large, book cluttered room that also featured an impressive variety of Brillo the Ram memorabilia. Pam was something of a Brillo fan herself. *At least she has good taste.*

Pam had expected to be confronted by a pretty little spoiled brat dressed in fluffy pink princess gowns, and diamond-studded tiara. Instead, she found herself looking at . . . a kid. A rather gawky one, at that.

The princess wore white jeans, a Power Puff Girls T-shirt and a West Virginia Mountaineers baseball cap that strained to hold back a cascade of flyaway brown hair. She looked more like a playground tomboy than a prissy princess, and her hawkish nose and huge brown eyes were several sizes too large for a thin face that hadn't yet grown into them.

"You're here! Thanks for coming! I'm Kristina!" The princess marched enthusiastically over to Pam and stuck out her hand to shake. Pam took it a bit hesitantly. The princess had a strong grip for such a frail-looking kid and there were even some calluses on that palm.

"Pam Miller."

"May I call you Pam?" There was a slight accent but, the princess was obviously comfortable with English.

"Uh, sure. So, I hear you are interested in birds, Princess."

"I am! I have heard about you from some of the kids at the school I know. I also quite supported your motion to move the American redbird as the USE's symbolic bird from unofficial status to official. I am quite tired of eagles. I think the new American birds are wonderful!"

"Apparently you do your homework, Princess."

"Pam, you *can* call me Kristina."

"I think Princess will do, for now." Pam's expression was politely impassive.

The princess looked a little taken aback by that, which was a good thing as far as Pam was concerned. She had been working with school children in the nature education program she had started, and although she was more comfortable than she used to be, she felt a need to keep them at a certain distance; especially those who obviously wanted to be treated as adults. *That, you have to earn, kid.* Pam's sixth sense told her she was going to be pressed into service somehow, so she was wary. Pam could be more than a little shy, and she guarded her privacy fiercely.

The princess smiled a bit thinly, and started again. "Please forgive me. I sometimes get a little excitable, or so I am told." That was said with a glance at Caroline, who responded by taking a close interest in the bookshelves. "Let's sit down and have a cup of tea, and I will explain why I've asked you here."

Pam nodded in what she really hoped was a gracious sort of way, and followed the princess to a table in the center of the room. A servant appeared from nowhere with the tea. Pam noted that Kristina thanked the servant, which spoke well of the child. Thorsten excused himself from the proceedings, and she saw Caroline roll her eyes as he made a hasty exit.

"Once a soldier, always a soldier," she said shaking her head with a mix of exasperation and affection. "My darling Thorsten is not much for tea time. He's going to go chew the fat with the guards."

"The men do love to shoot the shit," Kristina commented, eying Caroline to see her reaction. Pam couldn't help but let out a small laugh.

"Just because Lady Ulrike isn't here, don't think you can get away with murder, my dear," Caroline responded, favoring the princess with a crocodile smile. The princess flushed slightly, but still grinned at Pam, whom she had seen laugh at her little flirtation with adult language. *Darn it all,* Pam thought, *maybe I'm going to like this oddball princess. She sure isn't acting much like Snow White so far.*

Having had a sip of tea, Kristina focused on Pam with her enormous, soulful eyes. "Please allow me to cut to the chase, Pam. I want to consult with you on a very important matter concerning an endangered species."

Pam's eyebrows rose again, she had thought she might be here to supervise the building of a bird feeder, or to tend an injured chick fallen from a nest. She was also impressed with the kid's vocabulary, the sign of an avid reader. "What species might that be?"

The princess produced her copy of *Alice's Adventures in Wonderland*, opening it to the page of the caucus race.

"The dodo," she said with the breathy drama of a nine-year-old revealing a newly discovered wonder to her friends.

Pam studied the line drawing; the odd beak that stretched all the way to the back of the head in a long, skeptical scowl above which saucer-like eyes were mounted in bony turrets, looking more like some helmeted dinosaur than a bird. She shook her head sadly. "I'm sorry, Princess, but the dodo is extinct. There aren't any left."

Caroline looked as if she was about to speak but the princess gave her a quick glance that said *please, let me.* Caroline got the message, contenting herself with smiling encouragingly. Kristina went on. "So I have heard. And just when did that happen?"

Pam thought of her copy of *Birds of the World* and the sad little chapter in the back that detailed the loss of the passenger pigeon and the Carolina parakeet. The dodo was there, too, of course, a creature of remote islands, one that didn't have the sense to avoid hungry sailors. Pam had hated reading about such extinctions since she was a kid, the subject was sure to make her feel depressed. She started to answer, "Why, that was sometime in the seven . . ." and stopped. A bewildered expression came to her face. She looked at Caroline who was nodding knowingly, and the princess whose eyes were bright with excitement. Pam continued in a very small voice "The seventeenth century. No, you have got to be kidding me. The *dodo*? The dodo is still . . ." Her words trailed away into air as she stared at the picture.

"Alive." the princess finished for her. "At least we think so. There is not a great deal of information available in either the up-time or down-time books I've been able to find so far, but the last sighting was reported in the 1660's. That's some thirty years from now."

Pam felt the world spinning under her chair, her hands gripped the side of the table. *The dodo!* The charmingly strange bird she would never get to see because people had killed them all in her former time-line. They were still thirty years ahead of that tragedy.

"It took me a while to get used to it, too," Caroline remarked. "The world's most famous extinct animal next to the dinosaurs is still alive right now."

"And we must keep it that way!" Kristina announced fervently. "The dodo *must* be saved!"

Pam blew out a long sigh of air. "You know, the worst thing is, why the hell didn't *I* think of it myself? I've been so busy trying to protect the wildlife around here that I haven't even taken one minute to think globally. Or, for that matter, temporally." She looked a bit dazed by the news.

Caroline said, "Everyone who came through the Ring of Fire is still, to some extent, in a state of shock. We may never be able to adjust one-hundred percent. There are so many possibilities, chances to change history, but we are just a bunch of normal people dropped into extraordinary circumstances. Don't be too hard on yourself."

Caroline was right, there were times Pam felt as if she would never really be completely comfortable here in the past. She looked at the princess, whose face was a study of earnest determination.

"Okay, Princess, how do you intend to save the dodo?"

"I want to send a rescue mission. Bring enough for a breeding population back to Europe where we can keep them in a sanctuary. I've been studying up-time zoos and I am sure it can be done."

"Wow, that sounds really great but it's a massive undertaking. How will you finance it?"

The princess smiled cheerfully. "Well, I *am* a princess. I have access to certain funds, even at my current age, and I know *a lot* of people. And, of course, I intend to ask my papa for his support."

Pam looked at Caroline.

"You can't get much more connected," the woman answered.

Pam studied the princess from across the table for a moment. This was the daughter of the man who ruled a huge swath of Europe, including their little circle of America, and who seemed bent on increasing that real estate. From what she had seen of Gustav he was probably a pretty good guy, the "Captain-General" who had saved a bunch of schoolkids, including her own son from the Croat raiders, a real hero. Even so, it seemed unlikely that he would put much backing into something as outlandish as what the princess proposed, especially with the situation on the continent still so volatile. On the other hand, grown men often go to amazing lengths to please their darling daughters. So far, the princess had demonstrated that while she might not be a spoiled brat, she *was* adept at getting her way.

"Say you can get your father, the *emperor*, to agree to this. What do you want from me?"

"Why, to lead the expedition of course!" Those giant brown eyes were not blinking.

"What? Me? Why me?"

"Because you are a bird expert. As far as I know you are the *only* bird expert Grantville has."

"I'm no expert. I'm just a birdwatcher."

"You have identified, studied and cataloged every species of bird that survived the trip through the Ring of Fire that has established breeding populations here. You have done the same for every native bird species in a fifty-mile radius. You have led a very successful nature education program with an emphasis on conservation. You are an experienced hiker and outdoors-person, trained by a retired *jaeger* from what I understand. You are currently writing a book called *Birds of the USE* that you intend as both a field guide and behavioral study of every species in the country. In addition, you are working as a scientist in the Grantville Research Institute sponsored laboratory testing program, and have extensive up-time training in the scientific method. I have no doubt that there is no one more qualified than you."

It was obvious the princess had been practicing that little speech. The kid was one smart cookie, and scarily organized. Pam rubbed her temples, her mind racing. Lead an expedition? Impossible! She had too much work to do, she couldn't possibly! She looked down at the open book on the table to see the dodo handing Alice a thimble. For most of her life she had felt sad when looking at any painting of the dodo, a pathetic creature that was obliterated by human carelessness. It had made her sad, and angry. But now . . .

"Damn it all," she muttered beneath her breath. The princess and Caroline waited expectantly. "Damn it all! She said louder, frustration in her voice. "Just what island does the dodo live on? Is it near Europe?"

Caroline fielded this one. "No, I'm afraid not, Pam. It's Mauritius, the largest in a group of islands called the Mascarenes, lying some distance off the coast of eastern Africa, in the Indian Ocean. It also seems that there is another dodo species on Rodriguez, but this is a bit unclear."

"Africa!" Pam's voice held a note of laughing hysteria. "All the way around the horn of Africa? Of course! It couldn't be the Canary Islands, or in the Mediterranean, could it?" *The dodo is still alive, I could see one, I could save them* . . . Pam's mind whirled, trying to grasp this new reality.

Kristina and Caroline were beginning to look worried. Pam's hands had developed a slight quiver. A tremble entered her voice when she spoke again. "Look, this is all just too much to swallow in one gulp. I've got to be honest with you two. I am still getting used to the idea that Germany is just a few hills over from my American house, and not the nice, clean, modern Germany that produces fine machinery and has an autobahn, either. I feel like I'm in some old movie half the time! Asking me to leave Grantville to sail around Africa in a ship of the day, which has got to be damn dangerous, is an awful lot."

The princess looked down at her tea, crestfallen. "I'm sorry Pam, it's just that you are the only person we thought of who might . . . *care* about this."

Pam touched a hand to her forehead, her fingers kneading out the stress building there. "Well, you were right. I *do* care. And now I have to figure out if I can even say *no* to this crazy plan of yours. Saving the dodo, yeah, that's something important. Look, I have to think about it, give me a little time, okay?" This made the princess look hopeful again.

Pam stood up. "Thanks for the tea, Princess. I'll give you a call when I've made my decision, maybe in a couple of days." Caroline and Kristina both stood up as well.

Kristina went around the table to look up at Pam's rather pale face. "You're right, Pam. It will be dangerous, although I promise we'll do whatever we can to make it safe for you. I will send my very best men with you, they will protect you through any danger. I assure you, I am serious about this, and can make it happen. I am confident in this."

Pam managed a small smile. "I believe that you are, Princess. I just don't know if I'm up to it. Talk to you soon. Caroline. Princess." She made a small bow to the two of them, then hurried out of the room.

∞ ∞ ∞

That night Pam sat in her favorite spot at her writing desk looking out the window at her backyard's big birdfeeder. It was evening, and there wasn't much action, just a couple of blue jays having an argument while gobbling sunflower seeds. This was one of the species that had come through the Ring of Fire with Grantville that was proving highly successful. The gray-and-orange Eurasian jays were still around, but the blue jays were more aggressive, and tended to bully them at the feeder. Pam was barely paying attention to their noisy antics.

There was only one bird on her mind tonight, and it was thousands of miles away on an obscure island in the Indian Ocean. It was a bird she never thought she would see in her lifetime, unless some genius managed to clone it back from the dead. But, *that* was a different lifetime. In this time, the dodo was still alive, and she could prevent the catastrophe that had made it the symbol of modern extinction. Pam poured a healthy splash of *kirschwasser* into a shot glass; the cherry-flavored liquor would help calm her nerves.

Up-time, the farthest she had ever been from home was Vancouver, Canada out on the west coast, and a brief holiday in the Bahamas. Those were also the only foreign countries she'd ever visited, and hardly exotic. Now she was contemplating a long and dangerous sea voyage from Europe to the far side of Africa. A voyage that would give her the chance to do something wonderful, something she dreamed of in her youth: The chance to save the dodo. If she survived it.

A small voice in her head chided her; *what makes you think you can pull it off? You're just a frumpy small town divorcée. You're no Charles Darwin!* Pam scowled into her glass, sloshing the red liquid around. That was the old Pam Miller talking. The Pam Miller of that other life where she had been pretty much a nobody. Her marriage had failed, and her adult son was only now just beginning to talk to her again, the result of his new bride's insistence more than any desire on his part.

Still, that was something. In some ways, things really were better now. The one thing she had been good at in that other life was her job. She was a damn good researcher and was highly regarded for her skills, although never really popular socially. That was better now, too. Here, her abilities mattered a lot more. The projects she was working on for the Research Institute were helping keep Grantville alive in this new time. She was well respected by her peers, and had even tentatively made a few friends there. At least they didn't forget to invite her to the office parties any more.

Pam looked up to see herself reflected in the window as darkness fell. She was older, thinner, and most definitely tougher. God, how had she been such a marshmallow? Was this woman in the glass really her? Pam smiled as she brought the shot glass to her lips. This was a new life. There were new chances available. She had changed going through that Ring of Fire. It had tempered her into something harder. She had crushed a man's jaw with her grandmother's walking stick to save a friend's life, a fighting man, a dangerous man. She had found the courage. The old Pam of the year 2000 would have melted into a blubbering mass of goo in the face of such danger. Not *this* Pam, not anymore.

She got up from her chair to stalk around the living room, no, her *art studio and office*, looking at the evidence of her accomplishments. Thanks in part to her efforts, blue jays, Baltimore orioles, hummingbirds, and many other North American bird species were establishing themselves in Europe. Her favorite of them all, the bright-red eastern cardinal, now went by the colloquial moniker 'redbird' that her grandmother had used when Pam was a little girl. Redbird translated well into German as *rotvogel*, and didn't have any religious connotations. It had been the official bird of the state of West Virginia back up-time, and was now in use again as such in West Virginia County, here in the great State of Thuringia-Franconia, United States of Europe. Its survival here had helped Pam adjust to her new life in this century more than anything else, except perhaps the close friends she had made among the Germans.

Seeing the up-time birds that had come through the event with them thrive had inspired Pam to go to work raising public awareness about protecting native European species along with the up-time immigrants. Through her school programs, she was fostering a love of nature in the youth of Grantville that she hoped would spread throughout this new country as time went on.

But, would it spread fast enough? The fires of industry were burning bright, and she feared they would scorch this new version of planet Earth into an ugly cinder, just as they had the forests and plains of the up-time world. And, that process was starting earlier. If nothing were done about *that*, saving the dodo would be meaningless. She sat back down.

You need to be smart. Think this through. This morning when she woke up, she was a woman who had become well known, and fairly well regarded in the local community: "The Bird Lady of Grantville." At one time that nickname would have flooded her with embarrassment, but now she had come to realize she *liked it*. People actually *liked her*, and her "Save the Birds" campaign was succeeding in over a hundred-mile radius. So, she knew people now, and they listened to her, but when she wrote letters to the *national government* regarding conservation initiatives, all she got in return were official form letters thanking her for her input.

She had even considered taking the train up to Magdeburg, and giving that cock of the rock Mike Stearns a good old-fashioned talking to in person regarding his new country's complete lack of an environmental protection policy. He might even listen to her . . . Pam gripped the arms of her chair. The thought that had been forming in the back of her mind ever since her visit to Cair Paravel this morning pushed its way to the front and took shape.

Who does Mike Stearns listen to? That would be King Gustavus II Adolphus, the high king of the Union of Kalmar, the emperor of the United States of Europe, the Captain-General who earned his place as a folk hero in their little circle of West Virginia. Mister fast-talking union man listened to *that* guy, their lives depended on it. And, *who* did Gustavus Adolphus listen to? Who had the emperor's ear? A small smile came to Pam's face. She knew one person who would have that ear, and that person wanted something from Pam Miller, wanted it badly. Pam tossed down the rest of the *kirschwasser* and decided it was best just to sleep on it.

∞ ∞ ∞

Pam knew it was a dream because she was wearing a child's dress she wouldn't have been caught dead in, even at age seven; a frilly blue-and-white thing of a century that both had, and had not, happened. She stood in Wonderland with the Dodo beside the shore, the other participants of the caucus race having all wandered away. The Dodo regarded her with sad, heavy lidded eyes.

"Are you quite sure you've nothing else in your pocket?" it asked in a wistful voice.

Pam found her pocket and reached in. With some surprise her hand closed on something round and heavy. She pulled out what could only be the White Rabbit's pocket watch, and held it up to the Dodo.

"Ah, there's something *I* don't have," said the Dodo. Nodding sadly, it turned away and walked into the lake until its odd-shaped head passed beneath the still, black waters. Pam cried out, and started to wade in after it, but instead woke up thrashing in the sheets like a feverish child.

After regaining her senses, she laid her head back on the pillow, sighed at the morning light coming through what would always to her be the wrong window, and mumbled, "I'm so screwed." It was eight o'clock in the morning, she was on flextime at work, so she hadn't set the alarm. Sighing resignedly at her fate, she reached over to the nightstand to pick up the phone.

∞ ∞ ∞

"Cair Paravel."

"This is Pam Miller. I'd like to speak to Caroline Platzer."

"A moment, please."

"This is Caroline. Pam?"

"Yeah, it's me. Listen, I want to ask you something. In your opinion, is this save the dodo expedition something the princess could really pull off? Would these people she knows, and her father, really listen to her and help make it happen?"

There was a brief pause.

"Well, I can't make any promises, but I believe it's *very* possible. Gustav is, at heart, a pretty nice guy who loves his daughter very much. He dotes on her, as do her many admirers and friends. And, as I think you saw today, the princess is one smart kid, and stubborn, too—just like her father. He knows that, and is definitely grooming her to one day take his place. In any event, he will at least listen to her ideas, and give them serious thought."

"Okay, that's good enough for now. Can I talk to the princess, please?"

"Why, sure. Just a sec." Her voice could be heard turned away from the receiver. "Kristina, Pam Miller is on the phone! She wants to talk to you!" Next came the sound of swiftly running feet on hardwood floors. "Here she is." Pam could hear the smile coming through the phone. Caroline liked her, that was good. A young voice, out of breath came across the line.

"This is Kristina! Hi, Pam, thanks for calling!"

"You're welcome. Listen, I've spent all day thinking about your project, and I'm interested. If you can really make it happen, I'll lead the expedition." Pam heard a shrill shriek of excitement blast from the receiver and held the phone away from her ear until the princess' cheering subsided.

"That's wonderful, Pam, that's really wonderful! I'm so glad you will do it, you are the best person in the world for it!"

"Well, thanks for the vote of confidence. That said, we need to be clear that most of the work needed for this project is going to fall on your young shoulders. I have a pretty important job with the Research Institute, some serious responsibilities, and it's going to take a lot of work on my part to get to a place where I can even think of asking for time off . . . sheesh, it's probably going to take a whole year just to make this trip, isn't it? Anyway, it's going to be *you* and your people are who are going to have to do all the expedition organizing, okay?"

"Okay! I'll take care of all that. I've already talked about it with Ulrik, and some other people I know, and they have promised to help!"

Pam crossed her eyes a bit at the mention of the princess' youthful betrothal. That was an issue she decided was best not to think on too much.

"That's great, whatever it takes. Now for my part, I'm going to do all the necessary research. I need to know everything I possibly can about those islands, and I'm not too confident that Grantville's libraries will have much, so I'll probably have to use down-time sources as well. I'm also going to have to study up on how to transport live animals on a long ship journey. Hopefully that's something up-time science can help improve the odds on. I'm going to be honest with you, Princess, getting from here to there and back again is going to be very complicated. A lot could go wrong, and there is a chance we will fail. Can you handle that?"

"I can handle it. All we can do is our best. I have great confidence that we can save the dodo, Pam, but I do understand the difficulties. I can only promise that I and my people will do our utmost to make it succeed on this end." The princess' nine-year-old excitement had been replaced with the calm voice of a girl much older. That made Pam feel a bit better. Negotiations had been breakfast conversation all of Kristina's young life, and she already knew how to play the game. There were some shrill inner voices in the back of Pam's head telling her she was crazy, but she would have to deal with them later. For now, she focused on the princess.

"That reassures me greatly. Now listen, saving the dodo is very important, but it's just one corner of a very big picture. I want you to understand how and why tragedies like the dodo extinction happen in the first place. Are you willing to do some reading?"

"Of course! I enjoy reading anyway. I'll read whatever you ask me to."

"That's good to hear. Have you got a pen handy? Yes? Okay, write down these keywords: *Extinction, pollution, deforestation,* and *habitat destruction.*" Pam only had to spell out a couple of those terms, Kristina's skills in her second language were nothing short of amazing for one so young. "Go to the library and see what you can find. You don't have to read everything in detail, just try to get the main ideas. When you have, call me back and we'll go from there. All right?"

"Gotcha. Will do, Pam," Kristina agreed readily.

Pam mused that she was on the phone with a new kind of person, a child of the most powerful European royalty in the current century influenced and educated by Americans from the future. What might this eager young girl accomplish as she matured? For just a moment, Pam felt a little guilty at the rather unpleasant educational course she was sending the kid on, but it was for the best. Pam had never believed in hiding the truth from children. Better they find distressing things out in their youth, so they can be better prepared to face them as adults. Kristina would have to see that big picture, the sooner she did, the sooner she could use her influence to prevent the worst from happening in this time. If they were going to save the dodo, they had to start in their own backyard.

"Okay, Princess, do your homework and I'll look forward to hearing what you have to say about it. Good night."

"Good night, Pam. And thanks, I really appreciate your getting involved! Thank you!" The line clicked off.

Pam put the phone down. "I hope you still feel that way tomorrow," she whispered.

∞ ∞ ∞

The princess looked awful. The more she read, the worse she looked. Her assortment of ladies-in-waiting clucked their concern and disapproval in the quiet of the town library, but stayed in their seats, cowed by Caroline's cool gaze. Caroline was concerned, too, but she knew the princess had to see this course of study that Pam Miller had laid out for her through. She, herself, was somewhat irritated at the woman for opening Kristina's eyes to the darker side of the up-time industrial revolution so soon, but it would have happened eventually. At last the princess closed the final book of the sizable stack. She looked like she might cry.

"Pretty sad stuff, huh?" Caroline asked, taking Kristina's slender hand.

"It was so terrible! I didn't know how bad it was! I knew that life up-time wasn't perfect, and that there were horrible wars, but the things they did to the land, to the animals! It was cruel . . ." She sniffed loudly, and wiped at her prominent nose with the sleeve of her cotton sweatshirt, causing another round of clucking disapproval from the ladies in waiting, which she ignored, as usual.

Caroline nodded sympathetically. "Are you okay?"

"Yes, I suppose so. Anyway, I think I understand what Pam Miller wants from me now. I've seen her 'big picture' and I don't like it either. Something needs to be done soon, or all that awful stuff will happen in this time, too. This isn't just about saving the dodo, it's about saving *everything*."

"Well, no one can do that, Kristina, but there are things we can do to help. I'm quite sure Pam hopes you will use the advantages of your position to do so. But remember, these are adult problems and adults are responsible for them. You're still only nine years old, so let's take it slowly."

"Yes, adults are responsible all right. Look what a mess they make everywhere! I'm only nine years old now, but I'm also the king's daughter, and what have he, and you, been trying to teach me if not responsibility?" Her large brown eyes were sad, but there was also a certain hardness there, a determination. *She's so like her father,* Caroline thought, not for the first time.

Kristina took a deep breath and let it out. She spoke again, the quaver of near tears gone now. "The Lord tests us, Caroline, my father says. I believe this is my first test, at least the first adult kind of one. Let's find a phone. I'm going to call Pam right now and tell her thank you for educating me. Then we'll discuss our next steps." She stood and walked confidently out of the room, and down the hall to the library offices with her bevy of ladies following, looking every bit the royal princess of all the land.

∞ ∞ ∞

Pam cradled the phone on her shoulder while she started a new pot of coffee.

"Yeah, it sucks, doesn't it? Look, Princess, I really am sorry I didn't warn you first, but nobody understands things like that unless they see it for themselves. Now that I have your attention, I have some more subjects for you to study up on: *National parks, conservation,* and *environmental protection.* A smart kid like you is going to be able to see where I'm headed with that. There were a lot of *good* people up-time, too, people who worked hard to protect nature. I think there may be people who will do the same here and now, don't you?" Over the line the princess assured Pam that there were such people here and now, and that she was one of them. Pam smiled as she hung up the phone; the seed she had planted was sprouting nicely, hopefully it would take root and really grow.

Later, Pam walked among her rows of sunflowers in the sweet light of the afternoon, thinking of cabbages and kings. She had finally admitted to herself that it had been wrong of her to want the up-time animals to survive here, she had always known that deep down. Transplanted species were so often destructive. She had already begun her own research, and had learned that pigs, rats, and other invasive species had also played a part in the dodo's demise, creatures that nature had not intended to have on those islands, brought there by humans. Now, the Ring of Fire had unleashed a whole raft of North American animals into the European ecology, and she had personally helped them get established instead of eradicating them as a sensible modern conservationist would have. *Oh well,* she sighed to herself, *there's no undoing it now.*

For around the ten-thousandth time, Pam wondered if the Ring of Fire was something nature had intended, a so-called "Act of God," like a hurricane or an earthquake? Pam's gut told her that it wasn't, that it had been some kind of strange cosmic accident, or a secret government experiment gone terribly wrong—the circle was just too perfect. That debate would likely go on until they reached this universe's twentieth century. Whatever the cause, she and a six-mile round piece of West Virginia domestic and wildlife had ended up here, and their numbers were growing. The bird species she was so fond of didn't really seem to be doing any harm to Europe's ecology, just a little extra competition for similar birds in the available niches. The seventeenth-century ecology of Europe seemed capable of absorbing them all. Apparently there was room.

On the other hand, raccoons were spreading rapidly, and earning notoriety as a real pest. The down-timers called them *maskierte teufelchen*, the masked little devils. The coons could be amazingly destructive with their hand-like paws, and the down-timers had never seen anything like them. No garbage was safe, and you had better stand guard on the orchards and chicken coops! Yet another destructive invader. Pam expected the coon-skin cap would be making a big comeback soon.

So, there were definitely negative effects on nature thanks to their arrival here. Pam tried not to think too much about the early industrial revolution they had ignited, and the environmental disasters it was sure to cause. She hoped the up-timers involved would at least consider what a mess they had left of their former world, but it was a faint hope. Money ruled the day, and there was a lot to be made, a bunch of hillbillies suddenly finding themselves richer than Croesus because they had found a way to reproduce a flashlight battery, or a hundred other such examples of up-time ingenuity—they weren't going to care if entire habitats were slaughtered wholesale in order to make their profits. Measures to protect their natural resources needed to be taken, and soon.

Pam had long wanted to do something positive, something *big* that would wake more people up to what they could lose. Saving the dodo, despite all the difficulties involved, still seemed like the best bet. It was such a perfect poster child; cutely ugly, pathetically incapable of defending itself, already gone extinct once in human knowledge, but still here *now*, at least for a little longer. They would all die in this world, too, if something weren't done.

Another thought kept niggling at her and she finally had to face it: Bringing dodos back to Europe was great, but it might not be enough to guarantee their survival as a species.

Even if they were able to transport a breeding population of dodos to the USE, there were still too many things that could go wrong. Diseases, diet—Pam knew very little about the bird she wanted to save. Of course, she would take the time to study them in their natural habitat *if* she could get there, but the dodos she brought back to Europe would be the equivalent of a few eggs in a very small and fragile basket. The real way to be sure would be to protect the dodos in their own natural habitat. But how? She couldn't very well erect impenetrable glass domes over the islands.

Pam managed a cynical laugh at the thought of a couple of lonely guardsmen patrolling miles of empty beaches on the remote isle, in order to ward off potential threats to the dodos. If nothing were done, the humans would eventually settle there according to the up-time history books, along with the pigs and cats and rats they would bring with them. It was all going to happen again unless there were controls in place. So, who was going to do the controlling?

Pam didn't like to think it, but there would have to be people there, and they would need to be *her* people, people she had influence over who would agree that the dodo and the natural environment of the island would be protected. That meant colonists. Pam shuddered a little. Colonists had historically never been good for *any* environment. But, she couldn't erect a magical force field to keep people off the island, either. If dodos were going to be protected in their native Mauritius, there would have to be a reason for people to be there to enforce it.

She laughed bitterly again to herself. It was pretty risky. Save the dodo by colonizing their island with people who might, with a lot of education and coaxing, agree that protecting the dodo was their civic duty. Pam visualized herself with a coonskin cap and a sawed-off shotgun, holding off an angry mob of settlers bent on cutting down the dodo's forest to build log cabins.

Still, she had found an angle that she would have to think about. Pam Miller, leading the *Mayflower* to the Mascarenes. There were going to have to be some really good reasons to found a colony that far way. What would make such a venture profitable? An undertaking of that scope would also need money up front, and she suspected that the amount the princess could offer without her father's support wouldn't be enough. What could she do to sell a colony on Mauritius to Emperor Gustav? What was of value down there? She thought about what she had learned about the islands so far.

The Mascarenes were three paradisaical islands at just about the halfway point on the sea route from Europe to India, and the Orient, currently with no indigenous peoples, no permanent residents, and no firm claims by foreign powers. The Dutch had a tentative claim, but Pam read the papers, and knew that they were a bit too preoccupied now to be focused on things like future colonies. Besides, possession was nine-tenths of the law. In the long run, Mauritius would become a strategic military port, as well as a handy trading post. The Dutch had thought that, and later the French. It held true now, as well, since there wasn't going to be a Suez Canal any time soon.

The region was a fruit ripe for the picking. The Swedish and their allies had a chance to get there first, but would Gustav see that? In her research Pam had learned the Swedes had completely missed the Asian money boat in the other timeline, forming a Swedish East India Company far too late to be a competitive player in the region. Maybe they would have if Gustav hadn't died in battle in that reality, an event the Ring of Fire prevented. Colonizing the Mascarenes would pave the way for the Swede's empire to become an Asian power; another of many second chances for a man spared an untimely death.

It was time to do more research, so Pam decided to head to the library for a few hours. Besides learning as much as she could about farming the various tropical cash crops, she would read *Alice in Wonderland* while she was at it, too, somehow she had missed it in childhood, and the whimsical old classic would make a nice break from her studies, a distraction from the lunacy she was embarking on.

As she walked down the slowly disintegrating pavement of Grantville, it occurred to her that she hadn't bothered to tell anyone else she knew about her planned adventure yet. It was something she wasn't quite ready to deal with; she needed more time to let the reality of her choice sink in. She decided she would start with her best friends, Dore and Gerbald at dinner tonight, they were sure to be understanding. Pam tried not to think about what her son and daughter-in-law would say.

∞ ∞ ∞

That evening when she got home from her studies, Pam found Dore finishing up the weekly house cleaning and Gerbald lounging on the sofa watching *Gilligan's Island*. There was so much wonderful entertainment that sadly had not come through the Ring of Fire with them, it was painful to think of it, but someone in town had owned the complete series on DVD, insuring the castaway's goofy antics would continue to rerun in perpetuity across all space-time. After the round of greetings, Pam flopped on the sofa next to Gerbald. The show was almost over, she knew how much he enjoyed it, so she kept quiet until the credits rolled, then they both sang along with the rather catchy theme song, and laughed like kids.

"Pam, today I learned that there was a special episode of *Gilligan's Island* that didn't come through the Ring of Fire in which the castaways were rescued! Have you ever seen it? Oh, how I wish I could!" Gerbald's voice was full of excitement, he had become a diehard fan of TV and movies, they brought out the overgrown kid in him.

"Yeah, I saw it, Gerbald. The truth is you didn't miss anything. It pretty much sucked, and then in the end Gilligan screwed up and they all ended up back on the island again." Pam had long ago admitted to Gerbald that she had watched the show growing up, and was rather fond of it herself.

"Ah, such a shame. Still, I wish I could see it, perhaps one day when Grantville starts making new TV shows here we could do a remake. I think I would make an excellent Skipper, although I would have to put on some weight."

Pam looked at her enthusiastic friend and found it hard to believe that he had once been a very dangerous professional soldier. She decided to decline on commenting that there were a multitude of up-time shows that deserved a remake and *Rescue from Gilligan's Island* was not on that list.

Dore came in and shook her head at her husband, a look of disgust on her red-cheeked face. "Buffoon. Imbecile. Wasting your time staring at that picture box, it's almost as bad as the drink."

Pam decided to decline to comment that having the TV on in the background had been an important factor in improving Dore's once broken English, and it had certainly added to her impressive list of put-downs. She jumped in before the usual banter could get started.

"Hey, you two, I have something I need to talk to you about. Maybe you better sit down, Dore." Dore eyed her curiously as she took the desk chair, the only other piece of furniture in the room that was not covered with Pam's work. Gerbald, also curious, straightened his lanky frame up a bit and turned to Pam. It was unusual for their friend to look this serious during their weekly get together.

"Why, what's on your mind, Pam?" he asked in his much practiced West Virginia drawl.

"Well, it's kind of a long story. A few days ago I got a call from Princess Kristina."

That made Dore's eyes widen, the woman was quietly a fan of the Vasa royalty and doted on news of their young princess. "*The* princess?" Dore asked, trying not to sound excited.

"Yes, *the* princess. She's really a nice kid, very, very smart. Anyway, she has asked me to help her save a bird."

"Then she has asked the right person!" Gerbald said smiling, ever proud of his American friend.

"Well, yeah, I guess I'm the 'Bird Lady' after all. The thing is, it's not a bird from around here . . ." Pam paused to engage in a careful study of her shoes; suddenly not sure she wanted to be having this discussion right now after all.

After a while Dore grew impatient and asked "Well, tell us, dear Pam, where is this bird from?"

"Um. From an island." Another pause.

"An island. In the Chiemsee? Or perhaps one of those in Switzerland?"

"No, it's one near Africa," Pam answered in a rather small voice.

"Africa!" Dore exclaimed, then went silent, trying to parse that distance out.

Gerbald frowned, a serious look coming to his face.

"That's a long way to bring a bird," he said calmly. "It must be a very special one. When it gets here you will help save it, yes? Another protected species?"

"Yes, that's part of the idea. The thing is getting it here." Pam still wasn't able to meet her friend's eyes.

Gerbald's eyebrows had begun to rise. "Pam, who will bring the bird from Africa?"

"I will." Pam looked up at them and managed a bit of a silly smile. Gerbald returned it, but Dore was definitely *not* smiling.

"Africa! *You* plan to *go* to Africa? Yourself? Africa!" Dore's voice was rising to the incredulous pitch she sometimes used when grilling Gerbald about his adventures at the tavern.

Pam gave her a helpless look. "Yeah, that's it. Actually all the way around Africa, then over to some islands called the Mascarenes in the Indian Ocean. That's where the dodo lives, and if I don't go get some now, they will all be killed over the next few years. The princess has asked me to do this." Even that last bit didn't budge the incredulous expression on Dore's face, an expression that was quickly turning to a righteous disgust.

"Madness!" Her voice sounded half-strangled. "You *can't* go all the way to *Africa*, even to save some bird for the princess. It's madness!" Dore's arms, powerful from years of difficult labors, were crossed now in front of her impressive chest, the picture of a woman who had long suffered foolishness, and would brook no more. "You cannot go, Pam. It is far too dangerous. There are savages and pirates there, and wild beasts that can chew you up, I have seen it on the TV. You simply must not!"

"Now, Dore," Gerbald switched into German. "Pam is a grown woman and must make her own decisions. You cannot mother her so! You know how strongly she cares for the birds and other living things, and besides, one cannot take a request from the royal princess of the land lightly! Please see reason." Dore answered only with a dismissive caw, unable to find her voice she was so appalled at the events turning before her. Pam spoke up again, also in German; she had become nearly fluent having decided it was necessary to her life down-time.

"Dore, please my dear friend, I don't really want to go. Really, I don't. But I feel I must. Doing this will get the princess on my side when it comes to stopping an environmental disaster here. If I help her, she will help me. I have her word on this and believe it. I must go."

Dore shook her head, her initial outrage changing to sincere concern for her dearest friend. "Oh my, Pam, I can't bear to think of you making such an awful journey. When is this to happen?"

Her face was now so mournful that Pam walked across the room and gave her a hug. "I don't know yet. We've just started. It will probably be a few months, things don't usually happen very fast in this era. I need to go talk to the princess again tomorrow before she leaves town. From there most of it will depend on her. Whatever happens, I assure you I will be very careful, I intend to come back to you alive!"

"Well, of course you will! And that is why we are going with you!" Dore announced in a suddenly confident tone.

"You are?" It wasn't really a question; deep down Pam had known this was the likely outcome of the conversation.

"We are?" Gerbald turned to his wife, his face alive with anticipation.

"Of course we are! We can't let Pam go off around the world alone! She will need our help on such a long journey! We *must* go!"

Gerbald studied his wife as if she had suddenly transformed into something miraculous like a talking horse. This was too good to be true! "Why, of course we must!" he bellowed heartily. "I've always wanted to experience a sea voyage! Africa, the Dark Continent, land of adventure! How wonderful!"

"Actually we are just sailing *around* Africa as far as I know, but maybe we could stop and take a look around a bit . . ." Pam was starting to feel a bit giddy now; her hesitation at breaking the bizarre news to her best friends had past. *They are going with me. Now I really know I can do this.* She grabbed Dore once more in a bear hug. "You two are the best, thank you!"

Dore patted her friend gently on her back, her upset finished, her eyes smiling now. "You can't be rid of us, dear Pam. We will follow you everywhere. In any case, it can't be any worse than following this lout through all those wars."

Later, Dore was cooking the evening meal while Gerbald napped on the sofa. Pam sat at her desk, staring out her garden window, tired from too much reading, and way too much thinking. *God, how I miss the Internet.*

"I need to come up with a plan," she mumbled into the fist that supported her chin. "I need a reason for people to want to go live on those islands. Something that will sweeten the idea up for that fat king to insure his support."

"Dinner is almost ready!" Dore called from the kitchen, giving Gerbald a chance to wake up, and Pam a chance to reach a good stopping place in her work.

"Dinner . . . fat . . . sweeten . . ." Pam's eyes widened. Quickly, she pushed her chair back, startling Gerbald out of his nap, and rushed into the kitchen.

"Dore! Do you know much about the emperor? About Gustav?"

"Well, certainly I know some things, who doesn't? I read the newspapers and listen to the talk down at the shops."

"What does he like to eat?"

"I believe he is very fond of meat, as most men are, and also of cheese."

"What about desserts?"

"Why yes, I have heard he loves chocolate and sweets. One must be a king to be able to afford such. Why are you smiling in this funny way, Pam?"

"How much does chocolate go for these days at Johnson's?"

"Oh, it is much too dear, even if it is available at all. I do not understand what the fuss is about, it's so bitter tasting unless you mix it with cream and sugar."

"Sugar! How much is that?"

"Well, it has gone down somewhat thanks to sorghum, but it is still quite expensive. We are lucky none of us here have that 'sweet tooth' so many Americans suffer from."

"Yes, that wonderful sweet tooth that Emperor Gustav has acquired. Do you know where all those things grow? Let me tell you! In places like Mauritius." Pam sat back and smiled, proud of her ingenuity.

∞ ∞ ∞

Pam called the princess the next day. "I've been doing a lot of research on all this and I need to get you caught up. I'm afraid it's going to take more than one ship to *really* save the dodo and here's why."

The princess listened quietly as Pam explained.

"The problem is, the dodos might not survive outside of their native habitat. Even if we bring a whole bunch of them to Europe they might die anyway. And if they do live, they might not breed. Instead of the other Europeans and Africans who will eventually come to the Mascarenes and cause the dodo's extinction, we need to get there first with *our* people, people whose *duty* would be to conserve the dodo and its habitat, farming sensibly alongside the nature preserves. We need to found a colony."

Pam gave the princess a moment to absorb the knowledge dump before continuing.

"So, you see, I'm not sure you can afford all that on your resources alone."

"No, I probably can't do all that on my own, but with father's blessing and some of his money to help, I could pull it off. But how can we convince him it's worthwhile? I already know what he will say if I just tell him it's all to save a bird. I would be scolded for such foolishness. He's spending a lot of money on his wars right now, we have to come up with other really good reasons for him to support this."

Dang this kid is smart! Pam grinned into the receiver.

"Right. Okay, I've come up with some good reasons. There's not as much info in Grantville on those islands as I might like, but I have learned that they have a mild, tropical climate. Up-time they raised warm weather plants like vanilla and sugar cane. If they could grow those then why not chocolate, or coffee, or cinnamon? If Sweden had a colony down there producing all that good stuff, it would be a lot cheaper than we can get it trading with foreigners. Even with the long distance involved, I think it would be profitable. Ships are just going to get faster, and then someday airplanes! TEA Airways already flies to Venice regularly. Looking at the maps, it's really not that much farther if we could get some other stops laid out on the way. I know for sure the people of the USE are going to want to buy those goods, and we might eventually be able to produce extra to sell to other countries as well. It could be a real moneymaker for the empire. We could make the Mascarenes into Gustav's very own spice basket."

"Pam, that sounds perfect! I know my father loves his sweets. He and other sponsors will surely see the wisdom in this. We will get to work right away; hopefully it will just be a few months until you can go. Meanwhile, is there anything else you need from me?"

Pam cocked her head for a moment, gears turned inside there. "Actually, yes. Please get a piece of paper and a pen, preferably royal stationary if you have it. I'd like a little something from you, just in case I should ever need it . . ."

Garrett W. Vance

Second Chance Bird

Chapter Two: Personal Affairs

Over the next few weeks the reality of Pam's looming journey began to sink in. Favorable reports were coming from the princess and her staff, it sounded like the mission was going to be a go, and they would be able to leave a lot sooner than expected, maybe even the end of May. The initial giddiness of such a grand adventure was harder to feel now, more and more she found herself fretting over it. This was big, this was scary. She had plenty of vacation days coming to her at work and had decided to burn a few to have some time to think. Feeling hemmed in by her garden's cool confines, she decided to take a long walk to help clear her head. It was a bright, sunny morning, and that would be just the thing to help keep her worries at bay.

Soon she was climbing up a familiar West Virginia hillside, feeling the sunlight touching warmly on her back. She came to the hill's abrupt edge, marveling as always at the glass-sheened cliff left by whatever event had caused their journey through space-time, presumably slicing the strata on a molecular level. A Thuringian stream blocked by the new heights placed in its path had created a sizable lake below, cool waters lapping against the smooth walls of the transplanted hills.

Pam sat down near the edge with her back against a sycamore tree. She forced herself to relax, to go into what she thought of as "birdwatcher mode," a state of calm awareness, quietly paying attention only to the world around her, ignoring the incessant whispers of the inner. This odd place was where she felt most at home anymore, along this edge where two realities fused to make something new. She gazed contentedly at the lake and the comings and goings of its small inhabitants; birds, fish, frogs, insects. In a comfortable space, Pam allowed herself to drift inward, looking at herself dispassionately, as if examining some new species of life, not judging, just observing.

She had been changed by the Ring of Fire as much as sleepy old Grantville had been, the totally unexpected revitalization of a declining town. The experience of time travel had awakened something in her as well, she had seen it in other up-timers, too. *Second chances*. The old Pam, who lived in a gray zone of self pity in that other life and time, had metamorphosed into something different, something *better*, a being of energy and convictions. A small smile came to her lips as she realized that she *liked* herself better now, at least most of the time. Maybe this new Pam really was a person who could take on something as big as the wide world, do something as Quixotic as save a doomed species halfway across the globe.

She thought of the time she had passed by this spot on her way to save Gerbald, knowing she was heading into danger, but ignoring the fear, conquering it, finding the strength to fight and win against the evil men who threatened her friend. She clutched the solid weight of her grandmother's walking stick, her body remembering how she had used it to devastating effect on their attacker, used it to survive, to win, the seasoned oak wood channeling an inner strength she hadn't known she had. Despite her increasing unease at what lay before her, that power was still within her, the power to fight for what she held dear.

The mission to Mauritius would surely be dangerous. It would be frightening. It would also be uncomfortable. But most of all she knew it would be worthwhile. In Pam's mind's eye she saw herself, saw the sensitive girl she had been as a child, who had wept when reading the story of the dodo in those dreary back pages of the bird guides, that terrible roll-call of the victims of extinction. She felt that little girl somehow looking at her future self with her own steel-gray eyes, the message clear: "*Change this.*"

Pam stood up, shaking her head to clear her reverie; she had seen enough. She took a big, deep breath of the fresh breeze coming across the lake and smiled.

"All right, you dodos, hang in there, I'm a-comin'!" she shouted merrily across the lake.

A noisy thought suddenly crashed into her mind: She had yet to tell her employers at the Research Institute of her plans, not to mention her family, starting with her father. The world spun a little too fast beneath her feet for a moment. *Deep breaths, deep breaths!*

∞ ∞ ∞

Surprisingly, her father took it well. He had aged a bit since the Ring of Fire, but there was a sparkle in Walter Miller's eyes. Becoming the high school chemistry teacher had revitalized him. Being around kids could do that, in those cases when it doesn't age one faster. In Pam's experience, things always went better with other people's kids. Not to say her father hadn't done a good job of raising her. She had never wanted for anything, and even if he was not one for a lot of overt affection, she always knew she was loved. Most importantly, he had always been encouraging when it came to Pam's choices growing up.

This time, considering the dangers involved, Pam had expected, and maybe deep down, *wanted* him to be upset by the news, but he took it all in stride. He looked at her with eyes that closely resembled her own and told her "Pammie, I'm real proud of you. Always have been, but now more than ever. I like what you are doing with the school kids, I see it making a difference with them, and I like that you are taking a leadership role in environmental protection. I dabbled in it myself in my youth, and I'm glad to see I raised a daughter who is going to really do something to help this new old world. I know you can do it. When Pam Miller puts her mind to it, she can do anything!"

This unexpectedly stirring praise managed to make Pam cry, so her father held her and gently patted her on her head for a long, quiet time.

Unfortunately, it did not go so well with her mother, who wept for over an hour. Pam did her best to comfort her, then had to leave her for her father's tender care, deciding that was enough drama for one day. She went home to get a bit drunk with Gerbald in front of the TV set.

The next morning she went to see her daughter-in-law Crystal, who was bound to be today's designated crier. Pam was by no means surprised, and felt awful as a just-got-pregnant Crystal cried and cried as her mother-in-law looked on helplessly.

"Oh, Momma Pam, you just can't be gone for a whole year! What about the ba-ba-baby-y-y-y!" Her voice broke up into incoherent sobbing.

Pam grimaced, she had known Crystal was going to take it hard, but *yeesh*. So, she overrode her embarrassment at the outburst, and hugged Crystal tightly. Crystal Blocker had come through the Ring of Fire with only a single aunt for family, and was whole-heartedly invested in changing that. Now that she had married Pam's son Walt, and become Crystal Dormann, she had a mom again, and Pam, being very fond of the sweet, good-hearted girl, had encouraged the relationship, wondering what it would have been like to have had a daughter to balance her often stubborn and difficult only child. She buried a rueful grin that her grown boy Walt was Crystals' problem now instead of hers, and patted Crystal firmly on the back, then took her by the shoulders to very gently shake her out of her sorrow.

"Hey, hey, honey, listen! It's not as awful as you're making it out to be! It's just for a year, and that's a blink of the eye, trust me. Come on, what's a regular old *year* to a bunch of time travelers like us, huh? I'll be back before you know it."

"But you're going all the way to *A-a-a-africa*, it's so *far*, it will be so *dangerous!*" More tears poured from Crystal's bright green eyes down her pretty-as-a-penny, freckled face.

"It won't be that bad. Besides, Gerbald and Dore will be along, and you know they won't let anything bad happen to me, right?" Pam knew that Crystal regarded her new German "uncle and auntie" very highly. This served to calm her down a bit. "And, when we get back we'll all have a big birthday party for my new grandchild, I promise! I'm so proud of you, honey! You are the daughter I always wanted! Now, I need you to be strong for me. This is something I just gotta do!" They hugged again, and Crystal allowed as how she understood. Eventually Pam got her settled down enough to where she could leave her, still sniffly, but coming to grips with her mother-in-law's decision. As she left the house, Pam found Walt standing in the driveway, with a very dark look on his still young face.

Uh-oh, Pam thought, *this isn't going to go well.* Walt had listened silently to his mother explain about her dodo rescue mission. He had walked out without saying a word when Crystal's tears came. Pam's stomach clinched, no doubt her son was ready to have his say now. *Here it comes . . .*

"Way to go, *Mom*. Nice," he told her in well-practiced sarcastic tones. Pam was sure that he had been drinking some moonshine out in the garage.

"She'll be fine, Walt. I've got her calmed down. She's a strong girl." Pam stood up straight, meeting her son's eyes, so like her own.

"Yeah, right. Crystal lost everything coming through that fucking ring and now she's losing you, too, *Momma Pam*. Obviously, you don't give a shit." Walt glared at her, his flushed face full of disgust.

Pam took a deep breath. "I'm sorry you think that, Walt. You are wrong, of course. I care about Crystal and you, and your baby to be, very much. Even so, I am an adult and there are things I have to do— This is one of them. I'm sorry it doesn't fit into your plans for me."

"Oh yeah, sail halfway around the world to save some freaky looking bird that's too stupid to run away from hunters. And that is going to what? Somehow save the world from a new industrial revolution? Good fucking luck! What the hell does it matter anyway? This world is going to end up just as screwed up as the last one and there's nothing you can do about it."

"I'm very disappointed to hear you talk that way. I didn't think I'd raised such a negative person. I thought I'd taught you better than that."

"Yeah, like you were a ray of sunshine while I was growing up. What I remember is you were usually depressed, and only took a break from that to bitch at me about doing my homework. Now, there was a great waste of time, all that 'getting ready for college' is doing me a lot of good now, isn't it? They don't even have colleges back here in the dark ages. You made my life miserable for *nothing!*"

"Well, I am *so* sorry I wasn't some perfect *Leave it to Beaver* mom for you, Walt. God knows, your father wasn't exactly helping me any, nitpicking my every move. And actually they *do* have colleges here, not that you would know since you decided to make the Club 250 the extent of your down-time travels. Yeah, I wonder if Crystal knows about that? *'You're going to be home late from work again, Honey? Okay!'* " That got under his skin, he had been starting to say something and stopped. Apparently what she had heard was true.

Pam continued. "Ya know, sometimes I don't love our new reality much either, but I've come to accept it. It's whatever *you* decide to make of it, and it most certainly is not the Dark Ages, which you would know if you had ever actually bothered to give one tiny shit about your education. As for wasting time, I can see now that is exactly what I was doing when I made you do your homework. Nothing in my power could possibly stop you from your chosen course of becoming an ignorant, grass-chewing redneck, destined to work the mines and die of black lung at age forty. Well, don't let me stop you now. You're a real hillbilly. I can see that. Go kick some cow pies for me. I've got better things to do."

"You self-righteous bitch. You've never loved anybody but yourself. It was always all about *you*."

Pam took a long look at her son and then in a lightning quick motion stepped up close to him while landing a swift, hard slap across his face. It was the first time she had ever applied a hand to him in his life.

"That's for thinking I don't love you, son." While Walt was stunned from the first blow, she slapped him again even harder. "And that's for not living up to your potential, for not even *trying* to. Crystal deserves better than what you have become. God, I hope you see it in time and get yourself right before it's too late." Pam held him in a long, piercing glare until he looked down at his shoes, his face red-hot with shame and pain, the fight all knocked out of him. Then she turned and walked away.

Well, that could have gone better. God's own truth is I should have done that a long time ago. She ignored the tears that streamed down her face as she marched back to her little pink house in the sunflowers. She was ready to go now.

Garrett W. Vance

Chapter Three: Out the Door

Grantville, near the end of May, 1635

How does one go about leaving on a year journey? A journey around Africa on a ship about as technologically advanced as the Mayflower? Pam stood in her bedroom scowling at the things she had arranged on the bed, feeling very put out with the whole exercise. The clothes she had chosen were the most sensible and weather resistant she owned. She figured she would be facing extreme conditions so she had selected items for both hot and cold weather. She had gone through her medicine cabinet and put anything that might be remotely useful in one of her carefully hoarded ziplock bags. There were other things that she should bring; the flashlight from the bedstead drawer, and some of her precious batteries, needle and thread for repairs.... The list got longer and longer. She found herself gazing numbly into her closet, feeling confused and overwhelmed by the scope of the journey she faced. Shaking her head she blew out a long, plaintive whistle.

Well, I'd better bring along my best little black dress so they'll have something decent to bury me in when I'm shot dead by savages with poison blow guns, or succumb to some rare tropical disease.

Enough was enough. This could wait. She swept the closet door shut with a bang and stalked off to the kitchen to make coffee. Would there be coffee on the ship? There damn well had better be! She would mention it to the princess' clerks.

Pam set her coffee on her desk to let it cool off a bit, her mind still busy going over things. She had hired some friends of Dore's as caretakers, a young couple who were new to Grantville and needed the work. She had written careful instructions in German (with a little help from Gerbald) telling them how to harvest the sunflower crop, and how to keep the bird-feeder stocked. Pam's daughter-in-law Crystal would be their paymaster and check on things once in a while, which made her more comfortable with the situation. Once Crystal had come to terms with Pam's looming absence, she had proven to be a rock, helping Pam get ready in any way she could. Meanwhile, Pam and her son Walt had been avoiding each other, which was sadly the usual state of their relationship.

Things had gone amazingly well when she broke the news at work, much better than she had expected. She had managed to nearly finish her latest round of research, and smoothly pass what little was left to do on to her colleagues. Pam had expected to resign, but the director had insisted that she remain an employee, moreover, an employee on official leave of absence drawing a reduced salary, which was quite generous to her mind. They asked her to document anything she found along the way that may be useful to their mission in Grantville, and she vowed she would. In a flash of inspiration Pam asked them to look into the subject of artificially pollinating the vanilla orchid if they could find some live specimens. Apparently it was a lost art, and she wanted to revive it for use in her spice colony. They even threw a farewell party for her! That had really helped her mood, she had been lonely since Gerbald and Dore had left a week earlier to supervise the loading of their ship, especially the stowing of the many pounds of coffee she had made it very clear were an absolute necessity. Well, she would see them soon enough, she would try to enjoy the time remaining in her cozy little home as best she could .Now that it really was really getting close to being time to go, Pam had to once again face the fact that she was at heart a homebody. Sitting at her window watching the bird-feeder was her idea of paradise. Chasing around Africa in a seventeenth-century sailing ship had never been something she would have considered in her old life. She blew softly into the steaming cup to cool it down, making this peaceful moment last as long as she could.

The princess herself had called her the other day to let her know the issue of the colonists was finalized. "They aren't annoying religious nuts, are they?" Pam had asked, and was assured that they were nice, quiet Lutherans who were looking for a better life, and willing to take a chance. They would travel in a fleet of four ships; one for Pam and her expedition materials, two for the colonists, and one military escort. Once the business discussion was done, there was a long pause from Kristina.

"You still there, Princess?" Pam asked. She could hear a deep, child-sized breath being taken.

"Pam, I want to thank you for doing this from the bottom of my heart. I know it's not easy for you, and I feel a little bad now that I talked you into it." Kristina's voice was freighted with emotion as if she might cry, enough so that it made Pam wonder if things were all right at home for her.

"It's okay, Princess. I wouldn't do it unless I wanted to. You see I was once a little girl who cried when I read the story of what happened to the dodo. This is something I need to do, and in no way do I hold you responsible. In fact, I'm glad you came along to help me out the door. I needed a shove. You are a real good kid, and your heart is in the right place. I hope you will continue to work to preserve nature. It's going to need your help in the years to come. I've seen what a bunch of Americans can do to the land, and it ain't pretty. You keep at it."

She heard Kristina sniffle away from the receiver. "Thank you, Pam. I will try my best. Please come back to us safely!"

"You can count on it, kid."

"May God be with you!"

"He's welcome to come along. I could use the extra help." This made Kristina laugh, which assuaged Pam's concern for the girl's emotional state. Pam laughed too, said good-bye, and put the phone down, feeling pleased despite her continued anxiety over the coming voyage.

∞ ∞ ∞

The day had come. Pam took one last look at her beloved bird-feeder, full of sunflower seeds and currently hosting a pair of young, up-time descended Eastern bluebirds, fellow immigrants through the Ring of Fire. She wondered where the transplanted bird species wintered now. In their former homeland, it had been Central and South America. Here in Europe she wondered if they found the balmy southern reaches of Italy or Greece to their liking, or if they ranged farther, across the Mediterranean to Africa? Well, now maybe she would find out.

She became aware of a noise coming from up the road, growing louder as it drew nearer. She peered out the front window to see just what the ruckus was. She could hear . . . cheering? And some kind of music. A bit irritated at the disturbance, she went out on the front porch to gaze over the nodding heads of her hillside full of sunflowers, to the road below. There was some kind of a parade coming.

"Oh that's just great. Now the road into town is going to be all jammed up, and I'll be late for the train." She was about to return to saying her private farewells to her little pink house when an odd thing caught her eye. There was something large coming into view, what must certainly be a parade float. Today wasn't any kind of holiday that she could think of, but with all the different kinds of people living in Grantville these days it certainly could be somebody's holiday. It looked like it might be a chicken, or a turkey, or maybe a . . . Pam gave it a good study with her sharp eyes, her hand cupped over her brow.

No. It's a dodo.

Pam rolled her eyes. She had already said all her good-byes to family and friends, not wanting a scene at the train station. Now she considered quietly slipping the door closed, sneaking off over the wooded hill behind her house, and then bushing her way cross-country to the station. As a dedicated birder she knew every secret path and hidden hollow in Grantville, and figured she could go most of way without using a road, or even being seen at all, for that matter. *Yeah, no problem, I could do that, the baggage has been sent ahead, just my rucksack left.* . . . She looked back at the road to see that the parade mostly consisted of a large group of children led by Stacey Antoni Vannorman, a teacher who often helped Pam with the summer nature program, and who had kindly offered to take it over during Pam's absence. The parade came to a halt at the bottom of her steep walk, the kids bearing painted signs that said "Our Hero, Pam Miller the Bird Lady of Grantville!" and "Save the dodo, Pam!"

Oh. Dear. God. Pam nearly swooned from embarrassment. *I swear I'd rather be lost in the Congo than be the leader of a damned parade.*

"We're here to escort you to the station, Ms. Miller!" one of her favorite girls from nature program outings cried out between giggles, beating her teacher to the punch. Stacey, knowing Pam's fluctuating moods pretty well after several seasons of working with her, grinned merrily at her current discomfiture without regret, and said, "I'm sorry Pam, but they insisted." She definitely didn't *look* sorry. Pam did her best to maintain the deadly expression of bored disdain she favored disruptive students with during her planned activities, but it broke into a really silly, grinning girl giggle of her own.

"Gawd, you guys! I'm simply mortified! Okay, I can't possibly get more embarrassed than this, so let's have a parade! Maybe no one else will notice if we move fast enough. I have a train to catch! Just give me a minute to grab my pack!" With one last look back, she took in her living room and her desk by the window, beyond which her lay her little garden. She felt a sharp pang of regret blended with a murmur of fear at leaving this island of reason in a turbulent world, a world that all too often struck her as violent and incoherent. With an effort of willpower she pushed the uncomfortable feelings aside. It was time to go. She was ready.

Pam turned back toward the door, slipped her trusty rucksack over her shoulder. She spied her grandmother's sturdy walking stick leaning in its usual place beneath the coat hooks. It had saved her and Gerbald's life once, she had nearly killed a man with it in their defense. *Might as well take it with me!* She gripped it firmly in her hand. The solid oak weight of it was reassuring, lending its strength to her. *If you could just see me now, Grandma!* Pam stepped out her door, closed it tight with a twist of the lock, and took her place at the head of her parade, gamely raising her walking stick up and down like a grand marshal's baton as she led them forward.

Pam hadn't expected anyone to attend her departure. She had warned her relatives away, being as how it was going to be hard enough as it was. But now, to her great discomfiture, Pam found a host of noble types and local muckety-mucks waiting on the station platform, and it looked like half of Grantville had turned up! Her cheeks achieved a rosy red they hadn't known since high school. A stunned, and thoroughly embarrassed Pam Miller was escorted by gentle hands up the stairs onto the platform.

Stacey climbed up with her, clearly the master of ceremonies. She spoke up in the far-carrying voice of an experienced teacher. "Ladies and gentlemen, I am very proud to present Pam Miller; champion of nature, and soon to be rescuer of the poor, helpless dodo!" Cheers and clapping erupted, some of the town's original hillbillies shouting out "Way to go, Pam!" Pam inwardly cringed, but resolved to make the best of it. *This is all part of it, too. Smile, Pammie!* And she did.

Mercifully, before she could be asked to make a speech, the train conductor blew a loud whistle and hollered "Alllll abooooarrrrd!" with old-time American gusto, albeit with a slight German accent. Pam was ushered to the open door of the converted school bus that someone had repainted a day-glo lime-green popular in the 1970s, a hue still found on several brands of construction equipment, apparently in a misguided attempt to make the thing look less like a school bus. It certainly didn't make it look like a train, to her it resembled a giant caterpillar.

Pam waved at the crowd one last time, then stepped onto the ersatz train. She made her way to the very back, even though it turned out that this was a "special non-stop express" just for her. *Thank you, Kristina!* She thought, grateful not to have any company but her own for the ride north.

She collapsed onto a dull-green, vinyl school bus seat as the converted vehicle rumbled out of the station, the festivities' noise diminishing behind her as they picked up speed. She didn't look back. Instead, she studied the bright red-and-white up-time safety stickers. These urgent messages from another universe combined with the familiar smell of up-time plastics, metals, and artificial fibers, suddenly made Pam painfully nostalgic for her child-hood. This quickly grew into a longing for up-time life in general, filling her with an intense feeling of loss she hadn't felt since her very first years here in the 1630s. She watched as the landscape made its abrupt, unnatural change from West Virginia to Thuringia as they crossed the rim of the Ring of Fire, a round peg thrust into the wrong hole by forces beyond comprehension.

She began to weep silently as the now familiar German country-side, with its thatch-roofed barns, and half-timbered farmhouses sped by beyond the fingerprint smeared windows. She had spent many hours wandering this quaint, pastoral landscape in search of elusive birds. This, too, was her home now, and it wasn't until she was leaving that she had come to realize it.

She knew she now belonged to both worlds, this Germany, this time and place, was a part of her as much as that lost USA had been. Once a soft twentieth-century woman, she had been re-forged in seventeenth-century iron. Pam found a handkerchief in her pocket and wiped away her tears, then blew her nose so loudly it made the conductor in the front of the bus-train jump. With professional courtesy he refrained from looking back to check on his only passenger, giving her all the privacy she might need. Pam smiled approvingly at his good manners. She opened the satchel containing her many notes, maps and copied pages of useful books, studying the long journey ahead as they chugged their way toward the distant sea on the ever spreading rails of industry.

Chapter Four: Out to Sea

Port of Bremen, The North Sea

After the train ran out of track Pam enjoyed a variety of uncomfortable conveyances, including horse-drawn carriage, and river barge. She sometimes felt as if she were in a never-ending historical reenactment, sure that she would turn the next corner to find a visitor parking lot full of cars and tired tourists, but the bumpy roads of the seventeenth century just stretched on and on as did the days. She eventually arrived in Bremen on a windy, overcast morning, travel worn and weary. Dore clucked worriedly over her, and sent her directly to a hot bath. The princess' agents had made arrangements for them to stay in a decent inn, not too fancy, but clean and well maintained. Pam slept most of that afternoon away, then joined her friends for a hearty dinner of baked salmon from the North Sea, which Pam declared to be divine manna from the gods. The next day they would meet the colonists. Tonight was for good beer, a round or two of schnapps, and an early bed.

Time flew by like a whirlwind for Pam. She met so many people that their names and purposes became a hopeless blur. She put on her brightest smile, and tried to look heroic, but inside she felt old familiar fears beginning to creep around. That evening she met with the colonists at an outdoor picnic style gathering in a wide meadow on the riverside. Everyone was very polite and deferential to her, the princess' agents had made it clear to the colonists that Pam would be the leader of the venture, and should be treated with all due respect. They were mostly young couples, only a few children or people over forty in the group, which she estimated to be about a hundred souls. Their pleasant demeanor put Pam at ease, and when it was finally time for her to deliver her speech she was feeling pretty confident, aided perhaps by the numerous toasts she had engaged in during the party.

She spoke in her nearing-fluent Thuringian-style German, and kept it short, hoping that her translator (his name had already escaped her), a jovial merchant from Stockholm who had lived in Bremen for many years, and was fluent in several languages and dialects, would at least get close to her desired meaning. She reminded them all that their sponsor, the young and much adored princess, was very concerned for the future of the dodo bird, as well as the many other unusual animals found on the islands, and that it would be everyone's duty to act as stewards of the land, living in harmony with nature while enjoying its bounty. They would be growing many types of crops that would be new to them, and would have to learn new ways of farming. It would be surely difficult at first, but ultimately very profitable.

The Swedes listened with eager expressions on their faces, Pam hoped this was because they were tired of the old ways, and were ready to try something better, something she could definitely deliver. When she finished, she gave them all a polite bow, and everyone cheered, which caused her to blush and almost trip on her way down from the makeshift platform. Gerbald caught her with one strong arm, handing her a tankard of beer with the other.

"You have missed your calling I think," he told her with a grin, "You should be running for Prime Minister!"

"I'd sooner chew my leg off. Leaving on a creaky wooden ship for a long and dangerous journey tomorrow is far preferable to a career in politics." She tipped her tankard back, taking a long draught. There were merry cries of *skål!* around her, and she stood swaying happily as they all joined in yet another round of toasts.

∞ ∞ ∞

Pam walked slowly down the Bremen docks flanked by Gerbald and Dore, escorted by a retinue of Swedish soldiers. Her head felt twice as large and three times as heavy as it should thanks to their frolics the night before. After crawling out of bed with a moan, she had taken quite a bit more than the recommended dosage of that crumby Gribbleflotz aspirin, which was better than nothing, and probably why she could manage at all. A sharp, salty wind whipped across the harbor, capping the waves in white, and making Pam shiver even under her best wool sweater. A bit of winter was still hanging around Bremen this morning, even this late in the spring. She felt as if she were trooping toward the gallows rather than leaving on the adventure of a lifetime, and longed for her little pink house in Grantville with a surprisingly deep ache. Wrinkling her nose, she pushed such thoughts aside. She had wanted this, she had gotten it, and by God she was going to go through with it.

"There she is, Pam!" she heard Gerbald proclaim, his voice excited.

She looked ahead to see a red-painted sailing ship tied to the dock, with a group of sailors standing by the gang plank. One of them, dressed quite a bit better than the rest, stepped forward to offer his hand to Pam. He was tall, his angular, wind-burned face sporting a broad smile. Long, red-blonde hair with a touch of gray was tied back in a pony tail, blowing about his wide shoulders in the wind. He was pretty much what Pam had expected a Swedish sea captain of the era might look like, but a lot more handsome! She took his hand, and tried not to blink like a smitten school-girl.

"*Frau* Miller, it is such a pleasure to meet you. I am Torbjörn, your captain for the voyage. Allow me to present your ship, a Dutch *fluyt*, which has been refurbished to help make you more comfortable. We have renamed her the *Redbird*, in your honor. We are at your service." he ended his welcome with a charming bow.

The captain spoke an understandable, but slightly odd-sounding German, touched by northern dialects, and spiced with the music of the Scandinavian tongues. Even so, he pronounced *Redbird* in crystal clear English. Pam looked up to see the name painted across the aft in an elegantly curved font, bright crimson with gold trim. She paused then to take the whole thing in. There was some kind of lethal-looking, big gun mounted on her deck, the sight of its polished metal gave her a chill, and she hoped fervently its presence would prove unnecessary. Her gaze continued around the vessel. It was not quite what she had imagined, shorter, stouter, and despite the fresh coat of paint, a bit more used looking than the great old ships of days of yore she had seen in the movies. It didn't quite manage to be ugly, but it was by no means a graceful schooner. Was it really seaworthy? She hid her concerns, and smiled back at the captain.

"Pleased to meet you, Captain Torbjörn, and let me say that I am honored by the renaming and modification of your ship. That was all very thoughtful and no doubt an inconvenience."

This pleased the captain, who obviously saw something beautiful in his vessel that she didn't as he regarded the lumpy looking thing with pride.

"It is our pleasure, *Frau* Miller, merely a gesture to honor you and our beloved Princess Kristina. We hope to make you and your staff as comfortable as possible during the long voyage. My usual small crew has been augmented by a group of volunteer soldier-sailors from the princess' own guard, you might call them 'marines' in your American English." With a confident smile he switched into heavily accented English. "You will be protected by the very best during our voyage. Now, allow me to welcome you all aboard!"

The captain beckoned them to follow him up the steep gang plank, leading the way with a spry and well practiced step. Pam followed slowly, holding on tightly to the rail ropes, which she was pretty sure were not standard, and looked to have been hastily rigged up for their use. Making a point not to look down at the water below, she stepped onto the decks of the *Redbird* with a quiet sigh of relief. Mercifully, her hangover was mostly gone, dissipated by the salt air and excitement.

Once assembled in an area of the deck relatively clear of casks, coiled ropes, and sundry other nautical apparatus, the captain asked them to wait for a moment while he made sure their cabins were indeed ready.

As they waited, Dore's face had grown paler than usual, giving her bright red cheeks the appearance of two poppies on a field of snow. Pam smiled, and took her dear friend by the hand, hiding her own grumbling fear as best as she could.

"Don't worry Dore," she said softly to the older woman, "I think I like this captain, and I feel we are in very capable hands."

"Of course, of course!" Dore replied with her usual confident tones, but there was no mistaking the tremble in her well-calloused washerwoman's hands.

Gerbald, for his part, was grinning like a lunatic, looking around the ship as if it were the greatest thing ever to happen to him.

"Ah, the life of a seaman, braving the waves and winds in search of adventure!" he exclaimed, his exuberance bringing a dour scowl from his wife.

"Now he fancies himself a sailor-man, does he?" she said in a quiet tone, so as not to be heard by the busy crew going about their duties around them. "Well, from what I know of the breed, a scoundrel like my brute of a husband here will fit in well, although a pirate's life would suit him better!"

Gerbald merely grinned all the wider, smugly taking Dore's disparaging remarks as compliments. "Do you think so? How fun that would be, the yo-ho-ho and bottles of rum! With luck, I'll have the opportunity!"

"We'll just see about that, you black-hearted fool!" Dore rolled her eyes and blew her usual puff of disgust-filled air his way, while the unrepentant Gerbald continued his happy inspection of their new home for the months to come.

The captain returned soon after, along with a ruddy-looking fellow with a harried-expression on his rather chubby face. "This is my first mate, *Herr* Janvik. He will escort you to your cabins. We shall be setting sail in an hour's time. I hope you will join us on deck as we bid farewell to Bremen."

"This way, please," the first mate said in rudimentary sounding German. Pam vowed to herself that she would take the opportunity to add Swedish to her growing collection of languages during the long trip. Gerbald was still gawking at the sailors and their sails as they entered the dimness below-decks. Pam gave him a quick whistle.

"Come along, Smee," she called to him in wry tone, "before you get in the way, and they decide to make you walk the plank before we've even left the harbor."

"Ah, another pirate tradition! How grand! It wouldn't do much good though. I am quite unsinkable." Gerbald exclaimed, then chuckled, pleased with himself until Pam heard a dull thud and looked back to see him rubbing his forehead at the spot in which it had bounced off a low beam.

"I wouldn't be so sure, my friend. All those rocks in your head might take you right to the bottom," Pam retorted. She and Dore both had a laugh at Gerbald's expense. He gave them a sheepish smile, and bent low to follow them to the waiting cabins. Pam and Dore exchanged a guilty grin; annoyance or not, Gerbald's boyish antics had served to alleviate the fear they shared. At least they were all together in this mad endeavor.

∞ ∞ ∞

Pam looked down at her bed, which was a rectangular opening in the wall surrounded by storage cabinets, and drawers. It was narrow, and a touch claustrophobic, but the mattress and bedding had been shipped from Grantville, so it would be clean and comfortable. There was a one-foot-tall wooden wall along the outer bedside that must be to keep her from rolling out onto the floor in heavy seas, it had an opening in the middle wide enough for her to allow for exiting and entering. Suddenly tired, she sat down to try it out. She lay her walking stick down between the edge of her heavy, wool blanket, and the thick timbers of the outer hull, a good place to keep it safely out of the way until needed again.

Looking about at her rather a-bit-too-cozy cabin, she saw there was a thick glass porthole letting some of the day's bleak, northern light fall on a fold-away desk. She had requested both, and was glad to see them. She could live without a lot of things, such as a private bath, but a desk she simply had to have, and a bit of natural light was always a good thing. The heavy wooden chair accompanying it was ornately carved in a floral motif, and looked fairly comfortable. She moved over to the desk and sat down. *Not too bad! Time to get settled in.*

Pam started unpacking her books and writing supplies, which she had insisted on carrying herself in her rucksack along with other precious and irreplaceable items such as her field glasses, and birding scope. After a moment's thought, she stopped. Considering the inherent dangers of the sea voyage to come, she decided to adopt a policy of keeping her most important things in the rucksack at all times, only fishing them out when necessary, and then putting them back as soon as she was done with them. If things went wrong, she could grab that bag and be gone quickly, well worth any inconvenience in the meantime.

During the voyage she intended to work on finishing some of the text for her book, *Birds of the USE*, and upon arriving in the Mascarenes begin writing about the species she would find there. The thought of this sent a wave of happiness through her. Yes, it was likely to be a hard journey, but the prospect of seeing the unusual birds of far off lands held a current of electric joy. And then there would be the dodo, a creature out of legend, the bird that she was coming to save. The very thought of it made her feel dizzy.

As she put her books and papers back into the rucksack she noticed the stiff corner of a photograph protruding from a dog-eared notebook. She pulled out the up-time style publicity shot the princess had given her on their last meeting, a black and white glossy of a bright eyed Kristina smiling shyly out at her subjects. On a whim, Pam stuck it into the crack between the wall and the low ceiling, a bit of decoration in the otherwise featureless cabin. She found that she liked this strange little ship better now that there was an echo of home in it. Her things were here, she was here, this was her place. She was brought out of her reverie by Dore's knocking, time to go up on deck.

The trip up the Weser River toward the sea was pleasant. They watched Bremen harbor's stolid buildings recede, replaced by farms and villages in vibrant spring colors despite the brooding skies. The rest of their small fleet followed along behind. There were two more *fluyts* holding the colonists, *Annalise* and *Ide*, and their military escort, the modest sized, but well-armed *Muskijl* brought up the rear. The *Muskijl* had been a captured imperial warship; it was now close to retirement, and apparently the best the princess could do. When the bosun, a cheerful-looking fellow who had some English told her the name literally meant "muscle," Pam laughed.

"That's good, we might need a little muscle." she grinned at her jest, but only Gerbald, well schooled in up-time English, laughed.

As they came to the end of the bay, the unsmiling first mate came to ask them up to the wheel as the surf would be getting rough, and it would be somewhat drier there. Standing behind the pilot and chatting with the captain, they got their first look at the North Sea, a dark, brooding mass topped with white spray. The wind picked up and was reaching what felt to Pam like gale force as *Redbird* bounded over the rollers.

"Refreshing, isn't it!" the captain shouted over the wind to his guests, who were beginning to turn alarming shades of green.

"Maybe we should go back to our cabins," Pam managed to shout back. She had never been in high seas before, and felt that her internal organs were jumping into the air, then landing back in new and uncomfortable configurations.

"No, my friends. It is better if you stay here for now, keep your eyes on the horizon and breathe deeply. You will get used to the movement soon enough," he told them, smiling kindly, but with a crinkle of amusement around the corners of his eyes at the landlubber's plight.

"I hadn't expected to be tossed around like a doll in the hands of an angry child," Gerbald muttered, trying to keep his balance as the deck moved beneath his feet. He was struggling mightily to maintain composure, but his face nearly matched the sage-green of his many-pocketed long coat. Pam looked at him and started to laugh, which turned out to be a mistake as her breakfast rushed up to join her chuckles. The captain nodded at a nearby youthful sailor, who gently escorted Pam to the back rail, where she was shortly joined by Dore and then Gerbald in a chorus of retching and spitting.

"Speaking of tossing . . ." Pam said nonchalantly to her friends before another round of vomiting hit her.

The captain, politely declining to observe their suffering, called over his shoulder, "There, you have it out of the way. It happens to us all at least once, and now you shall begin to feel better. Pers, kindly escort our guests below-decks, and get them cleaned up."

The young sailor, who looked to be still in his teens, tugged gently on Pam's coat sleeve, and the three of them meekly followed him down the stairs, nodding at the captain on their way, but too ill and embarrassed to manage eye contact.

"Loving the life at sea now, Greenbeard?" Pam managed to croak at Gerbald.

"Having sacrificed our breakfasts, perhaps the sea gods will be appeased, and provide us with gentler waters."

"May merciful God help us, he has been out here less than an hour and is already becoming a heathen," Dore muttered irritably.

Chapter Five: Getting to Know You

The North Sea and the Atlantic Ocean

After a miserable night of suffering with each roll of the waves, the North Sea had calmed somewhat by dawn. Pam, her sea sickness in remission at least for the while, spent the morning wandering around the decks, trying to stay out of the way of the sailors, and working on getting her sea legs. The sailors were all very polite to her. Several of them could speak a form of German she could mostly understand, and Pers could speak a little English, albeit with a very potent accent.

The young fellow was handsome in a classically Scandinavian way, with pale-blonde locks and bright-blue eyes. He explained that he had lived some of his youth in the Faeros Isles, which were part of the British Isles, but shared close ties with Scandinavia. He was a bright and friendly kid, not much older than her son Walt. Pam soon determined he would make a good Swedish language coach for the voyage. During what seemed a relatively idle hour for the crew, she began going about the ship with Pers in tow, asking how to say things in Swedish, or *Svenske* as she must now think of it.

"What is the sky called?"

"*Himmel*," Pers happily told her, enjoying the attention of the foreign lady from the future.

"And the sea?"

"*Hav*."

Pam jotted the words down in one of her notebooks. *It's pretty close to German,* she thought. *That might make this go even quicker.* Soon, other sailors became interested, and fairly tripped over themselves to point at things on the deck, repeating the *Svenske* words for them slowly and loudly to aid in her studies. Many of the items were nautical gear that she didn't even have a name for in English, and so found herself scribbling descriptions such as "rope and tackle thingie" and "looks kind of like a winch." Eventually, the first mate came along, and without saying a word, directed the men back to their work with an exceptionally hairy eyeball. Pam smiled sheepishly at him. He nodded politely enough before turning his attention to a sloppy line. His growled order to secure it properly made young Pers jump into action as if lit on fire.

Pam decided it would be a good time to go below decks to check on her friends, who still hadn't been sighted. She found them milling about their little cabin, in an attempt to make themselves presentable. They were both still green-tinged, but some of the color had come back to Dore's cheeks, and Gerbald was wearing the stony expression that so expertly hid the impish joker within.

"My Pam, I am sorry we are up so late," Dore apologized.

"It's all right, Dore. You needed the rest. I'm really sorry I got us into this, I never expected we would get so seasick."

Dore clucked such nonsense away. "Think nothing of it. The captain says that it shall pass."

Gerbald added in a wry tone, "It reminds me of the kind of hangover one gets after mixing too much whiskey with beer. There was definitely a spinning sensation to it."

Seeing the daggers in the eyes around him, he made his escape to the door. "I think I'm well enough now, shall we go up?" he asked nonchalantly.

"I'm feeling pretty good, too," Pam said "Being out in the fresh air helps."

Dore narrowed her eyes at her husband. "The fresh air will do nothing for this oaf's foolishness, I'm afraid. The good Lord knows he's had plenty of fresh air in his time, and it hasn't helped any yet!" She shoved past him to head to the steep, ladder-like stairs, followed closely by a chuckling Gerbald. Pam smiled at the warm familiarity of their banter.

After a tour around the deck and introducing her friends to Pers and his mates, the three of them stood watching the waves pass by. This seemed to suit Gerbald and Pam, who were practiced observers of nature, but Dore grew restless and fidgety.

"I don't know how you two can stand there and gaze at nothing! I'm going to go down to tidy up our cabins."

Pam and Gerbald knew that their cabins were already as tidy as could be since there had been hardly enough time to clutter them yet, but kept mum. There was no point in trying to stop Dore who, with shoulders pulled back in stiff determination, marched below decks to rejoin her never ending battle against dust, dirt and her new arch-enemy, germs, real or imagined.

"These may be the luckiest sailors ever," Gerbald remarked.

"How's that?"

"The next thing you know, Dore will be up here swabbing the decks and polishing the brass for them. They might as well go on holiday!" The two friends laughed, their voices swiftly carried away by the North Sea's bracing breezes.

∞ ∞ ∞

That evening they were invited to dine with the captain. The fluyt was not a very large vessel, and the captain's cabin was a little more than twice the size of Pam's own, while also serving as an office and dining room. She, Gerbald, and Dore joined the first mate, *Löjtnant* Lundkvist, the leader of their marine guard, and Nils, the ship's bosun, a red-cheeked, fifty-ish gentleman who was an old friend of the captain's, all squeezing in around the cramped, yet carefully set table.

The captain poured wine from an odd round bottle, which Pam recognized as a signature of Franconia's wineries.

"I hope this will make you feel a bit more at home." the captain said to them graciously, "Now that Thuringia has joined with Franconia I assume you share wine as well as borders. To a successful voyage!" He raised his glass in toast, being sure to meet everyone's eye one by one in the Scandinavian style. A chorus of Cheers!, *Prosit* and *Skål* came from the diners, bringing a cheerful mood to the slowly swaying cabin.

"It's lovely!" Pam remarked, having sipped the dry, but still slightly sweet, white wine. "Thank you for your thoughtfulness, Captain. You have made us feel so very welcome, and we do appreciate it."

That brought a pleased expression to the captain's wind-burned face. Pam smiled inwardly to herself. It was hard to believe that she, a former recluse, had somehow learned to function so glibly in public. She tried not to think about the fact that the captain was not only charming, but also rather handsome.

After another round of wine, a harried looking crewman arrived at the door bearing the first of several covered pewter trays. The fellow looked to be in his late thirties, and had the demeanor of one who strongly wished he were somewhere, perhaps anywhere, else. After bringing all the trays in, he leaned over to whisper to the first mate, and then made a hasty, bowing exit.

The first mate's expression was less than cheerful as he leaned over to whisper to the captain. The captain frowned and looked around solemnly at his guests.

"At the risk of spoiling our dinner before it has even begun, I must make an apology to our guests. It seems the ship's cook we hired for this voyage, a very capable fellow, had been suffering from an extreme case of gout, and had to resign at a very late hour. I am told there was no time to find a replacement before leaving port, and so Mr. Janvik here assigned the job to a less experienced man, crewman Mård. And now I am made to understand that Mård, while an excellent sailor, is even less experienced at cooking than we had hoped, and he wishes to extend his apologies, fearing that your meals may be quite a bit less savory than desired. Mind you that ship's fare is never very fancy at the best of times, but in any case I must extend also my apologies in advance."

There was a murmur of "Never mind!" and "Don't trouble yourself over us!" from around the table as the meal began. All put on a brave face, but the truth was that the food was supremely awful. The potatoes were only half-cooked, and needed to be cut with a steak knife, while the meat, which may have once been beef, had been charred to a crispy lump. Everyone did their best to eat at least some of it, but in the end their plates were hardly touched. Pam looked over to see Dore poking at a bowl of soggy, salted cabbage with her fork, a thoughtful expression on her perpetually rosy-cheeked face.

The captain sat back in his chair and sighed. "Honored guests, I have spent most of my life at sea, and I shall be blunt. I have eaten things that even a pig might pass up, and this is one of the worst. I can only once again offer my sincerest apologies. Tomorrow we shall signal the other ships to see if they can spare someone with at least a rudimentary knowledge of the culinary arts to become our new cook." His face was bleak. This was the kind of captain who took personal responsibility for all that transpired on his ship.

Pam found herself admiring him all the more, and suddenly felt a rush of relief; seventeenth century sailing aside, they were in as good a set of hands as could be found.

Dore looked at Pam with a questioning eye that meant *May I say something?* in the nonverbal communication they had established over their years of friendship.

"Dore, what's on your mind?" Pam asked her, hoping it would be what she suspected was forthcoming from the doughty German.

"I don't wish to speak out of turn, Captain, but perhaps I can be of service."

The captain raised his eyebrows at the woman who, thus far, had been as quiet as a mouse in his presence.

"Yes, *Frau* Dore? Please, you may speak freely at my table!"

"Well, there's really no need to take a cook from another boat. I can do the job myself. I have a lot of experience. Please, let me try."

The captain looked at Pam.

"She sure is a great cook, Captain!" Pam exclaimed "I can vouch for that!" Pam prayed inwardly that the captain would accept her friend's offer, she missed Dore's excellent cooking already, and it would make the voyage a much more pleasant experience.

"My wife is the best cook in all the USE!" Gerbald chimed in "I'll wager in all the Kalmar Union as well!" he added with a husband's pride, making Dore blush, and elbow him lovingly in the ribs.

The captain smiled while the usually dour first mate looked on with great interest. He had barely touched his food, yet judging from his pear-like shape he was a man who thought much of dinner, and missed few.

"Your offer is very kind, *Frau* Dore, but surely I cannot prevail upon you. You are a member of *Frau* Pam's personal staff and it wouldn't be right to put you to work on a voyage in which you are a passenger."

"Just try to stop her!" Gerbald countered wryly, earning himself another, less gentle blow to the ribs.

Dore straightened in her chair, casting aside the meek act she sometimes put on in front of strangers. "The truth is, Captain, I would very much like to do the job. Please understand that I am a woman accustomed to work. I've worked my entire life, and when I pass on to the next realm, my sincerest hope is the good Lord will have work for me to do there. Spending the next few months lolling around in the confines of this ship with nothing to do would bore me to tears. Please, I *need* to work! Again, I offer my services as ship's cook for the voyage, with the hope that you will accept." She fixed her gaze on the captain with determination in every inch of her robust frame.

The captain laughed, and threw up his hands in mock defeat. "Very well then, if *Frau* Pam and your husband have no objections, I don't!" Pam and Gerbald both nodded their approval enthusiastically. "The galley is yours."

"Good! Then I shall start immediately! If you would all be kind enough to amuse yourself for an hour, I shall make what repairs I can to this dinner, as well as make you a simple dessert."

"Mr. Janvik, by all means escort *Frau* Dore to the galley, and send some men to bring along these trays!"

The portly first mate nearly leaped from his seat, and Pam thought the sour-pussed fellow might actually be attempting to smile. They exited the captain's cabin at a speed which must surely be hazardous in such narrow confines.

Pam and Gerbald were left behind, both grinning like alley cats picking their teeth with feathers from the bluebird of happiness. The captain laughed heartily.

"I see from your faces that I am going to be most grateful for my new cook!"

The four remaining diners passed the time in conversation, the Grantvillers telling the Swedes of life in their most unusual town, and the captain and his bosun regaling them with tales of high seas adventure. The time passed by quickly and pleasantly.

One hour later to the very minute, a rich stew of fully cooked potatoes and pieces of meat salvaged from the center of the burnt round of beef came to the table, seasoned with onions, caraway seed, and thyme. It was, of course, excellent, and as the diners scraped the last molecules from their plates, Dore and a very relieved crewman Mård brought in the dessert, a soft and chewy spaetzel in a sugared cream, simple and delicious.

"So, that's why you had so much luggage, Dore!" Pam laughed "It was full of ingredients!"

"Well, I didn't know what to expect, and I needed to make sure you two ate properly on such a long trip. As it turns out, it's lucky I thought of it."

Dore sat back in her chair with her quiet kind of pride, dutifully accepting the rain of compliments. After the party ended with a round of minty schnapps, they made their way up to the deck for a breath of fresh air before retiring. By the lantern light, the sailors, whom she had also cooked a new meal for, all cheered when they saw Dore emerge, shouting praise in German and Swedish. Dore simply waved, and told them to shush. There was more than her usual rosy blush on her cheeks.

"Well, you certainly are the big hero tonight, Dore!" Pam gave Dore's arm a happy squeeze.

"I fixed up the sailor's dinner for them, too. It seems they liked it well enough."

Dore making light of her contribution was belied by the extremely pleased crinkles at the corner of her mouth and eyes. Later, Pam fell asleep smiling at the improved prospects of their crazy voyage.

∞ ∞ ∞

The next day, as Pam tried to get used to working at a desk that felt more like a carnival ride, one of the sailors brought her a pot of tea at Dore's instruction. His name was Fritjoff, and Pam thought he was likely the oldest of the crew, seeming to be in his seventies, yet still hale and hearty, which was sadly not always the case amongst down-timers. Tall, thin and sporting a long graying beard, Fritjoff was a serious old fellow not given to talk much. He set the tray down gently where she motioned him to, and shyly mumbled a reply to her thanks. As he was about to leave, something caught his eye, and his face lit up in a very surprising way.

"The princess!" he said in halting German. "Princess Kristina!" Pam raised her eyebrows at him, then remembered the photo she had put up the day before.

"Yes that's right. It's a photo of Princess Kristina."

The older gentleman's eyes were moist with adoration. They never moved from the photo which he studied as if to commit it to perfect memory. "We love the princess," he told her. "She is our light."

"Yes, I think I can understand that. She's a wonderful child, and she has a lot of heart." Pam watched Fritjoff stand there entranced, and wondered how long he would stare. After a very long moment he came to his senses, and began to leave hastily, apologizing profusely for having disturbed her work. Pam gave him an understanding smile, he seemed like a real sweet old guy.

"Think nothing of it, *Herr* Fritjoff. Say, wait a minute." Pam stood from her chair and reached for the photo. She pulled it carefully off the wall and studied it for a second. *You imp,* she thought. *This is all your fault, bless your too big for that skinny body heart.* With a broad smile, she held it out to Fritjoff. "Here, I'd like you to have it. I can get another easily enough when we get back, and I can see you think so much of her. Please, take it."

"*Frau* Pam, I can't . . ." Fritjoff said, but his eyes were fixed longingly on the glossy image of his adored princess.

"Yes, you can. In fact, I insist. I have had the honor of meeting the princess in person, and I am sure she would want you to have it."

Pam gently opened the old man's trembling hands, and placed the photo gently on his palms. "Only pick it up by the edges or it will smudge, and don't ever let it get wet! Now take it. It's yours now!"

Fritjoff's long fingers closed gently around the edges, moving carefully to grip it as she had instructed. He looked at Pam as if she had gifted him with eternal life, then bowed his head deeply to her.

"Thank you, *Frau* Pam. I shall never forget your generosity. I am in your debt." And with that he backed out of the cabin quickly, closing the door behind him. Pam could hear him nearly running down the narrow hall to show his mates his new treasure.

"Well, looks like I made a friend." Pam laughed to herself as she went back to work. That evening on her way to dinner she saw that the photo had been hung carefully in a place of honor near the stairs. Several of the sailors were looking at it with worshipful expressions. They grinned at Pam merrily as she went by, and thanked her repeatedly for sharing her wonderful photo. *Yeesh, that kid is a superstar to these people!* Pam rolled her eyes a bit once she was past the giddy sailors, but was secretly pleased at the reaction to her little good deed.

Chapter Six: Salt Tears and Sea Legs

The Atlantic Ocean

The days passed slowly as they made their way along what would, in another universe, have one day become a clipper ship route. Pam had studied everything she could find regarding her intended voyage before she had left Grantville, and found the age of the great clippers fascinating. *Alas, the heyday of the tall ship won't happen here,* Pam mused in her cabin. Those magnificent constructs of rope, sail, and wood were destined to be passed by all together in favor of bluntly effective engine power, an almost naturally evolved technological butterfly crushed by the gritty steel, and growling motors from the future.

Sometimes, the *Redbird* came in close to the other vessels in their small fleet, and they were able to wave and shout brief conversations to each other. Pam's Swedish was still clumsy, but the cheerfully stoic Swedes on the *Annalise*, *Ide* and ever-watchful *Muskijl* all congratulated her on her growing fluency, which pleased her greatly. She found that, by God, she *liked* these civilized scions of the Vikings. There was something about them that attracted her. Sometimes she would watch the captain going about his duties, and would find herself blushing. There was definitely something about him that attracted her, but she pushed such thoughts aside sharply. *No time for that, idiot! Get back to work!*

One afternoon, she and Gerbald walked the deck for some exercise, the stiff breezes of the Atlantic a refreshing respite from the confines of their cabins. There was something moving in the water about ten yards off the prow, so they paused to see what it was. Two large seabirds swam along the waves, chasing fish, and occasionally calling to each other. Pam was pretty sure they were flightless, their sleek wings looked thoroughly adapted to swimming.

"Are those penguins?" Gerbald asked, having seen them in the movies and taped TV shows he enjoyed so much.

"No . . . not penguins. They only live in the southern hemisphere, and we haven't passed the equator yet." Pam looked closer at the pair of large, swimming birds. They certainly looked like a penguin, about thirty-three inches long, their markings black-and-white, with a prominent white spot on the top of their heads. Still, their beaks seemed rather big for a penguin . . . Suddenly she remembered, another page in the sad little chapter in the back of *Birds of the World* shared by the dodo.

"Oh, my. I know what they are. They're great auks. They were extinct up-time, just like the dodo was," Pam told him in a very small voice, her eyes staring at the sight of the unique creatures, a classic case of convergent evolution, and yet another species destined for extinction.

One of the sailors, paused from his work to join them in watching the great auks.

"I haven't seen those things for a long time, not so many as there once were. I hear they make good eating!"

Pam just blinked at him, feeling her face grow hot, and her eyes fill with moisture. Suddenly, it was all much too big for a bird-loving former housewife stuck in the wrong century, and she couldn't stop the hot tears from coming, blurring the sight of birds that were surely doomed, wondering if she could somehow save them as well as the dodo, or if it weren't too late already. She mumbled an apology, and fled back to her cabin, burying herself under her blankets for a long cry.

On the deck, the sailor, a pleasant enough fellow called Helge, turned to Gerbald, his face filled with worry. "*Herr* Gerbald, I did not mean to offend the lady!"

"It's all right, friend. It wasn't you. It seems the world grows narrower and crueler with each passing year, and Pam's heart is so big she feels the pain more keenly than most."

Gerbald started to go, then paused, a slight smile on his face. He spoke then, in low, confidential tones. "Perhaps you haven't heard! I must warn you, it is very bad fortune to kill the great auks! I saw one fellow who ate one die terribly, as if he had ingested poison! It was awful! His face turned green, and he coughed blood." He paused for dramatic effect, then leaned in closer. "But here's the worst thing: The *same thing happened* to that fellow's mates, and they hadn't even taken a bite yet! Very bad juju."

The sailor's face was very pale as Gerbald nodded his head knowingly

"If I were you, I would take those birds permanently off the menu. That is, if you want to live! Better spread the word."

Gerbald smirked to himself as he walked back to his cabin, not realizing that he, himself, had just taken a major step toward preventing the future extinction of the great auk.

∞ ∞ ∞

The long days at sea rolled on. And on.

"Does that hat of yours ever come off?" young Pers asked Gerbald as they stood watching the increasingly sunny skies of their southerly course. He spoke in Swedish; Gerbald and Dore had soon joined Pam in the effort to learn that musical tongue of the far north, and they were all picking it up fast, especially since there was not much else to do. Pam chimed in, also in *Svenske*, the words now coming swift and sure.

"Ha! He'd feel naked without it! I would have sworn that it's sewn to his head if I hadn't seen him take it off for dinner." Pam laughed. Along with his sage-green, many-pocketed wool longcoat, the ridiculous-looking, mustard-colored hat made up Gerbald's signature look, no matter how much they teased him about it.

"I insist on that much. He used to take it off in church as well, but his shadow never crosses that doorstep anymore," Dore added, with an admonishing look at her confirmed black sheep husband.

"But what about the wind? *Herr* Gerbald, do you not worry that the sea breeze will take it?" Pers asked him in a concerned tone. "I've lost my hats so many times I no longer bother to wear one."

"No, my friend, it troubles me not. If nature should take it from me, it only means that it is time for a new one," Gerbald reassured him in his usual, quietly self-confident tones.

Pam and Dore both looked at each other with wide eyes, which then narrowed into the slits of hunting cats.

"Nature nothing! Get it, Dore!" and with that, both women lunged at Gerbald in a bid to tip his ridiculous hat off into the wind. He dodged them both easily of course, reflexes honed to avoid the jabs of deadly pike and sword being no match for such innocent sport as this. Laughing, he gently kept his assailants at arm's length until they gave up, the offending headgear still safely in place.

"Oh well, it was a good try," Dore grumbled, flushed and slightly out of breath. "I have thought to burn it while he sleeps many times, but oh the fuss he would make, I would never hear the end of it! Men are such children about their precious things."

Pam shook her head in resignation. "Well, I guess he wouldn't be Gerbald without that stupid hat. It's like his trademark or something."

"There are still a few men in the Germanies who fear the sight of this hat, you know," Gerbald remarked matter-of-factly, adjusting the floppy mustard brim to no visible effect; the felt remained warped and ragged.

"A few men?" Pers asked, still in awe of the ex-soldier but curious.

"Yes, it is so. I had some notoriety on the battlefield, long ago," he said, his hand instinctively going to the hilt of his trusty shortsword, pulling it partially out of its scabbard to proudly show it off to Pers. "This *katzbalger* is feared by more than just cats!"

"Please excuse my forwardness, but with prowess such as yours, why *only a few*?" The cheerful young fellow's question held just a note of teasing, trusting in the good nature of his new friend.

"Because most who have met this sword are dead, young fellow! Some survived, but only a few." Allowing himself one of his very rare, proud-as-a-lion-and-twice-as-dangerous-smiles, Gerbald sauntered away, every inch the great warrior, leather boots to ridiculous hat. Pers grinned after him, in full blown hero worship.

Pam and Dore looked at each other with eyebrows raised. Gerbald seldom spoke of his soldiering past, much less bragged about it.

"All hail the conquering hero! Must be the sea air?" Pam asked wonderingly.

"He rarely speaks such words!" Dore answered in a surprised tone. "Perhaps it is the close company of other fighting men." She nodded toward the Swedish marines drilling further down the deck rail. "He is still very proud of those days, you know."

"I'm just glad he's on our side," Pam said, and meant it. Meanwhile, Gerbald had sauntered over to the marines. After a brief, and smiling discussion with the *löjtnant*, they watched him join in their drills, stepping and swinging the deadly katzbalger right along with the rest. Not long after that, they saw that Gerbald, an experienced combat veteran, was giving the younger men some pointers.

"Oh, here we go now." Dore switched back to German, frowning deeply as she pointed at her husband with her chin. "The great soldier will teach these Swedish boys how it's done. He will be full of himself tonight." With a long-suffering roll of her eyes, she headed back to her galley.

Pers had been standing with them quietly watching the drills until the ever-surly first mate walked by, and cuffed him lightly on the head, causing the lad to bend himself back to the nearest task at hand in embarrassed haste. Pam turned back to the view over the rail with a smile, and watched the gulls swoop and cry alongside the ship, her heart filled with a sudden, and surprising contentment with life at sea.

Chapter Seven: Under Southern Skies

The Equator and the South Atlantic Ocean.

The days were growing warmer. They were headed for one of their way-markers, the Saint Peter and Saint Paul archipelago, near the equator, and roughly halfway between South America and Africa. Darwin himself had stopped there, and described two species of bird, a booby and a noddy, so Pam was anxious for a sighting. She prowled the decks peering through her scope and binoculars, but so far had been rewarded with only common gull and tern species. The area was known for storms, but the breeze that bore them along was sultry today. The men had taken off their shirts to work in an effort to keep cool. Panning around to the bridge with her binoculars Pam saw to her surprise that this included the captain!

Unable to stop herself, she paused to study the man; his chest and back were a bit hairy, but it was of a fine, red-gold color, and not too long, maybe even attractive. He was definitely in good shape, she had seen him drill beside the marines with what looked to be considerable skill with a longsword. He could also often be seen pitching in at the ropes, he was the kind of leader who would get his hands dirty if need be, and the men loved him for it. Pam admired his lean physique, that of a much younger man. She was just about to turn away when he noticed her attention, and flashed her a smile and a friendly wave. *Ack! I've been caught!* Pam, blushing hotly, gave him a feeble wave in return, then pretended to be interested in a handy seabird flying by, hoping he couldn't see the scarlet hue her face had taken on from that distance. *Gawd Pam, you are acting like a silly teen-ager!* She chided herself. *Still,* she admitted to herself with a tiny smile, *he is pretty hunky.*

Later that day, Pam declined a stop at the rocky atoll. She had read Darwin's notes on it, and there wasn't much of anything she could add to them, so they might as well just keep going. It made her feel depressed. Here she was risking her life on an expedition in a world where someone else had already discovered almost everything in a future that wouldn't even happen that way again. Deep down she knew that any research she did would have value, but the feeling of being a dwarf following along in the footsteps of giants, even ghostly ones who would now never even be born, made her feel insignificant.

Pam was quiet through dinner that evening. After dessert, the captain asked everyone to join him up on the bridge for a toast. Pam looked at Gerbald, but her friend only shrugged. The bosun, however, had a knowing look about his ruddy face. The night was a bit cooler than the day had been, and very clear, the stars so thick and close they felt they could pluck them out of the sky like grapes from a vine. Once Dore arrived from the galley, the bosun passed out a cup to everyone into which the captain poured a very fine French brandy.

"I've been saving this for a special occasion. Today we crossed the equator, having now come a long way on our journey. I would now like to direct your attention to the south." He pointed with his brandy glass. "Do you see those bright stars there, low on the horizon, in a group? They are, I am assured, the Southern Cross, and it is the first time I have ever seen them. Perhaps it is the same with some of you. They are as beautiful as their reputation states, and I hope for their blessing. And so, we have arrived at an excellent time and a place for a toast." He raised his cup as the others followed suit. "Here's to the good ship *Redbird* and all who sail on her!"

A chorus of *Skål* followed, and Pam found herself feeling better as the warm night and the delicious brandy worked to soothe her soul. While Gerbald joined the Swedes in another round of drinks, Pam noticed Dore had drifted off to the rail by herself, where she gazed solemnly out at the southern sky. Pam joined her friend, giving her a friendly bump which made Dore smile.

"Penny for your thoughts, Dore?"

Dore smiled again, Pam could see that the usually doughty woman was quite moved, and needed to gather herself before speaking. Eventually she turned to her younger friend.

"I never thought I would see anything like this Pam. The Southern Cross, the great oceans; these are sights for men of adventure, for the brave and the mad. . . . I'm just an old washer-woman, a simple soldier's simple wife. I never thought I'd be in places like these. . . ." Her voice trailing, Dore gazed up at the winking lights of unfamiliar constellations, slowly shaking her head, her face having taken on an almost child-like look of wonder.

Pam nodded slowly. "Neither did I, Dore, not in a million years. I'm just glad you're here to see it with me. It makes it a lot easier to cope with. Thank you for coming along on this crazy voyage. It's a lot to ask from a friend, even one as dependable as you."

"It's nothing, Pam. I would not have let you go without me! I just didn't expect such beauty, such thrills. I am glad I saw this, I am glad we are here, doing these things. It's . . . fun."

At that revelation, it was Pam's turn to have her words catch in her throat, so she just looked back at Dore with wide eyes, and grinned her biggest grin.

∞ ∞ ∞

As they continued south and then eastward, the weather got cooler. It was still winter in the southern hemisphere, and the warmth of the equator was fading with each passing day. One chilly morning Pam got up before dawn to make her way to the deck rail. She hadn't been able to sleep for several hours, and figured she might as well get some fresh air. Looking out to the north she gasped. The flat horizon had been replaced with a purple rise of distant land. *That's Africa!* she realized with a rush of excitement.

"There's the Cape of Good Hope, *Frau* Pam," the bosun told her as he came over to lean on the rail beside her. "A lovely sight, isn't it?"

"It's like I'm in a dream sometimes, one incredible thing after another. I really never thought I would see a place as far away as this. None of us did."

They watched as the sun rose, bands of light and shadow lent the continent the appearance of some vast, enigmatic monument fashioned of gold, and ebony. After a few minutes spent drinking it all in, the bosun gave the scene an admiring little whistle before ambling off to his duties, but Pam stayed there, mesmerized.

A few minutes later, Dore, always an early riser joined her on the deck with two mugs of hot coffee, one of which she placed in Pam's eager hands. They gazed at the red vastness of dawn-painted Africa for a while, then Dore spoke aloud in a reverent tone:

" '*And God called the dry land Earth; and the gathering together of the waters called he Seas: and God saw that it was good.*' "

∞ ∞ ∞

They were getting close now. The weather turned from fair to foul, and Pam felt she was back on the North Sea again. Day after day they bounded across hair-raising swells. That morning, the captain had told her that they might sight Mauritius by afternoon, maybe even be able to land if all went well. Pam had become increasingly anxious over the last few days of unpleasant pitching and rolling. The rough seas had dampened her mood, even though the sailors said they were happy there were such strong winds to push them along.

Feeling cooped up in her cabin, and frustrated with what had come to seem a never ending journey, she decided that cruel waves and wind or not, she would spend the day keeping watch. She really couldn't just sit and wait any more. After a late breakfast from an ever sympathetic Dore, Pam bundled up in her best foul weather gear to go stalk the decks, binoculars ever at the ready. She even trusted young Pers with her precious birding scope in order to have another set of keen eyes on the task. He had been eager to climb into the crow's nest and help her keep vigil. The bosun had allowed it, and the first mate had apparently elected not to interfere, despite surely considering it a shameful waste of the lad's abundant energies. She looked up at the bridge to give the captain a hopeful smile, which he returned when he noticed her there. He had dressed in a fancier than usual coat today, and cut a fine figure.

"Come on up here, *Frau* Pam!" he called down. She climbed the steep ladder-steps carefully, grateful to be that much higher above the bitter cold, splashing seas.

"I see you are eager to get there, *Frau*. One hopes you have not grown unhappy with our service?"

"Oh, no, not at all! You're wonderful, I mean, you and your crew, all wonderful!" *Gawd, you sound like a total dork!* The captain laughed amiably, he had only been kidding, and fully understood her desire to reach their destination.

"Of course, of course. It's been a long voyage! I must admit I'm looking forward to some time on shore, maybe have some fresh fruit—not that *Frau* Dore's cooking isn't delicious, it's the best ship's fare ever! I don't imagine you would let me keep her on?" he asked, grinning in jest.

"No way, buddy. She's mine!" They shared a good laugh and Pam began to feel the knot of tension that had been forming in her shoulders ease. *We really are almost there! I can hardly believe it!*

"Dodos, here I come!" she said to herself as the captain turned back to his duties.

The hours passed by slowly. Behind them the weather from the south promised to turn surly, black clouds were building, and the wind had dropped a few degrees. Ahead of them the *Muskijl* tread solidly along, the *Annalise* and *Ide* just ahead of her. Their fleet might be few in numbers and made up of small vessels, but Pam now understood that they were also tough, the product of years of shipbuilding know-how in the wintry north. They were made for weather like this, and took it in stride.

"That's a real demon storm brewing down there," the bosun muttered darkly when he came up on the bridge to confer with the captain.

"Looks no worse than a North Sea squall," the first mate said, his voice full of tedium.

"Now it does, but this is the south, and the weather's different down here, meaner. I've seen it like this before down near Cape Horn. When she hits us tonight she'll be full blowing all right. Let's hope we're in the lee from it, behind the island."

As the weather worsened, Pam did her best to go unnoticed, hoping the captain wouldn't send her belowdecks. He and the pilot, sturdy Arne, both held the wheel steady, their eyes were only for the waves. The sky behind them darkened, in stark contrast to the bright skies to the North.

The afternoon was slipping by, the descending sun's rays slanting across *Redbird*, casting her in bronze as the shadows grew longer on her decks. Pam's eyes were aching from straining to see over the horizon, and she began to feel tired, regretting the foolishness of her long watch. She was just about to go find some tea, and possibly pour a little whiskey in it, when Pers' excited call came from above.

"There it is! The island! The island of the dodos!" Pam ran to the rail, fumbling to get her binocular straps untangled. The ceaseless rolling of the sea had a way of tying them up in knots. With her naked eye she saw something to the north, a blur of color above the sea's distant curve. Focusing in carefully, she had a clear view; pastel smudges of lavender and green, volcanic mountains rising majestically from the islands interior.

"Mauritius. At least that's what I'll call you until we give your new name to go with your new destiny." Pam grinned up at Pers' pale face high in the crow's nest, and waved crazily at him. Not letting go for a second even to wave, he grinned back, letting out a loud whoop of joy. They were moving fast with the blustery wind, and the mountains grew larger and higher above the horizon. The captain deemed it safe enough, so Dore and Gerbald were summoned to come join them on the bridge, where they all milled about, grinning like children at the county fair, nearly half out of their minds with excitement. Gerbald had remembered to bring along a bottle of schnapps and was passing it around merrily, careful not to let the waves ceaseless rocking spill any.

The captain soon caught their joyful mood, and told them in a very pleased voice, "Our colonists may be able to set foot on their new home this eve after all, if we can find a safe anchor before dark. We'll head up the east side. The storm is blowing from south by southwest, so we'll have more protection there. Your maps from the future show several suitable harbors. Let's hope they are right." The man turned back to the wheel, well earned pride in his every move. Pam made herself stop staring at his broad shoulders, and returned to the impromptu party at the rail. That was when Pers called again from the crow's nest.

"Sails in the east! A ship is coming around the island's east side!" The revelers quieted themselves, they hadn't happened on many other ships on their journey since leaving the North Atlantic, and the presence of another vessel here and now seemed a surprise. Pam held her binoculars to her face, hurrying to find the ship, which had now turned southward, headed directly toward them.

"It's big," she told them calmly enough. "And it's got guns. Big guns." She lowered the binoculars, then quickly handed them to the captain. After he found his focus he was quiet for a moment. He handed the binoculars back to Pam, his face ashen.

"It's a French warship. Their crew is readying her guns. We are about to be attacked."

Chapter Eight: Sacrifice

Near the Southern Coast of Mauritius

The captain's face was grim as he watched little *Muskijl* place itself between *Redbird* and the attacking French man-of-war, a David dwarfed by a terrifying Goliath. It was doubtful God could provide as lucky an outcome. *Muskijl* was far beyond her class in this match. Behind the looming warship, *Analise* and *Ide* were trying to flee to the northeast, but Pam saw several smaller ships with elegantly slanting triangular sails in their path. *Lateen,* she said to herself, remembering the word from her far too brief crash course in seventeenth-century sailing. The kind of sails used by the infamous Barbary corsairs. *That can't be good. What is going on here?* A thundering *boom* jarred her from her thoughts; the French had opened fire on *Muskijl*.

"Will we fight beside *Muskijl*, Captain? The men are ready at the carronade and cannons," Janvik asked, his face as pale as the wild, skirling clouds that blew before the tailing storm.

The captain watched the battle begin through his spyglass. After a moment of silence he shook his head. "No. Captain Lagerhjelm has waved us off. He will sacrifice *Muskijl* to give us a chance of escape. Hard to port; we will make for the west. Have the men—"

Before he could finish his orders an explosion somewhere below them rocked the *Redbird,* throwing Pam to the deck. She came to her knees but stayed there, not daring to move, hand gripping the rail. The French had trained a long gun on them, a warning not to flee or just a sampling bite of their next meal.

"*Jävla fransk kuksugare!*" the captain cursed, "Keep steady for the west!"

"She's coming around sluggish, sir! I think they've hit our rudder!" The pilot's voice was strained as he pulled on the wheel with all his strength. Another crewman leaped to his side to help.

Gerbald turned to Pam.

"We should get belowdecks, Pam. It would be safer there."

"I'm not so sure about that. I think I want to stay here. I'd rather know what's happening than wait in the cabin. You two go down; I'll be all right."

Dore nodded. "I have seen enough war in my time, a battle at sea is not so different. I will go to the galley and prepare emergency supplies, in case we must leave the ship."

"And I wish to go get my weapons. If we are boarded, I will stand beside these men." Gerbald's voice was barely audible over the cannon fire. Despite announcing their intention to leave her side, the two of them remained, looking to Pam for some signal that they really had her approval. After a moment she figured this out, and gave them both a gentle shove.

"Go, both of you! I am as safe with these guys as I would be with you. Better we prepare for the worst. Go, and be careful!"

Looking back at her with worried faces, Dore and Gerbald hurried down the ladder. Another shot from the man-of-war ripped through a sail, not doing much damage, but definitely adding to the tension.

"Shall we return fire, Captain?" Janvik's eyes had taken on a predatory character, Pam was surprised to see a boiling fury there. The man was usually so cold, showing no emotion beyond a constant irritation. They all turned their gaze to the ongoing battle, poor *Muskijl* was barely visible within a pall of cannon smoke. She listed now, tattered and torn like a toy boat forgotten on the pond for the winter. She had scored a few hits on the man-of-war, but the outcome was clear enough. The French soldiers were gathering now, readying to board her. Swedish marines stood proudly waiting on *Muskijl*'s heavily damaged deck, prepared for the inevitable. They would give their lives to buy the fleet under their guard more time.

"No, damn it all, we run!" The captain's voice was filled with pain. "This is a civilian ship, the princess' mission comes before anything else!" he shouted. His tone softening, he added "We would stand no chance, my friend. Let us hope we live to see revenge. Bosun! Report!"

"Sir!" The bosun was bent precariously over the stern rail attempting to see how bad the damage was. "Not good, Captain. We barely have a rudder left; she's held together by splinters."

Inch by painful inch the *Redbird* changed its course, exiting the battle with all available speed. Another shot from the French gun landed against her starboard side even as she pulled away. Pam started to get up to view the damage, but the captain saw her move.

"Blast it all, woman, stay down! I'd tell you to get below, but it's no safer there!" Behind them the roar of cannons had stopped, replaced by the lightning strike crack of musket and pistol fire. They were still near enough to hear the sound of men screaming in agony. Pam tried to watch the action astern, but the ever increasing power of the waves slamming into their side made it hard to focus. She felt sick, but not from the movement of the sea. Men were dying today, dying for her mission, for that damned dodo. She fought back angry tears, her hands pale and bloodless as they gripped the *Redbird*'s rails. The wind was picking up, the storm had arrived with untamed Antarctic wrath.

"We've got to find safe harbor before this gale blows us up on the rocks!" Janvik yelled over the howling wind.

"If the rudder holds we have a chance!" The captain joined the sailors at the wheel, they held *Redbird* on course with all their strength. "Bosun, tell that fool Pers to come down from the rigging before he blows away!"

Redbird pitched up and down like a roller coaster, cold spray drenching them. It became much darker all of a sudden as storm clouds overtook them. Pam saw Mauritius drawing closer, still lit by the setting sun, the waves pushing them toward frothing shores.

"Pam!" The captain called to her. She left her place by the rail to stand before him, steadied by one of his strong arms grasping hers. He was dripping wet, his muscles trembling from the cold, and the strain of man-handling the damaged rudder. "Quickly now, go below and get only your most precious things. There is a chance we may have to abandon *Redbird*; best to prepare for the worst! Don't tarry! Then I want the three of you waiting beside the ship's boat, understood?"

"Yes, sir!" she shouted back over the roaring wind. Their eyes locked for a moment, icy blue to cloudy gray. The captain managed a smile for her. "Fear not, my friend. Who knows what fate awaits? We have escaped those French bastards, and now we may survive the ocean's rage as well." Pam sensed that he wasn't as hopeful as he meant to sound, but gave him a smile back, anyway. This satisfied him, he gave her arm a squeeze before releasing her, and turned back to his struggle with the wheel. Pam knew she wanted him to do much more than squeeze her arm, but now was not the time for such thoughts. Still, she smiled again despite all the horror unfolding around her. *We are going to survive. We must!* she told herself.

Pam hurried down the ladder as carefully as she could. Everything was made slippery by the crashing sea and the icy rains that had come to join the winds. After a half-slipping half-sliding journey across the bucking ship, she paused at the rail near the hatchway to the lower decks. Pausing to catch her breath, she stole a look back at the battle they had left behind. There in the distance, still illuminated by the day's last feeble rays, the two ships were locked together, smoke streaming from battered *Muskijl* in long, orange ribbons. Pam saluted the brave crew that had sacrificed themselves to give *Redbird* and the rest of their fleet a chance to escape. A great swell blocked the view, then another. The sun set, storm clouds swept low over the world, and the tragic scene went to black.

Garrett W. Vance

Chapter Nine: Redbird Down

*P*am was about to begin crying for lost *Muskijl* when Gerbald and Dore emerged, so she held back her tears to show courage to her friends. Each was carrying a variety of baggage. Pam wasn't sure how anyone could haul so much stuff.

"The captain says we may have to abandon ship. Wait beside the ship's boat while I go get my things."

"I will go!" Gerbald told her.

"No, you stay with Dore! I'm smaller and I can move faster—three minutes!" Pam ran to the hatch, and somehow made her way to the deck below without falling.

Pam was thrown against the wall of her cabin as *Redbird* listed hard again. She hit her elbow right on the funny bone, which is never very funny at all. Gasping with pain, she pushed herself toward her desk. "I have seconds, only seconds," she muttered.

Her trusty rucksack was there already holding her most precious gear. *Good thing I thought of that. I wish I wasn't right about things so much.* She stuffed her notes from the desk and her pencil box in; everything else was replaceable. Her flashlight was on her bed; she grabbed it just as the boat listed again, this time throwing her to the wet and sloshing floor. She saw her grandmother's walking stick lying on the bed against the wall; sadly it would have to be left behind, there was no way she could hang onto it and get herself back topside. She would need both hands to navigate the dangerously tossing path. She shoved the flashlight into her rucksack, zipped it shut, and shrugged it onto her back. Seawater slapped hard against the small portal. She realized she was standing in eight inches of sloshing seawater now, the ship must have sprung a leak from one of the cannon hits. It was well past time to go!

Back on deck the scene was mayhem. The waves were driving them closer and closer to the rocky shores of the island. Dore was clutching a large wicker basket as if it were a darling infant, while Gerbald helped load the ship's boat, a long pinnace, along with several of the marines while the sailors struggled to keep *Redbird* alive. Pam could barely see the captain through the rain and darkness. She thought she heard cannon fire again but it was the impact of massive waves on cliffs. Mauritius towered over them like an unfriendly giant, illuminated by eerie flashes of blue lightning.

The bosun arrived, his usually cheery face grim and lined with worry. "We are abandoning ship! All hands to the pinnace!"

The sailors grimly dropped whatever they were doing to make ready for launch. Pam couldn't imagine how this was going to work in these wild seas. She told herself to breathe, and to trust in these good souls who had befriended her on their long voyage together. She was angry, too, but there was no time for that now. She knew she must focus on each moment or it might become her last.

"Come, my friends, get in, get in!" he ordered them. The first mate was holding tight to the line, his face gray with the strain, trying to keep the pinnace steady.

"The captain!" Pam cried, looking back at the man who now stood alone at the nearly useless wheel, buying them what time he could before the rocks could take her. "Captain!" she shouted, louder, frantically trying to get his attention.

He waved them off frantically. "Go! Go now!" His words were barely audible over the crashing seas.

"He will do as he must; you can't help him! Now get in or we all die here!" the bosun shouted. With a firm hand, he half pushed, half helped Pam into the swinging pinnace. The small craft bucked and leaped on its lines. She and Dore collapsed into the boat's bottom on top of the baggage. Gerbald arched himself over Pam and Dore, trying to stay out of the way of the sailors as well as using his own bulk to prevent the women from being pitched out.

They were lowered swiftly into the fast-moving water, which caused them to bounce even more crazily. Around them, the sailors and marines climbed in, readying themselves at the oars, their movements fluid and confident despite the raging waves. Pam looked up at the first mate who was still on deck, having seen them safely lowered. He favored her with a smile, the first she had ever seen upon his thin lips.

"May God be with you, *Frau* Miller." With a swipe of his knife he cut the pinnace loose.

Suddenly understanding the risk he was taking for them Pam shouted "Thank you, *Herr* Janvik!" as loudly as she could. The first mate granted her a sketch of a wave before hurrying to join his captain at the wheel.

The nimble craft moved rapidly away from *Redbird*, more steady now that she was free of the ship and fully manned. They rode fast, carried by the marching swells, surfing along like the canoe in that old TV show *Hawaii Five-0*. The show's dramatic theme song began to play in Pam's mind, and she wondered for a moment if she would wake up on her sofa in front of the TV, all of this just an awful dream.

"Thank the Lord! The cliffs stop here, there's a beach. Make for it!" the bosun shouted. The sailors and marines rowed for their very lives, silent and determined to beat the hungry sea.

Pam forced herself out from under Gerbald's protective weight to grasp the gunwale. She could see *Redbird* through the sheets of rain; some of her lanterns were still lit despite the gale. As the ship spun about and rolled precariously, she caught a glimpse of where the enemy cannon had punched a jagged hole just beneath her water line. No wonder she had grown so sluggish. It was a bullet through the heart of her. The captain and first mate were still trying to steer the badly damaged craft away from the rocky point toward the same possible safety the pinnace was fleeing to, but an unseen rock caught her, and sent her over on her side. Pam couldn't see if they had time to leap free or not. The *Redbird* rolled completely over; the sound of her wood scraping and splintering against the rocks was the screeching music of hell itself. Pam screamed over the gale, her voice lost in the curtains of rain that now mercifully hid the wreck of the *Redbird* from view.

Their troubles were not over. Sweeping twelve-foot rollers pounded against the narrow beach they were aiming for. Landing would be dangerous.

The bosun shouted to the frightened passengers and crew, "We are going to try to bring her all the way in but it's ugly—if we go over, you'll have to try to make it on your own!"

Pam looked down to see Dore's face was white and filled with fear, a sight that Pam would have given anything never to have witnessed.

"I can't swim!" Dore blurted out, a trace of sob in her voice that brought a gush of fresh tears from Pam's eyes. Thankfully, Dore couldn't see them as they were lost amongst the ceaseless raindrops.

"I can swim for both of us, don't worry!" Pam shouted back, injecting a tone of confidence she didn't really feel. Pam was in the grip of clutching fear, fear of an intensity she hadn't felt since the time she had stood between a badly wounded Gerbald and an evil man wielding a bloodstained sword, herself with just her grandmother's walking stick to defend them. She had lived through that; maybe she would live through this, too. The thought helped quell the worst of her terror.

The pinnace and her frightened passengers sped toward the shore, the white sands intermittently lit by cobalt lightning like some haunted dance floor beneath a spectral strobe. The bosun ordered the men to row harder as he used the tiller to guide the craft over the treacherous waves. Pam clutched Dore, and Gerhald clutched them both, grimly ready to swim if they must. The bosun let out a whoop that had something of joy in it as he turned the pinnace quickly to starboard. Through the rain and darkness Pam could see that the shore at that edge of the wide cove was somewhat protected by a jutting wall of rock, another arm of the same rocky point that had destroyed the *Redbird* farther out. If they could make it in to the calmer waters behind that, the chances of landing the boat safely would greatly improve; and if they didn't, they would crash against the very rock that could save them.

"Get ready to jump if I say so. It's going to be close!" the bosun bellowed over the storm and hollow booms of the waves slamming onto the shore. The sailors heaved mightily on their oars at the bosun's hoarse commands, now surfing again along the face of an awesome wave, growing menacingly taller as it reached the shallows. The rock wall loomed ahead of them, waves crashing against it in foaming white fury.

"Steady . . . steady . . . Now, hard to starboard, men, *heave!*" The nose of the pinnace jumped to the right, well away from the fast approaching rocks. The boat bounced dangerously across an area of roiling, white-streaked water deflected from the rock face. "Now, hard port!" the bosun shouted with all his might to be heard over the crashing waves. With a roller coaster flutter in their stomachs they slid over the hump of a smooth swell and into a patch of relatively calm water in the lee of the rock wall. "Brace yourselves!" The prow of the pinnace hit this gravelly section of beach hard, but stayed upright. "Jump to shore, hurry!"

Gerbald pulled Pam and Dore up by their arms and guided them to the prow, Pam leaping first. There were larger rocks amongst the gravel, she felt one scrape the side of her leg, and knew it had drawn blood. She turned to help Dore, still clutching her wicker basket. She landed with a heavy "*Ooomph,*" but managed to stay upright. They were up to their knees in clutching, fast-moving water that almost knocked them over, but Gerbald had arrived, and used his solid strength to keep them on their feet. Pam was towed along by the still very fit retired soldier, her arm in his powerful grip. Soon the three of them were above the tide-line, standing amongst driftwood and the hearty kind of low brush that thrives along the edges of beaches. Gerbald ran back across the gravelly sand to help the men secure the pinnace. The sailors had gotten lines out and were dragging the boat safely up and away from the angry sea.

Pam squinted through the rain at Gerbald and the sailors at work, almost grateful for the ghostly flashes of lightning that played across the scene. She wanted to help them, but how? She realized with relief that she still had her rucksack on and quickly doffed it, fumbling around within until she found the flashlight. She handed the bag to a stunned-looking Dore and said, "Try to find some shelter in those trees just above the beach!" Then she ran down to the waterline, following the narrow but powerful beam through the driving rain. Reaching the men, she tried to aim the flashlight at places she thought would help the most. Eventually, they had the boat nearly to the high tide line, and were tying her to the sturdiest trees and rocks they could find. After securing the craft as best they could, they opened up water-tight compartments containing emergency supplies.

Pam found Dore huddled in a relatively flat area of grass among the wind-twisted shrubs and small trees that lined the shore beneath rows of towering palms swaying like hula dancers in the howling wind. They did their best to help the sailors set up camp, using the pinnace's sail draped over lines tied between trees as a rain tarp. An oil lamp sprang to life, lighting the surroundings in a heartbreakingly warm glow. Pam could now see the faces of the sailors and soldiers she had come to count among her friends. They were exhausted and fearful, but there was relief there, too. They would live to see the dawn. Suddenly, Pam remembered the captain and the first mate left behind. She came to her feet quickly, feeling saltwater still sloshing in the toes of her boots.

"Get up! Get up! We have to search the shore for the captain and the first mate!" Pam told them. The weary men looked at her for a long moment; there was little hope in their eyes. Some of the marines started to stand even before their officer, *Löjtnant* Lundkvist could growl at them. The sailors stirred, but it was plain they were exhausted.

The bosun's gravelly voice cut through the noise of the raging storm. "*Frau* Pam is right. Move your arses, you lazy sots! We have a duty to perform." As one, the sailors rose to their feet, stifling groans. If there were any chance of finding the first mate and the captain alive, it must be now.

Dore also stood. "*Herr* Bosun, do you have any kind of foodstuffs in the boat's stores?"

"Yes, but not much, I'm afraid."

"Then I will stay here and make us a supper. You will all need something to eat to regain your strength after a night like this."

The wet, weary men gave her a grateful murmur of thanks as they shuffled back out into the night's cold rains. Pam favored her friend with a grateful smile as she ducked out from under the tarp. Her doughty Dore was back and working, a glimmer of good in all this night of loss and pain. *Better to be like Dore and stay busy, Pammie, because if you start to think too much about what's happened here you will lose it, and not be of any help to anyone.* The thought of the captain, her friend, and possibly the beginning of something more, sent a knife of regret into her heart, but the painful slap of the cold, rain-filled gale made her keep moving. *Please, oh please let him be alive!*

∞ ∞ ∞

The cove was about half a mile long. The gravel turned to softer sand as they left the rocky edge where they had landed. The waves had calmed somewhat, but were still dangerous. They made their way slowly through the darkness, fighting the fierce wind, forming a line from as near the pounding surf as they dared, up to the highest elevation the storm waves had reached. Two men carried lanterns, one up at the high tideline, and one halfway down to the water. Pam, walking between Gerbald and the bosun, stayed as near the rushing waters as they could, scanning the surf with her flashlight. Pam tried not to think about the long-handled spade the bosun carried, and what its purpose might be.

Flotsam and jetsam from the wreck of the *Redbird* were beginning to wash up on the shore. Anything that might possibly be useful, such as planks and pieces of rigging, the men dragged up to relative safety. A brief cheer went up as they recovered a large cask of potent Swedish *schnapps* liquor. Upon reaching the far end of the beach they found it ended in a jumble of massive volcanic rocks, making further exploration this night impossible. On the way back to their camp, they found a few more odds and ends, but no bodies, much to Pam's relief. Maybe the captain and the first mate had escaped the wreck and survived, ending up somewhere safe elsewhere up the island's coast. It was a faint hope, but better than none at all.

At their makeshift camp, they were surprised to find a roaring driftwood fire blazing a safe distance from their shelter. The storm had mostly blown itself out, and the rain had stopped. Dore was busy clucking over the old cast iron skillet Pam had given her so long ago. It sizzled delightfully on a bed of coals. The heavenly scent of pancakes wafted toward them, mingled with the fine perfume of wood smoke.

"Good gravy, Dore, how on Earth did you get a fire started in that rain?"

"Oh, that was nothing, Pam. Remember that I was once a camp follower. I have lived outdoors for months on end thanks to that oaf there." She gave a haughty tilt of her chin to Gerbald who returned it with his usual shrug of guilty-as-charged resignation. "I always keep flint and steel in my apron pockets, and I found plenty of dry tinder under all that driftwood. It was a snap!" The last line was in English, and she snapped her fingers loudly to punctuate her American vernacular. "Now, you men gather round and get dry, but don't kick sand on my cakes or I'll have your hides!" There was a murmur of assent as the exhausted men gratefully encircled Dore's bonfire. Soon they were eating the simple pancakes Dore had concocted with the help of that big wicker basket, and the other mysterious baggage she had brought along. Dore was not a woman to be caught unprepared! The pancakes were a little brown on the outside, and a little mushy on the inside, and absolutely delicious.

After dinner, the men with weapons huddled in a group under the sail's shelter to begin a rigorous cleaning process of their weapons and metal tools. It was vital to remove any sea salt from the firearms right away. From somewhere in the infinite secret pockets of his sage-green soldier's longcoat, Gerbald pulled out an up-time gun cleaning kit, which he shared with the grateful Swedes. Pam watched him deftly clean the "Snakecharmer" pistol-grip shotgun her son Walt had given him. His touch was noticeably tender. Pam had seen it before, the fanatical love men had for their guns, but this time, as she listened to the wind whisper through the fronds of the shore palms, she was glad to see it.

The important ritual of gun cleaning accomplished, and with a hot meal in their bellies, they all found places on the matted grass beneath the sail tent to curl up. Despite the chill damp, most soon slept the deep and silent sleep of those who have faced death and lived.

Pam lay awake, watching the fire dance in the wavering breeze still blowing in from the unquiet sea. Under decent circumstances, she would have reveled in spending the night on an exotic island, but now she just felt lost, a castaway in a hostile environment. Even surrounded by her closest friends and a group of highly trustworthy men, a desperate loneliness overtook her. Deep down in her heart she felt she was a woman out of time and out of place.

Chapter Ten: On the Beach

Pam awoke just after sunrise to find Dore preparing breakfast. She had cleverly arranged a pile of volcanic stones into a simple oven, and was using it to bake what looked like muffins. Pam decided right then that the woman was some kind of miracle worker. Nearby, Gerbald, *Löjtnant* Lundkvist, and the bosun were conferring about their situation while the sailors and soldiers slowly roused themselves. Pam, her legs and back stiff from the lack of a mattress, lurched over to join them. The Swedes greeted her warmly, glad that she was up and about while Gerbald flashed her a grin.

"Look, Pam, it is just like in *The Swiss Family Robinson*, isn't it? We are marooned on a desert island! How thrilling!" Gerbald told her in a far too chipper tone, obviously hoping to cheer her up, but only succeeding in annoying her thoroughly.

"Back off, Man Friday, I ain't had no coffee," Pam answered in a menacing croak. Gerbald nodded solemnly at her medical emergency, but didn't lose his smile. He always seemed delighted with adversity, often to Pam and Dore's chagrin.

Dore gave Pam a very apologetic look. "Pam, I am so sorry. The coffee was lost in the storm."

"It's not your fault, Dore! You have gone way beyond the call of duty! Look at this breakfast, it's fantastic!" All those gathered murmured their sincere agreement, and Dore went back to her ceaseless work, satisfied that she had done everything she could to ensure they had food to eat, and under very dangerous circumstances to boot.

Pam turned to the bosun. "Any idea where we are, *Herr* Bosun?"

The stout, windburned Swede scratched at his gray-streaked, red beard. He used a stick to draw a rough map in the sand.

"Not with perfect accuracy, mind you, *Frau* Pam, but I have some idea. We were approaching the southern tip of our destination when the attack happened. We fled to the north and west. The storm carried us some five miles, our progress slowed as we were taking on water. So, we are somewhere on the south coast of Mauritius. Even after looking at the up-time maps I have no idea where. They show very little of the island's topography." The sun could now be seen poking its head above tall, green hills.

"What do you think became of the rest of our fleet?" Pam turned to *Löjtnant* Lundkvist, a serious fellow in his early thirties, an adept leader who would likely go far in the royal service. She tried to keep a growing sense of fear and loss out of her voice.

"*Frau* Pam, when last sighted, the colony ships were fleeing the opposite direction from us, heading east toward the southern tip, and most likely up the island's east coast. They would have been looking for a sheltered harbor and I recall seeing one on the map. . . . I hope they made it that far. They weren't alone, I fear. We saw other foreign sails, of a kind the heathens use. No doubt mercenaries hired by the French to aid in this foul endeavor. There can be no doubt our little warship was captured, and most likely the colonist's ships, as well, God save their souls. They were flying French colors, and we are still effectively at war with the French."

"The fucking French. Those *bastards*." Pam was startled at the seething hate she heard in her words, but it was there. These weren't the charming, thin-mustachioed, beret-wearing fellows seen in daytime TV documentaries about wine, cheese and fine cuisine. This was another age and these were the *enemy*. She had lost nearly everything; the expedition was in ruins. They were just lucky to be alive and she wasn't sure how long that would last. She looked around at the men gathered, all grown quiet as the direness of their situation grew ever more apparent.

"Gentlemen, doesn't it seem a bit convenient to you that in all this wide ocean, a French man-o-war was lurking around a remote place like this, just in time for our arrival?"

They all nodded grimly.

"Richelieu," Lundkvist said the name as if pronouncing a particularly offensive obscenity, "has spies everywhere. He wouldn't have even needed them this time. Our journey was very public, widely promoted in newspapers and on radio while the princess and her offices were fundraising for it. As for why he would attack us, I think that's clear enough—"

Pam jumped in before he could continue. "Because in the up-time history this island became a French colony and he doesn't want to lose it to Gustav. Once developed into a way station on the journey around Africa to-and-from points east, I guarantee you this place will be an economically valuable, and strategic holding."

Lundkvist grinned at her. "Well put, *Frau* Pam. Have you ever served in a military? You seem to have the mind for it."

"Nope, I just did my homework. I spent more time at the library than at home before we left. But the thing I didn't think of that's killing us right now is how desirable this island might be to *other* foreign powers. I should have bugged the princess to get us a bigger warship."

"Pam, you ask too much of yourself," Gerbald told her gently.

Lundkvist nodded. "*Frau* Pam, we *are* military trained, and we didn't see this coming either. In any case, another ship would have been impossible. The king's assets are all tied up in Europe. We got the *Muskijl* only because she was being retired. It was to be her last voyage as a Swedish warship. We planned to donate her to the colony."

Mention of their ill-fated colony caused them all to fall silent, their concern for the colonists weighing heavy on their minds. What more was there to say? It might be another year or more before anyone friendly came looking for them. Meanwhile, they were stuck on an island where they were heavily outnumbered with no ship. *To put it bluntly, we're screwed.* Pam kept the thought to herself.

Still filled with anger, she made herself unclench her fists and looked around at the three men. She realized that now they were waiting for her to say something. Why were they waiting for her? The bosun's tired and bleary hazel eyes watched her patiently. Yes, this was a man awaiting orders, a man ready to go to work. More surprising, she felt the same vibe from the lieutenant. She realized that with the captain and first mate missing, she was ostensibly in charge, the brilliant up-time lady scientist appointed to lead the expedition by their beloved princess. *Oh, Hell! I don't want this job!* All Pam wanted to do was curl up under a tree and cry herself to sleep. With a kind of mental shove she made herself look up, knowing it was up to her to *do* something.

"All right, then. Thank you, gentlemen. We must hold on to hope that *Analise* and *Ide* won free. We may be shipwrecked but we aren't completely lost. We know what island we're stuck on, and the people back home will eventually come look for us here. We may be outnumbered and outgunned by the French and their allies, but we are far from helpless. I have great faith in all of you. Let's stay vigilant, and keep working while we ponder our next move." *That actually sounded pretty good!*

"We should make another sweep of the beach to see if anything has washed up overnight." She had hung on that word "anything" for a second longer than she wanted to, thinking of what things might have arrived with the tide that she might not want to see. "We are going to need fresh water. Gerbald, can you take that on? This sure isn't Germany, but you're the best woodsman we've got."

"Of course, Pam. We may be far from home, but this is still the world of our birth, and where there is greenery, there is water. I will find it."

"Good. As Crystal would say, 'You the man.' " They shared a quick smile, and Pam began to feel better. It was a small, weak kind of better, but still a step in the right direction. The Swedes were already heading off to organize the search party. She called after the bosun.

"*Herr* Bosun, can we take the pinnace out today to see what's left of the *Redbird*?"

"Yes," he said, coming back to her side "but we must wait for a better tide. Right now it is too shallow. See the coral reefs out there? In a few hours the tide will come in and we can go. While we wait, I will send the men down the beach."

"Taking the pinnace out to the wreck, that's exactly what they did in *Swiss Family Robinson*!" Gerbald was back to his boyish delight in being marooned. "I do wish I had that book with me now." He sounded like this was all a cheerful Sunday picnic, earning him a roll of the eyes from both Pam and the bosun.

Pam turned to the grizzled seaman. "Thanks, *Herr* Bosun. When you go, I want to come along. I have to see how bad it is with my own eyes. . . . It was kind of my ship, you know?"

"I understand completely. I am so sorry we lost her for you. It is a shame myself and all our men feel most strongly. Today the seas are calm and I believe it will be safe enough. And now, to work." The bosun, with tasks to accomplish before him, sounded almost like his old cheerful self as he rousted the still-sleepy men, and gave them their orders.

Gerbald stayed with Pam a minute longer, his always startling blue eyes regarding her calmly from beneath his monstrous mustard colored hat, which had unfortunately survived the wreck along with him. Pam met that stare with her own metal-flecked grays and said "What?"

Gerbald flashed her a truly sunny smile. "I am just pleased to see you have adjusted to the circumstances so quickly, Pam. You are truly the toughest, and most resourceful woman I have ever met, excepting Dore, of course. There is no one else I would rather be shipwrecked with . . . except, perhaps, Ginger and Mary-Anne." He had a dreamy look on his face.

Pam flipped him the bird that one doesn't find in any field guides, and marched off to join in the search.

Chapter Eleven: The Flood May Bear Me Far

Later that morning the sailors raised a shout from down the beach. Pam and the bosun rushed over to see they had discovered an old shipwreck high above the tideline. There wasn't much left intact, just a rotting, wooden skeleton. Nearby, pieces of it looked like they might once have been removed and used to make a temporary shelter.

"Apparently we are not the first to sail, or wreck, here," the bosun said, looking around the scene carefully.

"How long do you think it's been here?" Pam asked, a note of concern in her voice. Did they have neighbors?

"I have seen a lot of ships and a lot of wrecks in my time, too many of the latter I regret to say, but it's impossible to really tell for sure. The vessel's wood might be some kind of cedar, which could explain how well-preserved it is. From their overall condition, I'd make these pieces to be around a hundred years old, more or less. Just a guess, mind you." The bosun cast his eye around the scene with a worried expression on his face. "Still, we can't be sure we are alone here. No one should go wandering off by themselves, although I don't see any signs of recent activity. Best to play it safe, though." Pam was not comforted.

After a bit of digging around the decaying hulk, Pers let out a whoop of discovery. Full of youthful vigor he soon unearthed around two hundred pounds of wax bricks ensconced in a hollow under a heavy beam. To their surprise, each bore some kind of inscription.

"This looks like Arabic to me, but I'm no expert." Pam said. The bosun nodded, squinting at the strange script.

The men made a thorough search of the area but nothing else of use or interest was found. The bosun ordered the men to carry the bricks and whatever lengths of wood that might still be usable to camp. Looking back at the abandoned shelter, he told Pam, "Perhaps they were rescued!" with a well meaning attempt at good cheer.

"There's a good thought. We must think positively." *Easier said than done. I have to stay busy or I'm going to go nuts, this is really all just too much.* Pam put six of the odd bricks into her bag. Having been too uptight to eat earlier that morning, she returned to camp to see what kind of miracle her friend had produced for breakfast.

First, Pam gave the wax to Dore to see if she could find any use for it, keeping one for herself as a souvenir. Dore was well pleased. "Candles!" she exclaimed and began to bustle about trying to scrounge up something to use for wicks.

"There's a lot more where these came from, the men found them on an old shipwreck."

"A lucky find, we shall have light through the night now if we wish it."

Pam sat down cross-legged in the sand under the sun-dappled shade of the palms, studying her mysterious prize. *So, others have been here before us.* She wasn't sure if that was a comfort or not. She also mused that they were most likely going to be melting an important archaeological find, but pushed the thought aside, their survival came first. Dore handed her a muffin on a plate of plantain leaf. At the moment, none of the various fruits growing in abundance around the camp were ripe, but Pam looked forward to the day. She loved plantains, and there weren't any to be had in Thuringia-Franconia. *The plus side of being marooned.*

Pam ate her muffin slowly. It was utterly delicious, seasoned with a bit of sugar and cinnamon, and just enough to fill her. The real problem was coffee, or the terrible lack of it. Her head still felt fuzzy inside even though she had been up and about for hours, and there was a dull ache at her temples. These were the same telltales of caffeine withdrawal that she had experienced in the first year after the Ring of Fire, before Grantville had come into a fairly reliable supply of the blessed bean again. It would take a few more days, but the feeling would pass. Hopefully they would be rescued by then, but she wouldn't let herself think too hard about that.

Pam stood up from her place near the fire and tied the red cotton handkerchief from her back pocket over her head. The sky was the extra deep cerulean that can be seen sometimes after a storm has passed, and the climbing sun promised to be hot. It felt like it was already around eighty degrees Fahrenheit and it couldn't be much later than ten AM. The sea glowed the intense aqua of tropical waters; the sapphire sparkles at the surface almost blinding to look at.

At least it was beautiful here, and Pam began to feel just slightly better, the awesome pageantry of nature pushing her many worries to the back of her mind. *Its a nice day, just enjoy it for what it is, fool.* She made herself get up, thanked Dore, and wandered down the beach to rejoin the sailors in the ongoing search and salvage operation. Down at the water's edge, the sea was as gentle as a lamb now that the lion winds had ceased their roaring, so she took off her socks and boots and walked barefoot across firm pale sand, wading through the lapping wavelets.

From Pam's point of view the pickings were fairly slim, but the men seemed happy with every broken barrel and tangled mess of rope they recovered. They found a saw, and some wood-working tools packed in a water-tight wooden crate that had washed up, and they held a brief, whooping celebration at such excellent luck. The tide was all the way out now, and just beginning to turn; at the cove's far end it revealed a wide muddy flat dotted with slippery black volcanic rock. The upper beach here was made up of a coarser salt-and-pepper sand composed of tiny volcanic pebbles and bits of broken coral. Neither surface was particularly conducive to walking over, and Pam definitely didn't like the feel of the mud oozing between her toes. After rinsing her feet in the sea as best she could, she put her footwear back on, taking a moment to be very thankful she had brought her very best waterproofed boots along.

Shortly, Pam whooped aloud herself when she saw a small barrel floating along the water's edge. The sailors got there first and were checking its contents as Pam ran through the splattering muck to join them. *Please be coffee, please be coffee, Please be coffee!* she prayed earnestly. It turned out to contain sugar, which was no bad thing, so Pam did her best to hide her disappointment.

Pam continued to follow the waterline closely, scanning the shallows. There were countless black crabs scurrying about the rocks, Pam thought they might make a decent meal if they could be caught. She was startled for a moment by a long, brown tube shaped object half hidden in a clump of kelp. A sea snake? She approached carefully, then let out a peal of delighted laughter as she realized the menacing looking creature was in fact her grandmother's gnarled oak walking stick! After flicking off sticky bits of seaweed she found the tough old thing damp, but no worse for wear. Pam clutched the familiar item with both hands and held it to her breast.

Memories of her grandmother flooded into her mind, the long birdwatching walks they had taken through the peaceful West Virginia countryside, her grandmother's gentle voice listing the many birds and animals they found to her attentive grandchild. That was where a love of nature had been firmly planted in her heart. What would her grandmother have thought of Pam using it as a weapon in the seventeenth century? Pam had once broken a man's jaw, thus saving Gerbald's life with the dear old thing, it was almost beyond imagining. That incident had begun with trying to save a family of up-time wood ducks from poaching. Why? Because she had to save the natural world, that's why, Pam Miller, Mother Nature's Protector, "The Bird Lady of Grantville." She shook her head, thinking of the dangers her love of nature had led her to, as well as the friends she had made because of it. Now, she had led them into even greater danger.

She looked around at the men combing the beach, every floating piece of civilization they could find increasing their chances of survival just a bit more. Everybody was putting on a brave face, but she knew they were really in trouble. The bright burst of joy from recovering a personal relic from a lost future faded as the depression which had been whispering to her, biding its time at the edge of her consciousness, finally asserted itself in her mind, a dark cloud spoiling her sunny day. All the parades and good will speeches meant nothing now. Their ship was sunk, their expedition was over before she had even *seen* a damned dodo, and they were marooned on a remote island in the seventeenth century with no such thing as search-and-rescue planes. Pam fought back tears; they had been waiting their turn too, now threatening to spill. That was when she saw the line of sailors ahead of her farther up the beach had gathered in a circle around something floating in the shallows.

Her recovered walking stick proved helpful as she made her way across the muddy flats toward the now silent sailors. Young Pers saw her coming, and quickly came to cut off her approach. As he drew near, Pam thought that he didn't look quite so young anymore. Where was the happy fellow who had helped her pass the hours on the long journey around Africa? His rosy cheeks looked dimmed even in the bright southern sunlight.

"Pam, please, you must stay back. This would not be good for you to see."

Looking past him, Pam saw the men were dragging a soggy mass from out of the shallow water. Their movements were strangely gentle and spoke of deep respect. She saw a boot had come free revealing a bare foot, its color an unnatural shade of white, with a tinge of palest blue. Pam looked away.

"Who was it?" she asked in a small voice.

"Our first mate, Janvik. We must give him a proper burial now. It is better to do it quickly . . ." Pers paused, his face full of worry for a very upset Pam.

The tears that had been waiting impatiently behind her eyes burst loose now, and she swallowed a terrible sob. Her grief was made worse by a sharp sense of guilt that she hadn't liked the man much in life, and that was only because he was just doing his job, and keeping his men at their tasks while she flitted about the ship like a silly school girl, distracting them at her whim. Tears fell hard in a hot cascade down her tanned face, their salt and moisture joining the great Indian Ocean in tiny splashes.

Pers reached out to tentatively pat her on the shoulder. Pam stepped into the young sailor's strong arms, and clung to him, unknowingly pressing the walking stick painfully against his back, but the big, solid youth didn't mind. He did his best to comfort his distraught friend, who now felt she had added a death to her list of responsibilities. Maybe two, if she counted the missing captain. The thought made her cry so hard she shook. Pers patted her back gently, as a son would his weeping mother.

"There, *there*, *Frau* Pam. We who go to sea know death well. He sails silently behind us, waiting until he is called upon to bring us to the next world. It is just the way of things. Please, you mustn't cry so."

"It's all my fault. All of this fucking disaster is my fault."

Pers clicked his tongue to negate that statement. "You cannot think such things. Can it be your fault the French came with their warship, your fault such a terrible storm blew in when it did? You must not make this your burden, *Frau* Pam, *Herr* Janvik did his duty, and none could command him otherwise."

Pam stopped her tears and slowly drew herself out of her young friend's comforting embrace. She nodded and sniffed sharply. Finally, after doing her best to wipe her face dry on her sleeve, she asked him "How did you get so wise, anyway, kid?"

"I listen to those around me, and I remember what they say when it is of value. I only hope my words, simple they may be, are of some comfort to you. You are also my teacher, and I am grateful to have met you; I have learned much. We men of the *Redbird* all think the world of you, *Frau* Pam, don't you know?"

Pam gave him a squeeze on his arm. "Yeah, you're helping. I'll remember what you said. Thanks for being here for me, Pers. It means a lot to me to have such fine friends." This pleased the young sailor, who even as he blushed, smiled in his infectious way. Pam's personal storm having blown itself out *for now, for now,* she watched the solemn and timeless ritual of digging a grave. Such sad toil taking place on a sunny tropical beach seemed incongruous, like an odd twist of plot in a confusing dream.

"I'll go get everyone at camp and bring them back for the service," she told them, needing some time alone to pull herself together.

"It will take about an hour to finish our task here. We will wait for your return before we say any words," the bosun replied, sweating from his turn with the long spade.

Pam nodded and walked slowly back toward the distant white rectangle of their sail tent, leaning heavier on her grandmother's walking stick than she had ever remembered doing before.

By the time she returned, the grave had been filled, a fresh mound of sandy loam beneath which their sailing mate's mortal form would be returned to the earth. The funeral was simple and sincere. The bosun said the Lord's Prayer in Swedish, and Dore sang a Lutheran hymn in German, *Wie schön leuchtet der Morgenstern*, which Pam translated as "How Brightly Shines the Morning Star." Pam marveled at the beauty of her friend's strong alto voice. During the years she had come to think of this woman as an older sister, but this was the first time she had ever heard her sing. All held a respectful silence once the last thrilling notes of Dore's voice fell away with the sea breeze.

Pam clutched a simple bouquet of wild flowers, weeds most likely, but pretty enough, that she had scrounged together on her way back down the beach. She was about to place them on the grave when she looked up to see all eyes on her. *Oh no. They want me to say something!* The great woodsman Gerbald hadn't returned from his mission yet, and Pam felt vulnerable without his reassuring presence, the older brother to match Dore's role as sister to her, the two forming a much-treasured set. She realized she would eventually have to speak up. Her mind suddenly slipped down into a pleasant yet seldom used gear, and she found herself stepping forward, miraculously speaking up in a somber tone worthy of an ordained minister.

"I want to share with you all a poem I learned when I was a school girl. It's by a man named Tennyson, who might never be born in this world. He wrote it for sailors in particular. I only know how to recite it in English, but I hope the sound of it will still bring some comfort to us. The poem is called *Crossing the Bar*.

> *Sunset and evening star,*
> *And one clear call for me!*
> *And may there be no moaning of the bar,*
> *When I put out to sea,*
> *But such a tide as moving seems asleep,*
> *Too full for sound and foam,*
> *When that which drew from out the boundless deep*
> *Turns again home.*
> *Twilight and evening bell,*
> *And after that the dark!*
> *And may there be no sadness of farewell,*
> *When I embark;*
> *For tho' from out our bourne of Time and Place*
> *The flood may bear me far,*
> *I hope to see my Pilot face to face*
> *When I have crossed the bar."*

Pam looked up to see the men around her nodding their approval, even if they hadn't understood all of the words, they had felt the emotion of the piece. Dore regarded her with a quiet, beaming pride. Pam gently placed her simple bouquet at the foot of a stout, red-painted plank from *Redbird* the men had placed there as a marker, on which the first mate's name, nation, ship and the current year were carefully scribed with the wax they had found that morning. They hoped the water resistant substance would tell his story for many years to come. Pam turned away first, and they all walked together back to camp, seeking relief from the stinging noonday sun.

Chapter Twelve: Redbird's Last Gifts

A couple of hours later Gerbald arrived in camp carrying several full water skins, which were met with great cheer by the thirsty castaways. Their meager and stale supply from the pinnace, augmented by what little rainwater they had been able to capture in the confusion of the storm, had nearly run out, so Gerbald was just in time. After hearing the sad news, and paying his graveside respects to the deceased first mate, Gerbald led them to a delightfully clear spring about half a mile back in the forest that would provide more than enough water for their needs. If that ever failed, he had also found an actual river a few miles farther on, so they were no longer in any danger from dehydration. Everyone felt a piece of their overall tension fall away; the presence of potable water was crucial to survival. Even if all else was hardship, their thirst would be quenched.

Pam turned to the bosun. "It looks like the tide has come in. Have your sailors got enough strength left to go check out the wreck?"

"Why of course we do, *Frau* Pam. We are Swedes of the royal navy! Stronger than any ten other men, *ja*, boys?" The men all brought themselves to their feet with a creaky chorus of *ja*s, mustering smiles for the brave Lady Scientist.

Dore took Pam gently by the arm. "Pam, you must promise me to be careful, yes?"

"I will be, Dore. We all will be." Serious-faced Dore looked mostly satisfied at this promise, then clutched at Pam's arm again. "I know you go to look for things we can use from the broken ship. Please, if you can, and only if it is not dangerous, try to find me some more pots and pans! I can make do with only the one, but if I had more to cook with I could provide better comfort for these poor men, and we three as well."

Pam smiled at Dore's always earnest desire to help, and gave her a quick hug. "I will, Dore. That's first on our list—I'm sure the men will all agree. You are the best, Dore, always the best."

Dore blushed at the praise, and hid it with her usual bluff sternness. "Yes, well, I'll be that much better with a soup pot in my hand! Now go, and be careful. All of you!"

The salvage party, including the bosun, all murmured their "Yes, ma'ams" to the feared and revered Most Excellent Cook, as they went to drag the pinnace back into the water.

∞ ∞ ∞

Pam sat in the prow of the long, narrow craft where she could use her birdwatching trained sharp vision to locate any floating prizes while keeping out of the oarsmen's way. Gerbald had declined to come along, preferring to continue his scouting of their new, and hopefully temporary home. The water was incredibly clear, the tide having swept away the roiled murk from the storm. Below them a kaleidoscope of fantastical fish darted and cruised among branches of coral in an undersea garden of fancy. Pam looked back at the horizon, resisting the siren call of the mysterious realm beneath. She wished for a mask and snorkel, and regretted that she could put a name to only a few denizens of these exotic seas, such as the elegant Moorish idols, and the hearty little clownfish guarding their anemone homes. Maybe some day there would be time to study the aquatic world as she wished to, but for now she had other, more pressing matters.

The pinnace carefully approached the rocky point that had taken the *Redbird* in its crushing embrace. Pam's heart sped up as she waited with dread for the first view of her wrecked ship. She knew it had sustained heavy damage, but maybe, just maybe, they could fix her up, and she could sail again. As it came into sight, that hope was dashed. Pam bit her lip as she saw what little remained of her, the broken spine and ribs of her hull surrounded by splintered wood and damp scraps of torn sails. The men landed the pinnace on a relatively flat stretch of sand from which they clambered up slippery rocks to view the devastation first hand. Pam stood at the water's edge, gazing at the place where her great mission had come to its grievous end.

"So much for rescuing the dodo," she mumbled to herself. "Now *we* are the ones who are going to need rescuing." Shaking her head in resignation, she gingerly made her way up the tide-bared volcanic rocks. Most of the ship's contents had been smashed by the power of the storm into unrecognizable bits of flotsam and jetsam.

A flash of bright color against the dark stone caught her eye, a canary yellow plastic whistle, still intact. It had been the captain's, a prized possession from the future world he had come across in his travels. It made his absence all the more painful, but she tucked it safely into a pocket of her rucksack, holding onto a wispy hope that she might one day return it to him. She heard one of the sailors, kindly old Fritjoff, the princess' number one fan, calling to her so she made her way over to him. He grinned with his few odd remaining teeth as he pointed down into a wide shallow depression in the rocks filled with lukewarm seawater left behind by the tide.

"Look! Madame's bird wire!" Just under the surface lay one of the rolls of chicken wire that her old friend Willie Ray Hudson had managed to scrounge up for her, in perfect condition except for a festooning of seaweed. She hadn't thought of Grantville for days, and the memory of afternoon lemonades on the much-loved farmer's wide front porch flooded her with nostalgia. Suddenly she missed Grantville, badly, and wondered if she would ever see it again.

"You want us to retrieve it, don't you?" Fritjoff asked her shyly, having seen the sad look pass across her face.

"Yes, please do. It could still be of some use. We don't know how long we'll be here . . ."

Fritjoff nodded respectfully, then climbed down into the depression to manhandle the heavy roll up out of the pool. Pam was astonished at his strength and agility, considering his octogenarian looks. *He's probably only in his sixties! This world is so hard on people.* Soon he and another sailor, sturdy Arne, were hauling it down to the pinnace. Little by little as they sifted through the broken remains of *Redbird,* they found other small prizes; a length of good rope here, a box of copper nails there. To their eyes it was pretty fair salvage; they would by no means be coming back empty-handed. Pam saw the bosun and a few of the sailors standing near one of the ships' surviving ribs, a curved finger of wood pointing at the bright southern skies. Pam made her way over to see what they were up to.

"It is one of the cannon, *Frau* Pam!" The bosun announced with a bright tone of excitement in his voice, hoarse from shouting orders at sailors. "The new type, the *carronade* made with the Grantville designs! It is still usable! We just have to gather up the balls scattered about here, and we brought plenty of gunpowder with us on the pinnace!"

Pam looked down at the big metal weapon still connected to a section of broken ship's wood. It shone brightly in the sunlight, retaining its polish despite the rough handling.

"Okay . . . but what good does this do us? We don't have a ship anymore."

The bosun nodded. "Even with no ship, this gun can protect us. We can mount it on the shore. If an enemy ship comes to our cove, then *boom*! It is better than throwing coconuts!" This made everybody chuckle, even if a bit grimly.

"Can we get it back to shore?"

"Yes, I think so. It is very heavy, but we have tools. Tomorrow we will come back for it. Now the tide is returning and we must go. I think this won't be floating away!" They left the elegant-looking cannon behind for later retrieval, but the men didn't wait to haul the tremendously heavy barrel of ammunition back to the pinnace. They would take no chances there.

The sturdy little boat rode lower in the water on the return trip, burdened with the weight of their prizes. Pam smiled, looking down at the variety of metal pots, pans, and cutlery they had recovered. That would make Dore very, very happy. *Maybe our luck will change?* Pam mused, but didn't dwell on the thought, not wanting to jinx it.

That night they passed around a big bottle of *kirschwasser* that had miraculously survived the storm, and a bit of good cheer came back into the group. They were not in a good situation, not at all, but it could have been much worse, and they were all doing their best to improve it. Pam tried not to think of the dodos she had come to save, and the abrupt end of her quest to forge a colony that might truly coexist with nature, having learned from all the terrible mistakes of her own time. Instead, she swallowed as much of the cherry-flavored liquor as the men did, and drifted off into an exhausted slumber. If she dreamed that night she knew not.

Garrett W. Vance

Chapter Thirteen: Crazy for Coconuts!

The next day she woke up late. Except for a single well-armed guard, all the men had gone off to retrieve the cannon, including Gerbald, who had a knack for jury-rigged mechanics. Dore gave her a simple breakfast and remarked that they were going to need to do something about getting more food, soon. Pam nodded, feeling hazy and disconnected. *Caffeine withdrawal, bleah.* Dore made sure she drank some water and told her to take it easy for a while. Pam obeyed, lounging around in the shade, watching for the men to come back from their mission. She felt drained, like a balloon with all the air blown out of it, just a floppy piece of limp rubber. This was not a good feeling. After a while, she got up and decided to make herself useful, but ended up just wandering aimlessly around the camp, which evolved into collecting seashells. By the time the men came back she had a nice little collection, lovely, and entirely useless.

There not currently being anything she could do to help, she watched as the men hauled the heavy carronade up from the beach with a system of ropes and makeshift pulleys Gerbald had helped set up. Once the formidable-looking gun was safely ensconced above the high tide line, everyone sat down for some lunch. Dore had something special for dinner in mind, but they had to make do with the hard bread and dried meat from the ship for now.

"We need to have fruit," Dore announced, looming over where Gerbald, Pam, the bosun and the marines' lieutenant held council sitting sitting in a shady spot. "Pam, you have studied these islands; what can we eat here? I am going to run out of flour and such eventually, and I have learned about the need for certain vitamins during my time in Grantville. We can't survive on bread and water, especially since we are going to run out of bread."

Pam felt a bit put on the spot, but understood her friend's concern perfectly.

"Well, during my library research I made a list of every edible plant that grows or might grow in this region. I was going to encourage the colonists learn to use native species along with whatever we brought with us. I'll go through my notes. Off hand, we have plantains, they just aren't ripe at the moment. There's probably breadfruit here, too, I think I'll know it when I see it. These palms along the beach have coconuts, and there is are a variety of palm species further inland, including date palms. I haven't identified them all yet. Oil palm could be useful, although some types might be inedible. I was happy to see Indian gooseberries, an excellent source of vitamin C, so we should be safe from scurvy. All in all, I suppose coconuts would be a good place to start."

They all stood up to scan the camp. There were a few coconuts lying around, but they looked as if they had been there a bit too long, some were even beginning to sprout fronds. They could see what they thought might be several likely specimens up in the trees, but they were quite high up.

"Someone must climb a tree and bring some down," Dore decreed after careful scrutiny.

"Who is going to do that?" Pam asked, maybe just slightly irritated with Dore's bossy attitude.

"I know who," the bosun said smiling. "*Pers!*" he shouted.

The youth came running, looking around with wide eyes to see what might be required of him.

"Congratulations," Pam told him. "We have just elected you to be our resident *Gilligan.*" Gerbald and Dore laughed immediately but the Swedes could only smile politely.

"It's a *high* honor," Gerbald told the boy in English, trying to keep a straight face. They had been teaching the ever-curious Pers English and German throughout the voyage, and he was getting pretty savvy. He gave his older friend a suspicious look.

Pam snorted. "I'm sure you can *rise* to the occasion," she added, then burst into a fit of giggles.

By the time they had explained their up-time humor to the uncomprehending Swedes, who still didn't really get it, but understood someone like Gilligan's role in life well enough—a low-ranking youth who is a bit of a buffoon, and gets stuck with all the crappy jobs no one else wants.

Before they knew it, Pers had shimmied all the way up one of the trees, an accomplished climber by nature. "How about this one?" he called down, pointing at a large, light-green sphere one size again bigger than a bowling ball.

"Sure, send it down!" Pam shouted back. With a couple of whacks of Pers' knife the coconut plummeted, causing the bosun to have to jump out of the way.

"Sorry, *Herr* Bosun!" Pers called down.

The bosun grumbled something about having other things to do, and began ordering the rest of the men, who were taking their sweet time finishing their lunches while watching the entertainment at hand, to get back to work.

"Are there any brown ones?" Pam called back up.

"Well, try this one. Look out below!"

After a while they had a collection of coconuts of varying ripeness. After opening the outer husk some were still green while riper fruits were the more familiar brown. Pam knew the green ones were edible from visits to the Thai restaurant in Morgantown, and was pretty sure she had eaten a ripe brown one at some point, or at least had drunk a piña colada out of one.

It was a study of trial and error. Gerbald sliced the first one in half with his *katzbalger* shortsword as if it were an enemy's head, splashing the juice all over the place. That taught them to poke a hole in it first, using an auger from the ship's tool chest, then pouring the juice, or *milk*, into one of Dore's prized soup pots. It tasted a bit sour, but there was sweetness there, too. Pam thought she might grow to like it. The meat was delicious, and further research stopped as they gorged themselves. The ripe brown ones were even better, more meaty, with a creamy juice that much more closely resembled milk. Once the meat was removed, Dore suggested they clean and save the sturdy brown shell halves for soup dishes. Pers was sent on several more missions up the trees to make sure there would be enough for everyone's dinner.

Pleased with their progress Dore bestowed them all with a truly lovely smile. "Now we will survive," she said matter-of-factly, and returned to her makeshift kitchen.

Chapter Fourteen: Keeping Busy with Bamboo

The following days were spent trying to improve their situation as best as they could. They picked a relatively clear spot to build a much more substantial camp, well past the high tide line, and hidden from the beach by a belt of tall grasses and the stately row of palms that stretched all down their cove.

First of all, by unanimous consent, a sand-floored, palm frond-roofed "galley" was constructed for Dore, featuring a bamboo work table, and a bamboo latticework hung from the ceiling, a place to keep their food up high, and off the ground. There was very fortunately a large grove of the versatile tall grass nearby, which they weaved into walls between bamboo frames. A few yards outside the kitchen door, they built a primitive but functional oven and stove from volcanic rock. Dore was very pleased with it all, considering she had worked with worse in her years following Gerbald to war.

Next came a simple bungalow for Pam. The small structure, which she called "The Professor's Hut" was raised five feet high on bamboo stilts to avoid creepy crawlies, and provided a safe place to sleep and store her things. It was nothing fancy, but they did add a small sitting porch out front, with a very basic bench and desk in the shade of the roof's extended eaves, a comfortable spot for her to do her reading and writing at.

A similar structure went up for Gerbald and Dore, which Pam dubbed "The Howell Mansion," and then the men built a communal longhouse for themselves. On the tour, Pam was pleased to see that Fritjoff had lovingly hung his somewhat water damaged photograph of the princess on a beam near the entrance. Weapons and ammunition were carefully stored in cabinets fashioned from the best lumber salvaged from *Redbird*.

At a proper distance from their dwellings they dug two outhouse latrines, each with bamboo walls and a palm tree roof, the "Lady's and Gentlemen's Rooms." Pam used her art supplies to paint yellow moons on each door, which reminded of childhood summer visits to her uncle's rural West Virginia cabin.

Just behind the tall grass above the shore, the men erected a well-camouflaged platform where they mounted the carronade so that any unwelcome visitors would have a nasty surprise.

The bosun was very pleased with the progress. "The sailor's general wisdom upon becoming a castaway," he told Pam, "is to think long term and hope short term. Besides, the men are happier if they are kept busy."

"Great work *Herr* Bosun, please tell the men we are very grateful for their hard work!" Pam said, grateful for the greatly increased comfort.

Gerbald and some of the sailors were catching some very tasty fish lately, as well as digging clams and catching crabs in bamboo traps that Gerbald tinkered together. One day Pam was amazed to see Dore pull a slightly rusty red-and-white tin of circa 1983 Schillings brand curry powder from her wicker basket. Seeing Pam's astonished expression, Dore exclaimed, "You told me to bring anything I thought I might be able to use from your kitchen, so I packed up most of the spice cabinet. They don't weigh much."

"What will you make with it?" Pam's mouth was beginning to water, it felt so long since she had eaten anything one could call savory.

"Do you remember when we dined at Crystal and Walt's home a few days after their wedding? She served something called a 'fish curry' that I thought was quite tasty. I remember she said it would be better with coconut milk. Well, we have that, and fish, so I thought I'd try it. Is it a good idea?"

Pam hugged her so hard she almost knocked the sturdy woman over.

All in all, Pam couldn't help but think that things were getting better. She tried to put the real danger of their predicament out of her mind for now, there wasn't anything more to do about it than they were already doing.

Pam suggested to the bosun that they send the pinnace up the coast to scout, but the seasoned sailor told her that such a voyage would be dangerous, and he preferred not to risk it yet. While a sturdy little craft, it wasn't designed for long journeys in rough seas, and worse yet it could be captured easily. It was his opinion that they save that idea for a last resort if rescue didn't come after a few months, and she agreed.

Pam decided that meanwhile she and Gerbald would scout around on foot. There were mountains rising a few miles behind their cove, and by the looks of them they weren't much higher than those of West Virginia that she had climbed so many times over the years. They would definitely offer a broader view, and Pam was getting bored and depressed hanging around camp, anyway. She needed to walk.

It was too late to head out that day, she would have to wait until morning. Whistling an old Looney Toon tune she arranged her ever growing shell collection decoratively around the edge of her front porch to pass the time. *Well, Mauritius is definitely* not *better than the Bahamas, but today is a pretty good day anyway.* Satisfied with the results of her art project, she rested in her hut until dinner, still feeling antsy to get hiking. There was another thing fueling her urge to go walk about, something that she didn't dare think on too much due to the still fresh pain of losing her ship, and all hope of accomplishing the expedition's goals. The fact was, despite everything else, she was dying to see a dodo.

Chapter Fifteen: I'm No Darwin

Early the next morning Pam and Gerbald donned their rucksacks and left camp, promising to be back before dark. Rather than trying to follow the very difficult terrain along the shore leading northeast, they headed due north, inland, planning to gain the summit of the closest mountain, a fairly easy day's hike for them if the lay of the land cooperated. So far, it wasn't much worse than a West Virginia woodland, some thorny underbrush, but mostly easy walking through a very beautiful forest. There was a plethora of amazing birdlife at hand, but Pam resisted stopping to take notes and make sketches; they were on a mission. Despite natural wonders revealing themselves at every turn, Pam grew morose.

"I'm no Darwin, not even an Audubon. Everything I do has been done," Pam muttered. "I'm just following in their footsteps."

Gerbald, well familiar with this negative train of Pam's thought, tried to encourage her. "That was a different world, a different time, Pam. Darwin and Audubon probably aren't even going to be born thanks to the butterflies. I am told there is an awful lot of up-time knowledge that isn't in your library. The Ring of Fire brought back only a small amount of all the information collected in that other future. Right here and now there is still much to learn! Someone must seek out the discoveries waiting to be made on *this* world, in *this* time. Look around you. I don't see any human tracks here, do you? We are possibly the first people to visit this forest. *This* world needs a trailblazer, a scientist, a dreamer. We don't have Darwin. We won't need him, because we have Pam Miller."

Pam laughed aloud despite her dark mood. "Gawd, Gerbald, when did you come up with *that* speech? You sure know how to polish an apple!"

"I have been working on it, knowing the need for it would come. Were you moved?" He was grinning at his great cleverness now, which made it impossible for Pam to maintain her funk.

"Yeah, I was moved. I reckon I'll never know how or why I ended up here, but I can say it's not all bad. I know I have a purpose in this century. It's just hard to stay focused, especially when everything turns to shit like it has lately. Perhaps you may have noticed my most recent purpose has *literally* ended in disaster."

"Well, you know I am no religious man, but Dore is convinced that you were sent by God to help us improve this world. I see no reason to disagree."

"Thanks Pollyanna, you can knock it off now, I'm cheered up." Their laughter mingled with the cries and songs of unknown birds.

Chapter Sixteen: Gerbald, Dinosaur Hunter

They took a break before noon near a small, spring-fed creek. The water was cold and delicious.

"We've been walking for hours and still no sign of a dodo." Pam looked around the open forest, searching the leaf-littered floor for movement.

"Perhaps we did not land on Mauritius after all? Could this be Reunion or some other island?"

"No, we passed Reunion the day before we wrecked. It was far enough away that I didn't get much of a look, but I trust in our navigators. This *must* be Mauritius."

"Pam, as a hunter, I have spent days on end in the bush without seeing a single example of whatever game animal I was hunting. It's not unusual. I believe the American phrase is 'getting skunked.' "

"Yeah, well, I suppose. I'd just like to see a dodo, is all. I mean, we came all this freaking way. Remember, there aren't any left up-time, so it's kind of special. I will be the first person from my former century to see one, and yes, I am kind of excited about it."

"My eyes are peeled, Pam. If there are any around here, we will find them." They finished drinking their fill and continued on. The trees were getting bigger and more numerous. With mutual sighs, they made their way through an unexpectedly deep valley they hadn't known stood between them and their intended hill climb. The massive trunks and their chaos-patterned fretwork of high branches blocked out most of the sunlight, so they walked through a deep-green gloom. In the distance something squealed, the sound taking on a sinister ring in the primeval setting.

Pam began to get jumpy as they passed through the ancient groves. The raucous cry of an unseen bird high in the canopy startled her, causing her to miss her step. She sprawled clumsily onto the forest floor, face down into a bed of moldering leaves and twigs. Gerbald hurried to help her up. She clutched at him for a moment, her eyes wide with fear.

"Pam, what is the matter with you?" he asked in his most soothing voice, gently brushing the leaves off of her.

"Sorry! I can't help it. Damn!" Standing now, she took a deep breath, and tried to get ahold of herself. "I'm getting the willies out here, Gerbald. I mean, this isn't Thuringia. We're on a weird, remote, and uninhabited island looking for what I was raised to believe was an extinct species, *dodos*, for chrissakes! What if there are still fucking *dinosaurs* out here in these jungles? I mean, this place has been untouched since time began!"

"Now, that would be something to hunt, a true challenge!" Gerbald sent a piercing gaze out into the foliage, his face full of melodramatic wonder and avarice. "I could be the first man from my century to bag a dinosaur!"

"Oh, Christ, I wish I'd never let you read those Edgar Rice Burroughs books Walt gave you."

"*At the Earth's Core* and the rest of the Pellucidar series are fantastic, but I'm most fond of Sir Conan Doyle's *Lost World*. The movie was great, too, although the dinosaurs were men in rubber suits."

"Not to mention all those other hokey old movies you like so much. There were scads of film masterpieces we didn't have with us when we went through the Ring of Fire, but, Jesus wept, some dork had five years worth of schlock he taped off the Channel 13 Friday Midnight Thrillfest, and the Saturday Afternoon Matinee. What was that one you liked so much? Oh yeah, *Valley of the Gwangi,* featuring cowboys versus dinosaurs. Give me a break! How many times did you watch it anyway, twenty-five?"

"Thirty-two. A brilliant film! Ray Harryhausen was a genius! The tyrannosaurus rex menacing the town, prowling through the shadowy church—stupendous! I don't care what anyone says, Harryhausen's work was far more gripping than that silly *Jurassic Park* flick, ha! Oh, Pam, if only we could get a Hollywood going in Grantville, I would so like to be in the movies. People say I have a talent! Just think of it, *Gerbald, Dinosaur Hunter!*" Gerbald struck his most heroic pose.

It was true, Gerbald was one hundred percent pure ham at heart. The guy probably could have gotten at least some bit parts up-time; he did have charisma. Pam just laughed at him as she stepped around a particularly fresh and pasty animal turd, glad that she had not fallen into it. Seeing that she was ignoring his current heroic pose, Gerbald changed his patter down to a lower, but still melodramatic key.

"You know, Pam, I sometimes wonder—" He paused to look suspiciously at the leaf-screened sky, then continued in a somehow familiar creepy voice, while giving her a penetrating look of dread. "*What if* the event that happened to Grantville had taken you all even further back into history, or even *pre*history? What if you had fallen *much* further through the depths of time, say, to the Cretaceous period, when dinosaurs ruled the world? What would have become of you then?" He stood looking at her wide-eyed as if this nightmare might occur at any second.

"Knock it off, Jack Palance. You're already weird enough without talking like that guy. I'd probably be safer out here with a velociraptor than a nutcase like you." Pam, as usual, couldn't help but smile at Gerbald's antics. Once he got started it was hard to stop him. His goal wasn't really to freak her out, goofing around was just his way of passing the time on a long trip. She knew he also did it to distract her from her *moods*, and couldn't help but love him for that.

"You got it! That *was* Jack Palance! A master actor. I do miss movies. One day we will have another of those festivals where we drink beer, eat pizzas and watch movies all day like we used to."

"Yeah, that wouldn't be half bad. I miss the beer and pizza anyway." While humoring Gerbald, Pam had inserted a stick into the still mushy turd. It was full of smashed seeds and what might be crushed nutshells. "Although, one day we will probably look back at this jungle and say "Ahhh, the good old days."

Gerbald's face suddenly took on a sincerely wistful expression. "I would be glad if you were to one day think of our adventures together in that way, Pam. I certainly will."

"Yeah, we have fun, Ivanhoe, just don't get all misty on me. Let's see if we can find a damn dodo along the way while we are out here. Look, check out this turd, it's very exciting. It might be dodo scat, it's big enough and has the right consistency for a large-billed terrestrial vegetarian. Say, here's an idea, we can co-host a thrilling nature series, *In Search of Wild Bird Poop*."

"Always the romantic soul, our Pam, a woman who lives for adventure." Gerbald started humming the National Geographic theme loudly as they made their way through the underbrush. Pam joined in until they were laughing so loud it hurt their sides.

"I know! We shall do a remake of *The Valley of the Gwangi*! We could film it here on this very island! I will portray the heroic cowboy, naturally!

Lacking Ray Harryhausen, we will cast live dinosaurs, of course." He stopped abruptly and pointed at a tree, his face a model of terror. "My God, its an allosaurus! Flee!"

"Shh, I'm trying to think of what I will tell Dore when I come back without you tonight." Pam's scowl was fierce enough that Gerbald went back to his silent woodsman mode, but a hint of a contented smile still showed on his lips. He had cheered Pam up after all, always a very good thing.

Garrett W. Vance

Chapter Seventeen: Pam's Pot o' Gold

Leaving the forest behind, Pam and Gerbald arrived at an area of grassland, their planned climb rising before them. It was somewhat larger than it had looked from a distance, but they decided to try it anyway, as there was still plenty of daylight left. The slope was gentle, and soon they were high on the grassy mountainside. Reaching the mound of the summit they were rewarded with views east and west, as well as into the interior. One thing for sure was, that they were on a big, rugged volcanic island, and reaching the north end of it by any route on foot would be hard going for even the most experienced hiker.

Now that they had accomplished their task and weren't in such a rush, Pam wandered about the mountaintop, pausing periodically to make sketches of the views and various new species of birds they came across. It was sunny, but cool at this altitude, the breeze sweetly scented by the many wildflowers dotting the sub-alpine heaths.

Suddenly Pam let out a shrieking whoop. Gerbald rushed to her side to see what the matter was, his hand ready to unsheathe his trusty *katzbalger* shortsword.

"Pam! Are you all right?" He found Pam running around hugging the shrubbery, her eyes flashing with intense joy.

"All right? Am I *all right*? Oh hell yeah, I'm all right!" She kissed a leafy branch and began to perform some kind of celebratory dance through the plants as Gerbald looked on, thunderstruck.

"Pam, what in the world is going on?" He asked, as her delirium showed no signs of stopping.

"Don't you see it? Here, *here*! Look at this little tree! Do you know what it is?" She hugged the one closest to her.

Gerbald took a moment to study it closely; it was a pleasant enough looking shrub, with glossy green leaves, and yellow-shading-to-purplish berries. He had never seen one before in his life.

Pam stopped her crazy dance to stare at him expectantly. Finally he shrugged his shoulders in defeat. Pam laughed, the merry sound echoing around the hills.

"Gerbald, this is the most wonderful plant in the world. This, *this* is *coffee*! *Coffeeeee*!" She turned back to the shrub and hugged it again.

"*Coffee?* Coffee! Great Caesar's ghost, Pam, you found a coffee tree here at the ends of the earth! Are you sure?"

"Yes, I'm sure. I studied the hell out of this stuff before I left, trying to find crops for our colonists to grow down here. I couldn't get my hands on any viable beans before we left, but look! Coffee trees are growing *wild* here, and they are all over the place!" She swept her arm around and Gerbald realized that there were hundreds of the pretty little coffee trees thriving on the slopes of their antipodean mountain, all heavy with berries.

"Are you sure you can drink it?" Gerbald liked coffee well enough, but his knowledge of the subject didn't extend past asking for *"A little cream, no sugar."*

"Sure, why not? There's different species, but they're all drinkable. I'm not sure what type this one is, but it looks like the berries are in season! Sweet jumping Jesus, I have coffee again, hallelujah!" She returned to her ecstatic dance while Gerbald searched through his many-pocketed, sage-green coat to locate a cloth bag suitable for berries.

The two of them got back to camp later than expected. The extra weight had slowed them down since they had stuffed every hollow and pocket of their clothes and rucksacks with beans. Gerbald's coat was visibly lumpy with the things. They were just about on their last legs when they reached camp, but Pam couldn't wait until morning. Her exuberance was easy to catch, and soon everyone watched expectantly as Pam and Dore went to work on the treasure trove of beans. They roasted them as carefully as they could in Dore's makeshift stone oven, then ground them with the back of one of the sailor's axes. Pam used her cotton handkerchief for a filter, and soon enough a black brew simmered in the cookpot. Pam, no longer caring that she hadn't seen a single damn dodo all day, took the first sip of the newfound coffee from a coconut shell cup. She held the hot, bitter, liquid in her mouth for a moment before swallowing, as all eyes watched and waited for her reaction.

"Oh. My. God. This is the best thing I have *ever* tasted. It's coffee here in the middle of no-effing-where! It's coffee for castaways! Yippie-kay-yay!"

The men all smiled, pleased to see Pam so happy. Dore refilled her cup, followed by cups for herself, Gerbald and all the crew. The bosun determined that some of the spirits recovered from the late *Redbird* would make it taste even better, and the sounds of laughter and good cheer echoed around their little cove late into the night.

Garrett W. Vance

Chapter Eighteen: Birdwatching

Castaway Cove, South Coast of Mauritius

The days passed by slowly on their stranded shore, becoming weeks, and now nearly two months. Pam Miller, her companions Dore and Gerbald and the survivors of *Redbird's* crew busied themselves with various projects to increase their comfort and safety. The sailors used the tools recovered from the shipwreck to improve their shelters, Dore and Pam gathered the fruits and nuts they were sure were safe to eat, while Gerbald searched for game-birds (with Pam's rare blessing for such activities), and fished the bay along with the sailors. They were all alive, and in reasonable physical health; staying busy was what they did to remain sane. Despite these various distractions they all felt the world was leaving them farther and farther behind with each passing day.

Old Fritjoff had taken it upon himself to be Pam's caretaker. He had cut all the underbrush out from under her stilted hut, and made sure that there were no creepy-crawlies lurking there. He cleared a sandy trail from her door down to the beach, and swept it clear of leaves and debris every morning before she woke up, but not before leaving a coconut bowl full of cool water from the spring on her porch. Pam was embarrassed by the attention, and told him he didn't have to go to all that trouble over her, but the white-haired gentleman just shyly nodded and continued to look after her anyway.

"It is no trouble for me, *Frau* Pam. It is good for a man to have work to do, and even better when it is in the service of a fine and important person such as yourself. Don't fret now. You are doing the princess' work, and I serve you as I would her. Just call on Fritjoff if you need anything. I will be there for you."

Pam was touched by his eagerness to please, and thanked him profusely, asking if there were anything she could do for him. Fritjoff smiled with his few remaining teeth, his blue eyes still bright and sparkling in his long-lived and wind-wrinkled face.

"No, no, I am a simple fellow and have few needs. But, if it were no trouble to you, one day when you meet again with Princess Kristina, I would be greatly honored if you would pass my humble respects on to her. That would be a true kindness to a faithful servant of the Vasa such as myself."

Pam promised to do so, and didn't say it aloud but intended to make sure that on that future day Fritjoff would be right there with her to give his respects himself. *That would be a real treat for the old guy. I'm going to make that happen. He can get that precious photo autographed in person!* The thought gave her a very warm and pleasant feeling. She realized that she had grown very fond of these stouthearted men of the north, and that it was a blessing to be caught in such trying circumstances with these trustworthy people around her. *Someday I might even look back on this castaway life and miss it . . . but not too much.*

One overcast morning, Pam and Gerbald, finding they were stocked up with enough food to last several days and utterly bored with life at camp, decided to follow the river into the interior. They had been too busy to explore further since the triumphant discovery of coffee a few weeks prior, and Pam was absolutely itching to get back to her search for the elusive dodo.

The going was fairly easy. They followed a corridor of grassy meadows between the river and the forest's edge. The sun burned the clouds off around eleven, at which point it became hot enough to chase them into the shade of the woods. The forest floor was clear of thick underbrush, a mossy parkway through ancient tree trunks. Pam kept her eyes open for new birds along the way, occasionally stopping to observe and sketch one of the myriad species that inhabited the island. She had decided that her best bet on finding any dodos was to simply stop looking for them, contenting herself with the many other amazing birds that inhabited the isolated island. She wondered how she would ever manage to catalog them all. It would take ages to do it right . . . but then again she might have that kind of time, if rescue didn't come. She wondered if she could find natural substitutes to replenish her diminishing paper and art supplies.

That thought made her mood sour despite the beauty of the venerable groves, and soon she was just slogging along in a funk, not really paying attention to her surroundings at all. Just as she was sinking into a really bad mood, Gerbald let out the low whistle that meant "*Look at that*," one of the signals they had developed in their years spent birdwatching in the wilds of the Thüringerwald. Pam froze, carefully scanning the tree limbs for a choice specimen. Gerbald gave her a nudge with his elbow and pointed downward with a small movement of his head.

Pam followed his gaze to a large, odd-looking bird standing just six feet away from them on its sturdy legs and thick toes. It cracked a nut with a loud snapping sound in its grotesquely large and powerful bill. The bird regarded them calmly with a bright yellow eye turreted in a beak that covered nearly all of its head. Overall, it was awkwardly-shaped, and a bit comical looking, with fluffy white tufts of feathers puffing out at its tiny wings and arched tail, exactly as in all the illustrations she had seen, although it stood a bit more upright, and was slightly thinner than it had been portrayed in art. Pam's eyes were wide as she marveled at the living creature, its breath moving the downy gray feathers of its chest, its beak clacking softly as it swallowed the nut. It was the strangest bird she had ever seen, a bird she had once *never hoped to see*, a bird lost forever in her former world. The poster child of the doomed and extinct, *alive,* right in front of her: The Dodo.

The three of them stood still for a very long time, content to stare at each other. At last, the dodo gave them a dismissive coo *(just like a dove!)* and dipped its plated head to search for another nut. It soon found one, and the powerful beak went back to work. Pam felt her face grow hot and wet, she was crying, crying the tears of joy a child might if, through some happy magic, she found herself in the living presence of a *real* Santa Claus, stepped out of the chimneys of legend in jolly flesh and blood.

"It's so ugly!" she exclaimed with a joyous laugh in her voice, "And it's also the most beautiful thing I've ever seen!" She took Gerbald's hand for confidence, then together they took first one, then another step closer to the dodo, which simply ignored them as it continued its nut-cracking. At last Pam reached out with trembling fingers to gently touch the downy gray feathers. It watched her out of the corner of its bright-yellow eye, but gave no reaction other than to continue eating. "It's real." she whispered. "This is really happening." She gasped as she noticed two more dodos foraging nearby, blithely paying no attention whatsoever to the humans among them.

"Congratulations, Pam," Gerbald told her in the solemn tones of one who has witnessed something wonderful. "Now we know they still live and our sacrifices were not in vain. One way or another we will find a way to save the dodos from the fate they suffered in your up-time world. Your mission will be a success, Pam, I swear this."

Chapter Nineteen: Dodo Do's and Don'ts

The news of Pam finally meeting the elusive dodos face to face was met with cheers back at the camp. The sailors well understood that finding the odd-looking birds was very important to her, and to their princess, even if they were still a bit cloudy on why. They offered whatever services they could give in supporting Pam's efforts to study the creatures, although Pam couldn't think of much they could do beyond the daily task of making sure they had food and shelter, which they did with Scandinavian stoic good cheer.

Over the next few weeks Pam noticed that, although they tried to hide it, the men were growing more and more frustrated with their isolation. She realized they were keeping quiet about it in order to give her time to study the dodos now that she had found them, waiting for her to satisfy her needs before making any attempts to leave their encampment in search of the colonists, and possible escape from the island. For her part, Pam felt guilty at letting her desire to observe the dodo supersede looking for the very likely captured colonists, but it was a guilt she decided she would accept, at least for a little while longer. They had, after all, come all this way! Rationalizations well in hand, Pam and Gerbald marched off into the woods daily, enjoying their prize.

Pam was in a state of bliss as she went about her studies. It was as if beloved cartoon characters from her childhood had come to magical life before her eyes, their antics all for her own, personal entertainment. She sometimes shook her head in wonder that she was actually seeing living, breathing dodos. *Finally, something good about time travel!* Following quietly along behind the humorously waddling creatures, Pam observed their behavior with delight. Their rare cries reminded Pam of young geese, and they also chuckled to themselves while foraging, a sound much like a pigeon makes. Increasingly Pam thought they might be descended from, or perhaps cousins, of the pigeons and doves.

"Pam, are the dodos eating pebbles?" Gerbald asked, no longer bothering to whisper, since the dodos completely ignored their presence. As long as they didn't make too many sudden movements, the dodos were unconcerned at having large bipedal primates in their midst.

"They don't actually eat them, they swallow them down into their gullet to help digestion. The stones aid in grinding up the food." Pam answered, watching a young specimen in hot pursuit of a stumbling beetle.

"I should try that the next time we have dried squid for dinner." Gerbald remarked with his usual, wry drawl. He had really taken to becoming a hillbilly. Pam figured it must come natural to him.

To their surprise, the dodos could move surprisingly quickly in pursuit of scuttling prey. Like many bird species, they were opportunists, consuming whatever they could manage to get their ponderous beaks around. A sudden lunge, and the dodo's sharp bill might snap up a juicy frog, or wriggling worm. Pam was sure that their amazing appendage could deliver a nasty wound if a dodo was provoked, and stayed well clear of it, always moving calmly and not getting too near its business end. As far as the dodos were concerned, Pam and Gerbald were about as interesting as a big, gray rock. The humans were totally ignored as the clucking, contented dodos went about their endless, and not very difficult, search for food.

One day, Gerbald managed to find out just how powerful those beaks could be, when he accidentally stumbled through a dodo nest. The nest was rather unimpressive, a shallow depression dug into the mulchy forest floor, lined with a bit of down and twigs, but it was home to a magnificent white egg as big as a softball. The mother of said egg, who was eating some nuts nearby, let out a shockingly loud whistle like a tea kettle on the boil, and charged Gerbald with shocking speed, her beak clacking loudly, and downy feathers fluffed out to give her a more menacing appearance. She was a lot larger than a turkey, if not nearly as big as an ostrich, and her head rose nearly to his abdomen. Gerbald shouted "Yikes!" one of his vast vocabulary of American TV-isms, and backpedaled away from the angry creature.

Pam watched all this from the safety of a nearby tree. As soon as the ruckus started she had gone up the nearest one, standard procedure for non-climbing critter attacks in the Thüringerwald, good for wild dogs and boars, but not much help against bears. As Gerbald turned to break into a run, the outraged mother stretched her neck out farther than Pam would have guessed possible, and closed it sharply around his booted ankle. Gerbald yelped even louder, then managed to shake the dodo loose with a twist. Pam thought that the bill's sharp tip might have pierced the leather. The dodo seemed satisfied at having exacted her toll in flesh, and doubled back to make a big scene of stalking around the nest while squawking loudly, a clear message that anyone else wishing to disturb her precious egg was going to get the same treatment *that guy* got! By now Gerbald himself was up a tree, massaging his ankle.

"Jesus crippled Christ on crutches cut from the cross!" he cursed, his voice full of annoyance. Pam couldn't say her friend had been afraid during the encounter, Gerbald didn't do fear, but this was as discombobulated as she had seen him in a long time.

"Good gawd, Gerbald, where did you come up with that bit of blasphemy? Dore would pop a vein!" Pam suppressed a laugh, not wanting to further injure the great woodsman's pride.

"Thanks a lot. It's a Gerbald original. That hurt like hell! Mother Dodo put a hole in my boot, and even broke the skin!"

"Consider it a sacrifice for science. Ya know, I never would have gotten to witness that nest protecting behavior without you along, because I'm not dumb enough to actually piss a mother dodo off." Pam started laughing despite herself. The whole thing, from her safe vantage point, had been nothing short of hilarious. "Channel Thirteen Mega Monster Afternoon Presents: *Gerbald the Fearless Dinosaur Hunter vs the Menace of The Mad Dodo Mama!*"

Gerbald laughed along with her. It really was only his pride that had been in any danger. The dodo, despite its bluster and fearsome beak, hadn't been any kind of real threat to him, beyond a bit of a bruise.

They stayed in their trees for a while, watching as the mollified hen settled down on her lovely big egg, from which vantage point she favored them both with stern glares until, ruffled feathers at last relaxing into their normal softness, she fell asleep.

On their way back to camp that evening, Pam looked back on the mother dodo's defense and began to feel sad. Gerbald had been caught off guard, but if he had really wanted to, he could have dispatched the creature with ease. She realized now that all his actions had been to avoid having to injure the dodo rather than to protect himself. Pam now felt embarrassed at having teased him. Even an inexperienced woodsman, say a sailor, or a farmer, would ultimately prevail against the big, flightless birds.

A darker thought came then, something she knew she must eventually face. Even if she could control human depredations against the dodo, there was still the danger posed by introduced species. Humans had killed their share of the poor dodos, creatures evolved with no natural predators present, and completely unequipped to deal with any real danger. But from all Pam had read and surmised, the major threat to the dodo's future would be the foreign animals that would inevitably arrive with humanity, whether by design or not. Yes, she would try to stop that invasion, and she would make some difference. After all, she had not allowed her colonists to bring along any mammals other than some horses, cattle and sheep, but the rats would be on that ship, too. Even immaculate *Redbird* carried vermin, despite her and Dore's efforts to eradicate them. How many rats had swum ashore during the wreck? Would they find today's nest and break that pretty shell into a hundred sticky pieces, while the poor mother squawked and chased them about in vain?

Gawd, Pam, she thought, *there is no point in fretting about this now. We haven't even gotten from Point B to C yet in this mess, and here you are worrying about W.* She smiled, deciding to chew on the problem a little more anyway. *Well, it's going to come up eventually. Might as well have a plan.*

Dogs, cats, pigs, rats and, according to the books, monkeys, would be her enemies in the future, and she would have to come up with ways to control their populations on the island. She shook her head, knowing that, if she lived to see it, the day would come when she would find herself in the role of the island's animal control officer, and did not relish the prospect much. Getting the bats out of the Baptist church had put her off dealing with mammals of any sort. She had been able to manage that episode humanely without resorting to killing the poor little things, but it would be otherwise with stray invaders on Mauritius. She would have to be ruthless.

Satisfied with her initial studies, Pam began her next project, painting accurate portraits of the dodos. This was for scientific purposes, of course, as well as the genuine pleasure the art gave her. The problem was, despite their general appearance of ungainliness, the big birds covered a lot of ground in a day, sometimes traveling many miles on their sturdy, yellow, four-toed feet. Upon finding them in the morning she would get her bamboo easel, a hand-crafted gift from the bosun, and her precious watercolors all set up in a nice, sunny clearing, but before she could even finish the initial sketches the dodos would plow through the area's edible matter, then wander off, leaving Pam alone to repack her gear and follow. This happened again and again, and she was beginning to get frustrated until she hit upon an idea.

She and Gerbald spent the next morning gathering nuts, seeds, fallen fruits, beetles and whatever else they could find for dodo treats. After they had a sizable store in hand, they caught up to the dodos at their latest hangout. Overall, the birds seemed to move in a very loose, but discernible flock, groups and subgroups working over their various territories in what Pam thought must be a slow, weeks-long, loop, allowing the freshly foraged areas time to replenish before coming around again. Pam sat up her paints and got to work. A while later, just as the dodos were about to move on, Pam reached into her bag of goodies and threw a healthy handful of dodo treats across the clearing to the ever-hungry birds.

"Here you go, sweeties! Eat it up, yum, yum!" Pam called and cooed while Gerbald rolled his eyes toward the heavens. The dodos looked at Pam with their uncanny yellow eyes, then looked at the treats scattered at their feet. With what Pam felt for sure was a shrug of their tiny wings, they began pecking at the unexpected offering.

"I don't think this is a good idea," Gerbald muttered. "Didn't you say we don't want to make pets of them?"

"I'm not! I'm just feeding a few pigeons in the park, that's all! Just look at this sweet afternoon light, it's perfect for painting!" Whistling a merry tune, she went back to it. A quarter of an hour later, the dodos had eaten all of Pam's treats and were beginning to move off again, when Pam called out a friendly "Yoo-hoo!" and threw them yet another double handful. This time without a pause, the dodos began to eat while Pam continued to work on her latest masterpiece. After several more repetitions of the new ritual, Pam beamed at what was turning out to be quite a nice work of art, and she did say so herself! It might even be the one to use for the happy little afterward she would add to her book, *Birds of the USE*, detailing how the dodos *would not* be going extinct in *this* world, thank you very much!

After several hours, Pam decided that any more work on the piece would just be fussing, so she set about getting her gear ready for the hike home. The dodos were finishing up their latest treat as she woke Gerbald from the nap he had been taking, not part of his standard bodyguard and look-out routine, but then back in Grantville they hadn't been out in the field every day, all day, either. Deeming these woods safe enough, and Pam having developed nearly a good an eye and ear for intruders as his own, Gerbald got some extra sleep in the way of old soldiers from time immemorial, wherever and whenever he could.

"Come along, Rip Van Winkle. It's almost the eighteenth century. Let's get back."

"Wake me when its the twentieth century, or as soon as everyone owns a colored TV," he mumbled sleepily from deep beneath the wide and warped brim of his floppy, mustard-colored hat. With a groan, he rose languidly to his nearly six feet and stretched like some gray-whiskered, but still deadly, jungle cat. Pam marveled at his ability to sleep anywhere as she finished packing up her gear. As she made ready to leave the clearing, she noticed that the dodos, although finished with their snacks a while ago, hadn't moved on. Instead, they all stood around staring at her.

Pam smiled, a bit surprised at this new behavior. Then she laughed a bit as she realized what was going on.

"Oh, I see, you want another treat! Sorry, kids. I gave you all I had. You're on your own again!" She turned away from them, pleased with her cleverness and the nice piece of art it had yielded, and began to walk toward the trail leading home. Out of the corner of her eye she noticed that Gerbald had not fallen into step with her and was still watching the dodos.

"Um, Pam? You best have a look," he said in a very calm voice.

Pam turned around to see that the dodos, rather than melting back into the forest in search of food, had all moved closer to her, a group of six adults and a couple of youngsters now just a few yards away. They stood in a loose clump, their somehow disconcerting yellow eyes all trained unblinkingly upon Pam. Frowning a bit, Pam took another two steps toward the edge of the clearing. The dodos did the same.

"Shit! They think I'm going to give them more treats."

"One dares not utter the phrase 'I told you so.' Oops. I uttered it!" Gerbald said in a smug tone.

Pam screwed up her face to stick out her tongue at him. She took another step, and the dodos followed again. Exasperated, Pam waved her arms around in front of her in what she hoped would be seen as a gesture of discouragement and called out "Shoo! Go on now, I don't have any more for you, now *git!*" The dodos' heads bobbed around watching her arms gesticulating, then sniffed around their leathery feet to see if more treats had been let loose by those actions. Not finding any, their gaze returned to Pam. It then occurred to her how large the dodos really were, and began to feel a bit unnerved by their bright-yellow stares.

She looked to Gerbald for support but he just shrugged his shoulders.

"Don't look at me! You're *the bird lady*," he told her. "Let's just try walking away. They will get bored eventually."

Nodding nervously, Pam turned and headed down the trail at a brisk-but-not-too-brisk pace, followed closely by Gerbald. The dodos came along after, one-by-one down the narrow path through the forest. Pam was worried that the large, and in such large numbers possibly even dangerous birds might try to rush her, but so far the dodos were content to politely wait for more treats. Following the treat-giver seemed their best bet. Pam forced herself not to run, as she knew that despite their ungainly appearance, they could match her speed.

An hour later they emerged along the shore near their encampment. Pam and Gerbald, followed by a neat line of dodos. Pers saw them first and whistled up Dore from her kitchen to come have a look. Soon, all the sailors stood watching the bizarre procession.

"I feel like the Pied Piper," Pam grumbled.

"More like Mother Goose, I should think." Gerbald teased her, enjoying every second of his friend's well-deserved discomfiture.

Pam grimaced at him, but managed a calm smile for those assembled, looking for all the world as if she were completely in control of the situation. As soon as she stopped moving, the dodos formed a circle around her, waiting expectantly for their next snack.

"Are these the famous dodos?" the bosun asked, regarding the unusual creatures with wide eyes.

"Yes, indeed they are. Dore, do you happen to have any nuts stored away?" Pam's voice held just enough tinge of desperation to send her friend hurrying into the kitchen to find some. Dore returned shortly with a banana leaf basket full of nuts, which she cautiously passed over the dodo's heads to Pam's outreached hand, never once taking her suspicious eyes off the gathered birds.

"Gawd, I really hate further associating humans with food, but at this point I have to do something." Pam told Gerbald, quietly.

"I'm not sure why you are so edgy. They are just pigeons in the park, after all."

Pam silently vowed to have revenge later, then turned to her flock.

"Here, chicky-chickies, have some more nuts!" she called sweetly, throwing a heaping handful at Gerbald's feet. The birds ran to him, eagerly gobbling up their prize with a loud clacking of their bills.

"Here, hold this!" before Gerbald could think, Pam had thrust the basket into his hands. Just as he began to make his protest, she slipped around behind him, making a rapid beeline for her hut, leaping up the stairs, and slamming the door shut behind her with a loud slap of bamboo. In the meantime, the dodos had finished their latest round of snacks, and were now staring at Gerbald and the basket of nuts in his hands.

Dore began laughing, as did the sailors, all of whom were carefully backing away from the strange, hungry creatures in their midst.

"Ha!" Dore called out to her flummoxed husband. "It looks like Mister Funny Man is the one left holding the bag! It serves you right, buffoon!" she chided him, laughing aloud before disappearing into the safety of her grass-roofed kitchen.

Gerbald shook his head ruefully at being so easily duped. With a sigh, he smiled graciously at the dodos surrounding him.

"Come along then, my feathered friends. Let us see if clever old Gerbald can give you the slip." The dodos followed him as he led them away down the beach into the twilight. Pam wouldn't even come out for dinner that night, so eventually Dore sent Fritjoff off with something for her to eat, growling that she finally understood why the up-time phrase "for the birds" implied something foolish or worthless.

The next day, the dodos were hanging around a little ways down the beach, scavenging the tide flats for bits of seaweed and snails. Pam watched from what she considered to be a safe distance through her birding scope, as one of the larger dodos managed to catch a scuttling crab. Gerbald was taking the day off from scientific study in order to lick his wounded pride. He had been up well after dark playing a game of hide-and-seek with his erstwhile followers, and had little use for Pam at the moment. Pam just smiled. She knew he'd get over it sooner than later, understanding that no trickster ever enjoys being among the tricked.

And so, the dodos decided to make the beach their home for the time being, sleeping under the palms, and occasionally wandering through camp in search of a treat. Although Pam warned everyone not to feed them, they inevitably did anyway. The ugly-cute critters were just too hard to resist. The lonely sailors enjoyed the novelty of having pets about, even ones as odd as these. The only member of the party who was immune to the dodo's charms was Dore, who had no fear of their sharp beaks, and who shooed them away from her kitchen and gardens with the fearsome might of her bamboo-handled grass broom.

From the time of their arrival, the *Redbird* castaways had been relying chiefly on seafood for their protein. There were very few birds present that might be considered game. Gerbald had snared a few black-feathered marsh birds along the river which Pam thought might be some kind of moorhen, but they tasted pretty much like the mudflats they had come from, and had little meat on their sharp bones. They had also tried eating several species of sandpiper and gull, but the rubbery flesh stank of rotten fish, and was so unpalatable they ended up using it all for bait.

The dodos had been among them for several weeks now, and their novelty had worn off. Pam realized, to her horror, that the attitude of the men toward their pets had subtly changed. Pam now saw a look of hunger on their faces as they watched the fluffy dodos wander around the camp, nicely fattened up from their regular treats. Dodos were now the largest, and juiciest bird they had seen since being marooned, resembling in many ways a plump turkey. They no longer were feeding the dodos for amusement's sake, it seemed, but rather to fatten them up for the cooking pot! Even Dore was sneaking a predatory peek at them now and then, as she worked on the crab and coconut curry they were having *yet again* for the noonday meal.

Pam decided she had better head this disconcerting development off right at the pass. As the men finished their breakfast she walked out into the morning sunlight and *harrumphed* for their attention.

"All right, everyone," she announced in her now well-seasoned Swedish, "I know you all are hungry for meat. I've been watching what's happening lately, and I *know* what's been going through your minds, but just let me tell you one thing: Don't even *think* about eating a dodo, not even *one*! Anyone who does is going to be in big trouble with me, and you better believe that is a place you do not want to be! Besides, the books all say they taste terrible!" She was really getting mad now, and stomped around among the stunned sailors, making sure they all got a good look in her eyes, and that each and everyone fully understood that she meant business! Finally, she rose up to her full less-than-a-third of their average height, crossed her arms self-righteously, and said "You lot know how to fish don't you? Well, get off your butts and start fishing! *Now*! *MOVE!*"

The men, hardened naval seamen all, leaped up at her fiery command, rushing off to prepare the various fishing tackle they had contrived, while Gerbald hastily retreated into the underbrush to gather materials to weave into a new fish trap. Dore hunched over her coconuts with a guilty expression, while Pam continued to stalk up and down the beach keeping a watchful eye on the oblivious dodos. *We had better get out of here before history repeats itself*, Pam thought darkly, refusing to admit to herself that she, too, was beginning to wonder what a nice fat dodo might taste like.

Garrett W. Vance

Chapter Twenty: Strangers Come to Call

Pam and Gerbald were climbing over the steep southern bluff to explore the adjacent stretch of beach to the north, in search of more new species and possible new food sources, when an unexpected splash of color out on the water caught Pam's ever-watchful eye.

"Gerbald! Look!" Pam hissed back into the trees. She was now on her belly in the tall grass, crawling toward the cliff's edge. Gerbald slithered up next to her with practiced grace.

"A ship! What kind?" his eyes were bright as they focused on the vessel dropping anchor in their bay. Pam carefully grasped the black neoprene strap at her neck to pull her precious birding scope out. She cupped a palm over the outer lens to prevent any reflection from the bright southern sun giving away their position. Focusing in, she gasped in surprise. It was a brightly painted vessel, with elegantly carved ornamentation on its woodwork, featuring dragons, and sea turtles, and cranes. The back and front were both high-set, and the sails were an unusual rectangular shape, ribbed like a hand fan.

"Hmmm." I think it's some kind of a junk," Pam said.

"Really? I am no seaman, but it looks like a perfectly seaworthy boat to me, although shaped rather oddly." Gerbald squinted at the vessel curiously.

Pam stifled a laugh. "No, not *that* kind of junk. I mean a *Chinese* junk, a type of ship from the Orient."

"Ah, another one of those *homonyms*. A rather annoying feature of English, I must say."

"I agree. Christ all mighty, we have to get back down to the camp. Do you think they've seen it, too?"

"Master Bosun always sets a watch. The Swedish sailors are resourceful and well-trained men. We are lucky to have them."

"Darn tootin'!" If one were to be shipwrecked with someone, a friendly band of resourceful Vikings was definitely the way to go.

Pam watched the swarthy-complexioned men on the junk's decks going about their tasks. "They don't look Chinese," Pam whispered, even though it was very unlikely they could be heard against the wind at such a distance. She handed Gerbald the scope.

"Indeed, at least not any such as I have seen on TV or at the movies, although I think some of those were actually white people in poorly-done make-up. These fellows look to be some kind of a Moor. By their white robes and headgear I would say they are followers of Allah the Merciful." The last came with an ironic chuckle from the old soldier.

"Arabs?"

"Perhaps, or some relative. Turks, possibly. They are well armed with those curved blades, and handle themselves like fighting men. Several have firearms, although those look rather primitive. Oh— Oh my." His tone turned dark.

"What?" Pam asked, growing more and more uneasy.

"It's ugly, but you had best see it for yourself. Look there, hanging from the bowsprit."

Pam looked, and to her horror, saw several severed heads with long, silky, black hair hanging there, grisly trophies swinging in the sea breeze. Despite the advanced state of decay, she was sure their features were Asiatic.

"My God, they killed the Chinese who owned the ship! These guys are some kind of pirates!"

"Indubitably." That was one of Gerbald's favorite two dollar words, gleaned from watching TV, of course. "This is not good," he added with a frown.

"Have you ever fought any like them before?"

"There were some such as these amongst the Spanish. They were fierce fighters." He handed the scope back to Pam. "Don't worry, they will bleed as well as any man," he added, his voice taking on a cold edge. Pam looked at the former soldier, still fearsome in his fifties, his hand resting instinctively on the hilt of the deadly shortsword attached to his belt.

"No doubt they will. Let's git."

Very carefully, they eased back from the cliff's edge through the grass, leaving little trace of their presence. They made haste through the shadowed wood, down the rocky hillside to their castaway camp. They arrived to find Dore clutching her biggest cleaver, waiting anxiously near the hidden path which was their designated escape route, leading to a refuge in the forest they had prepared for such emergencies. Seeing her loved ones arrive, she puffed out her typical exasperated breath. Before they could begin to tell her what they had seen, Dore addressed them in hushed and serious tones.

"You are late. We know about the boat, too. We were not seen, and the *löjtnant* has already set up his men in an ambush. They think those men out there will come ashore for fresh water. They are no Christians by the looks of them. The bosun says they are murderous pirates."

Gerbald nodded, allowing himself a grim smile at the prospect of combat. Pam leaned on her grandmother's walking stick, catching her breath and calming her nerves as she watched Gerbald slip silently into the brush to confer with the men, becoming invisible to any onlooker within an instant. Thanks to his training, she knew how to do that, too, and in a situation like this she was glad of it.

"Come on, Dore, let's get undercover. This is one time where I am more than happy to let the boys do their macho warrior thing, and stay out of the way."

"And such boys they are! They relish this, you know. Fools."

Chapter Twenty-One: Pam Hatches a Plan

Pam silently led her friend farther down the escape route, a narrow trail with an entrance imperceptible to any who didn't know it. Dore followed with remarkable grace. For the first time it occurred to Pam that Dore had lost a lost of weight since their voyage had begun. Her sturdy, buxom build had taken on a bit of youthful slenderness. She moved as silently as Pam did. Having been a soldier's wife and camp follower for many long years, Dore was no stranger to slipping behind cover when the weapons came out. They paused at a fallen log in the shade of the trees, not far from the hideout, and waited there silently, listening for any sounds of struggle from back at the camp. An hour passed and then two, according to Pam's self-winding, waterproof Timex, more valuable than a chest of jewels in this century. They began to get restless.

"What if they don't need fresh water?" Dore asked quietly.

"Then they won't need to come ashore. I sure would like to take that boat from those bastards, but I don't think our guys can win an attack by sea, even with the pinnace. By the time they got it in the water, those Arabs, or whatever they are, would have plenty of time to either pull anchor and scram, or prepare to hold them off. They would have a huge advantage." Pam rubbed her chin and began to think about the problem at hand. If they didn't do *something*, the ship might just sail away without giving them any opportunity to capture it, which was beginning to seem like a very important goal. Pam thought they were all ready to take a chance to escape in a seaworthy craft at this point, even if the risk was high.

The pinnace just wouldn't cut it on a long voyage. According to the bosun, it was really only supposed to hold half their number safely, being designed as a close range, ship-to-shore ferry and lifeboat. Short of being rescued by a friendly ship, which was extremely unlikely this year, they needed to get their hands on something big enough to carry all of them away from this lonely coast. Ideally, something big enough to mount that lovely up-time inspired cannon, which would give them a fighting chance next time they encountered bad guys. Pam squatted on the fallen log, going into what she thought of as thinking cap mode, working the problem in her head.

After a while a grin came to her face. "Oh, goodness . . ." she mumbled.

Dore's ear's pricked up. "You have an idea," she stated, knowing Pam's nuances well by now.

Pam nodded carefully as if afraid to lose it. It was ridiculous of course. It was *utterly* ridiculous, and it would probably work. She took one of Dore's firm, wash-worn hands in hers.

"Yes, I have an idea. I think I saw it in an old movie, or maybe on *Gilligan's Island*, that old TV show Gerbald likes so much. Now, it's pretty crazy, but you are going to have to trust me on this, it's going to work. It's going to work because it *is* crazy!" She leaned closer to her older friend and outlined her plan while Dore listened, eyes growing larger and larger.

"*What!*" Dore almost shouted when Pam had finished, then caught herself and hissed, "You want us to *what?*" Dore's face had a look of shock that Pam had rarely seen before, the look of a very conservative Christian woman who has been asked to do something beyond the pale. Pam continued to nod, now more sure than ever.

"Listen, Dore, honey. It's the only plan I've got and I know it sounds bad. It's totally nuts, in fact, but we have to do it. There's not much time. The guys' ambush isn't working. It needs bait. It's time for us girls to step up. I know you are made of strong stuff. Now please put your misgivings aside and help me do this. I *need* you, Dore. I need you to do this with me."

Dore narrowed her icy blue eyes at Pam, her best friend, her adopted little sister, in some ways the child she never had. The formidable, all-purpose, soldier's wife harrumphed mightily, and fiddled with her apron strings, lost in thought. Disapproval and mistrust showed in every twitch of her powerful fingers. Pam waited for her to work it out, hoping that Dore would realize the necessity of her bizarre proposal. Seeing the look of fading hope on Pam's face, Dore gripped Pam's hand hard and said, "For *you*, my dear Pam, only because *you* would have it. May the Good Lord forgive us."

Shortly she and Dore were in a huddle behind the camp with Gerbald, the bosun, and Pers, while the other sailors kept their positions. The anchored ship's crew had finished most of their work, and looked as if they were getting ready to either set sail or take a late afternoon nap.

Having heard Pam's plan, the bosun exclaimed rather loudly, "You want to *what*?" His face was a study in astonishment. Young Pers had turned a new shade of pale, his eyes wide as China plates. Gerbald laughed silently into his hand, his entire frame shaking with mirth until Dore slugged him in the bicep; *not* on his sword arm, Pam noted. Gerbald let a laugh escape rather too loudly. There were tears in his eyes, he was so struck with the pure outrageousness of what Pam proposed. Barely controlling his hilarity, he announced, "I *like* this plan!"

Dore glared at him menacingly. "As you would, you disgusting goat. To see your own women folk half-naked and dressed like these *harlot dancers* would appeal to an impious sinner like you. May God have pity on your black and shriveled soul."

"Not *harlots*, Dore, *hula! Hula* dancers. Big difference. It's a cultural thing. They live in a warm climate, so they just don't wear as many clothes as we do. Come on, let's go get dressed. It's time to lay the bait."

Gerbald continued to chuckle impiously at the proceedings, making Pam snarl at him with uncharacteristic vehemence. "That's enough out of you, dumbass! I need her calm, and you are *not* helping!" She slugged him in the arm, hard, just like Dore had done for good measure. *I didn't hit him in the sword arm either. We're going to need that*, she thought darkly. Pam was sure he was immune to any physical pain she could inflict, but her fierce tone and epithet silenced him immediately, his mirth replaced by a pitiful, chastised look, which, even so, still smacked of insincerity. Sometimes the man could be infuriating when he got into his teasing mode.

Pam turned to the bosun. "Tell *Löjtnant* Lundkvist what we're doing. I want the men ready to get between us and them *fast*." The bosun nodded his understanding somberly. "I'm sure I don't need to tell you fellows that *anyone* who makes fun of us is going to have to deal with *me* when it's all over, and I won't be as nice as the bloody damn pirates!" Pam growled as she led Dore away to the costuming department, her gray eyes brooding like a dangerous storm front. Two voices came back with very earnest "yes, ma'ams" and one made a strangled cough, trying to cover a fresh round of chuckles. *Men can be such pigs*, Pam thought as she stalked off. *Thank God they're here.*

Dore's face was miserable as Pam led her into the cool dimness of their camp's main hut, where they held meetings, stored food, and ate their meals during inclement weather.

"Come on, Dore. You need to buck up and get into character. We need to be good actors." Her voice was full of false, but hopefully convincing, cheer.

"*Actors?* Those sin lovers who appear in all manner of un-Christian garb in your up-time entertainments. Oh Dear Lord, strike me down where I stand." Dore looked up at the thatched ceiling of the hut with imploring eyes.

Pam suddenly lost her patience. There wasn't much time and the stress was becoming too much to bear. She grabbed Dore by the arms and shook her with quite a bit of strength, Dore being a very solidly built individual. Pam raised her voice as loud as she dared. "Damn it all, Dore, *listen!* We are *not* sinners. We are doing this to save ourselves and get off this fucking rock, got it? God is merciful, right? He would want us to fight for our lives, right? So whatever we do today, He's going to forgive us! Now grow up and help me pull this off!"

Dore's eyes focused on Pam with startled wideness. Her dear Pam, shaking her and lecturing her as if she were a stubborn child, was an unpleasant first, another of what was shaping up to be a very long day of such unpleasant firsts.

Pam released her grip to hug Dore tightly as she would have her own mother, and spoke in a shaky small voice, all trace of anger gone. "I'm so sorry, Dore, but I can't think of *anything else to do!*" Dore, her arms now released from Pam's surprisingly powerful grip, hugged Pam back for a moment, then gently untangled herself from her friend's frantic embrace.

"It is I who should be sorry, dear Pam. Sorry for questioning your sincere efforts and being such a pious old fool. I know you would only ask such of me in desperate times, as these are. It is indeed time I 'grow up' and be a help to you." Dore took a deep breath and let it out slowly. She even managed a small smile. "Now tell me, what must we do to appear as *harlot dancers?*"

That made Pam laugh, her tone still a little desperate, but warming quickly to the intrinsic hilarity of their situation. She stepped back and eyed her old friend who now stood courageously ready for Pam's orders. Pam, relieved, got started. "Well, first you have got to lose that apron. It's *so* last century."

Chapter Twenty-Two: Harlot Dancers

As Dore began untying the many clever knots she made her husband navigate through in the private hours, Pam reached up to set free the pony tail she usually tied her flyaway hair in an effort to keep it mostly under control. She shook her head to loosen up the wavy, dishwater blonde locks, *fly, be free!* then mussed it all up with her hands to make it look even wilder. Next, she carefully emptied her pockets of any valuables such as her scope, and put them into her trusty rucksack, which she hid carefully behind a rafter in the shadows of the grassy ceiling. She took off her shirt and stood a little self consciously in her bra, careful not to let Dore see her own shyness. Dore looked at her approvingly as she hung her apron on a branch of one of the hut's primitive support beams.

"You are such a lovely girl, Pam, and still so young. If I were your age and still single, I might let the men know it, in a properly modest way of course. You are a candle that hides its light."

Pam was forty-five years old and didn't consider herself either *lovely* or a *girl*, but smiled at Dore's praise anyway. She had never been a bombshell of any sort, but she was attractive in a "step or two ahead of Plain Jane" sort of way. Her years tromping around the forests and fields down-time had trimmed away any trace of the fat that she felt had made her so unattractive in her late thirties and early forties, the self-pity-cherry-bon-bon-eating years that had followed her divorce. She took a deep breath, sucked in her proudly hourglass waist, and stuck her ample-enough-for-another-look chest out. It seemed things were still holding up well there. She allowed herself a rather pleased grin.

"Maybe I do still got something, huh? Let's hope it's something an Arab pirate type might appreciate." She took a careful step toward Dore. "Now it's your turn, darlin'." Dore made no move and simply nodded to Pam with a *do what you must* look, so Pam gently reached out and began loosening the complex knot-work of braids Dore kept her hair so severely bound up in. To Pam's great surprise, long, lush locks of auburn laced with strands of silver fell down to nearly her waist.

"Talk about holding your light under a bushel! Good golly, what I would give to have hair like yours! You keep it tucked up so tight, I had no idea!" Pam reached out and felt a lock, it was thick and smooth, nothing like the thin, dry feel of her own hopeless mane. Dore blushed a little, and quietly admitted that Gerbald was quite fond of it and that's why she kept it long for him, despite the nuisance of its required care.

Pam nodded approvingly. "I'll bet he likes it. It's gorgeous. *You* are gorgeous, Dore!" Pam shunted aside the bit of jealousy that crept into her mind, and said in what she hoped was a firm yet comforting tone, "Okay, next we got to free up your bosom. Take off the smock." Dore complied, and the drab, gray piece of utilitarian clothing came off.

Like many down-time working women Pam had seen, Dore kept her bosom tightly confined. Accomplishing this was what appeared to be some kind of wrap made of sturdy canvas. At Pam's silent nod, Dore loosened the straps on the dour down-time version of a modesty-defending brassiere. Pam's eyes widened. She knew Dore had plenty in the chest department, but the reality was, well, larger than expected, the envy of any Hollywood starlet. Dore's chest thrust out heroically like that of a mighty warrior queen, nothing at all like the grandmotherly flaccidity she had expected. Dore, bare to the waist with her hair down had ceased to resemble the humble washer-woman Pam had grown accustomed to thinking of her as, and was revealed as a Wagnerian goddess, a lovely and fearless Valkyrie. Dore was solidly built, certainly, even after the island diet the hourglass was perhaps a bit thick, but now that her true buxom, healthy beauty was revealed, the effect was something close to ravishing.

Pam let out a long, almost catcall of a whistle. "I'm going to call you 'Wonder Woman' from now on. You are a hottie!"

Dore blushed even harder. "Gerbald, he tells me I am beautiful, but you know him. His sweet talking is shameless. When I was a young girl in my teens I remember the village boys thought well of me, and I often felt their lustful looks, but that was so long ago."

"Girl, I'm here to tell you, you still got it and then some! Gawd, Dore, you look fantastic, and not just in a 'for a woman your age' kind of way. You could make the village boys get down on their knees and beg right now! Shit, I guess that makes me Mary Ann 'cause you got Ginger nailed."

Dore's face burned the scarlet of a summer sunset. At last, she smiled widely in an open way that Pam had never seen before. A day for firsts indeed. A bright bit of Psychology 101 popped into Pam's head and she put it to *The Plan's* advantage right away.

"Look, Dore, just pretend you are a silly seventeen year old again and these pirate types are the village boys! It's perfectly all right to be a bit naughty in a situation like that. We are just pretending, to save our skins. So just let go and be a little more flirtatious than you would have allowed yourself back then. Well, a *lot* more flirtatious. We need these clowns to want our bodies badly!"

It was Dore's turn to laugh now, in a shy but pleased way. "The village boys! Yes, I was a flirt sometimes, oh the shame. Very well. I can do that, Pam. We will make this work."

"Right. Now, off comes the bottom parts." Dore's face changed rapidly from glowing sunset to kitchen flour again. Pam thought she heard her mumbling a prayer for forgiveness under her breath as she began to unclasp the ties of her exceedingly modest dresses.

A short time later the women emerged bare-chested, wearing simple grass skirts over their under-garments made from materials hurriedly reallocated from the hut's walls, making sure to show quite a bit of leg. Dore's legs were those of an athlete, well-muscled from years on the road and standing at work for long hours, but still shapely. The strings of clam shells they had made to decorate the place while fighting the sheer boredom of their existence were now draped around their necks, and bunches of hapless orchids growing nearby had been firmly woven into their free-flowing hair. Each carried a large basket full of that evening's dinner fruit, and Pam had used some of the berry juice to brighten up their lips.

"We are some glorious and sex-starved hula harlots in need of some male attention, and we always get our way!" Pam announced bravely, and they both nearly lost control to a fit of nervous giggles.

"Now, Dore," Pam said breathing deeply to retain composure, "remember these pirates are dangerous. We don't want them to get too close. Let's try to lead them back up the trail where our guys can get the jump on them and the fight can't be seen from the ship. When the killing starts, we run like hell, okay?"

"Got it." Dore resembled some kind of seductive and dangerous heathen chieftainess, a tigress of lust. If Pam had a mirror she would have been both shocked and proud of her own wanton and wild appearance. She figured she at least somewhat resembled a Caucasian

Hollywood extra made into a faux-Polynesian girl, last seen throwing flower petals in the path of *Fantasy Island's* latest guests. A counterfeit *wahine*, but still easy on the eye. A sudden burst of confidence filled her, *Goddamn it, we are looking fine!*

As they sashayed down the path to the beach as seductively as they could muster, Pam began to feel eyes on her. She tried not to look right or left in order to avoid giving away her men's positions but out of the corner of her sharp and well trained birder's eyes she could make out some of the sailors hidden in the bushes, their mouths open in pure astonishment, tinged with a bit of dawning appreciation. *You goofballs better keep your eyes on the pirates when we come back this way*, she tried to radiate back at them. *These treats are not for you!* All too soon, they left the cover provided by the last line of palms perched along the high tide line, and sauntered casually onto the still uncomfortably hot sand. Pam stifled a grimace and whispered loudly, "Remember, we want them to come ashore. We must be alluring sirens. Let's get their attention now."

Dore called out sweetly in German, "Come, oh wretched and lustful goats from yon ship. Come and feel my ample breasts in your greasy, godless hands!" Pam almost lost it again, but realized they would be better off not revealing their identity as Europeans beyond the paleness of their skin, which she hoped would pass for pleasingly exotic in these latitudes. She stage-whispered to Dore, "Don't speak German or English to them. We want them to think we are savages."

Dore's brow knitted below her wreath of exotic blossoms. "What should I say, then?"

"Just use nonsense talk, like to a baby. Boo-loo ooh-loo gaga waga! But make it sound sexy!"

"Boo-loo ooh-loo! Rhumba, rhumba, rhumba!!" she crowed back with unfettered heathen delight. She whispered to Pam, "A *rhumba* is one of those shameless dances Spanish-speaking papists engage in up-time. I saw it on TV."

"That's perfect, Dore. More like that!" Pam whispered back. "Calypso bistro, bongo wongo marimba hoochi-koochi!" Pam shouted at the top of her lungs while performing her best imitation of a parade float beauty queen's welcoming wave. In the distance she could see the junk's crew beginning to rouse to the racket they were producing.

About halfway down to the water's edge, they set their baskets down on the sand. Pam squinted to see if they had the pirate's attention, and found that, oh yes, they did. The sheet-wrapped goons were beginning to chatter excitedly, and point at them. Pam motioned to Dore to follow her lead and set the baskets down, slowly to make sure there was a nice long view of that which was unfettered and freed to gravity's whims, then began motioning to their abundant offerings with alluring gestures of invitation that would put any game-show co-hostess to shame.

"Ooga, beluga! *You swarthy schmucks!* We got'sa some big froota-loopas for you-ah!" She turned again to Dore who was mimicking her gestures. "And now, we dance!" Pam whispered to her blushing, but gamely seductive, friend.

"You start!" Dore hissed at her.

"Koo-lookoo-kookoo-lookoo-koo!" Pam yodeled at the top of her lungs as she began to shake her belly and her breasts as hard as she could in a move she had seen on a Don Ho TV special when she was a kid. She continued to vibrate, as she slowly turned around to give them a three-sixty degree view of all the available goods. Dore followed her lead, turning in the opposite direction. Her shaking was a speed or two slower, but she added a warbling bird-like cry in her powerful church choir alto. *Go, girl, go!* Pam grinned at her as they came back around again. Next, Pam stopped shaking and began a circular swaying of the hips while her arms lithely made gestures of come hither toward the boat.

To both Pam's relief and growing trepidation at what would come next, she saw their ploy was working. Several of the junk's invader crew were slapping each other on the backs in what was surely an exchange of lascivious dares. Several more worked to untie a small craft lashed to the deck, a longboat that they proceeded to lower into the water. *They've swallowed the hook, line and sinker! Time to reel in!* Pam and Dore continued to shake and gyrate their scandalously half-clad bodies as if trying to stay upright in a fearsome earthquake.

Suddenly, an older captain-type fellow emerged from the upper decks. Upon seeing what was happening, he began shouting at the crew. He had an enormous, white handle-bar mustache, and wore a ridiculous oversized turban from right out of a storybook. The men just pointed at the beach, and looked back at him with shamed but imploring grins. The captain-type narrowed his eyes to have another look at the distraction across the water, so Pam and Dore both waved coyly and blew kisses to him. With a dismissive snort and wave of the hand, he marched back into his cabin. Whatever happened next would be no responsibility of his.

The majority of the men immediately began crowding into the boat, stepping on and over each other as they vied for a spot. Still, a few others remained on the deck, either unimpressed by the beach-side burlesque show, or under strict orders to remain on watch, their faces scowling fiercely. They would have to deal with that fun bunch of fellows later. At least most of the moths were flying to the flame.

"Oh shit, here they come!" Pam hissed out of the side of her mouth to Dore, who had really gotten into the spirit of the thing, and was busy pushing her prodigious breasts up with both hands, in offering to the oncoming boatload of hormones. Pam's eyes widened at this impressive display of wantonness, and not to be outdone, she began a snaky, pelvis-thrusting, dance that included some low front bends complete with jiggling. She couldn't be completely sure, but she thought the pirate types were now rowing faster. *If this wasn't so damned dangerous, I'd be having a pretty good time,* she admitted to herself ruefully. *Thank the Lord, the good Methodist ladies of Grantville aren't seeing any of this!*

When the boat hit the shallows, and the pirates were just starting to clamber out into the gentle surf, Pam and Dore began their backward retreat to the trail. They left the fruit baskets where they were, hoping to slow them down a bit more. Walking backwards as rapidly as they dared, while still beckoning and cooing coquettishly, they reached the line of palms just as their admirers reached the baskets. Pam and Dore both began pantomiming eating the fruits and a fair number of the men paused to fill their hands with the offering, biting into the luscious fruit with sly smiles that anticipated more delights to come, their eyes never leaving the women for very long. *Good, now most of them have their hands full of nice, juicy, slippery fruits instead of on their weapons.* Pam had caught a good look at the wicked scimitars, daggers, and several exotic-looking pistols they wore shoved into their belts, and lost any doubts she might have had that they were facing dangerous pirates, or whatever passed for a seagoing scoundrel in these parts.

Pam winked at Dore, mission almost accomplished, and began to edge back into the trees, still cooing and beckoning to their prey. *Come on, you assholes, follow the pretty ladies!*

There was some discussion amongst the pirates, undoubtedly as to whether to proceed into the trees or not. This didn't last long, as they appeared to feel they were in no danger, if any unfriendly "natives" appeared they seemed confident they would be able to make short work of them. Such overconfidence and lust proved to be just the right combination. The pirates assumed they were being led to where the real party would start, and gamely followed along.

Pam and Dore had not quite reached the spot where the ambush awaited. Unfortunately, some of the pirates had grown impatient, and were catching up to them more quickly than expected, their hands eager to get ahold of offerings intrinsically more alluring than fruit. Pam gave Dore a small push, a signal to move faster. A pirate caught up to Pam just then, grabbing her wrist, hard. Pam felt a note of panic ring through her, but kept smiling. Dore paused, to look back, worry creeping onto her face. Pam gestured with her chin for Dore to move on, but she knew her friend wouldn't leave her behind. A second pirate was closing fast. The plan was in danger of falling apart, and Pam's heart began to race. The one holding onto her used his free hand to grab one of Pam's breasts, causing her to yelp.

That was all the signal Gerbald and the Swedes needed. Pam watched in amazement as a large, sage-green and mustard-colored blur came rocketing out of the brush. Suddenly, the man pawing Pam was sporting a bright red gash where his throat had been, the work of Gerbald's deadly *katzbalger* shortsword. Pam brushed the dying pirate's still clutching hands away from her, they were all that was keeping him upright. He collapsed into a growing pool of his own blood as if all the bones had gone out of him. An identical fate met the next pirate closest behind, who hadn't even had time to begin to think of pulling out his own weapon before the *löjtnant* drew an ornately-decorated longsword across his throat. *Good!* Pam thought, her blood running cold. The decaying, tortured faces of the beheaded Chinese sailors flashed in her mind, and any shreds of guilt at planning the death of these people evaporated.

Pam and Dore began running, Pam pushing Dore ahead of her as much as Dore was pulling Pam into the tall grass, away from the action. From a relatively safe distance, she saw Gerbald down a third pirate with his *katzbalger* as the bosun shoved his cutlass deep into the gut of a fourth. The *löjtnant*, not to be outdone, skewered another through the chest. As planned, no one fired a shot, keeping the inland action a secret from the remaining pirates at anchor. One or two of the pirates managed to get their weapons out, but Gerbald and the Swedes made quick work of them. It was finished as rapidly as it had begun. The sailors dragged the pirates' bodies off into the brush to hide them, then scuffed fresh sand and scattered leaves across the trail to cover the drying pools of blood just in case anyone else came looking. Pam hoped they would, since the same fate awaited them as befell their brother pirates.

Pers, for his keen eyes, and Rask and Torgir, both experienced marines, remained on watch at the ambush site, while the rest of them went back to the camp to regroup. The bosun, in his early fifties, although aged prematurely by years of sea-winds and the relentless sun, was doing his level best not to look at Pam in her "harlot dancer" get-up, and losing that battle. This was possibly the most bare female flesh he had ever seen outside of a dimly lit dockside whorehouse, and the poor fellow was obviously shaken. Pam smiled at him patiently, and quickly got back to business as he did his best to focus his interest on a nearby palm tree.

"Good job, everyone!" Pam praised them, "That worked really well! I have an idea for part two, so tell me what you think." All the men listened intently to Pam's next plan, mostly managing not to stare at the ladies' exposed expanses. Dore stood unashamed beside her, a lioness proudly standing with her brave and clever young companion, head, and other assets, held high. Gerbald grinned like a fox in a henhouse, obviously pleased to see his Christian wife of so many years standing before him in unfettered heathen glory. Dore saw his look and rather than become annoyed as she once would have, gave her husband a serene smile. Pam saw this exchange out of the corner of her eye. *Oh gawd, what have I unleashed? I just hope he doesn't make her dress up like Princess Leia!* When Pam finished outlining her plan, the men, heads safely down, all mumbled their agreement before fleeing the sight of so much female flesh. Pam giggled as she and Dore retired to the main hut to get ready for their next show.

Garrett W. Vance

Chapter Twenty-Three: Boarding Party

The shadows had already grown long. Dusk followed quickly, so they didn't have much time to prepare. The pirates onboard the anchored ship had grown increasingly agitated, but it seemed there was only one landing craft, and it was out of reach on the beach. So far, no one had volunteered to swim ashore to check how their comrades might be enjoying their shore leave. The mustachioed, and ornately turbaned captain was close to having a conniption fit. He stomped around the deck, sometimes shouting at the empty shore in a menacing bellow.

Just after sunset, during the last few minutes of natural light, a procession of the island's inhabitants came down the trail to the beach carrying torches and more baskets of fruit. The two women were joined by a slender male youth dressed in the same grass-and-flower style, whose shyly downcast face was a study in red. The captain shouted himself hoarse at them in his unintelligible language, but all they did was wave, as the youth pushed the pirates' longboat back into the water. The two women climbed into the front, while he sat in the back, paddling the unfamiliar craft clumsily toward the junk, canoe style. The women stayed seated so as not to tip the odd craft over, but put their upper bodies to good effect in a shimmying and swaying dance, all the while crooning sweet nonsense. Slowly, they drew nearer to the larger craft. The youth's piloting was unskilled, but they were making headway. Nearly all of the crew aboard were gathered at the rail to watch the bizarre shore party's approach.

"It's working, it's working," Pam said just loud enough for Dore and Pers to hear. The giddiness that had helped her get through the first round had faded. Fear ran through her, a cold tingling in the balmy night. She had washed the spattered blood from her face, but she still felt unclean somehow. Her smile was forced, and she began to worry that the enemy would see through their act too soon. She jiggled her scantily-covered breasts a bit harder in an effort to distract these frightening, and undoubtedly ruthless men from the terror that was threatening to creep across her painfully smiling face. Whatever mad confidence had taken hold of her earlier had fled. She was literally half-naked, and felt completely exposed.

I can't believe this is really happening, it's some kind of a nightmare, oh God, oh God! As they drew nearer the boat, she took a deep breath and forced the inner voice of her fear to stop its nattering. Now was when it mattered most that she stay cool. This was the part that really counted. She could see Dore reflected in the water, waving the torches in a graceful arc. The more distraction the better, plus the light might blind the pirates somewhat to the darkness beyond. They were only a yard away now, Pam coyly fluttered her eyelashes up at the captain, whose outrageous, curled mustachios dripped with sweat. She instantly regretted doing that as it sent the already upset fellow into a rage, eyes bulging, and face cartoonishly crimson, reminding her of the garrulous Nome King from the Oz books of her childhood.

With a nerve-jarring shriek, the corpulent old pirate captain vaulted over the rail to climb deftly down a rope ladder with a grace that belied his awesome girth. He jumped the last few feet to land in the front of their longboat, his prodigious weight causing the craft's back end to rise dangerously out of the water. Dore accidentally dropped one of her torches into the water while hurrying to take hold. Pam was bounced upward and back, landing painfully on her bottom between her and Dore's bench seats. She received another nasty jolt when the pirate captain began making his way toward them, causing the craft's rear to fall to the surface again with a slapping splash. Suddenly, Pers leaped over her, placing himself between the women and the invader, armed only with his paddle. Pam looked on in horror as the enraged captain knocked the paddle from his hands, and then began pummeling poor Pers with meaty fists. The youth got a few good shots in himself, which only made the horrid creature angrier, laying into Pers with increased vigor. Pers was knocked backwards just as Pam had been and was in a bad position to defend himself. A kick of the pirate captain's boot knocked the wind out of him, and he slumped into the boat's planked bottom.

Pam felt something hard and cool jamming painfully into her shoulder blade. She knew it was the butt of the up-time Smith and Wesson .38 caliber pistol Gerbald had insisted they bring with them for this part of the mission, which Dore had hidden in her fruit basket. She thrust the pistol into Pam's hand.

"Shoot, Pam, shoot! I *know* you know how!" Dore hissed in her ear.

Pam's eyes narrowed. She was filling with a deep and powerful anger. Pers was no more than a boy! *So much like my own Walt!* She had naturally grown very fond of the lad and his sunny disposition. The fat captain had stopped beating the boy now, and was reaching for a nasty-looking curved long-knife at his belt. A cold rage she was sure was founded in maternal instincts went through Pam, a partially physical sensation, electrified emotions buzzed through her blood and brain. *You really do see red!* she thought as tiny red stars began to sparkle in her vision. She gripped the pistol firmly, feeling its weight, clicked the safety off, and pointed it at the approaching foe's chest.

I've shot pistols a hundred times back at Uncle's farm. Hold it steady, get your target in your sights, deep breath, squeeze slowly . . . Pam felt as if she were moving in slow motion, but the pirate captain, angling his knife for a murderous stab, paused when he realized Pam was armed. His cruel eyes widened. There was a flash and loud crack as if lightning had struck.

Pam watched, half in horror, half in glee, as the pirate captain fell, a bullet through his heart. He hit the boat's side heavily at his waist, then tipped over into the water, turban first, with a sizable splash. The heavy pistol had kicked back into her hands hard, jarring her muscles painfully, but she kept it under control as her uncles had taught her, despite her awkward position.

"*Argghhh!*" Pam's wordless, primal wail was lost in a wider cacophony. The bitter gunsmoke stench helped clear her head. With a twist and a heave, Pam began to extricate herself from between the seats, carefully keeping the pistol pointed away from her friends. Dore helped lift her as best she could with her free hand, she was holding up the last torch, its light flickering crazily across the boat as it swayed and bounced with their frantic movements.

Pam saw that the second part of their ruse was in full effect. During the noisy show they had put on, Gerbald and the Swedes had launched the pinnace, carefully circling around to the seaward side of the anchored junk. They had succeeded in boarding, and were now locked in close combat with the Arab pirates.

There was a loud *boom* as Gerbald downed one charging pirate with one barrel of his pistol grip Snakecharmer shotgun while sticking his *katzbalger* shortsword deep into the gut of another. He moved around the deck with the practiced grace of a ballerina, dodging and killing with silent precision. Another *boom* from the next barrel, and two more charging pirates fell, screaming and pawing at their shot-destroyed faces before dying. This is what Gerbald was trained for, how he had made his living from his youth to just a few years ago. War was his first calling, and he was very damn good at it. *I'll have to remember to thank Walt for giving him that crazy shotgun pistol,* Pam mused as she watched him quickly reload it. The Snakecharmer soon fired again, killing one pirate and maiming another, which the *katzbalger* finished in a single, swift stroke.

Not to be outdone, the *löjtnant* parted a burly-looking fellow from his head with a swift slice of his elegant longsword, sending the appendage rolling across the deck like a ghastly, black-bearded bowling ball. The night was filled with the sounds of clanging metal, angry shouts, gunshots, and death.

Dore grabbed Pam's shoulder and pointed, a pirate trying to flee the losing battle was halfway over the rail and poised to drop into their longboat. Pam shot him in the back, his falling body struck their bow with a sickening *thunk* before splashing limply into the water. Pam let out a long, low stream of curses under her breath.

Dore gripped her shoulder harder, bringing her face close behind Pam's ear. "It is good, Pam, you help our men! There, shoot that one!" Dore pointed at a pirate who was closing in behind the bosun, who was currently occupied with another opponent, his cutlass clashing and clanging against a blood-streaked scimitar. Pam stared for a moment at the wet, red blade in the sneaking enemy's hand. *That's the blood of one of ours.* She took aim carefully, supported by Dore's firm grip on her shoulders. Her finger squeezed. Now accustomed to the bang and flash, she didn't flinch afterward. She calmly watched as the pirate trying to get the drop on the bosun dropped limply to the deck, a bullet through his neck. *My shot went a little high, but he's still dead as a door nail.*

The bosun separated himself from his momentarily distracted dueling partner with a mighty shove. The taller, thinner pirate skidded backward on the blood-drenched deck. The bosun glanced a question at Pam, with a barely perceptible nod she drew on the bosun's opponent as he regained his footing, and shot him in the gut. Pam looked away from the messy results, her own gut suddenly sinking, as if meeting a sudden drop on a roller coaster. The deck went abruptly quiet but for the moans of the dead and dying. No pirates were left standing. *Löjtnant* Lundkvist looked down to see Pam still holding her smoking pistol. He saluted her. Pam's hands lost their strength, and she laid the pistol down heavily on the seat in front of her as Dore eased her grip on her shoulders.

"It is all right now, Pam. It is over," Dore told her. "You did well, my friend. It was you who turned the battle's tide. You never missed once!"

Pam thought of each man she had shot and fought throwing up. She had barely eaten a thing all day so it wouldn't have helped much anyway. She looked to the deck where Gerbald had finished hurrying the enemy injured along on their journey to hell with a quick slice to their throats.

"Let us leave none alive," he said to *Löjtnant* Lundkvist and the bosun as calmly as if he were ordering a hamburger at the Freedom Arches. They nodded their solemn agreement. The Swedish marines took the lead in searching the ship, cautiously entering the captain's cabin, then the lower decks, pistols ready. While Dore went to the aid of injured Pers, Gerbald motioned for Pam to join him on the deck. Somehow she managed to climb the rope ladder with nerveless fingers until Gerbald dragged her over the red-lacquered rail. Dore clambered up onto the deck next. Standing unsteadily, Pam saw bodies in the flickering torch light, and not all were dressed in bloodstained white robes. Gerbald looked at Pam proudly.

"Nice shooting, Tex! Four shots, no misses! It was you who ensured our triumph!" he told his ashen-faced friend, who just blinked at him, half in a state of shock. He saw where Pam was looking, and his voice took on a serious tone. "Rask is injured very badly. We have lost Mård. Fritjoff is sure to follow him. He is asking for you, Pam."

Pam felt a knot tighten in her stomach. *Not the nice old fellow who loved that photo of "The Princess" so much!*

"You are sure about Fritjoff? Not making it, I mean?"

Gerbald nodded sadly. "I am sorry, Pam. He fought bravely. Please, follow me. Dore, see what you can do for our wounded."

"Pers has also been hurt, but not too badly. I shall tend to Rask first," Dore replied calmly, being used to aftermaths such as these.

Gerbald led Pam to where Fritjoff lay, his head cradled by an exhausted bosun. Fritjoff's face was pale except for a line of blood trickling into his white beard. Someone had placed a cloth over his wounds, Pam could see that it was dark and soaking wet. Her gorge wanted to rise, but she forced it down.

"Fritjoff, *Frau* Pam is here to see you," the bosun said softly into his ear. The old man's eyes opened, bloodshot and wild, darting about in search of her.

"I'm here, Fritjoff," Pam told him, kneeling next to him and taking his hand. Although they were cold and bloodless, his long, thin fingers grasped hers with surprising strength.

"*Frau* Pam, thank you, thank you. I haven't much time now. I am no longer the fighter I was when I was young, but I take two of these dogs to their graves with me."

"You are very brave, Fritjoff. I am so proud of you. I know the princess will be, too." Pam told him, tears forming in the corner of her gunsmoke-stung eyes.

"The princess. Will you tell her? Will you tell her that I served her to my last?" His sentences were now punctuated with heaving gasps as his punctured lungs fought a losing battle for every breath.

"I will. I will tell her all about you, Fritjoff! How brave you were, and how you loved her and how you kept her photo. I will tell her of our good Fritjoff, loyal friend and fearless soldier!" Her voice caught, and she fell silent, trying not to lose her composure, not yet. Fritjoff tried to say more, but his gasps were coming rapidly now, stopping him from further speech. Pam took the damp cloth from the bosun and began to wipe his face, tears streaming now, mixing with the cool water and drying blood. The touch of her hand seemed to calm him, and he was able to speak again.

"Thank you, *Frau* Pam, thank you. I see the faces of my ancestors now. They have come for me in the ships of the old times. I see their sails, red and gold. Soon I shall join them." His grip on her hand tightened, and his eyes were able to focus on her for a moment. "You were always kind to me. It is you who are the brave one, *Frau* Pam. All we men see it. It was *you* who captured this prize. I am glad to have you as my captain here at my end." Before she could answer, Fritjoff convulsed, a final ragged breath, then silence. His grip loosened, and his hand fell limply to the deck. Pam let out a low wail, still wiping his forehead with the cloth. The bosun gently pushed her hand aside, and closed the old sailor's eyes.

"Fritjoff lived a long life, *Frau* Pam, longer than most who go to sea," the bosun told her, his voice rich with utmost kindness. "He is with his people now in the next world. Don't weep so."

Pam somehow ceased her keening cry and took a deep breath. She wiped her tears with her arm, her hands shaking.

"Come, good lady. Let us now help those who stay with us in this world of trials and troubles." The bosun stood up, his movements those of one bruised and battered in cruel battle, but still filled with strength. He took her trembling hands in his and lifted her to her feet. Pam embraced him fiercely, nearly knocking the wind out of the poor fellow, then released him to peer about the deck with tear-burned eyes. She shook herself, then spoke from an icy, calm place in the maelstrom of grief and disgust heaving about her mind.

"I'll go check on Pers. I think he's all right, just badly bruised."

The bosun saluted her, then turned to place a cloth over the face of their fallen comrade.

Pam returned to the rail to see Pers was beginning to come around in the junk's longboat. The boy was black and blue, and he had a bloody nose, but his eyes focused on Pam, and his pupils weren't dilated.

"How do I look?" he asked cheerfully.

Pam let out a laugh, more of a growl really, and told him, "You look like an elephant stepped on you, but you'll live. Stay put there and pinch your nose shut until I come back and tell you to stop." He did as she ordered while Pam went to join Dore where she ministered to Rask.

"Oh, dear. It is not good. A deep cut to the thigh here, and a gash to the side of the belly. I must find out how deep." No stranger to battlefield medicine, Dore went about her examination with the same deft swiftness she would preparing a chicken for the boil, ignoring the man's gasps and moans of pain. Pam was suitably impressed that Dore had developed such sophisticated first aid skills during her years as a camp follower. She knelt down to assist however she could. Under Dore's direction they made quick progress and stopped the bleeding.

Pam cursed under her breath, and wished for up-time antibiotics. Back at camp she had a precious plastic bottle of Bactine, an over-the-counter antibacterial and mild local anesthetic she kept in her birding pack's tiny medkit for cuts and scrapes on the trail. She had been hoarding it, using it only sparingly, but she knew she would give it all if needed to help this man. With Rask stabilized and resting as comfortably as they could make him, they stood up wearily.

"I have some antibacterial medicine in my hut," Pam told Dore.

"Good, we will use it. Here come the men. Let us thank the Lord we have prevailed and pray that He welcome the souls of our brave men in His heavenly kingdom." Dore lowered her head and clasped her hands in silent prayer, a common pose for the upright German lady made utterly unearthly by her half-naked condition. This night Dore was a grass skirted, savage warrior queen with flowers in her hair, blood spattered and brooding as she sent the power of her unwavering faith to aid the souls of their fallen on their journey to Paradise.

Chapter Twenty-Four: The Prize

Captured Oriental Junk, South Coast of Mauritius

Pam watched while the sailors cleaned the blood from the decks of their prize. The flickering light of the torches made their shadows leap and dance, lending the scene an eerie, otherworldly quality. An hour had passed since their success in capturing the junk, its original, presumably Chinese merchants having perished at the hands of an organized gang of pirates she thought must certainly be Arabic in origin. She based that guess on their clothing and behavior, but most of the denizens of the seventeenth-century Indian Ocean were still a mystery to her. She had a hunch that she would be learning a lot more about this part of the world in the days to come, and, based on what she had experienced so far, doubted it would be pleasant.

Just twenty minutes ago she had watched her men cut down the severed heads of the junk's former owners from where they had been hung as trophies, a gruesome display courtesy of the now dispatched pirates of the Indian Ocean. It was a grisly task. Pam felt pity that they had died in such a horrible way. She had asked that they be wrapped in a sack and given a Christian burial at sea. No one had any idea what their religion in life might have been, so Lutheran would have to do. Having borne witness to that brief but dignified ritual, she now waited to be returned to their beach refuge.

The uncomfortable feeling that none of this was real that sometimes swept over her came again. She felt as if she had wandered into some live-action period drama, a terrible tale of fighting seamen and ruthless brigands of days gone by. Any minute now, the lights would come up, and the actors would shed their costumes. She closed her eyes hard for a moment, wishing with all her might that she would wake up back in the future age she had been born to. But when she opened her eyes, she was still there on the blood-splattered deck. *Damn!* Forcing herself to stay calm and make the panic subside, she thought *This is not "days gone by." This is now days! These are new days, these are my days and I must live them, like it or not!* Gritting her teeth, she felt her head begin to clear. The scene came back into focus. Although lacking somewhat in sophistication, the current age certainly brimmed with action.

A watch of marines under the command of *Löjtnant* Lundkvist was assembling on deck. All the sailors could fight, and fight well as she had seen, but these men specialized in it. They would stay aboard to guard their new ship, a bizarre, and brightly-painted three-masted vessel that dwarfed lost *Redbird* in size and complexity, while the rest of the tired crew and Pam's personal staff returned to the beach camp. There was a lot of clean up left to do, but once the gory decks had been swabbed, the rest could wait for morning. The slain pirates were to be thrown overboard with the outgoing tide just as they were, with no wrapping or ceremony.

"Those poor Chinamen were one thing, but these lot don't deserve any such respect." the bosun said, his voice surprisingly cold. "Let the crabs have them, the murdering sons of dogs."

Pam nodded, trying not to look at the sheet-wrapped body of their friend Fritjoff lying nearby. Fritjoff and the bosun had been close, sailing together for many long years. The injured look on the normally jolly bosun's face was enough to make Pam cry. She briefly considered weeping again, but the tears wouldn't come. She was all cried out for this night. Maybe in the morning. Meanwhile, dark thoughts like *I've killed men with my own hands!* and *More good men have died for my cause this night!* tried to push themselves into her consciousness, but she was too tired, so she ignored them until their shrill accusations fell away. She knew they would return, demanding to be heard in the early hours of the morning when she would stare at the shadow-filled ceiling of her hut and remember. But *not* just now.

Looking around the deck, she saw that not all the men's faces were grim. Some were beginning to admire their prize, and clap each other on their backs in celebration of a hard-fought victory. Pam made herself smile for them. She knew that for some reason they looked to her, so she allowed herself to share some of their pleasure. They had won, they had a ship, it was foreign and weird, but definitely seaworthy. Now they were *free* and able to take action! Pam turned her gaze away from the orange glow of the torch-lit deck to peer at the dark mass of the coastline. Her colonists were out there, somewhere, and they were certainly in trouble.

"We'll come for you," she spoke into the night in a voice beneath a whisper. "We're ready now, hold on!"

A few minutes later, Pam sat in the rear of the pinnace as the exhausted sailors rowed through the tranquility of a wind-less night. She was heading back to the simple comforts of her bamboo hut with her most trusted friends, Gerbald and Dore, as well as young Pers, injured Rask, and the earthly remains of poor Mård and Fritjoff. Mård had been a shy fellow, the hapless sailor who had ruined dinner their first night out. Pam hadn't really gotten to know him very well, but she recalled that he had always spoken gently to Pers, even when the lad was being a teen-aged idiot, and so she thought highly of the man for that. She would miss his face, and dear old Fritjoff's. Their places would be empty at breakfast.

These fallen heroes would be given a proper burial on the grassy mound beside the first mate in the morning.

Dore turned to see Pam looking at the shrouded corpses with an expression that held all the world's cares. She reached for Pam's hand and squeezed it. Pam returned the squeeze gratefully, and the two of them looked back at their prize. The vivid colors of the junk's lacquered woodwork and fanciful carvings under the flickering torchlight made her seem like something come sailing out of a dream, a phantasmagorical craft from beyond the edge of the world.

"What a day," Pam said, while Dore solemnly nodded in agreement.

Chapter Twenty-Five: Breakfast of Champions

Castaway Cove, South Coast of Mauritius

Pam slept like a stone. The marvelous aroma of coffee brewing wafted through her little window, and summoned her from slumber just half an hour after dawn, bringing her forth to blink at an already too-bright sky filled with enormous cotton clouds. She managed to stagger down to the cook-fire to join the men waiting for breakfast. The Swedish crew always treated her with deference, but this morning they all leaped to their feet, except Rask who was still nursing his injuries. He looked much better as he smiled widely at her. They made much fuss about finding her the most comfortable seat next to the fire. She leaned over to Gerbald and quietly asked him in German, "What's up with these guys? Since when do I get the star treatment?"

Gerbald smiled his best "You have asked the Fount of Wisdom" smile at her. "Pam, do you mean to tell me you really don't know? Think about what you did yesterday! It was *you* who lead them to victory! You even killed four of the enemy yourself. More of those bastards died at your hand than by the hand of any one of us! You are their hero!"

Pam blinked at this revelation, and then smiled, though her brow remained furrowed. "Well, Howdy Doody," she muttered in English. "Now I'm a hero. I just wish I felt like one." Dore handed Pam her coffee, but she just stared into its steaming darkness for a while, savoring the aroma along with a growing feeling of pride.

Dore seemed completely unfazed by the wild events of the day before, and was going about her tasks with her usual efficiency. As Pam began to sip the wonderful native coffee from her coconut-shell mug, she was pleased to see that her friend had concocted some kind of culinary miracle from the final remnants of *Redbird*'s food stores, ingredients Dore had been jealously guarding, doling them out slowly over the months of their isolation.

"No point in saving all this now! Much longer and it would have all gone bad anyway," she said brightly, stirring a rich broth of salt pork, beans, dried onions, and butter, thickened with the last of the flour, and seasoned with a variety of herbs and spices. Everyone was beginning to crowd around the cook-pot, staring at it with hungry eyes.

"Stay back now, you fellows. There's enough for everyone, and we need to save some for the men on the ship!" Dore chided them, but in a tone set at a less stern pitch than usual.

Pam, beginning to achieve caffeinated consciousness, now noticed that Dore hadn't put her beautiful auburn and-silver streaked hair up in its usual severe bun this morning. Instead, she wore it in a loose braid over her shoulder, tied with a string to keep strays out of her eyes. Pam smiled to see this development. Dore was definitely wound a bit less tight today. Evidently a little "harlot dancing" had been just the thing for her ever-serious friend.

After filling themselves with the delicious and hearty soup, they all stood up, stretched, and made ready for the solemn duty they had to perform this morning. Singing a Christian hymn that was ancient even in the seventeenth century, many of the words of which Pam couldn't catch, the Swedes carried their dead down the beach with all the respect one might have afforded the kings of old.

The dodos followed along behind the procession, forming a peculiar kind of honor guard, cooing and chuckling softly, but keeping a polite distance instead of engaging in their usual snack begging. Pam thought they must be able to sense the somber mood, and once again was surprised at their intelligence. The dodos really were not dummies. They had just evolved in a place where there was no need to fear bands of roving carnivorous apes. The sight of what to Pam was almost a mythical creature, alive and thriving right before her wondering eyes, made her heart race yet again, and brought a modicum of good cheer to her heavy heart. *All this fuss, all this trouble is really for you, funny birds!* she thought at the exquisitely odd creatures.

At their lonely little seaside cemetery, Pam saw that two graves had been dug already. Getting up early for hard work was nothing new to sailors, and Pam respected them all the more for it.

There were four grave markers now, all made of sturdy boards salvaged from *Redbird*, their epitaphs neatly painted by Pam with her waterproof acrylics, and further protected by a coating of amber-tinted tree pitch. Each bore the name and rank of their fallen and, if known, their birth date and birthplace, followed by their country, *Sverige,* the date and, lastly, the name of their ill-fated ship.

The fourth marker had gone up this morning along with Fritjoff's and Mård's but there was no grave at its feet. It was a memorial to their captain, Pam had been putting off looking at it now that it was in the ground, and finally decided she would just have to face it. The marker read: *Torbjörn, Captain of the Redbird.* After the official names and dates, Pam had added, "*He stayed behind to save us all. Lost at sea, we pray this brave man yet lives.*" She had done the work alone in her hut, not wanting the others to see her tears as she painted this memorial to their lost friend, a man who, if he was still with them, maybe, just maybe, would have become something more to her. Now, standing among her band of castaways, all gathered for a funeral yet again, she sent a brief thought across the rolling waves. *Torbjörn, if you are out there somewhere please know we haven't forgotten you! I haven't forgotten you! Please be alive!*

The burial ceremony was brief but emotional. The bosun spoke the Lord's Prayer and the twenty-third Psalm in Swedish, his voice cracking, the loss of his long-time friends and shipmates having hurt him deeply. Pers stood beside him, lending his quiet support. The bosun then asked Pam to recite Tennyson's *Crossing the Bar* as she had for First Mate Janvik. She managed to get through it in a calm, clear voice despite the great sense of loss within her. Pam had brought along the photo of Kristina that Fritjoff had prized so much. She considered burying it with him but decided the fine old gentleman would have been more pleased to have it hanging proudly in a place of honor on their new ship. Holding it to her breast she spoke quietly to her fallen friend as he was gently lowered into the sandy grave.

"I won't ever forget you, Fritjoff. I will do as I promised and tell the princess of your bravery in battle, and your dedication to her cause. I will tell her of the great love you felt for her, and how you served her so well, just as soon as I see her again." An unwelcome thought intruded. *If. If you see her again.* Pam looked out at the captured Oriental junk floating in their lonely bay, its vivid colors glowing ethereally in the morning light. *Our chances have improved by a lot.* She left a small bouquet of wildflowers beneath each of the four markers, whispering "thank you" to each. Then she walked back down the beach, trying hard not to think too much on all they had lost, and concentrating instead on what they might now hope to gain.

Gerbald caught up to her, and gave her the look that said "*Is this a good time?*" He knew Pam's emotions ran deep, and that sometimes she just needed to be alone. She saw his cautious approach, smiled and took his arm, something she rarely did. He patted her hand in an awkward, big brotherly way, glad that she wasn't taking things too hard. They walked together in silence for a few minutes then Gerbald said, "Pam, this morning the bosun told me it will take a day or two to make this *junk* ready to sail. They 'need to figure out if this fancy-painted contraption can be sailed by Christian men.' I believe those were his words." They both laughed. Pam had watched the bosun studying the junk from the shore during breakfast, and couldn't tell from his expression if it was love or loathing he was feeling for the strange new ship he would be responsible for.

"He's a smart guy. They all are. They'll figure it out."

"Indeed, I have the highest confidence. In any event, it seems we have a little more time to spend here, and I thought of something you might like to do."

Pam's eyebrow's arched up at him, her gray eyes sparking with curiosity. "Ooh, what, do tell! Do you have a box of chocolate cherry bonbons and a bottle of *kirschwasser* hidden away for me?"

"Nothing so immediately gratifying." He laughed. "We are getting low on coffee, and who knows when we might come across it again? I thought we might hike back up the mountain and resupply ourselves. We can also bring back some live specimens to grow in pots on the ship until we find a more permanent home for them. That is, if you feel up to it." Gerbald's face was perfectly straight, but she detected the tiny wrinkle around the corner of his mouth that revealed he was terribly pleased with his idea.

"I take back everything I said about you, Gerbald. You are a real stand-up guy, a real pal," Pam kidded him, slapping him on his sturdy bicep with her free hand. They both grinned, Gerbald knowing the teasing praise was really sincere.

Pam noticed that the dodos had fallen in around them, cooing contentedly, spread out around their path in search of sand fleas and bits of seaweed.

"I have an idea that will go well with yours," she said, nodding at their avian companions "Let's take *them* with us. I don't want to leave them hanging around the beach looking like dinner to the next ship that comes this way."

"I'll get some nuts and dried fruit from Dore for the bait. I'm sure she will be happy to provide. She won't be missing what she has come to refer to as 'those flightless pests!' It is only her deep respect for your wishes that has kept them out of her stew pot." Gerbald grinned.

Chapter Twenty-Six: Ups and Downs

A while later, as Pam gathered supplies for their trip, she found a rather depressed-looking Pers carrying odds and ends from the sailor's longhouse down to the beach for transfer to the ship. He was still bruised from his encounter with the pirate captain, but had been deemed fit enough for light duty. Pam stopped him as he hurried by without so much as a greeting for her.

"Hey, Pers, are you all right?" Pam asked him, first checking to make sure they were out of earshot of his boss, the bosun.

"Oh, yes, Pam, I'm fine." The boy managed to give her a small smile, but still didn't look fine. Pam figured he was just tired and feeling bad about losing two more comrades, as they all were. Pers was a real good kid, and had been very brave, not to mention a good sport, dressing up for their friendly natives act, and Pam wanted to do something to cheer him up.

"Well, maybe so, but you look like you could use some fun anyway. Gerbald and I are going to hike up to the mountain to get more coffee today. Would you like to join us? We could use your help carrying the beans back. That is, if you're up to it. You took a pretty good beating last night!"

Immediately Pers face lit up. "Oh yes, I feel a lot better this morning! I'd like to come with you very much!"

"Great! It will be a good chance for you to work on your English, and your German, too. We haven't had much time for your lessons lately. Let's go talk to the bosun."

Pam led Pers straight to the very busy gentlemen who was just about to board the pinnace to be rowed out to their gaudy new vessel.

"*Herr* Bosun, I wonder if you can spare me Pers for the day. Gerbald and I are going for a resupply of coffee, and could use some help carrying it back."

The bosun smiled, having become an aficionado of the bitter drink himself. "We are likely going to be all day figuring out how that floating fancy is sailed. I think we can spare the lad." He turned to Pers, who was looking brighter by the minute, and told him, "Now, you mind *Frau* Pam, young fellow, and stay out of trouble!"

"Yes, sir!" Pers looked like his usual happy-go-lucky self again.

"Thanks! We'll be back by sundown," Pam told the bosun. He gave her a salute, and stepped into the pinnace which immediately pulled out into the gentle surf. Pam was sure it was the first time the bosun had ever used that particular gesture with her, and it made her feel a bit uncomfortable.

A few minutes later she, Gerbald, and a much cheered-up Pers, were heading down the beach to collect the flock of dodos that had decided to become their permanent neighbors. The problem was that their current humans were leaving, and future visitors were not likely to be so gentle.

"I just can't leave them here on the beach," Pam said as they handed out treats to the now nearly tame animals. "The next people who land here might put them on the menu. We have to lead them back up into the forests where we found them, and then throw them off our trail."

"No problem," Gerbald said confidently.

The dodos, having determined that these three humans were today's most promising food source, followed them as they left the shore for the interior, encouraged along the way by frequent treats.

"I have heard dodos are supposed to be quite foolish," Pers mused. "But they don't really seem so to me. They always seem to know who has food, and who is likely to give them some!" He chuckled as a dodo gingerly took the nut he offered with its massive beak, yellow eyes bright with what Pam took for pleasure.

"We have made them into terrible beggars," Gerbald added. "I wonder if it was situations such as this that helped lead to their extinction back in that other world you came from, Pam. The dodos getting used to people, and coming around for handouts, until one day they find themselves in the stew pot."

"Well, based on what we have observed, it all fits. It was very selfish of me to give them food just so they would sit still for a portrait. No true wildlife scientist ever baits their subjects. I feel awful that here I am trying to save them, and ended up putting this flock in more danger instead." Pam's face drew down in a deep frown.

"Now, now Pam, you mustn't think that way!" Gerbald told her, knowing that it would be best for them all if he could improve her mood quickly. "No one else on the planet cares about these creatures as much as you do, and ultimately it will be you who prevent their loss in this world. I am confident in your abilities."

"As am I!" Pers chimed in "You will save the dodos Pam, it is your destiny!" Pers' exuberant sureness in her made Pam laugh, the frowns forgotten for now.

"Well, it feels like we're making progress again. Maybe we can still give the dodos their second chance."

"Come along, you second chance birds!" Pers called happily, starting to walk up the trail with the dodos in tow, waving a plaintain in his hand like a parade baton. Several of the larger dodos crowded around in front of him, stretching their necks up after the banana and blocking his way up the path. Pers eventually had to push past them, and scowled at the insistent panhandlers. "Argh, you stupid creatures! I take back the nice things I said about you! You are too greedy!" Pam and Gerbald enjoyed a silent smirk at the youth's expense, they had both had the same thing happen to them after all.

Soon enough they were sorted out and on their way again. After conferring with experienced woodsman, Gerbald, they decided to lead the dodos to a similar, but different part of the forest than they had found them in. Hopefully, the dodos would be disoriented by the purposefully convoluted journey. Better yet, if the same kind of foraging were available in the new territory, the ever-hungry birds would be distracted enough to make finding the beach again not worth the bother. Reaching the top of the first rise, a couple of miles from camp, they looked back to see the junk sailing around in a tight circle out in the bay, the small forms of the sailors running about her decks like angry ants beneath the red sails.

"Shhhh, listen!" Pam told her companions as she leaned on her walking stick and pointed toward the obviously misbehaving ship. The wind was blowing inland, and even at that distance it carried a faint stream of curses from the bosun. She put a hand over her mouth to stop from laughing.

"Sounds like they are having a wonderful time," Gerbald whispered, unable to keep from chuckling at the foul language. "The bosun could make a career in the opera. His voice certainly carries well."

Pers gazed at the humorous scene with a wistful expression on his face even though he chuckled along with Gerbald. Pam saw this, and knew something was still eating the kid. She vowed to find out what before the day was done.

∞ ∞ ∞

The temperature grew uncomfortably hot as noon approached. The near-daily rains seemed to have spilled themselves dry for a spell, but Pam suspected they would be back. Today it felt like high West Virginia summer here in the Tropic of Capricorn, and they were grateful when they finally entered the moist depths of the forest. The shade of the great trees was a cooling balm. The dodos became excited, scuttling through the underbrush and squawking in what sounded like happy tones to Pam. She sighed despite the pleasure at escaping the too-bright sun, remembering that back in her original century Mauritius had lost nearly all of its original vegetation through rampant logging and uncontrolled agriculture. *Not this time* she vowed. *The colonists agreed to follow the modern sustainability practices I researched. We can't let that happen again!* Then another darker possibility entered her mind. *It will only work if my colonists are still alive.* She pushed the thought away. She knew better than to start stacking up her cares too high; it just made her feel overwhelmed. *One step at a time* she reminded herself, and breathed deeply to stay calm.

To further distract herself from her endless list of cares, Pam set about identifying what trees she could. While Grantville had by no means contained a plethora of information on such a remote place, Pam had found out quite a bit about the Mascarenes in her studies, surprisingly more than she had thought she would. She spoke aloud as she led them across the forest floor, sharing the knowledge with her companions.

"Let's see, what tree have we here! I think this is *Foetidia mauritiana*. It's named for the strong smell of its oil. Straight trunk, gray bark, a bit of red in the leaves. I'm pretty sure that's it. This fellow over here must be *Diospyros tessellaria*, one of the ebony trees. It's nearly twenty meters high, black bark, long glossy leaves. If we are careful, and harvest its wood wisely, we can make a lot of money for the colony. It's perfect for piano keys, and from what I've seen there's going to be a booming business in those things back in the USE."

"It's beautiful," Pers commented, gently running his fingers across the bark. "I've always hated cutting down trees, but I know we must sometimes."

Pam favored the youth with a beatific smile. "A necessary evil. If things go our way, we will protect a great many more trees, such as these here, and those that we do harvest we will replace with new. That way we can have wood for generations to come instead of just lopping them all down and leaving nothing for later, as so many fools have done. That's what happened in my other history, here and a lot of other places, before people wised up to the concept of sustainability. Even once we knew better, far too many people continued clear cutting, only interested in what they could get for themselves, not about the future. It was awful. We made our world ugly and sick."

Gerbald nodded his solemn agreement. "There are many hunters in the Germanies such as myself who would see it done in your way. But every year the forests shrink. Unfortunately, greed usually wins, and the trees come down. There will be no animals left to hunt if it continues."

"Well," Pam said with a sigh, "and I do hate to say this, it's probably already too late to save much of what's left of Germany's old growth forests. In an ideal world, the arrival of Grantville might have slowed things like uncontrolled logging down. But from what I see, most of us Americans are dancing around the fires of industry as if they were the Golden Calf. The people concerned with the ecological impact of our industrial revolution come early I can count on one hand, starting with me."

"Well, that's a start," Gerbald said. "If you add me, you will have six. As a hunter, I'd like to see the Thüringerwald preserved. Surely we can do better."

"And I seven!" Pers chimed in. "I don't believe that when God gave man dominion over the Earth He intended for us to destroy all in our path, yet I have seen such in every port. It is shameful."

Pam's eyebrows rose high on her forehead at such an erudite statement from their young Gilligan. Pers, though still in many ways a carefree youth, was paying attention to the world around him. Her fondness for the boy deepened, and she allowed herself a bit of pride in knowing that she had played a significant role in his education. She gave them both a big smile as she sat down on a large round rock to take a breather.

"Well, looks like I've made two converts to the Pam Miller Tree Hugging and Marching Society. A good start indeed." After taking a quick look around to make sure the dodos weren't close by, she reached into her pocket to pull out the shaved coconut, dried fruit and nut gorp trail mix she had brought along, carefully unwrapping its leaf container so as not to spill it.

"Here, help yourselves!" she invited her companions, lifting her open hand up in offering. Pers and Gerbald both took a step forward but then stopped, eyes wide. Even though neither of them were anywhere near her palm she felt a pressure there and heard what could only be a chewing sound. Shifting her eyes to her hand she was stunned to see a very strange face; a wide beak of a nose shaped like a rounded ship's prow with two holes for nostrils beneath which a wide, lip-less mouth was chewing gorp. Dark, liquid eyes regarded her calmly from behind droopy lids set in thick, scaly gray skin. This startling visage was at the end of a very long neck that snaked down into a horn-like saddle heading a large, smooth, green-gray plated shell. A shell she happened to be sitting on!

To her credit, Pam didn't panic, successfully conquering her first instinct to jump up with a startled shout. If she had been in any real danger, Gerbald would have taken care of it by now anyway with his warrior's reflexes, long before she could react. The creature was obviously harmless.

"What is it?" Pers asked in a hushed tone.

"It must be a dinosaur!" Gerbald answered, laughing with delight.

Pam felt the large "rock" beneath her shift slightly as the long-necked creature took another gentle mouthful of trail mix.

"Gentlemen," she announced with some bravado, "meet the giant Mascarene tortoise. I remember reading about them and wondering why they weren't as well known as the Galapagos version. The answer was, of course, that they had become extinct along with the dodo, but the dodo got the starring role in the tragedy."

"The dodo is a most engaging creature," Gerbald said. "But this fellow has personality as well. I am a hunter by nature, but I confess I wouldn't be able to kill such a soulful-eyed beast unless I was in utmost need of sustenance."

"Yeah, he's pretty cute, huh?" Pam carefully slid off her living seat to kneel beside the placid creature, offering it more gorp, which it took daintily from her palm with a wide, bluish-hued tongue. "Unfortunately, a lot of hungry people who aren't as kind as you will end up here in the years to come, unless we get in control of things first." Pam gently stroked the tortoise's shell. "This must be the saddle-backed version. They were . . . or, I'm pleased to say . . . *are,* inhabitants of the forests, adapted to stretch their necks up in search of leaves and fruit. There's another closely-related type with a shorter neck and rounder shell that live in the grasslands." Pam gave the tortoise the last of her gorp as she rubbed it gently on its scaly skull, which it seemed to like. Its heavy-lidded eyes half closed in delight.

After a long minute of deep thought, Pam stood up and looked at her friends. Her face was pale in the arboreal shadows and filled with cares.

"Ya know, guys, sometimes it just seems like too much. This island is so complex, we are barely scratching the surface of understanding how these ecologies work, and now we are introducing human settlers even earlier than they came here in my other history. I hope I've made the right decisions. I hope I can make all this work. It's really a lot on my plate. Sometimes I just feel overwhelmed." Her shoulders were slumped, and she looked at the tortoise with a helpless expression.

"Pam, you must not forget that we are with you in this. You do not face these burdens alone," Gerbald told her. "Can you not see that myself and Dore, this fine lad Pers, the bosun, and all the men of the *Redbird* support you wholeheartedly? You carry too much on your shoulders. We lend you our strength. Please, take it."

Pam took a deep breath before speaking in a low, but controlled tone. "I know you do. I'm stupid for forgetting that. It's just that sometimes I get scared by my new life here. If you had seen me back up-time in Grantville you wouldn't have recognized me. I was a failure as a wife, as a mother . . . it seemed like no matter how hard I tried nothing worked. The only thing I ever got right was science, so I got some education and went to work, and that helped, but now I'm not a lab tech. I'm the lead scientist. I'm the one who has to make the big decisions, and it's freaking me out! I feel like I hold the lives of all these living creatures, the lives of all these people who came here with me, in my hands. And so far, I've sucked at it." She had started calmly, but by the time she finished her voice was freighted with emotion.

Pers had a good grasp of up-time American English vernacular, thanks as much to Gerbald's wise-cracks as Pam's lessons, and knew what "sucked" meant.

"Pam, you do not *suck*. I can assure you none of we Swedes think that. We *admire* you. We think of you as the brave lady, our wise woman, a warrior! You must not think of yourself in such a bad way, please. Listen to *Herr* Gerbald! We will all help you succeed!" There was no mistaking the deep concern and sincerity in Pers' young voice.

Pam visibly pulled herself together, rubbing her flushed face and clearing flyaway locks from her brow. She nodded, favored them each with a tiny, but sweet smile, gave the giant tortoise a final pat on the head, then turned and started walking. Pers and Gerbald watched her go, giving her the time and space she had silently asked them for.

After a minute Gerbald clapped a still worried Pers companionably on the back. "Well done, my boy."

Pers stood tall, feeling as if he had just been knighted.

Chapter Twenty-Seven: Farewells and Beginnings

Pam's mood improved as they left the gloom of the forest behind to begin the ascent into higher country. The sun was still bright, but there was a cool breeze dancing across the rocks and shrubs that made the afternoon heat bearable. Gerbald and Pers picked their own paths nearby. They traveled in a silence that she knew would be up to her to break, but not just yet. She paused, looking back to see that the dodos had stopped at the edge of the forest. Apparently the open hillsides were not to their liking, or maybe the long walk had tuckered out their stocky legs.

This was good-bye to the flock that Pam had gotten to know so well. They would return by a different path so the birds wouldn't follow them back to the perils of the beach. She took a long, last look, a kind of mental photograph she was sure she would never forget. In her heart she had a comforting feeling that it wouldn't really be the last time she would see these birds. Satisfied, Pam gave the dodos a smile and a farewell wave, then turned away to continue her climb up the gentle slopes of what they had dubbed Coffee Mountain. A mile or so later, she looked back once more and the dodos were gone, returned to their former life hunting for nuts and grubs amongst the great trees of this innocent island paradise. Pam envied them.

Upon reaching the top, Pam opened the picnic lunch she and Dore had concocted, which included a small flask of *schnapps* to celebrate with.

"Come and get it, fellas!" she called as she lay the offerings out on a broad, flat boulder conveniently placed near the summit. They would enjoy their meal with a fabulous view. Somehow, Dore had managed to bake a simple bread in her stone oven. They filled each loaf with crab meat, thinly sliced Barbel palm hearts, bamboo shoots, and a generous helping of spices mixed in melted butter from Dore's larder. The results were delicious, and Pers liked his so much that Pam gave him half of hers. The portions were more generous than she could handle anyway.

Around them the lush, green mountains of the island's interior marched away into mists in the north. To the south they could see the sapphire sparkle of the sea. They passed the flask around while enjoying the spectacular views, and then lay down in the soft grass to take a short nap before gathering their coffee beans. After an hour passed, Gerbald estimated it was around three in the afternoon. It would take them at least an hour to gather their beans as well as some young trees, then they would begin the long walk home, reaching camp at dusk. Time to get back to work.

First, Pam gave Pers a lesson in coffee-bean picking. The trees bore a variety of ripe and unripe fruits, making it a bit tricky, but the youth was a quick study, and was soon filling his sacks with the purple-yellow coffee beans faster than Pam and Gerbald could. Seeing his rapid progress, they turned their attention to bringing some young trees back alive. Gerbald had brought along a short spade from the *Redbird*'s toolchest, which made the work go fairly fast. They placed the roots in moist canvas sacks surrounded by their native soil, then wrapped the leaves in sailcloth and tied them together in a bundle that would be easy to carry down the narrow forest trails.

With all their bags and pockets once again bulging with beans, they began the long walk home.

"Ugh. This stuff is heavier than I remember it." Pam groaned. Her shoulders already ached from the unaccustomed weight in her rucksack.

"Well, you were about out of your mind with joy last time," Gerbald reminded her. "That must have made the burden feel lighter."

"Now I think I'm just out of my mind," Pam muttered darkly.

"Yes, I recall you pranced down the mountain like an alpine goat in spring." Gerbald chuckled, stifling a groan of his own at his even heavier share of the burden. "I'm sure you will find it all worthwhile again months from now when you still have coffee to drink," he added, trying to sound encouraging.

"Here, *Frau* Pam, allow me to take some of this." Pers came beside her, reaching for the extra sacks she carried draped over her shoulders.

"Naaw, come on, I loaded you up like a pack mule, Pers. You're already carrying a lot more than your share, even taking the age difference into account. I know how strong you are, but I don't want you to get injured."

Pers grinned and took the sacks from her anyway, ignoring her protests.

"Nonsense! This is nothing compared to the tortures the bosun has put me through. Believe me, as far as I am concerned, this is still a 'light duty'!"

Pam gave him a grateful smile. "Well, at least it's all downhill from here." she said as brightly as she could manage. Pers stepped into the lead, walking with a spring in his stride that belied the many pounds of coffee he carried.

Gerbald and Pam looked at each other, silently admitting that they were both already tired, and knowing they had a long way to go yet.

"Youth. If only there was a way to steal it from the young," Gerbald said as they watched Pers scamper down the trail. With a tandem sigh they followed, placing one well-worn boot in front of the other.

Just before sunset they were back on the familiar trails near the beach camp with less than half a mile to go. They paused again at the rise they had observed the ship from that morning to watch the sun go down. The junk now lay at anchor on the high tide, once again resembling a fanciful toy more than a real ship, its bright colors darkened to deeper, eldritch hues in the evening glow. Lanterns were lit one by one. Pam thought she could hear the quiet murmur of the men on deck in the evening hush. As twilight surrounded them, Gerbald started walking again, and Pam began to follow. After a minute she realized that Pers was still standing on the rise, his head hanging low, and his face long in the dim purple light.

Pam tapped Gerbald on the back, speaking to him in a low whisper. "Hey, something's wrong with the kid. I knew something was bugging him this morning, he put on a brave face all day, but now . . . I'm going to stay and talk with him. Do you want to join me?"

"Hmmm. I know he looks up to me, which is very flattering, but I also know sometimes a young man needs the comfort of a woman instead of a man. Lord knows when last he saw his mother, or if he ever has. Go see what's troubling him, Pam. It would be good for him." He carefully didn't add *and for you,* but he certainly thought it as he started walking again. The last mile was easy even in the dark, but he would wait in the brush below the rise until they passed by, then follow them back, just in case. *The bodyguard's job is never done.* He smiled with satisfaction despite his earnest wish to be back to camp and put to bed.

Pam walked back up the rise and over to Pers. He saw her, and started to walk again, but she motioned for him to stop. He was trying to look cheerful for her, but she could see plainly enough in the remaining light that he was troubled.

"All right, you can't kid a kidder, pal, so tell me what's wrong." Pam gave him her best sympathetic smile.

Pers smiled back, but his brow was still downcast.

"Well, it's nothing really . . ." He paused, tongue-tied.

Pam waited, continuing to smile encouragingly. Seeing that there was no escape, the young man continued.

"Well, I shall have to tell you a little about me. My parents were poor farmers on the coast near Norway and, already having several sons, they sent me off to sea when I was but nine."

"Just nine! Jesus!" Pam was appalled, but had heard far worse since her arrival in the 1630s.

"Please don't think badly of them. They could barely feed us all. Besides, I was glad to go. I wanted to leave that stupid village and see the world! The work turned out to be harder than I thought, but the men usually treated me kindly. It's just that life on a ship, well, the faces change, and once you get to know someone they die, like poor old Fritjoff, or move on to another ship . . ." He stalled for a moment, but Pam nodded her understanding, signaling for him to go on.

"My dreams have changed. I've seen a lot of the world. You may be surprised how much. I want a home now, to stop traveling, to get to know a place. And the truth is, even though we got stuck here against our will, this is the first time since I was that boy of nine that I've lived in a *home* instead of a ship, here on this island with all of you. And now, we are all leaving . . ."

Pers was struggling to keep smiling, but Pam could see he was very upset. She took his hand carefully, afraid the simple act might make him lose his composure and start crying, a terrible thing to have happen when you were a proud youth becoming a man.

"Pers, I'm sorry. I didn't know you felt this way. I want you to know I completely understand. When Grantville came through time I was all alone. Like I told you earlier, I was divorced, so no husband. I still had my son, but he doesn't like me much anymore. If I hadn't met Gerbald and Dore, I don't know what would have become of me. Well, I'd probably be living as a shut-in, and weigh fifty pounds more than I do! At least until my supply of cherry bonbons ran out. Anyway, everybody needs a home sometimes, and Gerbald and Dore gave me one."

She paused, trying to gauge the young man, trying to see if what she wanted to say would be the right thing, the thing Pers needed and wanted. She had all his attention, and knew that he looked up to her far more than she had realized. *Well, you have never been Miss Congeniality, that's for sure.* She took a deep breath, and placed a hand on Pers' wide shoulder.

"Pers, I'm sorry I didn't see how strongly you felt sooner. I want you to know that you will *always* have a home with me if you wish it. You have been my very special friend all through this voyage, proving your love and loyalty a hundred times over. I have already come to think of you as another son. I swear to you, it's true! When that pirate was beating you, that was what made me mad enough to shoot him. He was hurting *my boy*! In my heart *you are* my boy, you've earned your place! Whatever you want, I will make it happen for you. If you want to go to school, I will see to it. If you want to work with me, I will have a place for you. If you were to think of me as your family, why, it would make me very proud." Now it was Pam who was in danger of tears. The hope dawning on Pers' face, still a boy as much as a man, made her heart beat double time.

Pers stuttered a bit, and then, in a small child's voice said, "I'd like that very much, if you will have me. I would like to have a mother again."

"Awww, come here, kid." With that, she grabbed Pers, who was a good two feet taller than herself, and gave him a bear hug. "Let old Pam be your momma. I'll try my best, but I'll warn you I'm not always too good at it. I'm not sure where all this is going from here, but you just stick with me, we'll figure it out together, all right, son?"

Pam could feel Pers shaking. He was weeping now, but she could tell from the vibration that these were good tears, the tears of relief and discovered joy. She joined right in, and they stood there for a while, a mother and son, which to Pam's great pride she knew they had become, not by blood, but in all the ways that really mattered. After a time, Pam stepped gently back from the embrace to look at the bright, lovely youth who had entered her life. She patted him gently on the cheek.

"Don't worry, Pers. I won't tell anybody what a sweet kid you are. They already know anyway. Now, let's go home. I'm so hungry I could eat coconut crab curry, heigh-ho!"

"Yes, ma'am . . . er . . . *Mom*!" He gave her a snappy salute, his usual grin back in place and grown a size bigger.

Garrett W. Vance

Chapter Twenty-Eight: The Last Day of Camp

It was their last day at the beach camp. That evening they intended to dine on the ship, and spend the night aboard before sailing with the dawn. The bosun, despite an initial raft of complaints about the many oddities of their new vessel, had deemed her seaworthy enough, and ready to go. Toward the end of their conversation around the dinner fire the previous evening, and with more than a bit of liquor in him, the bosun had began to wax so poetic on the junk's capabilities that Pam suspected he was beginning to fall in love with the thing, and thought that must happen between all sailors and their ships eventually.

After an early breakfast, Pam sat on the porch of her hut, sipping her third cup of coffee. Pers had been drafted by the bosun first thing. She had given him a wave and a wink as he set off for the beach, which made him blush. *Looks like I'm a mom again. Well, good for me.* The thought filled her with a deep, comfortable warmth. Pers had come to think of their beach camp as home, and she realized she had, too. She would miss her funny little bamboo shack at Castaway's Cove, and wondered if she would ever come this way again. They had been very lucky to make a safe landing here when the *Redbird* went down. All in all, they had enjoyed a much higher level of comfort than could be expected, thanks to the island's natural bounty and the many skills of her companions. At times, it had felt more like she was on summer holiday than marooned, especially during the heady days that followed her finding of the dodo flock. Those were good times, and she wouldn't forget them.

"Maybe someday we can make this a research station and spend some time here again," she said to herself, a habit that she was careful not to let others overhear. "I would like that. Yes, we shall." The sailors had built to last, and she thought the buildings could survive a few seasons without human care. Finishing her coffee with a gulp, she went inside and put the coconut-shell cup on a shelf, leaving it there for that possible someday. The tiny room was mostly empty. She had already sent her baggage out to the ship, and only a few island gewgaws remained; a shell collection along the window sill, and some sketches she had hung on the walls that weren't important enough to take with her.

One piece of art, placed in a prominent place over her cot, was a message to any who might take shelter here in the future, a painting of a dodo with the words "Please do not kill this bird! Bad luck follows those who do!" written in English, German and Swedish. "Can't hurt!" she said, chuckling at her own cleverness. Assuming they could read, sailors were by nature superstitious, and she had no bones against using a bit of psychological warfare in her cause. *In fact, I should probably do that more.* She brushed against some of the shell necklaces hanging from a peg beside the window. She and Dore had worn these with their native getup. On a whim she took one and put it on, a bit of beach-camp style to remember the place by. Pam took one last look around, backed out onto the porch, then closed and latched the door shut against the wind. It was time to go.

She found that Gerbald and the men had already moved the heavy carronade from its log mount and were now loading it onto the pinnace with a complicated affair of poles, ropes, and pulleys. Gerbald had proven many times to have a knack for that sort of thing, even impressing the sailors who worked with such tools on a daily basis. They had made him the foreman for the task, and he was basking in the glory of leadership, one of his few foibles.

"Show off," she teased as she sauntered by the proceedings. Gerbald just grinned, as pleased with a ribbing as he was with positive attention. Pam thanked the Lord she had found such a good-natured friend. She knew that he had become an expert in deflecting the worst of her moods, and she usually allowed him to do so with silent gratitude.

Pam wandered up to the kitchen to see if she could help Dore with her cooking things. Not too surprisingly, the incredibly efficient woman was already packed up and had drafted sturdy Arne and another sailor, dark-haired Lind, into hauling the boxes and bags down to the pinnace. Pam was given a fairly light basket to carry, and returned to the beach with it. The pinnace had already left on its mission to deliver their special gun to the new vessel, so Pam put her basket down on the pile of goods waiting for the next trip and decided to take a walk. She didn't want to go by way of the cemetery. Her good-byes had been said, and the pain was still too fresh, so she went the opposite direction, ending up on the high cliff lookout she and Gerbald had sighted the junk from just a few days days ago. It felt like weeks! Pam sat down with her back against a gnarled, wind-tortured tree to watch the proceedings. The job of getting the carronade onto the junk and mounted looked like it was going to take a good long while, so she let herself drift off into a nap.

Chapter Twenty-Nine: An Unexpected Promotion

After an hour of dozing filled with dreams featuring swords, blood and the screams of the dying, Pam shook herself awake with a sour taste in her mouth, feeling unrested and anxious. She hurried down to rejoin those at the beach, comforted by their dependable presence.

The bosun and two of the more senior sailors, Vilfrid and Lind, awaited her on the shore along with Gerbald and Dore. They would make the trip in the *Redbird's* pinnace, which the sailors would then haul up onto the junk's wide deck. The modest little craft was quite dear to them, having proven its worth time and again. It took her a while to realize it, but the sailors were once again being especially polite to her. Of course, they always had been, but there had been some kind of a change since they had captured the Oriental junk.

"The big gun has been mounted on the new ship. Are you ready to board, *Frau* Pam?" the bosun asked.

"Yes, just let me take one last look." Pam scanned their home for all those long months, the realization that her stay in this remote place was at an end finally sinking in. A fierce joy filled her. *We did it. We are getting out of here.* She climbed into the pinnace, where she was ushered to a seat in the prow. She watched their beach recede until they began to draw in close to the junk. After one last, long, look she turned her back to the shore, ready to begin her journey again.

Pam looked up to see all the sailors and marines were lined along the gaily painted rails. As the pinnace drew close the men sent up a cheer, whooping and hollering with a gusto rarely seen in the cool-tempered, well-mannered Swedes. Pam saw Gerbald on the bench down from hers waving back at the sailors like some teen-age state fair princess in a parade, full of winning smiles and gracious bows. This made Pam and Dore both burst into laughter. They joined in with the merriment and waved and shouted greetings back to the cheering crew.

Soon they had clambered aboard with the help of many friendly hands, accompanied by the high, keening tune of the bosun's whistle. Their entire company stood assembled on the deck of the fanciful junk they had acquired at such bloody cost. The men opened a space around Pam and her staff, all the while clapping and cheering. After a while, the bosun raised his hands and brought the men down to a hush. Pam smiled warmly at all of them, the men who had brought her to the far side of the world, the men who had worked so hard to make her safe and comfortable during their castaway days, the men who had become like brothers to her.

"*Herr* Bosun, you fellows shouldn't put up such a fuss!" Pam said, her West Virginia twang creeping into her Swedish. She was beginning to feel shy, and a bit overwhelmed, as she always did when finding herself in the public eye.

"It is from our hearts that we do!" the bosun told her. "We have been delivered from our sojourn on that wretched shore, and are in possession of a fine craft. All of this is because of the great courage and many skills you, *Herr* Gerbald, and *Frau* Dore have lent to us. We never would have been able to live as well as we have while lost, or to have captured this vessel without your help, and especially *your* leadership, Pam."

The men broke out into a cheer again, clapping their hands for Pam, who felt as if she wanted to dissolve into the deck.

The bosun nodded happily, and fixed a toothy grin on her. Before she could make a break for it, he said, "In the tradition of the sea, a captured vessel becomes the property of the victors, in particular the leader of the victors, their captain. Pam, *you* made the plan which ensured our success. *You* led the attack like some warrior queen from out of the old tales!" He paused to dramatically sweep his arm across the decks in a gesture that included all the grinning men standing at attention. "This is *your ship*, we are *your crew* and *you* are *our captain*. We await your orders, *Captain* Pam!" He gave her a long salute, his eyes meeting hers with admiration. Ending the salute, he gave her a polite bow, and took a step back to join his men silently at attention.

Somewhere a seagull cried, and the sound of gentle waves lapping against the red-lacquered hull became intensely loud in the silence. Pam's eyes were as wide as porcelain plates, their steely gray having attained a glazed cast. After a while, Gerbald reached out and poked her in the arm, a deep chuckle coming from beneath the shade of his ridiculous mustard-colored hat's floppy brim. Pam looked back at the men, *her* men, and managed a kind of stunned half-smile. She nodded slowly a few times, taking it all in. Somewhere inside the turmoil of emotions whirling through her brain she heard a calm, clear voice, the one that always came when she really needed it: *You have earned this honor, Pamela Grace Miller. Now acknowledge their faith in you. It is yours by right!* Suddenly, her eyes came into focus, she drew back her shoulders and in an unexpectedly loud and commanding voice bawled, "Make ready to sail!" The men jumped at her order, spreading out through the ship. These men were eager to be back to their profession, they had grown tired of life onshore, and bent to their tasks with relish. The bosun stepped forward to pump Pam's hand in the American-style Gerbald had taught him.

"Was that the right thing to say?" she asked, relieved that the show was over, and reeling from the ramifications.

"Absolutely! Well done, Captain Pam. I knew you had it in you!" The bosun beamed at her.

"Look, I'm not so sure about this 'captain' thing, Nils." she said in confidential tones, leaning into him closely and using his Christian name, which she rarely did. "Isn't it a job that's better suited for you, or the *Löjtnant*? The extent of my boat piloting experience is rowing a boat around a lake as a kid. I have only a vague idea how to sail a ship, much less captain one."

"No, ma'am, I wouldn't have it. This ship is squarely yours, and you command her. There's a lot more to it than the sailing, you can leave that part to us! You just tell us where you want to go, and we will take you there! This is your expedition, and we will follow your lead."

Pam's eyes were moist, she was supremely touched by the confidence these brave men had shown in her. The bosun saw that she needed time to let it all sink in, and motioned toward the aft cabins.

"If I may be so bold, Captain, might I suggest you and *Frau* Dore have a look around the ship?" He started to go, but then stopped, with a bemused expression on his face. "Perhaps I have grown a bit rusty. You ordered us to make sail but what is our destination?"

Pam looked out at the sparkling azure sea to think for a moment. "Well, the plan was to anchor here tonight. We know its a safe harbor. Why don't you just take us for a spin up and down the beach, a little demonstration of what we feel like under way. Then let's anchor back here, and give everyone a rest. I think the men need one before we go off into the unknown, chasing French warships and the like."

The bosun beamed. "Very wise, Captain, very wise. Now, leave it all to me, and make yourselves at home. What I believe serves as the captain's cabin is at the top of those stairs, and meaning no offense, ma'am, but you might find more comfortable clothing there, although it will be of a foreign cut."

Pam looked down at what was left of the clothes they had landed in, barely rags, and held together with grass stitching in places.

"I think that's the best idea I've ever heard, *Herr* Bosun! We look a mess. We'll try to find some new clothes, and some for you and the men as well. We are all a bit worse for wear."

"Well, then, I'll get back to work. May I ask *Herr* Gerbald here to come help with raising the pinnace? He has an eye for rope work, and is the only one of us who can make some sense of this foreign tackle." Then, he and Gerbald just stood there looking at her. After a long moment it dawned on her. *Oh, good Lord! They're waiting for you to say yes, dummy!*

Pam quickly muttered her captainly assent.

"I would be delighted, Captain Pam!" Gerbald answered enthusiastically. "I have always loved a good puzzle." Gerbald had been in Pam's service for a number of years, and knew the high quality of her leadership well, even if she herself didn't see it. Even so, as he left he didn't neglect to give his friend and employer a smirk, pleased at her discomfiture. She stuck her tongue out at him.

"Ever hear of walking the plank, buster? Yeah, *you* in the funny hat!" she called menacingly after him. She turned to see that Dore was smiling broadly at her, face bright with excitement. This rare sight filled Pam's heart with a shiny kind of joy, and she grabbed her friend's hand.

"We need new clothes, sister. Let's go find some booty!" Pam said to her.

"Yes, ma'am, Captain Pam!" Dore replied in English with her thick German accent, coming to comically straight as a board to attention, and adding a snappy salute. This made them both start laughing, and so in high spirits they began their exploration of the exotic and alluring foreign ship.

Chapter Thirty: Galley of Celestial Delights

They began their tour below decks, deciding to save the captain's cabin for last. No point in putting on something new, then getting it all dirty down in the holds. The junk was certainly unusual-looking on the outside, but a ship was a ship, and belowdecks offered a layout not too terribly different from those built in Europe. In Pam's opinion, it was even more spacious and well-thought out in its design. The cabins were larger, and the hallways surprisingly higher. None but the tallest of the men would have to crouch as they moved about. Everything was clean and dry, the wood well-caulked and painted with some kind of preservative stain. They found a large storage bay with its deck doors open to let in the bright southern sunlight. Pam walked around its shadowy recesses, lifting tarps and poking at oddly-shaped barrels marked with the wispy brush strokes of strange languages.

"We should find out what all this cargo is," Dore said, peering into the shadows at a plethora of crates and sacks neatly made fast to the walls and floors. "We may have something of value here. It's likely we will need to trade for supplies sometime in the voyage to come."

Pam made a slow turn, the light from above catching her hair and bringing out flashes of silver amongst the dishwater blond locks. She was smiling, and Dore thought she looked like an angel. Dore was greatly pleased to see her friend happy after such a long ordeal.

"There's enough room here to make a pen for a flock of dodos," Pam said brightly. "They would have fresh air and light when the weather is good, and be well-protected when its not." Her voice was filled with a hope she had not felt in a very long time. "We have another chance now. Maybe I can still save the dodos, bring a breeding population back to Europe, if we accomplish nothing else."

"Of course you can, Pam. We will help as always," Dore encouraged her.

They left the cargo hold to continue aft. After climbing some steep stairways that could have passed for ladders, they arrived in a room that made Dore emit a gasp of delight. It was the ship's galley and it was . . . wonderful! There was a brass pipe built into the wall from which either stored or freshly-caught rain water in barrels on the deck could be drawn with ease over a deep, porcelain sink. Next to this was an open window, its square panes made of a thick, ivory-colored laminated paper that would let in plenty of light to work by even when closed. There were fat candles placed here and there for after dark. Pam and Dore entered the seemingly cluttered, yet actually highly-organized space, not sure where to begin their exploration.

Hundreds of small drawers and cabinets dotted the walls, and filled the spaces under the wide, wooden counters. A peek into some of these revealed dry goods, what might be flour, sugar, and many dried herbs and spices. A variety of unusually shaped pots and pans hung from a rack above an iron wood-stove. Pam recognized a wok and a steamer. Even though their shapes were strange, she knew Dore would be able to put them to use. Latched drawers held a dazzling array of cooking implements and tools, including ladles, skewers, meat forks, and many items less easy to ascertain the purpose of. The room was filled with a delicious aroma of woodsmoke, strong scented herbs, and fresh salt air. Immediately adjacent lay a pantry chock-full of dried meats, fish, fruits, vegetables, and many more as yet unidentified items. There was even a row of pots with live herbs growing on a shelf beneath a window. Dore and Pam both clucked over these, and immediately watered them with a teapot. They had obviously suffered under the ship's pirate occupation.

"Good gawd, Dore, it's like a modern kitchen! More like a restaurant kitchen than something you'd have at home. It has everything but an electric dishwasher!" Pam exclaimed, overwhelmed after months of coconut-shell soup bowls and clamshell spoons. She didn't say it to Dore, but vowed to herself that she never, *ever* wanted to eat coconut and crab curry again. *Ever!*

The galley of the *Redbird*, despite being built with several up-time style conveniences, was a greasy hole in the wall compared to this. Pam noticed a cylindrical ceramic pot filled with what must certainly be chopsticks. She pulled two of them out to study them; they were about eleven inches long, one quarter of which was squared and the rest rounded, cut flat at the ends, made of a smooth, yellowish wood that had been stained darker on the rounded, food grabbing end, presumably by use.

"Hey, Dore, I think I know what country this boat is from— China, or, whatever they call it in this century."

Dore looked at her friend with eyebrows raised in interest.

"These are called 'chopsticks' and they're used for eating. When my son Walt got old enough to behave reasonably well for an hour or two, we started going out to eat once a month, and tried a lot of different kinds of restaurants. There were lots of Chinese places around and even a couple of Japanese joints over in Morgantown. Once we tried Korean food up in Pittsburg, but it was a bit too spicy for the guys. Anyway, I'm pretty sure these are Chinese-style chopsticks. The Japanese versions are shorter with pointy ends, and the Koreans make theirs from metal. I have no idea why, because they sure were tricky to use. The metal was slippery!"

Dore looked on with a certain amount of amazement. "It's sometimes hard to believe that you lived in such a world, Pam. You make food from the Far East sound commonplace, available just down the road, when in our time most know little about the world beyond a few miles!" She reached over to the holder to pull out two of the slender wooden rods herself. "I don't see how these could be used to eat." she remarked after giving them a careful study. She ended up holding one in each hand like drumsticks with a mystified expression on her face.

"I'll show you!" Pam began to demonstrate. "You put them both in one hand like this, and pick up the food between the ends. It's tricky at first, but you get the hang of it pretty fast. Especially when you're hungry!" She opened a few drawers until she found what must certainly be dried peas. "Here, watch!" Pam deftly picked up one pea at a time and made a row of six across the counter as Dore looked on, wide-eyed. "I think we left all the clamshell spoons back at the beach, so I guess I'll have to teach everybody how to use these. My ex-husband never could get the hang of it, he always had to ask for a fork." With several flicks of her wrist she returned the peas back to their drawer and slid the chopsticks back into their container with a satisfying wooden click. "Yup. Must be Chinese. They like their food all right, pretty fancy stuff! I'm not too surprised they had this nice a setup even in these times. Well, lucky us!"

She turned to Dore, who was allowing herself a tentative smile at the prospects of cooking in such an odd, yet practical galley.

"Welcome to your new kingdom, Chef! I can't wait to see what you come up with first!"

Dore grinned at her enthusiastic young friend. "Well, I can promise you one thing, my dear Pam— it will *not* be coconut and crab curry!"

Garrett W. Vance

Chapter Thirty-One: One Man's Junk is Another's Treasure

Captured Oriental Junk, South Coast of Mauritius

Pam and Dore climbed out of the cool shadows of the lower decks to stand blinking beneath the Tropic of Capricorn's blazing sun. Squinting against the glare, Pam saw Dore looking wistfully back down toward the wonderful galley they had discovered—a paragon of luxury and abundance after their long sojourn marooned on a remote shore. Pam smiled at Dore's almost child-like eagerness to play with her new toys, and motioned her to follow. "Okay, pal-o-mine, you'll have your chance to do your thing in there soon enough. Let's go check out the upper cabins."

The junk was cruising slowly down the length of the cove, pushed along by a summery breeze in her slatted crimson sails, engaged in another practice run. Sailors rushed to and fro, sometimes pausing to puzzle over her unfamiliar designs. The bosun's voice could be heard on the foredeck, by turns roundly cursing any man who was slow to grasp the intricacies of the foreign rigging, then damning the mad heathens who had built such an unusual craft in the first place. Pam had full faith that her crew would manage; they were moving forward in any case, which must surely be a good sign. Now that they had a ship, she didn't want to dally. The fate of the colonists weighed heavily on her, as it did on all aboard, and all possible haste would have to be made. But not tonight, tonight they would rest, they had certainly earned one.

Their eyes now somewhat adjusted to the brightness, she and Dore headed to the high aft tower that Pam thought of as "the castle deck." Standing in its shade, they peeked into the bottom cabin. The windows had been opened to freshen the air inside, which had a pleasant woody scent. Earlier, the sailors had reported that they had performed a very thorough cleanup, removing all evidence that the pirates had ever lived aboard. One of the cleaning-crew sailors, Hake, had remarked that the heathen pirates had been remarkably neat and clean, except for some bloodstains here and there, very likely from tortured captives. "Once they've dried, they're hell to remove."

Pam had grimaced at that, but didn't fault the fellow for his honesty. "Let's go inside!" Pam said, Dore nodding eager agreement.

The cabin was no disappointment even after the delights to be found in the galley. These were the quarters the bosun had suggested for Gerbald and Dore. The door opened near the bottom of the castle deck's ladder. As the only married couple of the expedition, they would be given the second-nicest room on the ship, the first being reserved for the captain. They found a spacious, wood-paneled apartment, elegantly furnished with the same kind of heavy, ornately carved and lacquered wood furniture found in the lobbies of fancier Chinese restaurants. It most certainly had been reserved for distinguished guests, or perhaps used by high-ranking ship's officers. They found fresh bed linens neatly folded and ready for use in sandalwood scented cabinets. Pam was very pleased to see they were made of silk. The bed was, much like the *Redbird*'s, built into the walls. It was a lot wider, yet a bit shorter than what they were accustomed to. There were plenty of large cushions and pillows if they needed to spread out onto the carpet strewn floor.

After the initial inspection, Dore wrung her hands and exclaimed, "We can't possibly stay here!" She was obviously shocked by the level of opulence. "This is a room for a prince or a duke, not a washerwoman and her old soldier husband!"

"Nonsense," Pam replied firmly. "You're the chief cook and Gerbald is my personal bodyguard, as well as an acting sergeant in our fighting force, so you get the good stuff. Enjoy it!" Dore looked unconvinced, but Pam added "That's an order!" and gave her friend a playful grin.

Pam wasn't surprised when the upper quarters were double the grandeur and four times the space, occupying the entire floor of the tower. Pam looked around, quickly deciding she would make the area near the door the dining room and office. The back third of the capacious room would be made private, since that was where the bed was, as well as the bathroom. She was pleased to see those facilities were a bit more advanced than on the ships of Europe. There was more than enough space for her needs. Placed along the dark-stained, wooden walls were many beautifully painted, movable screens. These would be perfect for dividing the room.

The two friends grinned like fools at their change of fortune. To go from roughing it, stranded on a deserted shore, to occupying ship's quarters that oozed with comfort was a pleasant kind of shock. Pam shook her head slowly, gazing at the luxurious space as if she were in a dream, daring it to be solid. Pam and Dore began rearranging the place to suit Pam's needs, taking one of the three-sectioned screens from the wall and placing it in front of her bunk, to make it a sleeping alcove. The wood bases of the five-foot screens were quite heavy, and certainly designed to stay upright even in the worst storms. Pam was also pleased to find that this ship would provide a gentler ride than poor old *Redbird* had. They were under way at a fair clip now, and she could barely feel it. As they went for another screen, Pam bumped into a pile of pillows leaning against the wall and knocked them over. When she bent down to straighten them, she noticed there was an opening in the wall—a thin, dark crack running from the floor to a height of about three feet.

"Hmm, what do you suppose this is?" She pushed the pillows away, and felt along the crack with her fingers. To her surprise, it was a small, hidden door that had been left just slightly ajar. A thrill rose in her. *So, our lovely craft has secrets. Wonderful!*

"Dore! Try to find a knife or something we can use to pry this open!" Dore began to scurry around the room in search of a suitable implement. Pam kept tugging and pushing here and there until she discovered a tiny spot the size of a man's thumb that appeared to have been worn smooth by years of touch. She pushed it, and the door popped open as neat as could be. "Never mind, Dore. Bring a candle!"

Dore, well-practiced with the flint and steel she carried in her apron pockets, had a candle lit faster than Pam could strike a match. She handed it to Pam, and they both got down on their hands and knees to peer into the space they had revealed.

To Pam's amazement, there was a deep closet there, a secret room. Among the various fascinating items within the dark space, the one that caught her eye above all was a large wooden box reinforced with metal bands. Crawling over to it, she tried to pull it toward the door. It wouldn't budge. There was something about the thing. . . . The very heaviness of it made the teeny-tiny hairs at the nape of her neck stand up and do the mambo. Sticking out of an ornate-looking brass lock was the back end of a tarnished silver key. Apparently its last user had left in a hurry. . . . Possibly the ill-fated original owners, or the fat, turbaned pirate captain they had sent to his rightful reward in Hell. The box looked like a certain kind of container all right, built like a safe, massive, and thick. It was darkly age-stained and covered in a faded but flowing white script. She didn't dare think the words that were screaming to be heard in the back of her mind. It simply couldn't be . . .

"Open it, Pam! Let us see!" Dore urged her on, her voice a bit higher-pitched than normal, more like that of a child's than a serious-minded, late-middle-aged woman of God. Pam marveled once again at the amazing youthening effect adventure was having on her friend. They kneeled in front of the mysterious box, both giggling, holding on to each other for support.

Pam hesitated, her hand trembling near the key until Dore gave her a gentle push. They both jumped a bit, their nerves as taut as guitar strings.

"Oh, we are so silly!" Dore said, laughing "It's probably full of ship's papers, all written in that ridiculous squiggle these Easterners use instead of decent letters." Even so, her face was full of expectation.

"Right!" Pam agreed. "It's not like we would actually find anything valuable on a real pirate ship! This isn't a movie, right? I'll bet it's empty." They both laughed while Pam turned the key. There was a muffled click deep within the mechanism, then the lid popped up a few inches as it released from a spring. Pam and Dore's eyes were as big and round as harvest moons as they gazed at the rainbow of colors glinting within.

"No, it's a treasure chest!" Pam announced with comic nonchalance. "Holy shit," she murmured as she raised the chest's heavy lid until it caught some kind of stop and held open. "Holy shit." she said again as her hands touched cool metal and smooth stone. Despite her amazement at such an unexpected discovery, Dore managed to give Pam a quick look of disapproval over her blasphemous language. Suddenly, Pam's mouth was a bit too dry, and she nearly croaked, "I can't believe this."

Dore murmured something incomprehensible as she peered over Pam's shoulder. This was replaced by a funny kind of squealing noise, and she held onto Pam to steady herself. Scarcely believing what she was seeing, now *touching*, Pam filled her hands with a shining mixture of gold and silver coins, glittering jewels and pearls. The box surely held a fortune, a small one perhaps, but a fortune nonetheless. As if to make sure it wasn't a figment of her imagination, she pried one of Dore's hands from its painfully tight grip on her arm, and poured lucre into it. They knelt there staring silently into the chest's gleaming contents for a very long time.

"It's real. A real treasure chest on a real pirate ship. Yo-ho-ho." Pam's voice was hushed and full of wonder.

"One might say that our fortunes have changed," Dore said, her head shaking slowly as if to dispel her disbelief.

"Go fetch Gerbald!" Pam told Dore, now feeling dizzy as if she were on some kind of wild carnival ride, the thrill switching to terror and back to thrill again. She dug deeper into the chest, scooping the contents to one side. Besides the coins and gems there were some larger pieces buried within: tiaras, combs and other less easy to identify objects, all a-glitter with precious stones.

Dore ran so fast that she might have shot out the door and off the top floor like a cannonball if she hadn't caught herself. Pam had never seen her friend move like that, but then chalked it up to her years surviving in the rough following Gerbald in and out of battles. Dore was certainly full of surprises, but then these days surprises had become the norm.

Shortly, a huffing, puffing Dore returned with an amused Gerbald hurrying after. His ever-present goofy hat was knocked from his head by the low door casing as Dore literally pushed him through. Before he could bend down to retrieve the hat, he froze in place, seeing Pam holding a double palm-full of treasure. His eyes widened, and he just stood there staring while Dore picked up his hat, long the object of her scorn, taking care to scrunch and twist its seemingly indestructible mustard-yellow felt between her strong hands with malicious intent.

Second Chance Bird

Failing to make much of a dent, she stood on her tip-toes and plopped it back onto his head where it looked no worse for the attempted wear and tear.

"There, he is speechless! If only we had one of those video cameras to record the moment for ages to come," she said, laughing at her husband's flummoxed state.

Pam smiled to see a bit of the feisty old Dore back in play.

Gerbald straightened the much-abused and well-loved hat over his salt-and-pepper hair, taking a moment to digest what he was seeing. With a regal sweep of her arm, Pam escorted him to the closet, which he crawled into with easy grace. He pushed the box to gauge its considerable weight and was able to move it a quarter of an inch. Then he scratched his chin and grinned.

Pam grinned back at him. "I think this might have belonged to that fat, old pirate captain. The writing on it looks more like that swirly Arabic script than Chinese characters. This wasn't the first ship he'd captured, I'll bet. We are probably looking at years of plunder here. I guess you really can't take it with you."

Dore, who had managed to compose herself, quoted scripture in her old, familiar Christian soldier's tones: " *'Treasures of wickedness profit nothing: but righteousness delivereth from death. The Lord will not suffer the soul of the righteous to famish: but he casteth away the substance of the wicked.'* Proverbs 10:2-3."

Gerbald nodded in sober agreement with his pious wife, buying some always useful good will with the gesture, then turned to Pam.

"Pam, when your luck changes, it *really* changes. What do you intend to do with all this?"

"I've decided already," Pam said, while letting a handful of gleaming coins slowly fall back into the chest with a musical tinkling. "We should divide it equally among everybody on this ship."

Dore nodded in staunch approval. "That is the right thing to do, my Pam!" Dore told her. "We are all in this together. Shall I summon the bosun now?"

"Allow me to tell him," Gerbald cut in. "After all, I missed out on the thrill of first discovery. I would very much like to see our good friend's face when he hears of this windfall. I will keep it between we four for now. We can divide it all up and then pass it out to the men before tonight's party. I'll bet they will be over the moon."

"Tonight's party?" Pam asked. She saw Dore deliver what must have been a painful blow to the small of her husband's back.

"Oops!" Gerbald said in English, followed by a long-suffering sigh.

"Spiller of the beans!" Dore growled at him, also in English. After many years together they used English and German interchangeably, and sometimes mixed the two together in one sentence, despite their best efforts not to. Pam mused that this habit was evolving into a creole some were calling "Amideutch." Dore continued in German, which would always be the most comfortable for her, "It matters not. We have all had enough of surprises by now anyway. We have earned a bit of fun after our many troubles, and so tonight is for celebration!" she said expansively, her face alight with pleasure.

"Who are you, and what have you done with Dore?" Pam asked, but Dore didn't seem to hear. She was now pushing her husband toward the door. "Go now, oaf! We must make ourselves presentable. Now that our Pam is a captain, she can't go about dressed in these rags! Out with you!"

Gerbald didn't resist. This time he was careful to duck and keep his hat on.

"Maybe you can buy a new hat now!" Pam called after him. It never hurt to hope.

"What? Waste such riches on everyday items? No, I shall use my share to do something truly wonderful. I shall buy my own television set."

"Not until I have a decent house you won't, foolish man. If the Lord has seen fit to gift us with riches, we must use them wisely!" Jumping, Dore took a swipe at the much-hated hat, but Gerbald was too fast. Her hand flew through thin air as Gerbald disappeared from sight, launching himself out the door and dropping from sight in a blur. No crash or injured call for help came, so Dore and Pam, now giggling like schoolgirls again, began rummaging through the room's many drawers and cabinets, laying out exotic garments on the bed and divans as they went.

Garrett W. Vance

Chapter Thirty-Two: Counting their Blessings

Soon after, the bosun was brought in to view their unexpected bounty. He let out a long whistle as he squatted in front of the brimming chest. "I've sailed the seas since I was ten years old," he said, "and never have I seen this kind of wealth. I will be able to buy some land and retire now. Truly, your generosity is great to share it with us, Captain. We would never ask it of you." His eyes glistened moistly.

"You've earned it, my friend," Pam told him. "You all have. Let's count it out, the four of us, and the *Löjtnant* as witness, equal shares for all." The bosun nodded, but Pam still had some idea that she would somehow end up with more. The men of the sea had ways of doing things, and she knew the captain traditionally got a larger share of the booty, a much larger share. She intended to protest, of course, but wheels were already turning. Pam had projects lined up for years to come, and now she had that most critical of all resources: funding. One thing was certain, the first thing she would do with her share of the take was to make damn sure her colony succeeded, which went hand in hand with saving the dodo.

When the *löjtnant* arrived, he expressed much the same sentiments as the bosun had, but Pam told him to just accept what was coming to him and be happy. He smiled, and replied, "As you wish, Captain." No doubt he was as glad to get his hands on such a large chunk of change as they all were.

Together, Gerbald and the *löjtnant* managed to drag the chest out of its closet, and bring it over to the large table Dore had cleared of Oriental knickknacks for the purpose.

"Okay, here's what I think we ought to do," Pam said, after considering the situation for a few minutes. "Let's start with the coins. We will group them by types first, and then the ones that don't match any others we can group by material and weight." She reached into the chest to scoop up a double handful of coins which she piled onto the table's surface.

"Here, these two are the same, they look like copper, and they have square holes in the middle. Chinese, maybe. I bet they're not worth much." She pushed them off into their own area. The next coin she held up to the light, and made a long whistle. "If this isn't a gold doubloon, I'll eat Gerbald's hat. I always think of the Spaniards hanging out in the Caribbean, but I guess I remember reading something about the Philippines as I was getting ready for this trip. Let's hope there's more of these."

It turned out they weren't able to recognize most of the coins, but the bosun had an old sailor's eye for metals, and was able to make what Pam thought were pretty good guesses about the value of each. Gerbald, as an ex-soldier, had also seen his share of foreign coin, and did his best to help the bosun make identifications. They sorted the coins into gold, silver, and other less identifiable metals, or blends of metals. Piles sprung up around the table as they worked. Pam could scarcely believed they were engaged in such a project. Once they finished with the coins, they turned their attention to the loose precious stones.

"Could this be a ruby, Pam?" Dore held up a red gem the size of her thumb.

"Well, maybe. I really don't know much about this stuff." As it turned out, no one else in the group did, either. "Where the hell is a jeweler when you need one?" she muttered. They ended up grouping the gems into pretty little mounds by color. Overall, the coins were quite a bit more numerous, but they still ended up with a respectable amount of possibly precious stones.

Next came the jewelry. The *löjtnant* carefully handed Pam a fanciful gold tiara encrusted with what must surely be blue sapphires. Pam placed it on her head and grinned.

"Look, I'm Wonder Woman! Now we just need to find the bullet-proof bracelets!"

Gerbald, a dedicated student of American pop culture, laughed. Dore just rolled her eyes to signify *How much of such foolishness must I endure?* while the Swedes wore the painful smile of wanting to show approval for a joke they just didn't get. Pam tried to explain Wonder Woman and the concept of a super-hero to them in Swedish. She was getting pretty good at the language, but would need more time to really become fluent. Finally, after several long minutes of word searching and gesturing, the bosun and the *löjtnant* both nodded with the satisfaction of understanding.

"We see now," the *löjtnant* said, "This is just like the sagas from the old days! This woman is as strong as Thor, she can fly like a bird, and she has enchanted accoutrements to aid her in battle. It's obvious! Wonder Woman was one of your gods before you Americans became Christians! It's just as in our Norselands where the stories of the old gods still survive in the tales we tell children!" The bosun agreed heartily, while Pam just smiled and gave up.

"Close enough," she said, and remembered to take the tiara she was still wearing off, feeling like an idiot for having it on throughout her lengthy explanation. She held it in her hands for a moment, admiring its sparkling beauty. "Hey, I know someone who we should give this to. Princess Kristina! Look, it's even in the Swedish colors, blue and gold." The Swedes clapped their hands at this suggestion. A generous percentage of the treasure, in the form of jewelry, was put aside to donate to the princess' crown jewels, a gift from her admirers. A pang of sadness came to Pam as she thought of poor old Fritjoff, and how much he would have approved of such a gesture. Even so, Pam didn't give everything to her patron. There was a certain pearl necklace that called to her in a siren song, and she claimed it without apology.

"I heard there's a party tonight and a girl has got to have something to wear!"

It took another hour to divide all the shares out of the various piles. As Pam had expected, the Swedes insisted that she take a larger portion. Since it was harder to gauge the value of the gems, she took a lion's share of those and fewer coins, figuring that some of the pretty stones might be worthless, while others might be worth more than the entire find. She would have to wait until she found a qualified jeweler to find out, and that would likely be a while. And so, despite her many protests, she ended up with a larger pile of loot than the rest.

"Look, I know you mean well, fellows, but really, I wanted everybody to have an equal share."

The bosun listened to her patiently, but his answer was always the same: "You are the captain, you get more. It's tradition."

Finally, Pam conceded. "Fine, but I want you all to know I'm going to use most of my take to help make this colony work. I really don't need this much money for myself. I'm already pretty well off."

This was met with warm smiles from her companions, which made her feel better about it. Smiling back, she dropped her take back into the chest, locked it, and put the key in her pocket.

The bosun summoned the men. One by one, they filed past the table receiving their share, their eyes bugging at the size of the unexpected windfall. Apparently sailors of the day were not very well paid. The shares weren't really that big; it hadn't been that large a box. Even so, each seemed overjoyed, and thanked her profusely before making way for the next.

When the task was all finished, Pam shooed everyone out of her cabin and fell down on the bed, very much ready for an afternoon nap.

It's better to give than receive, but it's lot of work, too.

Chapter Thirty-Three: The Captain's Ball

As the breezes died with the evening calm, the junk was anchored back where it had started, not far from their camp on Castaway Cove. Dore had come back to wake Pam, and help her get ready for the party. After some fussing, they stood on the narrow deck outside Pam's door, both dressed in fine Chinese silks. Some of the garments they had chosen were most likely designed for men, but they had made do, with pleasing results. Dore had found a long skirt which she belted with a sash and a simple tunic top, all in deep reds which suited her well. The tunic must have belonged to a large man as it had plenty of room for Dore's buxom figure. Pam, who was slight in comparison, wore a pair of knee-high black silk pants, a simple black shirt that buttoned at its collar-less neck, and a cerulean blue silk jacket ornately embroidered with gold pheasants and cranes, with large gold buttons and teardrop-shaped clasps. She left the jacket open to show off the lovely pearl necklace from the treasure chest.

"Look, I'm wearing the Swedish colors!" she said to Dore as she preened in the jacket. "The men will definitely approve. Plus, it's got birds!" She felt as if she were sixteen again, and headed for the high school's spring dance.

"Really, Pam, these garments are far too fancy for me. I am embarrassed to be seen in them! Tomorrow I shall have to find something simple that can withstand the galley. It would be a shame to ruin such finery as this."

"Yeah, yeah, tomorrow, fine, but come on, tonight's a party! Live a little! I now know that you *do* know how." Pam gave her friend a sly, knowing grin which made Dore blush, took her by the elbow, and guided her toward the ladder. At the bottom, Dore told Pam to go ahead, she would check on her foolish husband before rejoining her.

On the main deck, the men had placed a long, low table near the second and largest of the three masts. It was covered from end to end with food, a collection of dried meats and fruits found in the galley, fresh fruits from shore, and a row of very large fish they had barbecued with spices. The aroma was utterly delicious, and drew Pam closer. She thought the seasoning might be a mix of garlic, Chinese five spice, cloves, and black pepper. *Is that sesame oil and a dash of rice wine splashed on, too? Heaven!* Pam's mouth watered. It was hard to believe the men had managed such an ornate dinner without Dore's help! It had been a very long time since she had smelled such a savory meal, and she felt delightfully hungry.

Pers saw her and hurried over. He slowed when he noticed Pam's change of clothes and smiled approvingly.

"You look very nice," he complimented her, despite his obvious shyness about such things.

"Why, thank you, Pers! You look very nice yourself!" He was dressed in a canary-yellow version of what Pam wore, but without the jacket. The pants were too short on the long-legged youth, riding well above the knees, but he still looked handsome in the exotic outfit. Pam took his arm to give it an affectionate squeeze. She nodded toward the table "It looks like you fellows found your way around the galley! Well done!"

Just then Dore joined them. Pers gave Dore, the indisputable ruler of all things to do with food, a nervous glance and hurriedly told them, "We wanted to give *Frau* Dore here a night off from cooking. We men of the sea are not wholly without talent in that arena. I hope you like what we have prepared. We were very careful not to make a mess."

Dore scanned the table, sniffing warily at their offerings. After a long, tense moment she smiled, finding the sailor's efforts to be to her satisfaction. After all, it was nice to have a night off, and now she need not feel guilty for it.

"It looks fine, Pers," she told the nervous youth. "You men have done a good job. I thank you."

Having met Dore's approval, Pers immediately brightened, and led them to the place of honor, a line of five comfortable-looking chairs placed on a temporary platform raised three feet above the deck. Behind the stage, the clever sailors had hung a variety of flags and banners decorated with all kinds of fanciful motifs, to very festive effect. Pers ushered Pam into the middle seat, which was practically a throne; intertwining serpentine dragons of ebony with ruby eyes and ivory teeth framed a plush velvet cushion in scarlet-and-gold trim. Found amongst the cargo, it had been undoubtedly headed for some exotic sultan's palace.

The men were still going about their tasks under the watchful eye of the bosun, although many a glance was stolen in the direction of the food. Pam had arrived a bit early, but no one seemed to care. She was delighted to see they had all managed to trade their island rags for new clothing from the hold. No two were dressed the same, and they looked more like a band of circus performers than a ship's crew. Pam was smiling at the bustling scene so widely her face began to hurt. She turned to Pers, who was apparently assigned to be their maître d', and asked,

"You got any booze?" Pers smiled his sunniest smile, and disappeared from her side in a Pers-sized gust of wind.

He returned shortly with two elegant ceramic bowls garnished with fresh flowers, full of fruit juice and a very healthy shot of what tasted like rum. "I believe *Herr* Gerbald called them mai-tais. He says he will be your bartender tonight," Pers told them as they each took a careful sip. Even Dore smiled at the delicious taste, and took another, bigger quaff. Pam looked at her friend and grinned. *No teetotaling for the Christian soldier tonight. Looks like we won't have to play our usual game of "Let's get Dore drunk." She's leading the charge for a change! This is definitely going to be fun!* Pam thought with glee. She was fairly vibrating with excitement, and drank again, deeply, with intense pleasure.

"Tell Gerbald he's a genius and to keep these coming," Pam said. "I intend to get loaded. Party on!" Pers had enough English by now to get the gist of her meaning, and smiled with professional grace as he disappeared again. *The kid has a future as a great waiter, he's a natural!* Despite her proclamation, Pam tried to pace herself somewhat. She knew she was going to have to give a speech or two, and wanted to be well-relaxed for that, but not to the point of word-slurring wasted. She could do that after the speeches were done.

The sun was setting, and various torches and lanterns were being lit. The men were assembled on the deck, ready to commence the official celebration. Someone had found a very large gong, which Lind struck with a cloth hammer, the deep, vibrating tone signaling everyone to be quiet. By now Gerbald was sitting next to Dore, who was on Pam's left. The bosun and *Löjtnant* Lundkvist soon joined them, sitting to Pam's right.

The bosun stood up, causing the crew to settle into silence.

"Good evening to you all. Here at last, we find ourselves delivered from our isolation, aboard a ship that, while strange-looking, is a nimble and sound vessel worthy of the Swedish Navy!" He waited while a hearty cheer went up from the men, Pam and her retinue joining in. After a few moments he silenced the men with a certain gesture, and continued on. "And though some of us gathered here are not Swedes by birth, they have earned their place in our ranks through their great courage and dedication to our beloved princess! All hail Pam, Gerbald and Dore!" The cheers were louder this time, which Pam didn't think was possible. The attention made her face flush redly as usual, but she smiled, and took another big gulp of cocktail to steady her nerves.

The bosun, once again cutting the cheers off with an effortless gesture, turned to the two Germans and the American, a woman from a country that didn't even exist in this world and probably wouldn't. "As far as we are concerned, you three are every bit as Swedish in your hearts as we are, and I welcome you as brothers and sisters. Hurrah!" The men went wild this time, and the three of them found themselves urged to their feet to take their bows. Gerbald and Dore returned to their seats, but the bosun beckoned for Pam to join him at the front of the stage.

"And now let's hear it for our fearless captain, Pam Miller! Three cheers!" Gerbald must have coached them in the English-style he'd gleaned from watching old movies, as "Hip-hip-hurray!" sounded across the deck. When the traditional cheer finished, the bosun, who was proving to be quite the expert master of ceremonies, gave Pam a courteous bow and asked her, "Please, Captain Pam, a few words for your men, if you would." He stepped back then, leaving Pam in the figurative spotlight.

She smiled at all around her, not feeling as nervous as she usually did. She was comfortable here; these were her people, as much as any she had ever known. There was nothing for her to be shy about. She spoke out loudly and clearly, "My beloved brothers and sister, my dearest friends in all the world. You are the best of the best, and it is my supreme honor to be chosen as your captain. I will work my hardest to earn your trust in me, and lead us on to victory. In Princess Kristina's name, I swear!"

She paused and another cheer went up, everyone clapping as loudly as they could. She felt as if she were a rock standing in a sea of love, each wave that washed over her filled her heart with perfect joy. Deep in her mind she took some of that feeling and put it away for safekeeping. She knew she would need it someday when the doubts returned. The love she felt tonight would be a talisman against the darkness that sometimes tried to steal her few joys. *Maybe that won't happen so much anymore. Things have changed. I have changed.*

With what she thought might be the sweetest smile she had ever worn, she raised her hands and shouted over the din, "Let the party begin! I order every man aboard to drink as much as he likes and then some more. Let's raise some toasts!" She felt like a rock star.

There was a bustle about the deck, and soon she saw that everybody was holding some kind of a cup. They still had quite a bit of their carefully-rationed rum left, almost an entire barrel, which she figured they would be finishing off this night. Gerbald told her they had also found a number of very large ceramic jugs filled with a palatable alcoholic beverage he thought must be rice wine stored in the ship's hold, along with a collection of jugs and barrels containing strange-smelling and rather less reputable-looking liquors. *We aren't going to run out of booze in any case, God bless us one and all! We'll be needing His mercy when the hangovers hit tomorrow!*

The crowd was very quiet now, waiting for her lead. Pam held her cup aloft, and in what she had been taught was the Swedish way, made a point of meeting the eye of every single person aboard. Once she had accomplished that feat she shouted, *"Skål!"* and downed her cup in one swallow, quickly followed by everyone else. As soon as the cups were refilled, she began working through a long list of toasts, to the men, to their country, to their king and princess, to the lost men of the *Redbird*, and finally to their new ship. She paused then, looking a bit perplexed. She turned to the bosun who was beginning to list a little bit thanks to the quick succession of shots. There was little doubt that everyone was starting to feel pretty darn good.

"*Herr* Bosun, what is this ship's name?" her voice had grown just a tad thicker, but still could be heard clearly all across the deck.

The bosun stepped over to her and scratched the back of his head as if it would help him think. "Truth to tell, Captain, I have no idea. I think that's it painted there on her aft, but none of us can read it!" Then he laughed, and everyone joined in, the raucous sound echoing all around the bay.

Once the hilarity had subsided, he said, in as serious a tone as he could muster, "Captain Pam, she's your ship so you must name her," and gave her a slightly wobbling, but deferential bow.

Her mind a sudden blank, Pam turned to Gerbald and Dore for help. Those two had been drinking almost double time, and were already about two sheets to the wind and starting to let out the third. They both broke into fits of laughter when they saw Pam looking at them so seriously. That almost made Pam start laughing, too, but she kept in control.

"This is serious, you guys, we need a name for the boat, and we need it quick!"

"How about *The Hungry Dodo*?" Gerbald offered, trying hard to keep a straight face. His goofy hat was tilted nearly sideways on his head, and Pam figured the only reason it hadn't fallen off was because of the longtime bond of affection they shared. The hat, in combination with the incongruous fuchsia silk blouse he wore, made him look like something out of a Dr. Seuss cartoon and Pam struggled to keep a straight face.

"No, no . . ." she told him. "Dodos aren't exactly symbols of good fortune, not yet anyway." She turned to Dore, whose perpetually rosy cheeks blazed like fire engine lights on the way to a three-alarm fire.

Seeing that it was her turn, Dore sat up nearly straight and said "How about *Chinese Chopsticks*?" with sincere earnestness, except it came out sounding more like "Shineeze Shopstigs." She waited expectantly for Pam's certain approval, her big, blue eyes as wide and glassy as a stuffed toy's.

Pam had to look away from the two of them before she lost it. Meanwhile Pers had come onstage bearing yet another round of drinks, (someone should tell him to stop . . . well, maybe later) and her face lit up; an idea was coming.

"Pers! The other day, when we were taking the dodos back to the forest . . . what was it that you called them?"

"Ummm, 'stupid creatures'?" he blurted out, too late realizing that wasn't likely the answer Pam was looking for. He looked embarrassed.

Pam had to laugh then, but stayed in control. Everyone was still waiting on her decision.

"No, no, something about them being lucky, or something." Pam started to chew on her pinkie's sometimes-abused nail.

Pers, who quite sensibly hadn't been drinking at all, being sentenced to take the night's watch after the party, thought hard for a moment, and then raised his hand hesitantly. "Do you mean when I called them the 'second chance birds'?" he asked in a hopeful tone.

"That's it!" Pam suddenly rushed over to hug him. If not for his quick reflexes and fast feet, she would have knocked him, and the small drink staging table he had set up, right off the stage. After a good squeezing of surprisingly bear-like strength, no doubt augmented by the high octane content of her blood, she let go of the scarlet-cheeked Pers and turned to those assembled.

"The *Second Chance Bird*." She worded it in English as Pers had. "That's what we'll call her!"

Pers quickly translated this into Swedish and another great cheer went up. Pam took the fresh cup Pers held out to her and raised it. "Here's to the *Second Chance Bird*! God bless her and all who sail on her!"

Pam thought the sound of the cheering had grown a bit hoarse, but they bellowed away at full volume once again anyway. Feeling her duties had now been performed, she gave everyone a deep—almost too deep—bow, managed somehow not to pitch headfirst over the side of the stage, and returned to her seat amidst thunderous applause. She was smiling so hard and so wide that her face would have hurt had she been able to feel it.

The *löjtnant*, who was seated beside her and who rarely said anything beyond that which was required by the ever-diligent prosecution of his duties, turned to Pam, and addressing her in the most genuine and admiring tones, said: "Captain Pam . . . you sure know how to party!" Pam raised her cup to his and they knocked them together with a sloshing clunk, drank them down, and in unison signaled for more.

Off the hosting hook, Pam began to relax and really enjoy the festivities. It was hard to believe these jolly fellows were the same intent and sometimes a bit dour men who toiled so hard in silence throughout the day. *They have been through a sea change*, she thought and then started laughing. The *löjtnant* asked her what she was laughing about, and she tried to explain, but just got more and more mixed up until they were both snorting with laughter, him still clueless as to the phrase's meaning. Gerbald pitched in, trying to help, and soon they were all laughing so hard they could barely speak and weren't even sure why.

Pers looked on, frowning with a mother-ish kind of concern, wondering how he was going to get them all to bed, and praying no enemies would come across them in such a debilitated state.

During their exploration of the *Second Chance Bird*'s many holds and storage rooms, the men had found musical instruments, and were now bringing them out. Pam saw something slightly resembling a violin, but round-bodied and with only two strings, what might be a hammer dulcimer, some long-necked apparatus that could be distant kin to a guitar, oddly-shaped drums, cymbals, and other unidentifiable noise makers. Apparently, the junk had once boasted a small orchestra, very likely for the entertainment of its august owners and their distinguished customers. Many of the Swedes could play an instrument, it was a seaman's tradition, but their own fragile pieces had been lost with the wreck, except for a tin flute or two.

The men started warming up with the foreign instruments, creating a cacophony that would make an alley full of amorous cats cover their ears with their paws. After a few minutes, this transformed into something resembling a tune. Soon enough, they were playing a rollicking sea shanty that Pam could recognize as one she had heard many times on the voyage around Africa, a real foot-tapper made somehow thrilling by the unusual sounds forming its melodies and harmonies. Now that the band was in full swing, the five luminaries managed to get down from the stage without falling. Anyone who wasn't playing music was dancing. The *Second Chance Bird* was a floating party, the long suffering crew indulging at long last in the comforts of civilization.

Pam clapped as she watched Dore and Gerbald spinning about in some kind of folk dance. Suddenly Dore grabbed Gerbald by the scruff of his neck and dragged him into a passionate kiss. Gerbald's eyes went wide for a moment, but sensing there was nothing to do but enjoy this shocking public display of affection from his wife, he embraced her and kissed her back. When they finally parted, both looked as embarrassed as kids caught necking in the library. The men raised a ribald, but also encouraging cheer. Pam felt like the Queen of the May, surrounded by a bunch of men, some of whom were not bad looking at all, no sir, all eyes on her, and appreciative of her charms in a delightfully non-threatening way. *Ahh, what fine gentlemen,* she thought as she took turns whirling about the deck with every hand on board. *Another good thing about time travel! In this century they still make them like they used to.*

The party wound down as the hour grew late, and the revelers finally tired, or in some cases, became completely incapacitated. It was well past midnight, and Pam thought she should probably have passed out by now herself, but she had somehow fed on the positive energy around her. She felt stupendously drunk, but also calmly aware. She turned back to the bosun, who she had been talking with just a moment or three ago, to find him curled up under the mainmast like a big gray tabby cat. It was finally time to admit the party was over.

Head held high, but beginning to feel drowsy, Pam allowed the attentive and long-suffering Pers to escort her to her cabin. She walked with the careful, mincing steps of the intoxicated, cautiously stepping over the snoring sailors who hadn't made it to down to their bunks. As she slowly climbed the stairs with Pers literally bringing up her rear, Pam chuckled to herself that it was the only teenager in the group who had got stuck with taking care of all the drunk adults. *What a fine example we are setting for today's youth!* Pam thought with pride. *Someday I hope Pers has children of his own to put him to bed when he gets shitfaced.*

Pers guided her to her bunk and gently aimed her so that when she fell, her head was near the pillow, and most of her body off the floor. He picked up her dangling legs and placed them on the bed, then located a light blanket which he covered her with. Even a balmy night like this could get chilly before dawn.

Pam was still awake, or semi-conscious at least. She reached up to take Pers' hand and squeezed it softly.

"Yer a goo'boy, Perzzz." she mumbled, eyes mostly closed, her face the very portrait of pickled contentedness.

Pers smiled down at her and gave her hand a squeeze back, which he doubted she could even feel.

"I didn't know my real mother very well," he told her as he very carefully lifted her head and slid the pillow under it. "I was so young when I left . . . but I do know one thing: You are a *lot* more fun than she was. Sleep well, dear Pam." He stroked her hair lightly for a moment, then headed for the door. Before he closed it behind him, he could hear the gentle breathing of the fast asleep.

A little while later, Pam opened her eyes again, awakened by noises nearby. Listening carefully she heard muffled thuds and giggles coming from the cabin beneath hers. Gerbald and Dore's cabin. *Dear Gawd!* She grabbed a couple of pillows and crammed them over her ears to shut out the far too intimate sounds emanating from below. It must be like their second honeymoon. No, it was probably their *first* honeymoon. Pam looked up at the cabin's ceiling, softly lit by dim starlight reflected off the waves and through the open windows. Yes, she was happy for her friends, and yes, maybe just a tiny bit jealous. To distract herself, she reviewed the day's triumphs. Memory became mixed with dream as the waves rocked her back to sleep and the last clear thought she had before drifting off again was, *I'm Perilous Pam Miller, pirate captain! Who'd have ever thunk it?*

Chapter Thirty-Four: Anchors Aweigh

The decks of the Second Chance Bird at anchor in Castaway's Cove

Nobody was up early the next morning except the few unfortunate marines assigned to the watch. Pam woke to a splitting headache, and after some debate swallowed a couple of her precious aspirin with the carafe of water Pers had thoughtfully left for her the night before.

"I'm giving that kid a promotion," she mumbled through dry lips.

After a while, the drum and bugle corps marching around in her head settled into a less driving beat, and she decided she might be able to get dressed. This took much longer than usual, considering the clothing was of an unfamiliar design, and her hands felt like she was wearing oven mitts.

"That's the last time I drink that much," she growled, ignoring the annoying voice in her head reminding her that she said that every time she drank that much. Finally managing to pull her new boots on, Pam made her way to the door. She opened it, allowing a shaft of bright sunlight into the room, then closed it again as quickly as she could. The beam of light still seared in glaring orange across her closed eyes.

"Dear God, I swear, I'm going straight." She sat down for a while, cursing herself for not thinking to bring her up-time sunglasses on this little jaunt. Looking around, she found a floppy hat with a wide brim that resembled the ones she had seen Dutch merchants wear. She put it on, trying not to think about how it had ended up here. It was a bit large, so she tied a scarf around her head to make it fit better. She caught a glimpse of her red-eyed, exotically-clothed self reflected in a silver platter on the table, and laughed aloud.

"I'm either a pirate or a pimp! Grandma would be so proud." Pushing her hat's brim low over her eyes, she made her way out of the door into the late-morning sun.

The decks below resembled a zombie movie. Everyone seemed to be stumbling along in slow motion, their usually tanned faces bleached a deathly shade of gray. Except for Gerbald.

Gerbald was the proverbial cat who had dined on canary. Pam watched him swagger around the decks, grinning as only a man who had totally gotten laid the night before can. She rolled her eyes at him as she gathered him up, and went to go look for the bosun. They found him running his hand over the junk's delicately curved, crimson-lacquered railing. Pam wasn't sure over the noise of the surf, but she thought he might be softly cooing. He looked up with a grin that made Gerbald's giddy expression seem droopy in comparison.

"Captain Pam, *Herr* Gerbald, good morning! What are your orders, ma'am?" The bosun, a cheery sort to begin with, was as bright as the new dawn, in the highest of spirits. Apparently he was immune to hangovers, and Pam stilled an annoyed twinge of jealousy.

"Well, I think we ought to discuss that. Let's have a meeting." Pam saw that the bosun was now distracted by the sails, which resembled giant Venetian window blinds to Pam's eyes. "So, *Herr* Bosun, what do you think of our new ship now that you've gotten to know her a bit?"

"Oh, Captain Pam, she's lovely." And then he really did coo, making Pam and Gerbald's eyebrows arch in surprise. "Sure, she looks ungainly at first glance, but there is a swan hiding within this duck. See that high aft deck? I thought they were mad, but now I think it's there to keep us dry in a following sea. The bottom is flat, but she's got a kind of a wedge keel, we can go shallow with her, and even beach her with ease, but she should go confidently in high seas as well. I'll wager she's watertight, too. The hull is some kind of a sealed box. I'm not sure yet how they did it, but they're a clever lot, all right! And look here, these paneled sails and rigging are going to give us far more control than a regular rig, once we master their ways. We haven't sailed her as much as I'd like, nor have we had any foul weather to try her with, but I'm already sure she's the best damn vessel I've ever set foot on! We've nothing like her in the North Sea, and I'd take her into those cruel waters with no fear."

Pam nodded, catching a bit of the bosun's boyish enthusiasm despite her hangover. She understood many of the nautical terms from her hours pacing the decks of the *Redbird* on the long journey around the cape, watching and listening to the sailors at their work. She was very pleased the bosun had a new love in his life, and left him to his bliss to go find the *löjtnant*.

Eventually, the senior crew were all gathered on the dizzy heights of the junk's castle deck. It was time to make some serious decisions. Pam felt calm despite the mantle of authority that had somehow found her shoulders to fall on, definitely *not* something she had ever expected, nor wanted.

"Okay, we've got a real good ship, the bosun tells me. We can sail her?"

"Yes, Captain Pam!" The bosun's pride in his shiny new vessel resounded in his voice. "Our men are learning her ways quickly. We shall master her."

Löjtnant Lundkvist spoke up, "Captain, you should know that this ship is not without teeth. If we are attacked, we can fight back. There are two guns of Chinese make on each side. They are unusual, of course, but they look well-made, and surely operate on the same principles as our own. With your permission, we would like to test them."

Pam nodded her assent.

"Also," the *löjtnant* continued, "We have mounted the Redbird's carronade on the foredeck on a swiveling turret we were able to improvise. Its range is short, but its firepower is devastating. The perfect thing for cutting those French assholes down to size." This was definitely the happiest Pam had ever seen the fellow, a military man with shiny new weapons on his way to test them out on a much-despised enemy.

"Please, do your tests. I don't need to tell you to be careful. It's good to know we can give somebody a bloody nose if need be. Although, it makes me wonder how the pirates originally captured this vessel. There would surely be damage, like what we saw happen to *Muskijl* when the French took her."

The *löjtnant* answered, "The *Second Chance Bird* is in fine condition, no signs of battle damage. They probably captured her in the same way we did—through subterfuge."

"Yeah, must have. I suppose we'll never know." Pam pushed the thought aside, yet another mystery. They had things to do here and now. She gave them all a determined smile. "All right then, gentlemen, which way do you think we should go?"

The bosun rubbed his chin, considering.

"Well, Captain Pam, the colonist fleet was last seen headed northeast up the coast. Undoubtedly, they, too, were captured. I would suggest we follow that course slowly, looking for signs of wrecks, begging pardon for saying so, and hoping to find our folk in good health in some safe harbor. On your maps of the island from up-time, there are several places to check. We believe the site of Vieux Grand Port will be the first such we meet, followed by Poste de Flacq, among others. It would be best if we were not seen, and if we are sighted, to have plenty of distance to run in."

Pam nodded her approval.

"Sounds good to me, *Herr* Bosun. Let's do it. Slow and steady."

Gerbald spoke up then.

"We must consider what happens when we do find the colonists." Gerbald's face was stony, the mood Pam had come to think of as his warrior mode. "*Muskijl* was badly outgunned by those bastards, and though our new vessel may be better armed than *Redbird*, I doubt she can match a French warship. We must be prepared to face a stronger enemy—one that has possibly captured a source of slave labor for establishing a military stronghold on this island—with the comparatively few men we have."

Löjtnant Lundkvist nodded his agreement. "If that is the case, we must do what we can to help our people. We may be small in numbers, but we have proven ourselves in combat! Please, Captain Pam, whatever happens, let us make rescuing the colonists our priority!"

"Absolutely! Maybe we can't fight a sea battle, but we can go in by land and we can hit them hard. They won't be expecting us. They must have been sure we went down, and didn't even bother to come look for survivors after the storm, figuring it would have finished us off if their hits didn't. Well, guess what, *messieurs*! We ain't dead yet." There was real steel in Pam's voice. A powerful anger had grown in her over the months since her expedition had been upended by the French. She intended to make them pay.

"Up-time, the French had control of this island for a hundred-odd years, and now they have decided to stake their claim early. Their spies must have found out about the Swedish colony plan, and so they sent their warship in a bid to beat us to it. Well, they succeeded, for now, but we are back in the game. Gerbald, *Löjtnant* Lundkvist, please work on plans of attack for any situation you can think of." She smiled a smile that any she-wolf on the hunt would be proud of. "Think sneaky and fast. The element of surprise is what's going to do it for us, just like when we captured this ship."

After a moment's thought, Pam said, "Bosun, have all the men continue to wear the Asian clothes and have them tie up their hair in scarves. We want to look local from a distance."

"Aye aye, Captain!" The bosun looked positively jolly, a man back in his element and ready to work. "We'll look like real heathens, and run before anyone can get close enough to see we are good Christian soldiers."

They all grinned at each other. Some of the tension of the last months was melting away, replaced by a healthy excitement. The odds might be steep, but at least they were back in control of their destinies, free men and women with a good ship to carry them on their mission.

"All right, let's get going! Anchors aweigh!" she shouted at the top of her lungs into a rising antipodean wind. On the decks of the *Second Chance Bird*, the men smiled as they made ready to sail.

Chapter Thirty-Five: Smoke on the Water

They followed the coast warily, always prepared to turn tail and run if they saw another vessel, since it was unlikely that any such would be a friend. They looked for signs of human activity along the shores. Perhaps the other boats had been wrecked by the battle, and the storm and their passengers now castaways such as they had been. They took their time, anchoring quietly at night in what safe coves and cover they could find, keeping their lights dim and their voices down. The *Second Chance Bird* was on the prowl.

On a slightly overcast morning, they saw their first sign of people. They had set sail at first light, heading for the large, natural harbor at Poste de Flacq, one of the proposed destinations for the colony ships. Pers knocked politely on Pam's door to summon her to the wheel. She hastily put on one of her new Chinese suits, and arrived on the bridge sleepy, but resplendent in red-and-gold brocaded silk. Before she could greet the bosun, Pers reappeared with coffee for her, served in a deep ceramic bowl decorated with evergreen trees. She took a long, grateful sip before trying to speak.

"Good morning, *Herr* Bosun. Report, please."

He spoke in the hushed tones they had adopted during their hunt.

"We've sighted a lot of smoke coming from behind that point, Captain. Looks to be from a number of what might be cook fires or possibly land clearing." That made Pam grimace. The bosun continued, "It's a pretty certain sign there are people there. Plus, we are fairly sure this is the site of Poste de Flacq on the up-time maps. A good place to build a fort."

"Okay. Yeah, that could be good or bad, depending on just who it is having breakfast over there." The caffeine, in somewhat less concentration than the coffee up-time, began to kick in. The discovery of a possible human presence made Pam's heart race with excitement.

The *löjtnant* spoke next. "May I suggest we row the longboat that we captured with this ship along the shore and have a look around? We can keep close in, and stay hidden among the rocks along that point. The seas are fairly calm today." He was obviously eager to find out what was coming.

"No, I think it's too risky that you'd be seen. Gerbald and I will go have a look overland. You can put us in over there behind the point. It's wooded, and will give us plenty of cover."

The bosun didn't look very happy at that prospect.

"Begging your pardon, Captain, but it's likely going to be very dangerous. They will have sentries."

"Don't worry, friend. *Herr* Gerbald and I are very good at staying hidden in the woods. They will never know we were there."

Gerbald nodded his assurance, his eyes gleaming at the opportunity to do some scouting in his favorite environment, the forest.

After a quick breakfast—which Dore insisted on, and to which there was no saying no—Pam and Gerbald arrived on deck ready to head out on their spy mission.

Pam was dressed in whatever green and preferably not-too-shiny clothing she could find amongst the ship's unusual collection.

Unfortunately, it was all pretty gaudy. With a grim smile she strapped on the leather gun and ammo belt Gerbald had fashioned for her from materials found on the junk. The Smith and Wesson .38 caliber pistol she had used on four pirates was officially hers now, and Gerbald insisted she bring it with her. The truth was, she liked the feel of its deadly weight at her side, and would not hesitate to use it again when the time came.

Gerbald, of course, had on his perennial outfit of sage-green wool long-coat, a black T-shirt featuring a faded Lynyrd Skynyrd band logo, brown breeches, knee high leather boots, and crazy old mustard hat, along with his trusty *katzbalger* shortsword and pistol grip Snakecharmer shotgun hanging from his wide belt. He was the very picture of a new-fangled USE bad-ass, the toughest stuff of up-time and down-time rolled into one dangerous package. He took a look at Pam's bright green silks, and laughed aloud.

"You can fly, you can fly, you can fly!" he sing-songed as he pointed merrily at her undeniably elfin-looking outfit.

"That's pretty funny coming from a guy who looks like he's just come from *Beyond Thunderdome*. By the way, Dr Seuss called, and he wants his hat back."

They shared a brief laugh, then boarded the trusty pinnace, sitting quietly until they were put ashore. The sailors wished them luck and a safe return. They watched until their two spies had vanished into the trees before rowing back to *Second Chance Bird* with worry etched on their well tanned faces.

Garrett W. Vance

Chapter Thirty-Six: Contact

French slave colony near the site of up-time Poste de Flacq, Mauritius

"This is not good." Gerbald peered through the scope, scowling while Pam did the same with her binoculars. They were on top of the high bluff that formed the point, laying under ferns, and watching the harbor below, a deep one with a fairly impressive set of docks already in place. Their would-be guardian, the *Muskijl*, was heavily damaged, but still afloat, tied up to the dock behind the massive French warship that had claimed it. There were also several medium-sized lateen-rigged boats, certainly belonging to Arabs, or other such denizens of these far seas. Their hearts sank as they saw the *Annalise* and *Ide* laying at anchor nearby. Now they knew how these people had accomplished so much building in the months that had passed: Swedish slave labor.

There was a town taking shape on a gently sloping hillside behind a five-meter wall of heavy timbers running some twenty meters back from the shoreline, the beginnings of what would eventually be an imposing fortress. They could see sturdy Swedish men tethered together in work crews making it all happen. To Pam's surprise, their overseers looked like black Africans dressed in white robes with their heads covered, nearly the same garb as the Arabic-looking pirates they had defeated to take *Second Chance Bird*. Pam was no history expert but, like many Grantvillers, she had become a lot more interested in the subject since she had been thrown backward through it. She knew the African slave trade was largely run by Africans themselves, and that must have been where the French had found these fellows. Pam bit her lip as the slavers shouted at the colonists in what sounded like broken French; the snap of a whip echoed across the quiet bay, making her cringe. Out on the end of the dock, she saw several French soldiers passing around a wineskin, and enjoying a little fishing, while their mercenaries oversaw the work for them.

"Scumbags," Gerbald muttered under his breath.

"There are a lot of them, aren't there?" Pam muttered darkly.

"Yes. Not just the French, but their hired slave drivers as well. At least a hundred of the enemy would be a good guess."

"We'll need help, then." She bit her lip as she scanned farther back from the harbor. There she saw men and women carrying barrels, and performing menial tasks, their feet bound or chained. "We have to free the enslaved colonists and the crew of the *Muskijl,* and use them against their captors." Gerbald looked doubtful. Pam gave him an encouraging nudge with her elbow. "Come on, that's how they do it in the movies! It's worked for us so far."

Gerbald gave her an unconvinced smile.

"A risky proposition at best. The Swedes will be tired and weak from ill use. Just trying to contact them at all while they are under guard will be risky. They are bound. The ropes we can cut through quickly, but the chains will require either more time, or a key. It will be difficult." Gerbald's expression was grim.

"Okay. We told *Second Chance Bird* to give us a week out here in the field before taking further action. Let's take our time, lay back and watch for a while. Once we know more about the routines here, we can make a move."

Gerbald grinned at her with wry amusement.

"Yes, ma'am, Captain Pam!" he said in his best West Virginia drawl. He was always full of pride in his mastery of the accent and American slang, and seldom missed a chance to show it off. "And when we're ready, we can open up a king-sized can of whoop-ass all over them suckas! *KA-BLAMMO!*"

Pam rolled her eyes as the two of them vanished back into the shadowy forest, sly and silent as foxes.

∞ ∞ ∞

Pam and Gerbald watched the slave colony from various vantage points over the next three days. The Swedish colonists looked fairly healthy despite their ordeal, at least from a distance. They were a robust lot, and were weathering the hardships as well as they could. At night they were housed in makeshift huts in an open meadow fenced with an imposing array of ten-foot high bamboo stakes. The few children they had brought along were kept in the enclosure all day, tended by the expedition's small number of elderly. Pam saw that even this group was given work to do, weaving rope and baskets. The sight of the children and the old folks put to work by their new masters made Pam's blood boil.

Oh, I'm so going to put the hurt on those froggie bastards just as soon as I am able! she thought redly, a part of her shocked at the depth of her own wrath. Most of the men had been put to work logging and constructing the growing fort. Many of the women were sent out to the fields to tend newly planted crops. Other small groups of women were made to forage for fruits and nuts along the forest's edge, always under the watchful eye of a slaver.

They decided it was one of the latter groups they would approach, since they were the least heavily guarded, and cover was nearby. They were confident in their ability to remain unseen by the enemy among the trees and brush. Gerbald stayed back, prepared to distract or even kill the guard if necessary. Pam did her best to disguise herself as a colonist by wrapping her head in a dirty gray cotton towel she had taken from *Second Chance Bird*'s galley and draping a brown wool blanket from *Redbird*'s pinnace over her shoulders. Slipping silently out of the underbrush with the practiced stealth of a long-time birder, she joined the group of foragers.

Walking slowly, as if bound, she made her way from the deeper woods to the forest's edge, joining the women at the trailing end of their party farthest from the guard. She stayed low, endeavoring to be seen but unseen, just another slave. Ahead of her was a tall, statuesque woman in her late twenties, her fair features now deeply tanned and careworn, her golden-blond hair tied back in an unkempt pony tail. Pam studied her for a while, before making the decision to approach her. She looked like the calm sort, not someone who would react loudly and stupidly to a stranger in their midst. Pam, following her gut, came up behind her, keeping the tall woman's larger frame between her and the guard who stood some twenty yards off.

"*God dag, vän.*" "'Good day, friend,'" Pam greeted her quietly in Swedish, and continued in that language, her months with the sailors serving her well. "Please don't look back at me, just keep working while I talk."

The woman instinctively turned to look over her shoulder anyway, but caught herself, and looked forward again, one sea-green eye having regarded Pam from its corner for just a moment. She nodded her head slowly, continuing to pick small berries. Pam briefly wondered how they knew they weren't poisonous, but didn't want to think of the likely answer.

"I will listen," the woman replied quietly.

"Good. I'm Pam Miller, the American from the United States of Europe who led this expedition on Princess Kristina's behalf. Do you remember me?"

"Of course I do!"

"That's good. There are more of us who remain free. Can I trust you not to betray us?"

The woman nodded firmly, her shoulders tightening under her ragged blouse.

"Good, good. I knew I could. We have some soldiers, and we intend to free you colonists, but there aren't enough of us. We have to find a way to set your men free to fight with us when we make our move. We will probably want you women to create a diversion to distract your captors while we do that. Are there those among you who are brave enough to help us?"

The woman turned slightly back toward Pam and hissed proudly under her breath. "*All* of us! We will do anything to be free again."

"I thought as much. I've come to learn Swedes are just as tough as us West Virginia hillbillies! All right then, I need you to spread the word that we are coming, but only to those who really need to know. You can let the rest in on it when the time comes; the secret will stay safer that way. We will make our move from a few days to a week from now; we need some time to get prepared. I'm not sure yet how we are going to pull this off, but I will get word to you people the same way I am now. Make sure it's you, or someone trustworthy taking up the rear of your foraging expeditions from now on."

"It will be so. I can hardly believe it, here I am with Frau Miller, the Bird Lady of Grantville, still alive!"

"Heh heh, yeah, for now, anyway. Call me Pam."

"I am Bengta. I am very happy you made it. We feared the worst."

"Nice to meet you, too, Bengta. Just hang in there, we are going to do our best to get everybody out of this, I promise."

"Thank the Lord!" The woman's voice was quiet but filled with emotion. Suddenly she lowered it even further, a furtive hiss, "Pam! The guard comes this way; you must go!" Bengta continued to pick berries, keeping her head low, trying not to attract the surly man's gaze. No answer came, and she soon realized that Pam the Bird Lady was already gone.

∞ ∞ ∞

That evening, after a quick celebration over dinner at Pam and Gerbald's safe return, the senior staff gathered on the high castle deck. The Swedes' faces were a study in smoldering rage as they heard the news of their colonist's enslavement.

Löjtnant Lundkvist shook his head slowly. "I don't see how such a small force as ours can take on so many, even with our skill and experience. But if you order it we shall try, Captain Pam."

"Actually, Gerbald and I have been working on a plan. Trickery has worked so far, so we intend to stick with it," Pam said, her voice full of an uncustomary, sly eagerness.

"It seems that it is our turn for a masquerade, gentlemen," Gerbald told the men with a positively wicked smile. "Beware Greeks bearing gifts."

∞ ∞ ∞

The next morning Pam and Gerbald were rowed to the shore again. They made their way quickly through the forest to where the foraging party was again working their way along the freshly cut forest's edge. Pam winced at the destruction of so much timberland. These renegades were definitely not following her zoning plans. She quickly spotted her contact trailing along at the end of the group. Pam came up behind her, hidden in the underbrush.

"Hello, again, Bengta. I have news."

"As do I."

"Tell me."

"We have done as you asked. We are prepared to make our break. We have hidden weapons, tools, stones, whatever we could manage. When your signal comes, we will fight."

"That's great! I forgot to ask you last time, what became of the *Muskijl*'s crew and soldiers?"

"The sailors are working on building the fort. The officers and marines are being held captive in the French warship. We all fear for their health greatly; no one knows what condition they are in. Those filthy French bastards and their foreign dogs care nothing for our lives. If we weren't so useful, I doubt any of us would have been spared." Bengta's voice was thick with controlled anger. "Do you see that heathen devil who guards us? When the signal comes, I intend to stove his skull in with a stone, may God forgive me."

Pam nodded solemnly. "I shot four like him myself with a pistol a few days ago. First time I'd ever killed anyone. It was necessary, God forgives. Just be careful." Pam reached into her rucksack to pull out a bundle filled with sharp knives, a few hammers, and some chisels she had collected from the *Second Chance Bird*. "I've brought these for you; can you keep them hidden? They may help."

"Yes, indeed they will. I will make sure they get to those who can use them best. Thank you, Pam. You are our savior!"

Pam blushed at the woman's fervency. "I'm just doing my duty. I got us all into this mess, and I'm going to get us all out. So, here's what's going to happen. Make sure only your most trusted leaders hear this part.

Tomorrow afternoon you are going to see a strange-looking ship pull into the dock; it's called a Chinese junk, and you won't be able to miss it . . ."

As Pam outlined the plan, the woman's face grew bright beneath the grime of the brutal captivity she suffered.

Pam finished up. "The signal to raise holy hell is going to be 'Save the dodo!' When you hear that, go to work."

" 'Save the dodo!' Yes, the princess' funny birds. They are rather cute, I think. We have done as you asked, and try to protect them, driving them into the woods when we find them so the heathens can't eat them."

This bit of news almost made tears of joy erupt from Pam's eyes.

Bengta stole a quick glance back to smile at her. "It shall be as you say. We will be ready. You have our gratitude, Pam Miller. You are a very brave woman. We have seen that these swaddle-headed fools greatly underestimate women, and they shall die regretting it." Bengta turned briefly to check on the guard, who seemed to be dozing at his post. When she turned back, Pam was gone.

"Go with God, Pam," Bengta whispered into the trees.

Chapter Thirty-Seven: Hair Today, Gone Tomorrow

"You want to what?" The expression on the bosun's face was a mixture of horror and astonishment. Pam had expected this, and repeated herself in a calm voice.

"I want all you men to shave your beards, hair and eyebrows off." Looking around at the sailors gathered in the early dawn on the main deck, Pam realized that while she didn't quite have a mutiny on her hands, what she had to say was not at all popular with the crew. *Tough*, she thought, feeling firm in her resolve.

"Look, I know it sounds awful, but honest, it grows back! If I'm going to make you guys look like Orientals of any stripe, we have got to lop off those golden locks, like it or not! We are stretching the boundaries of believability to their limits, and this is the best way I can think of to start making you look non-European. Hopefully, the make-up will finish the job, and we can pull this stunt off."

A sea of unhappy, and even a few downright angry faces, glared sullenly at her, the sound of grumbling emanating from their midst. She looked to Gerbald for support, but found that he had made his way to the back of the crowd, where he was attempting to hide behind the mast. Now that he was actually having to go through with the plan he had helped hatch, it seemed his enthusiasm had taken a powder. Pam grimaced, and was about to start to speak when Dore stepped up beside her, brandishing a sturdy pair of scissors and a straight razor as if they were sword and dagger.

"That's enough whining, you silly boys! What are you, cowards?" Dore bawled at them so loudly it made them all take a fearful step back. "The captain has given her orders. Now line up, and get ready for your haircuts! You, there hiding in the back, the celebrated German sergeant, front and center. You shall be first! Make a good example for these men, or you might find my hands become shaky!" she ordered him, making a threatening gesture with the straight razor.

The sailors all parted to make a path for Gerbald, whose usually unflappable face had turned a flushed shade of red. He nodded resignedly, and came forward, head held high, to sit on the chair they had placed on the deck for the day's barbering.

"Here, let me take your hat!" Pam said a little too eagerly.

"I think not. I shall hold it myself," he replied, giving her a wary look while clutching the misshapen monstrosity to his breast.

"It was a good try, Pam," Dore told her as she set to work. Gerbald kept his salt-and pepper-hair close-cropped, and he shaved regularly in the up-time style, so the task didn't take long. When Dore came to the eyebrows, he flinched.

"Must you, Delilah?" he asked in a pleading tone.

Pam patted him comfortingly on the arm. "Yes, Samson. It will make you look incredibly odd, and that's the point. We need to do all we can to convince these renegade French and their lackeys that you are some kind of Asian traders. Look at it this way, Gerbald. You are playing a part in a play, and simply doing what is needed to complete the costume. You'll be a real actor after this! Hollywood could be next!"

That seemed to mollify him, and he closed his eyes tightly as Dore carefully shaved his eyebrows off. When she was all finished, there was no trace of blood, and Gerbald resembled a shiny new dodo egg. Some of the gathered men couldn't resist a chuckle, including the bosun.

Gerbald gave them a fierce glare.

"Ah, *Herr* Bosun." he said darkly, "I'm sure you will want to go next. Here, have my seat."

All good humor evaporated from the bosun's face as he realized there was no escape. He managed a weak kind of smile for the benefit of the other sailors, and took his turn in the barber's chair, looking for all the world as if he faced the gallows. It was Pam's turn, and she started by snipping his chest-length gray beard right to the chin. She thought he might start crying, so she moved around in front of him, and was as gentle as she could be. When she was all done, she paused to admire her work.

"My goodness, Dore, doesn't he look like a younger man now?" she asked her friend with just the slightest eyebrow twitch in her direction.

Dore caught the signal, and nodded her agreement enthusiastically. "Oh, *yes*, Captain Pam! You have cut at least twenty years away along with all that fur. *Herr* Bosun, you are truly a handsome fellow!"

When it came down to it, they weren't kidding. The bosun had a good, strong chin, and he sincerely did look a lot younger without all the gray hair. He pointed that masculine chin forward proudly, and grinned as he rubbed it, his cheeks a brighter red than even their usual cherry flush.

A couple of hours later, the entire crew was lined up for inspection as Pam and Dore admired their work. At first glance, they faced a collection of strangers, a very good start indeed.

"All right, take a break and get something to eat. In half an hour, be back on deck for your makeup, and don't be late," Pam ordered.

She and Dore took their leave, retiring to Pam's cabin. Once the door was closed they both broke into helpless fits of laughter.

"You thought that was fun," Pam managed to gasp, "just wait till we paint them all bronze!"

Chapter Thirty-Eight: Man Down

Pam would never forget the sound of the scream, followed by the sickening thud. Her heart stuttered a beat as an intense chill arced through her body. She tried to get up to run to the door, but her legs felt like rubber. Something terrible had happened, and she thought she recognized the voice behind the terrified shriek. She hoped she was wrong, and felt guilty for it, but if it was the boy . . . Pam felt as if she were trapped in a nightmare, and knew there would be no waking up.

Somehow she managed to make it to her door. She wrenched it open to find the men gathered below, surrounding a still form on the deck. She tried to shout, but could only muster a painful croak. The bosun stood up from the crowd, and looked at her, his face ashen. Summoning his own voice, shaky and pitched too high, he called out the answer to the question on Pam's stricken face.

"It is Pers! He has fallen!"

"Dear God, not Pers!" Pam whispered, and found it hard to breathe. Somehow, she climbed to the bottom of the ladder and made her way toward the men. They opened a space for her, all of them wearing the same pale look of fear as the bosun.

There was Pers, lying on his side, blood leaking from his ear. His right arm lay akimbo, broken. Beside him was a shattered ship's spyglass, its shards gleaming in the sun. To Pam's amazement and relief the teen-age boy was still alive, breathing loudly in ragged gasps. Pam knelt beside him and gently touched his forehead, but Per's eyes were rolled up into his lids, he was, perhaps mercifully, unconscious.

She turned to the bosun. "How?"

"He was climbing the mainmast to spy ahead for us, you know what a monkey he is! His foot became tangled in the unfamiliar rig, and as he was trying to get himself loose the line slipped. He fell . . ."

"How far?"

"From up there, just above the third sheet. A good thirty feet at least! His feet landed on that coil of rope there first, which took some of the impact, but his head hit the deck pretty hard and his arm is broken. Damn my old eyes, I was the one who sent him up there." The bosun was starting to tear up. Pam fought the urge to cry as well, but somehow a part of her that she was coming to think of as "Cool Captain" stayed in control.

"Bosun, go get Dore, now!" she ordered him, partly to give him a chance to pull himself together and not be seen weeping by the crew. Without a word he jumped up and headed for the galley where Dore would be preparing the skin dye they would apply to the sailors after lunch.

Gerbald appeared over Pam's shoulder. With remarkable gentleness he took the boy's pulse and pulled back his eyelids to view his pupils. They were dilated as big as saucers.

"He is concussed. I've seen symptoms like this in men thrown from horses or hit with blunt weapons. His pulse is good, but the blood from the ear is bad."

Pam could barely speak. "Will he live?"

Gerbald took her shoulder in a firm, encouraging grip.

"I won't lie to you, Pam. It's hard to say just now. The head injury may be very serious, or it may not be, only time will tell. I have seen men with injuries like these pass away suddenly without ever waking up, and I have seen some up and about within a few hours. We must think positively for him. There is plenty of hope. He's young, and the rope helped break the fall. I saw the whole thing with my own eyes. There is hope."

Dore arrived, plowing through the crowd like a bulldozer. Although they were trying their best to get out of her way, the men couldn't move fast enough, and the unlucky were bowled over by her fast-moving, low center of gravity and sturdy mass. She knelt beside Pers, clucking and softly praying under her breath as she gave him a thorough check. She was no trained nurse, but years following a soldier had taught her many first aid skills. Her methods were mostly homespun remedies, but effective ones. When she moved Per's broken arm he moaned, and his legs kicked slowly as if to flee the pain.

"He can feel the pain, and move his legs, that is good. His neck isn't broken, Thank the Lord!" she announced. "But, I am most worried for what may be damaged inside his head." She had brought her home-made first-aid kit with her, and began to splint the boy's arm with expert skill, Gerbald assisting her. Pam gently stroked Pers' flaxen hair as they worked, telling her dear, sweet boy that he would be all right, and trying her best to believe it. Sailors arrived with a make-shift stretcher, and many hands lifted Pers onto it, as softly as a cloud.

"Clear that storeroom two doors down from the galley. It will be our sickbay." Dore ordered them. The men jumped to the task without question, knowing that in a situation like this Dore held supreme authority with the captain's blessings. For her part, the captain was beginning to cry, and she let Gerbald steady her as they followed Dore and the stretcher-bearers down into the cool shade belowdecks.

****

An hour later Pam called her senior staff together for a meeting on the castle deck. All the fun and excitement of the last few days had drained out of her, and she was left with a bleak sense of foreboding. Her life had started to feel like she was the star of some wacky adventure show, but the sight of Pers lying bleeding on the deck had brought home to her the real desperation of their situation. The truth was, she wanted to go curl up in her cabin and wait for it all to be over, but these people had come to rely on her. She had accepted their allegiance, and now she had to be strong for them. Physically pulling herself together with a deep breath, and unclenching her fists, Captain Pam Miller turned to those gathered around her, all waiting for her to speak.

"How is Pers now?" Pam asked Dore.

"He is sleeping and his breathing is normal. I think it's best we just leave him be, and let his body do what it must to heal."

"Thank you, Dore. That's good." Pam let out a long whoosh of breath. She was still terribly worried about her adopted teen-age son, but they had done all they could, and there were a host of other problems to face this day, all of them deadly dangerous.

She turned to Gerbald, the bosun, and *Löjtnant* Lundkvist. Despite the gravity of the situation, she did allow herself a small smile at their shaven heads and faces, they looked like three cue balls lined up in a row.

"Gentlemen, we were going to make our attack today. After what happened to Pers, I'm not so sure. We haven't had a very auspicious beginning. Should we wait another day? *Löjtnant* Lundkvist, you are our military leader, please tell me, am I out of my mind? Do you think this plan will work?"

Her earlier confidence had faded away, Pam felt like she was participating in vitally important events that she was highly unqualified for, but somehow she had ended up in charge.

"Well, Captain Pam, I think it's highly unorthodox, reckless, perhaps even quite mad. But, as you said, that's precisely why it might work. In this situation, normal military strategy has no chance. Our only real hope is the element of surprise your trickery gives us. So, yes, I think we should go ahead with your plan. Despite today's misfortune, our men are wound up and ready for battle, we should use that to our advantage. I say we go in today."

The other two nodded their agreement.

"In addition to that," Gerbald added, "I can already feel my hair growing back. If we wait until tomorrow you will have to shave us all over again. I for one prefer to play the part of a hunting wolf, not a sheared sheep." Gerbald's face was a perfect picture of distaste at the thought of having his head shaved again.

They all shared a quiet laugh, humor so often being the best way to deal with stress. Pam was silently thankful to her old friend for his good cheer in the face of danger.

"All right then, let's do it." she told them, feeling her resolve grow again. "Dore, let's get the make-up ready."

The three men all moaned in unison, dreading further torture at the hands of these formidable Valkyries. Despite their concern for Pers, they made the effort to play their parts by cackling and rubbing their hands with threatening glee.

As the men went to round up the crew for their make-up session, Dore motioned for Pam to wait. She produced a folded cloth, one end of which she handed to Pam. Together, they opened it up to reveal a hand-sewn flag.

Pam gasped with delight. It was made from silk, of which there was plentiful variety and supply on their captured Chinese junk. The base was a rich sky-blue and over it was sewn a golden cross, in the Scandinavian style: the flag of Sweden. Behind the cross a black saltire ran from the corners with two gold stars on each band, just like the flag of the United States of Europe. Finally, to Pam's great delight, a gray dodo outlined with black thread occupied the center, complete with a shiny, gold button for an eye.

"Wow!" she exclaimed in English, then switched to German, which Dore was more comfortable using. "Dore! It's fantastic! How did you manage to do this?" Pam asked her grinning friend, who was a-glow with one of her very rare demonstrations of pride.

"I have some talents beyond the galley, you know. That oaf of a husband of mine was always tearing up his clothes in battle, or while running down some poor creature in the woods. Someone had to mend them! If left to his own devices he would go about in nothing but rags. Just look at his hat! I became fairly handy with the needle and thread," she said in modest tones, although it was plain she was highly pleased with her work, which was perfectly executed.

Pam hugged her, the flag squished between them. "Thank you, Dore. It's wonderful! We needed something like this, it will help morale. A fine flag for our new colony. Really, you are a wonder!"

Dore took it gently from Pam to fold it neatly up again.

"Today, when the time is right, we will raise it here from this deck," Pam promised her. "Then, we will fly it over the colony once it has been freed! Dore, you have outdone yourself, you are the best!" Pam was deeply moved at her friend's clever thoughtfulness, and felt some of the fear that had been building in her throughout the day ease its clutches. "Now, let's go paint our men yellow."

Chapter Thirty-Nine: A Ruse By Any Other Name

Pam and Dore stood before their first unhappy subject, Gerbald of course, whose sad, hound-dog face was now a rich, yellowish orange, not quite what they had in mind, but it would have to do.

"It goes well with his hat," Dore remarked, enjoying her beloved husband's discomfort.

Pam studied their victim thoughtfully. "I think a bit more turmeric paste around the ears. He looks more like a *Star Trek* Romulan than an Asian, but I think it will fool the French long enough."

"My people are declaring war on your Federation," Gerbald grumbled. He had, of course, seen every episode of the classic 1960s version of the show, one of his supreme favorites in the Grantville Library's video preservation archives. He made an effort not to flinch as Pam applied the turmeric they had found amongst the galley's many spices, and had worked into a soupy paste with rice flour and water. She prayed there wouldn't be any rain this afternoon.

"Just be glad I decided not to color you blue and glue some antenna to your forehead. There now, it's staining nicely," Pam said, smiling at her handiwork. "I think it will last a few hours, maybe even a few days!"

Gerbald groaned. "Must you do more? Am I not heathen looking enough yet?" he pleaded.

"Ha!" Dore interjected "Why not look like a heathen? You have always lived as one! Those such as you who have turned their back on Our Savior, Jesus Christ, deserve far worse than this bit of discomfort!" Dore's face became the very embodiment of confident self-righteousness. "Pray The Lord doesn't strike you down at the very sight of you."

Tuning out his devout wife's pious haranguing, Gerbald sighed deeply as Pam painted a highly realistic Fu Manchu mustache on his long, hang-dog face with an ash and ink paste. It was too bad something couldn't be done to hide his blue eyes, but Pam just didn't have that kind of technology available. She shuddered at the thought of trying to maintain a set of contact lenses down-time, since she knew that any pair of glasses in her possession would end up lost or irreparably broken within a few days, those would have been her choice. It was her opinion that the Lord hadn't given her much, but she was truly grateful for her excellent vision.

Two hours later, Gerbald was not alone in his oddly colored misery, he stood nearly indistinguishable from the crowd of orange-yellow-skinned Swedes. Pam laughed, thinking they looked like spear carrying extras wandered away from the set of that goofy old movie *The Conqueror,* which had cast an unlikely John Wayne as Genghis Khan.

"Okay, Jason and the Argonauts, it's time to get dressed!" Pam announced, pointing at the pile of cloth and clothing they had assembled from the foreign goods aboard their prize.

The men went to work pulling on colorful silk robes embroidered with glowing scenes of cranes and sunsets. The best of the finery and some sparkling jewelry went on Gerbald, whom they had unanimously elected to be their great and powerful Khan. He was a good choice, with his gift of mimicry and natural penchant for hamming it up, Pam thought he was their best chance to carry this charade off. The Great and Powerful Gerbald was to be carried on a beautifully carved palanquin they had found, no doubt belonging to the wealthy merchant who had once been this ship's master. Its satin pillows would be the perfect place to hide his shotgun pistol, the deadly Snake Charmer. According to Gerbald, when Pam's son, Walt, had given it to him, he had asked him to protect his mother with it. She and her son were not exactly on good terms, and she thought that might be a polite fiction, but she was quite glad to have the thing along. In any case, Pam hoped that its services would not be required, but knew in her heart that they would.

Pam and Dore hurriedly added the finishing touches to the costumes. Soon, they stood facing a mysterious envoy from what Pam declared to be *The Far-Out East*.

"I would not recognize them if I didn't know them so well! Dore exclaimed "Even that foolish husband of mine!" She was well pleased by their handiwork, cleaning her hands on her apron in a gesture of job well done.

"Gosh almighty, don't you fellas look a picture!" Pam gushed, lapsing into West Virginia hillbilly-ese for a moment as a rush of excitement coursed through her. *I can't believe we're really doing this; it really is like something out of some crazy old movie!* Her giddy grin turned serious as she thought of poor, badly injured Pers lying in a coma below, and what might happen to these men, her friends, in the coming hours.

"All right, we all know what to do. Good luck, my friends!" She regarded them with an intense pride for a moment, then shouted, "Battle stations!"

Pam and Dore kept a low profile on the castle deck. They were both wearing white linens draped over their clothes, with their hair tied up under makeshift turbans. They had decided against dying their own faces and hands since they were going to be far enough back from the action and, truth to tell, couldn't bring themselves to do it out of simple vanity, although they would never admit it, even to each other. Pam felt the heavy weight of her pistol at her belt, the weapon she had used so effectively in the capture of her ship. It both terrified and comforted her.

On the foredeck, Sten, one of the older sailors and experienced in firing cannons, waited for the bosun beside the formidable carronade deck gun salvaged from *Redbird*. It was currently hidden beneath a tarp, and Pam hoped that they wouldn't have to unleash its deadly force. If all went well, little blood would be shed this day. The marines and sailors not immediately needed to sail *Second Chance Bird* up to the harbor's wide dock, stood in attendance of the Great Khan Gerbald, who sat in his palanquin regally fanning himself with a bored expression. Every man had a sword, and several had pistols, all carefully concealed within the folds and sashes of their outlandish garb. Around them were placed brightly lacquered boxes and barrels of rice wine, the "gifts" they had prepared to lure out the renegade French officers. Pam shook her head dubiously, and frowned in a moment of doubt. Yes, it was a variation of the old Trojan Horse trick, hopefully these guys had never read Virgil. *Beware orange-skinned weirdos bearing gifts.* Pam knew they were taking a desperate gamble, but no better choices had presented themselves. It was completely nuts, and it had to work.

The bosun brought the junk in slowly, giving everyone on shore a nice long look at it. The captive Swedes paused in their work for a moment, while their captors gaped at the brightly painted boat approaching . The enemy had set up a grass-roofed rest area in the middle of the long,wide dock; several sailors loafing there began making their way out to the T-shaped end the junk was pulling up to, starboard side facing the shore. Pam saw that *Annalise* and *Ide* were still anchored out, well away from easy reach by any would-be escapees.

The bosun, silently guiding the crew manning the sheets with gestures and whistles alone, skillfully piloted *Second Chance Bird* up against the dock with a light groan of timber. He had wisely chosen their position, lateral to the shore. This move gave them a big tactical advantage, their hidden deck gun as well as their Chinese cannons had a clear sweep of the entire dock and shoreline, including the warship tied up stern out to their right some twenty yards inland.

At last they could read the enemy ship's name, *Effrayant*. Tied up just past its bow, the much smaller and badly damaged *Muskijl* floated, mostly hidden behind *Effrayant's* massive bulk. Hopefully, if cannon fire started, her crew was imprisoned aboard that vessel rather than the enemy's. Down the left side of the dock the slave-master's menacingly graceful lateen-rigged crafts were tied up in a line, looking like a scene from out of the *Arabian Nights*. All their guns would have a lovely, clean shot at them. Pam smiled wolfishly, pleased with whatever advantages they could get.

Five French sailors, who Pam noted were armed with what looked like flintlock side arms, had arrived at the end of the dock and were shouting at them. Pam was pretty sure they were ordering them to cast off and leave, and smiled to herself again, because that was not going to happen. Several of the African slave-masters began to venture towards them from the beach, but the sailors waved at them to stay back. The Africans were obviously very curious about the newcomers, and did so reluctantly. It was now completely clear as to who was running this operation.

Not for the first time, Pam felt sickened by the horrors mankind could inflict on one another for a profit. She knew there had been slave-owners in her own ancestry, amongst the Virginians on her mother's side. The very idea disgusted her, but she still tried not to think of these men as monsters. These were terrible times she had been thrust into. She knew that she would likely have to do things on this day and in the days to come that would have utterly appalled the old mild-mannered Pam Miller. There was nothing for it but to accept that, and act as she thought best. She would try to minimize loss of life on all sides, but deep down in her gut she laughed at her own naiveté. *You're a killer now, Pam Miller, and you're gonna do it again! Admit you like it, you love the power!* a sly inner voice teased her. She shook her head sharply to clear her mind, almost dislodging the ridiculous turban nesting there. Exercising another growing trait, a surprisingly strong force of will-power, she made herself concentrate on the events unfolding in front of her. There would be plenty of time for probing self-analysis of the inner demons she had set loose later; right now she was too damn busy leading a hostage rescue mission and slave rebellion, thank you very much! *I'm one of the good guys damn it, just let me work!*

The men of the *Second Chance Bird* remained stoically silent as the sailors noisily gesticulated at them. It was agreed that Gerbald would do *all* the talking and that time hadn't come yet. Completely disregarding the protests of the lowly dock crew, Gerbald waved his hand lazily, signaling the disguised Swedes to throw lines at the surprised sailors, who now found themselves tying the junk up to the dock despite themselves. Now, Gerbald regally motioned that he was ready to disembark. Two of their strongest men climbed over the rail and waited on the dock, ignoring the confused and increasingly nervous sailors gesturing frantically at them to stay onboard their vessel. The palanquin was lowered gently into their care, passed down by two more men stationed on the junk's narrow step-ledge halfway between the rail and the rough-hewn, uneven planks below.

Watching the scene unfold as scheduled, Pam fingered her pistol in its holster, hidden under a sash at her hip, awaiting the worst. She had tried to make Gerbald give the weapon to one of the men going onto the dock, but he had insisted she keep it, saying that she was a better shot than most of them, and it was best she have it just in case things went badly. She prayed fervently that it would not prove necessary. That new, and rather disturbing part of her that had appeared in recent days was darn glad to have it. Pam rolled her eyes to the heavens, thinking that it was bad enough to be going into a conflict without being conflicted about it to boot.

The disguised Swedes had begun passing the various prepared offerings down to the dock. This caused the sailors to cease their frantic fussing and become very interested in the arriving packages accompanying their bizarre visitors. They whispered amongst themselves loudly, pointing at the brightly-colored wooden boxes. They were especially interested in the barrels and casks. Perhaps they had run out of whatever rotgut a French sea-dog prefers?

Once the entire shore party was assembled on the dock, Gerbald harrumphed loudly for attention. He pointed at the sailors, and commanded in a deep, resonant voice, "*Sous capitaine!*" The sailors just stood there staring at him, wondering what they should do, not quite sure that they had just heard the leader of these strange folk say something in French. Gerbald repeated the order forcefully, adding a jabbing, pointing finger. "SOUS CAPITAN!" Then, with a sweep of his arms to their "gifts" he said "*Sous capitaine!*" in a cordial tone, while smiling graciously. Acting as if everyone had understood him perfectly, he clapped his hands twice and folded them regally across his chest, waiting expectantly for the men to get moving.

A brief discussion followed, after which the fellow who was apparently the highest-ranking of the group shook his head in resignation, and sent one of the group to go find their captain. Seeing this, Gerbald let out a loud grunt and his palanquin began following the messenger, the rest of his men gathering up packages and falling in behind. This caused a fresh hail of protests from the sailors, but they didn't reach for their guns, and now found themselves reluctantly escorting the determined strangers toward their own ship.

Pam started to laugh at their consternation, a kind of giddy, hysterical laugh, then forced herself to stop.

"Thank God, it's working so far. Please let us pull this off, please!" she prayed under her breath, joined by Dore doing the same in German. Pam looked over to see the bosun standing by the sailors assigned to man the gun on the foredeck. If that kind of shooting started, Gerbald's group had orders to hit the deck and hope the cannon shot sailed safely over them. The fancifully high decks of the junk looked tall enough, but Pam really didn't want to put that to the test. She hunkered down behind the rail, and used her scope to see what was going on ashore.

Up on the hillside she could see women working in the fields, while their men were busy constructing the town, and the fortress walls growing along the beach. Apparently, the renegades and their allies intended to make this a long term base, and why not? They had free labor, and all the supplies necessary captured along with the colonists. This would be a golden opportunity for an enterprising corsair to create a little kingdom here. During her research for the journey, Pam had read about pirate havens sprouting up on Madagascar and Isle St. Marie off to their west in the century to come. She wondered now if rather than being a plot of the hostile French government, perhaps up-time tales of lucrative piracy in the 1700s had inspired this bunch to start the game on their own a century early.

"Well, here comes a little wrench in that plan, *mes amis*," she hissed, scowling coldly.

The palanquin was now a few yards away from the *Effrayant*'s long, steep gangplank. The procession came to a stop at The Great Khan Gerbald's raised hand. They wanted to be close enough to storm the enemy ship if they must, but still have some room to duck if it came to cannon fire. Gerbald waited with an impatient expression as several officer types emerged from a shady spot on the ship's main deck and began yelling at the men on the dock below. These yelled back, again with much gesturing, recounting the story so far. After a minute, the yelling stopped, and the original welcoming committee stepped quietly back, relieved that their superiors were coming to deal with the problem. Gerbald took this opportunity to announce his intentions to the officers. "*Sous capitaine!*" he bellowed in a voice full of generosity and good cheer, sweeping his arm extravagantly toward the enticing boxes his servants bore.

After another long moment of consternation, one of the officers nudged another, likely sending that one off to fetch the captain. The man chosen for the task had a decidedly unenthusiastic expression on his face, which Pam thought probably spoke volumes about the personality of the captain. After a few minutes, and a bit of angry shouting emanating from the captain's cabin, a grouchy-looking fellow came swaggering out to the rail with an expensive looking sword at his belt, and a many-plumed, fancy hat on his head. He looked annoyed, but couldn't hide some interest as he squinted at the bizarre envoy assembled below. The officer who had stayed at the rail announced with proper respect, if little love, "*Capitaine* Leonce Toulon de Aquitane!" while the sour-faced man paused in what he must think was a heroic pose. Pam thought he bore more than a slight resemblance to your average Hollywood Captain Hook, and fought back a snicker. Sometimes it all just seemed unreal to her, and she had to remember that their lives were very much in danger, even from such an unlikely looking character as this.

"*Capitaine!* Gerbald exclaimed with glee "*Por vous, pour vous! Mon ami! Allez, allez.*"

Pam silently thanked whatever accident of the cosmos had ensured that a citizen of Grantville was in possession of the complete *Hogan's Heroes* on VHS when they got sucked through the Ring of Fire, thus allowing the voice of Corporal Louis LeBeau to emanate from a German soldier in another universe. Gerbald's fractured *Francais* was outrageously funny to hear, plus it was working.

The captain cocked his head at the insistent potentate who had so unexpectedly appeared, but favored him with a thin smile. Giving those gathered a curt nod, he stalked down the gangplank, followed by his chief officers. Pam whistled softly in relief, so far so good. Dore frantically took hold of one of Pam's shaking hands, pushing all the blood out of it with a single squeeze. The men of the *Second Chance Bird* stood perfectly still, a set of bronze statues in the late afternoon sun.

The sneering officers, certainly no real gentlemen, but pirates through and through, stepped primly onto the dock. They sauntered confidently over to Gerbald and his men, all of whom bowed deeply in unison at Gerbald's unspoken cue. This pleased the officers greatly. They smiled and chuckled to themselves, smug in their superiority. Gerbald the Great Khan graciously swept his arms once more toward the gathered gifts. With an openly condescending nod of acceptance to Gerbald, the captain bent down to open one of the boxes. This was filled with some of the treasure they had found aboard the junk, and a gleam of avarice came to the captain's scheming eyes. His officers bent down as well, opening up other boxes to find more of the same. As they became engrossed in the windfall, the odd-looking visitors began to surround them, cutting them off from the nearby sailors.

Chapter Forty: All Hell Breaks Loose

One of those sailors realized what was happening, and pushed the nearest visitor out of the way as he tried to rejoin his captain, one hand on the back of the disguised Swede's neck. His hand slipped off the sweaty skin, and with an expression of astonishment he held up his palm to show that it was stained the same shade of orange-yellow. There was a moment of silence as everyone stared at him.

"The jig is up," Pam sighed to Dore, her heart sinking.

The man with the stained hand began to shout at the top of his lungs, presumably to rouse reinforcements. Pam realized the Swede he had pushed was actually *Löjtnant* Lundkvist. Thanks to their disguises it was hard to tell them apart at this distance. The *löjtnant* calmly produced a very sharp sword from within his loose silk cloak, and stopped the shouts by slicing the man's throat wide open. He pushed the corpse backward to fall into the other sailors who had started to follow him. These now hesitated at the sight of so much blood. Even so, it was too late. An alarm bell began to sound on the *Effrayant*. Within moments, around forty surly-looking marines surged onto the deck from various quarters, all armed to the teeth. The Swedes were now well outnumbered.

"Christ, they have a freaking army with them!" Pam exclaimed. She thought fast, ignoring her terror.

"*Carronade!* Sweep that deck," she screamed at the top of her lungs. Her men were ready for that signal and all of them dropped onto the dock. Gerbald leaped from his palanquin, knocking down the French captain and landing on top of him, it having been decided they wanted to keep that one alive if they could. The other officers, realizing what was happening, flung themselves down onto the dock as well. The bosun swept the cover off the carronade and aimed it directly at the marines heading toward their gangplank. Not a second later its load of anti-personnel shot sprayed death and destruction across the *Effrayant*'s deck. Around half the enemy fell dead or dying to the deck, their moans of agony awful to hear. Still, that left at least twenty alive, who hurried across the gangplank or swung to the dock on ropes.

Knowing it would take time for the bosun to reload, Lundkvist and his Swedish marines, who had mostly been stationed near the front of the procession, leaped back to their feet and opened fire on the advancing soldiers, along with any sailors who had dared to draw their arms. Several of the enemy were mowed down while crossing the gangplank, while others were parted from their ropes as the bullets ripped into them, all falling limply into the water with a great splash.

Pam gasped as a musket ball hit the *löjtnant*, shattering half of his left knee in an explosion of blood, and white bone chips. He started to fall, but was buoyed up by two of his men, who continued to fire their up-time-make pistols into the charging soldiers even as they dragged their commander backward to the line the men were forming around Gerbald. Stunned by the amazing rate of fire, the enemy quailed long enough for the *löjtnant* to reach safety before finding their courage and mounting a charge. The French soldiers swiftly closed with the Swedes, who stood fast, and the dock rang with the clang and crash of close quarters sword fighting.

Meanwhile, Gerbald had pulled out his Snake Charmer, and had the nasty little shotgun pointed directly at the captain's head. The rest of the palanquin bearers had their swords and pistols aimed at the prone officers. The prisoners were quickly relieved of their weapons, while the Swedes tightly bound their hands behind them, and their ankles together; they wouldn't be going anywhere for a while. The captain was pulled roughly to his feet by the Swedes, the double mouths of Gerbald's shotgun-pistol jammed up under his chin. Given the chance by their first line of engaged marines, the circle fell all the way back to the *Second Chance Bird* with their captives. Pam could hear Gerbald loudly taunt the captain over the din of combat.

"Surprise, surprise, surprise!" Gerbald exclaimed cheerfully in his best Gomer Pyle imitation, the skill of which would sadly be lost on the captive captain. "I'll bet you speak English better than I do French, eh, *mon capitaine*? Well, don't you?" Gerbald gave the trembling man a painful prod with the barrels of his weapon. "Speak up, quickly! German will also do," he added in his native tongue.

"I speak English. What do you want, you stinking buffoon?"

Gerbald smiled broadly at the insult, respecting the man's courage for uttering it before slapping him so hard across the face that the man fell to the ground and had to be lifted up again. Now Gerbald brought his face within a few inches of the captain's, and his voice turned as cold as Germany's winter skies.

"Call your dogs off, now! If they don't surrender immediately I will take great pleasure in killing you, you son of a jackal. I may yet. It's best to do as I say. Understand? Now tell them, tell them to lay down their arms if you want to live!"

Pam suppressed a groan, she could hear *The Terminator* loud and clear in that last line. *We really do need to get him an acting job someday. He has truly missed his calling.*

"Yes, yes, I will do it," the captain cried, cowed by Gerbald's menacing presence and the shotgun barrels now resting against his cheek. With panic in his eyes, he began to scream orders. Some of the enemy paused at the sound of his words, but the battle continued. Pam saw to her horror that two Swedish marines had fallen to the dock's knotted planks, undoubtedly beyond help. Even so, their side's weaponry was superior. The dock was littered with enemy corpses, rivers of blood running off the edge to make pretty little crimson waterfalls, expanding into billowing red clouds in the clear waters below. The captain continued to shriek at his troops to stand down, and slowly the combat ground to a halt.

Pam had been so caught up with the action nearby that she had completely forgotten about the colonists. She looked to the shore to see that they had another problem. Two dozen of the African slavers had arrived, each wielding a nasty looking scimitar. They were running down the dock, straight toward *Second Chance Bird*.

"Gerbald, look!"

"Tell them to stop!" he ordered the captured captain. The captain shouted hoarsely at the charging men, but they ignored him, blood-lust flashing in their dark eyes. The Swedes had formed a circular line around *Second Chance Bird*'s lowest point, and were reloading their weapons. The men at the carronade were frantically trying to do the same, but were having some kind of trouble with the weapon. As usual, Murphy's Law was in effect. The bosun's curses echoed loudly around the bay. The enemy marines started to advance again but the terrified wail of their captain made them stop. Never taking their eyes off their foes, the Swedish marines rejoined the rest of their men, and made ready to resume fighting. Obviously against their will, the enemy fighters were backing away toward their own ship, disgusted with their leaders for getting captured so easily, but unwilling to sacrifice them for a certain victory, either. They stepped silently aside as the slavers trampled past them, whooping an eerie war cry.

Dore grabbed Pam and shook her. "Your gun! Shoot them, Pam!" she implored her friend. Pam nodded, pulling the heavy pistol from its holster as quickly as she could. It tangled on her sash for an agonizing moment, but she managed to free it. Below her, Gerbald kicked the captain's knees out from under him, sending him crashing face-first to the dock along with his officers and out of the way. He stepped over the man into the front of the line and unleashed the Snake Charmer with one hand while pulling his *katzbalger* short sword out of its scabbard with the other. The two leading slavers fell beneath the shotgun pistol's wrath and the third had his scimitar knocked out of his ruined hand before receiving the *katzbalger* in his gut. The Swedes joined in the fray, pistols firing and swords flashing.

Pam decided to shoot at men farther down the dock so as not to hit any of her own by accident. She was too excited, and her first shot went wild. She felt Dore grasp her shoulders from behind to help steady her, just as she had done during the fight for the junk. Pam gripped the pistol in both hands, firm, but not too tightly, just as her uncles had taught her, and took a deep breath. She took aim at the chest of a lumbering brute holding a scimitar in each hand as he shouted bloody murder in his incomprehensible tongue while running headlong at her friends. Breathing out, she pulled the trigger. There was a red explosion in the center of the brute's chest, and he went down like a sack of rocks. The man behind him tripped and fell onto his back, as he started to get up, he received Pam's next bullet through his left eye; it continued right out the back of his head as brains spurted out like watermelon innards at target practice.

Pam took a moment to get her bearings. There were no clear shots now that the enemy and her men were locked in combat. Gerbald was dancing through the slavers with his short sword, thrust-and-slice-and-step-and-kill. Pam was astounded once more by the old soldier's almost dainty grace in combat. Having cut himself clear of the fray for a moment, he calmly reloaded the Snake Charmer, looking all the world as if he were taking a breather from nothing more than a healthy morning walk. Just as he snapped the weapon closed, a wild-eyed slaver ran straight at him, scimitar held in both hands over his head, ready to chop Gerbald in two. Gerbald destroyed his assailant's face with one barrel, gracefully stepping aside as the dying man's momentum carried him past, off the dock and into the water. Pam couldn't help but laugh aloud as he nonchalantly wiped the man's sprayed blood from his face with a billowing silk sleeve, smearing the makeup on his forehead. She stopped laughing as she took aim at another enraged slaver headed directly for Gerbald. She shot him squarely in his side above the ribs, puncturing a lung. Gerbald frowned at her, raising the remaining barrel of his shotgun to as if to say *"I had him!"*

The enemy marines had been watching all this, and couldn't stand aside any longer. Despite their captain's imploring shouts to stand down, five of them decided to enter the fray, and began running down the dock toward the action. Perhaps they thought the invaders were distracted by the slaver attack enough that they could win their captain back. Perhaps they had simply decided they didn't care if their leader lived or died after all, and wanted to make sure their lucrative little kingdom continued with or without him. These were desperate men, men who probably couldn't, or didn't intend to, return to their homeland anyway.

Pam knew she only had two shots left before she would need to reload. She drew a bead on the first in line, but he saw her, and tried to dodge. Her bullet hit him in his sword arm and he fell down, gasping in pain. Next in line was a rangy-looking fellow with a really bad mustache. He tried to duck but she was ready for that, and aimed low, catching him in the center of his forehead, an instant death.

"I'm out!" she cried, feeling both horror and elation at her kills. *Four out of six, not too bad! That brings the count of men dead by my hand to eight, yo-ho-ho.*

Gerbald took down the next fellow with the Snake Charmer's second barrel. The remaining two decided that the odds were against them, and came to a skidding halt as Gerbald advanced with his *katzbalger*, its steel stained scarlet. One of them turned, and fled back to his ranks, while the other simply dove into he water, taking his chances with the sea rather than face the deadly German.

Pam reloaded her pistol, taking deep breaths to stay calm. By the time she was ready for action again the attack had drawn to a close. A Swedish sailor lay gasping, horribly wounded, and all the slavers were dead or dying. *Not bad, really*, she thought to herself with the cold, cold part of her mind that was Captain Pam doing her bloody work. *We got more of them than they got of us.*

She turned to Dore. "It's time!" she said. "They will have heard all the gunfire by now so if they haven't started their revolution already, they should do it now!"

They nodded to each other and in unison let out a ringing shout as they raised Dore's colonial flag.

"SAVE THE DODO!"

Dore gave the ship's gong a powerful thump with its heavy mallet for good measure, when its deep metal tone faded they could hear shouts coming from the town, and the fields above. More shouts of "Save the dodo!" echoed across the harbor as the colonists and her fighting men took up the battle cry. Up on the fortress walls Pam saw two Swedish farmers throw a slaver off the gangway running along its top to fall to his death. One by one, men were shedding their chains and taking up the scimitars of the dying slavers, who they now outnumbered.

Gerbald walked over to where the captain still lay on his stomach, he and his fellow officers bound and placed in a row like railroad ties. Gerbald turned him over with his boot as he reloaded his shotgun pistol again. The Swedes all reloaded their pistols as they reformed their defensive circle. Seeing what the orange-painted invaders were capable of, the remaining enemy marines and sailors decided to lay down their arms, then shuffle back with their hands raised, all the while keeping a wary eye on the fearsome deck gun of the *Second Chance Bird*.

Captain Leonce Toulon de Aquitane began to beg for his life.

"Please, know that my well-being has a rich value in gold; there will be rewards for my safety!" the would-be pirate king pleaded, quivering with fear.

Gerbald gave him a sharkish grin.

"Your riches are meaningless to us! As long as you continue to do as we say, you will continue to live! Now, send one sailor each into the warships. I want Swedish prisoners freed and sent out first, unbound! Then, all the rest of your crew must exit the ships, unarmed, with their hands on their heads. If they don't, I will take great pleasure in killing you. I may yet. Understand? Now tell them!" Gerbald lifted the man roughly to his feet. The captain gave the orders as instructed, speaking in a high, nervous pitch. Two of his men obeyed, jogging up the gangplanks to disappear into the *Muskijl* and *Effrayant*'s lower decks.

Dore turned to Pam. "Now that the fighting has stopped may I go down onto the dock to help the injured?"

Pam allowed herself a smile. "Of course, Dore. Please see to the *löjtnant* first, his leg is in bad shape." They gripped each other's hands quickly, then Dore ran for her first aid kit.

Pam turned to see a line of dirty, gaunt, but smiling, men come down the gangplank from the *Muskijl*. The freed Swedes carried weapons taken from their former captors who followed behind, heads bowed and afraid. More Swedes emerged from the *Effrayant,* shielding their eyes from the bright sun, but their faces were filled with joy. The captured enemy were directed to lie down in a line to be bound hand and foot beside their officers.

The half-starved, but elated, Swedes gathered near the *Second Chance Bird*. At first they stood a little way off, blinking and muttering amongst themselves, wondering at the identity of their strange looking rescuers until Pam's crew realized how odd they must appear, and began to laugh and joke in Swedish.

"Do you not know us? We are your brother Swedes! We have disguised ourselves as heathen Easterners to fool this trash!" The freed crewmen started laughing too, and a few happy minutes of embracing and happy back slapping followed.

The *löjtnant*, who had come to his senses despite the terrible injury to his leg, ordered his men to help him stand, despite Dore's insistence that he stay laying down lest the bandages come loose. For once, her orders were ignored. The man was too proud perhaps for his own good, but Pam understood his feelings. She caught Dore's eye, and subtly motioned for her to let him do as he wished. The formidable German scowled deeply, but kept still.

Lundkvist saluted *Kapten* Lagerhjelm of the *Muskijl,* a tired-looking fellow with a scruffy blond beard, who barely resembled the proud officer Pam remembered meeting in Bremerhaven so long ago and far away. Lundkvist quickly told him a very brief version of their adventures, and introduced him to the leader of their rescue, Captain Pam Miller.

Lagerhjelm looked up to Pam where she stood on the junk's castle deck and saluted her.

"Madame Captain, you have my deepest thanks. Please consider my men yours to command until this crisis is resolved. I'm afraid we are all half-starved and too weak to do you much good, but we shall try."

Pam saluted him back. "Thank you, *Kapten* Lagerhjelm! It is so very good to see you all safe!" Pam felt a sense of growing elation. They had lost good men, but they were winning the day, their sacrifices would not be in vain.

The *löjtnant* turned to Gerbald.

"*Herr* Gerbald, I am giving you a field command in the Royal Swedish Marines as a sergeant, the rank you once held when you fought for our king in the Germanies. Since I am out of action, the men are yours."

The orange-skinned Swedes all slapped their well-loved German comrade heartily on the back. Gerbald gave Pam a hugely pleased grin. Pam couldn't stop herself from emitting a rather un-captain-like squeal of glee. *Yes, we are winning, but it's not over yet you fool. Save it for later!* she chided herself.

With the dock in order, *Sergeant* Gerbald to began the next part of their plan. He assigned *Kapten* Lagerhjelm and six of his newly freed Swedish sailors to guard the captured officers and sailors, holding the enemy's own pistols and muskets to their heads. The enemy were not going to offer any resistance; they had seen the power of the *Second Chance Bird*'s men and guns, and feared for their lives. Gerbald led his shipmates, and those freed men who were strong enough to fight, through the carnage littering the dock, and on to the shore.

Upon reaching the open gate of the unfinished fortress, they split into two groups, one entering the town, the other going around the walls and up the slope toward the hillside fields. They were angry men who moved like tigers on the hunt, men on their way to undo terrible wrongs, men with blood on their minds. Pam swelled with pride to see them, her fears for their safety evaporating in the glory of the moment.

Pam turned to Lagerhjelm. "Are all your men all accounted for?"

"Yes, but a few who are quite ill still remain on the *Muskijl*, they need the attention of a physician. There is one we know is being kept out on the *Ide* who you—" Lagerhjelm was interrupted by an imploring call in English from near his feet.

A man who looked to be in his late fifties, wearing neither the garb of a sailor or an officer, turned a pale, mustachioed face up to her.

"*Mademoiselle Capitaine, please, May I have a word!* It is most important that you hear me!"

Pam looked down at the man like a circling raptor would mark a lone duckling peeping on a pond.

"Yes, sir, you may. I'm listenin'." she replied in a danger-filled, but cordial, drawl, her West Virginia Hillbilly accent in full twang as sometimes happened when she was keyed up.

"Allow me to introduce myself. I am Doctor Arnaud Henri Durand of Normandy. I am a physician, lately finding myself trapped in the service of these wayward men. Please, I can help your wounded, I swear to you on the holy cross! Allow me to assist; lives can be saved."

The man motioned toward Lundkvist with his chin. The *löjtnant* was lying on his back again, his face a mask of pain as Dore wiped his brow and worried over him.

"Your fine young officer there. His injury is most terrible, he may lose his leg today. Please, if you don't let me apply my skills, he will certainly lose his life before the sun sets! Let me help him!"

Pam gave the man a long, considering look. Sincere-looking, sad brown eyes met hers with a steady gaze, imploring her to see reason. She believed him.

"All right then. If you make yourself useful, *Doctor*, you will live. Try anything funny, though, and I'll shoot yer head clean off myself and make you number nine."

Pam lifted her pistol in front of her chest for dramatic effect. She switched back to Swedish.

"You men, go ahead and untie this doctor here, and let him do his work, but keep a close eye on him."

The *Muskijl*'s sailors cut the man loose, and helped him to his feet. Once free, the French physician bowed deeply.

"Thank you, *Mademoiselle Capitaine*. It is best we don't try to move the gentleman yet, please allow me to get my surgeon's tools from the *Effrayant*."

Pam sent him on his way with two guards. Durand fell politely into line in front of the watchful Swedes, walking as quickly as he could without running, which might alarm his escort.

Kapten Lagerhjelm turned to Pam again.

"I can vouch for that man, Captain. He was captured by these creatures and forced into duty. He tried to help us when he could, whenever this son of a whore allowed it, or behind his thrice-damned back."

The *kapten* gave the bound captain a sharp kick in the side for emphasis, making him howl. Pam didn't stop him. She figured the deposed tyrant deserved whatever he got, and concepts like the Geneva Convention were a long stretch of space-time away from the Indian Ocean of the seventeenth century.

"We begged them to let the doctor help when they found—" He was about to say more when their attention was drawn away to a commotion on the shore.

Pam and her borrowed crew had been watching what they could of the land battle, occasionally able to see Swedes and the cruel African slave-masters locked in combat. Pam prayed fervently that none of her people would lose their lives, but knew that some would. The battles they had been through today were too big, the foes too numerous. The slavers fought fiercely, with the tenacity of cornered animals struggling for their very lives. To Pam's great joy, shouts of triumph in Swedish could be heard, the whoops and hollers of free people released from months of painful captivity. A band of some thirty of the slavers, the fight taken out of them, were fleeing down the muddy track to the dock, calling to each other in voices filled with fear. They were in a panic, running pell-mell as they headed for their swift, lateen-sailed craft.

The bosun called out to her. "Captain Pam, the carronade is ready for firing!"

She turned to see him and his gun crew waiting for her command. Pam looked back at the would-be escapees hastily untying lines and readying their sails. They were utterly terrified, looking back over their shoulders at their pursuers with wide, frightened eyes. She hesitated. Should she just let them go, let them carry word back that Mauritius was free, and the Swedish colonists were strong? So much blood had been shed already today, should she be merciful to these men despite what they had done? Yes, she had learned to kill, but she still didn't think of herself as a killer; she was a soldier in war-time now, doing what she must.

A large group of Swedes were in pursuit, a mix of sailors and colonists berserk from wreaking their bloody revenge on their former tormentors and ready for more. Their bellowing shouts rang with hatred, the very sound of them sent a cold shiver up Pam's spine. *This is what happens when you push these calm, congenial folk of the North too far. The giants have awakened, and they are full of wrath.*

Following the men came a group of women, wailing and cursing as they carried their wounded on makeshift stretchers, lifting the injured to the heavens as if to say "*See? This is what has been done to us! We must be avenged!*" Pam saw one young woman born aloft by her kinfolk, splattered in her own blood from head to toe. Pam raised her binoculars for a closer look. It was Bengta! The woman was suffering from awful wounds, her face pale and distorted by agony, but her eyes were bright, burning with the flames of vengeance. Pam was aghast. The harm inflicted on Bengta was enough for her to make up her mind. This was war, and war is hell.

"You men down there, everybody get down! *Bosun*!" Pam's voice cut through the smoky afternoon air with a cold steel edge. "Target those boats trying to get away and *fire at will*!"

The bosun hadn't waited for her order to target the fleeing Africans; they were already locked on. His shouted reply of "Yes, ma'am!" was drowned out by the nearly immediate blast of the deck gun, its lethal projectiles mowing down the would-be escapees by the dozen. Before the smoke could even clear they were reloading.

Pam called down to the gun crew waiting below decks with the Chinese cannons. "Gun crew! Fire Number One and sink that ship that's getting away." She heard only half of a "Yes, ma'am!" as a *boom* sounded, heralding the exit of a heavy Chinese cannon ball. The projectile plowed through the bow of the light craft in a shower of splinters. "Number two! *Fire*!" Pam bawled. Shortly, another blast tore into the enemy ships still lined up along the dock, breaking apart the boats as if they were cheap toys. Lost *Redbird*'s fearsome carronade sounded again, shredding the slavers into a gory mess of bone and blood. The boats were sinking beneath the harbor's calm waters in a widening stain of blood and grease.

The Swedes on shore had stopped to watch the destruction happen, cheering the *Second Chance Bird*'s gunners on from a safe distance. Dore climbed back up to rejoin Pam, she looked at the scene dispassionately, sweat running down her strong, proud face.

"My God, we tore them all to shreds! I've never seen anything like it," Pam said in a small voice, stunned by the deadly force she had directed this day.

"I have." Dore's voice carried the chill as the winter wind. "Better like that than with the swords, Pam. Better those *dogs* die quickly than our people be hurt or killed in more fighting. Those savages made their choice, and now they have paid for it."

Pam nodded quietly in agreement. She winced at the awful carnage, but also felt a burning pride. *Fear us! Fear the people of the dodo!* The tribalistic epithet that had come to her mind made her smile; she might just use it some time. The truth was, the fury of the Norsemen was running in her, too. She had caught it from them, and found she liked its burning taste. She rejoiced to see their enemy obliterated, humiliated, defeated. *Blown to smithereens!* she thought with a cold satisfaction. Whatever demons these days of blood and conquest had loosed in her, she would have to wrestle with later. Today she was a fighting captain; today she was victorious in war.

Garrett W. Vance

Chapter Forty-One: Victory Lap

"Let's go ashore. Bosun, you are with me. Gun crews, stay on watch. Come, Dore, let's go ashore." Giving orders was coming naturally now to Captain Pam, and while it still made her a bit uneasy at times, she played the role she had been given as properly as she could.

Pam had shed her white robes, and straightened her royal blue, gold embroidered Chinese jacket, the Swedish colors which she wore with pride. They had adopted her, and she had accepted their kinship. She was one of them now. She pushed wisps of loose hair back behind her ears, and stood up straight. Dore grinned at her, carrying the colonial flag she had made fastened to eight-feet of bamboo pole. Pam slapped her friend on the back just the way the men always did to each other, and led her and the bosun down onto the dock.

The doctor had returned, and seemed satisfied with his work on the *löjtnant*, who was visibly more at ease, his leg smothered in bandages.

"How is he, Doctor Durand?" Pam asked him politely, having decided the man was indeed who, and what, he said he was.

The doctor's warm, brown eyes were full of relief that she had accepted him. "I may have saved his leg; we will know better tomorrow. Even so, he will never run again, and will need to use a cane to walk. I'm afraid his days as a fighting soldier are over."

"Perhaps. I have a job in mind for him where that won't pose too much of a problem. As is my right as victor, I'm claiming the *Effrayant* for the crown of Sweden for use in guarding this colony. She will need a captain." She looked down at the *löjtnant*, whose hazel eyes brightened at her words.

"She is yours to command if you will have her, my friend," Pam told him, her voice trembling with pride just to be a friend of this brave man before her, a man who would have gladly sacrificed his life for their cause, and almost had.

Lundkvist looked up and gave her an exhausted, but proud smile. "It will be my honor. Thank you, Captain Pam. Your deeds today will never be forgotten. You truly are our hero."

Lundkvist's praise made Pam's eyes mist up, but she fought back the joyful tears, and put a stern face on. There was another person she needed to speak to before any celebrating could take place. She turned to the doctor again.

"Come with me. There is a woman on shore who needs you right away. Once you do what you can for those most badly injured, I want you to see to a young boy on my ship. He fell from the rigging yesterday, and I fear for him. He is dear to me, and if you make him well you can consider me your new best friend."

The doctor bowed to her with courtly grace, and fell in behind her.

They walked past the rows of captives. Pam came to a stop over the corrupt French captain, the architect of all their suffering. His reckoning day was near. He was the helpless captive now, a tyrant deposed. He eyed her uncomfortably from his trussed-up position, cold, frightened sweat beading on his face.

"Hey, fuck-head!" Her voice seared the air with a heat she hadn't known was within her, a voice that could burn an evil man like this with its very sound. His eyes were bleary, swimming with dread. Pam found she relished his fear, it was delicious. She pressed the pointy tip of the odd, patent leather Chinese shoe she wore into the captain's long nose, making him grimace.

"I'm going to see to it that you pay for what you have done here, do you hear me? *Pay*! Your worthless, scumbag life now depends on how many ways you find to make yourself useful to me. We'll start with a full account of just *who* you and those slave-master fuckers doing your dirty work are, or, in their case, *were*. If you don't tell me everything I want to know, I'll throw you to those people you have been torturing for all these months, and laugh while they tear your arms and legs off. I'll make sure they do it nice and slow, too. So, *capitaine*, we'll talk later, at my convenience. Asshole."

The thoroughly humiliated villain didn't even try to speak, just nodded his assent as best he could with Pam's shoe smashing his considerable nose. Pam sneered at him, then walked on, her steel-gray eyes glittering with wrath and exultation, chin held high, hardly believing these things were happening, and that it was she herself who was making them happen. *Who are you and whatever did you do with meek and mild birdwatcher Pam Miller of Grantville, West Virginia?* a voice in her head mused. *Oh, she's still around, but right now it's a bad-ass warrior-queen of the Norsemen we need, so shush up, it's time for the victory lap!*

They stepped onto the shore before the rescued Swedish colonists. Pam suddenly grew shy and stopped. Pam's fighting men, their orange skin smeared with blood, grinned at her like fools. She winced as she counted them, yes, some were missing. There would be time for mourning later. Her heart swelled as they came, led by Gerbald, to stand beside her.

"Who is she, who is she?" the colonists whispered to each other.

Then, Pam saw Bengta among the crowd, watching from her stretcher, sea-green eyes full of triumph despite great pain. Pam ran to her, towing the doctor behind her. She gently took the young woman's hand while he went to work.

"Oh, Bengta, I am so sorry. What have they done to you? It's all my fault!"

Bengta smiled at her, gripping Pam's hand back with what was left of her strength. Pam tried not to look at the woman's awful wounds, the doctor was already muttering what sounded like prayers and curses under his breath as he did what he could.

"No, Pam, *you* have *saved* us. If you hadn't come who knows how long we would have suffered? You gave us hope, made us brave."

The women attending the grievously wounded young woman turned their tear-streaked faces up to Pam. "Please, who are you?" they asked.

"Why, don't you recognize her?" Despite the pain of the effort, Bengta spoke in a loud voice so all could hear, "She is our own Pam Miller, the Bird Lady of Grantville who led our expedition from the start! She has revealed to us that she has the heart of an eagle, the courage of a lion! She is our hero, the liberator of all our people here on this lonely isle so far around the world from old Sweden, this beautiful paradise which we will make our home!"

Pam saw looks of recognition and adulation forming on their haggard faces. She found her voice and spoke up.

"Thank you my friend, but it is *you* who are the true hero. It was brave Bengta here who led her people to fight for their freedom! All hail Bengta!" she cheered at the top of her lungs, so that it rang all around the harbor. The crowd took up her cry and then added "All hail Pam Miller! All hail the Bird Lady!" to the chant.

All of this made Pam blush, and smile broadly; a rakish, fearless kind of smile, one that she was quite sure she had never felt on her face before. She found it quite to her liking though, and wore it as she was enfolded into the joyous embrace of her people.

Chapter Forty-Two: There's Got To Be A Morning After

Bengta died during the night. Doctor Durand had done all he could, but she had lost too much blood. Pam sat beside her to the end. She passed quietly, with a soft smile on her lovely face. Pam wept, held by Dore as Gerbald and the bosun stood behind her while Durand gently closed Bengta's pretty sea-green eyes. A tear rolled down the French doctor's tired face. He was visibly devastated to have lost one so young and brave. Pam decided that she would indeed be his new best friend even if he couldn't help Pers.

The butcher's bill had been high. Of the colonists, they had lost twenty-three total. Twelve had succumbed to the long months of captivity under cruel conditions. The rest had been killed fighting for their freedom, eight men and three women, including Bengta. The details of Bengta's torture when the slavers discovered she had started the revolt made Pam draw blood from her palms as her nails bit into her clenched fist. By the time the colony's men could rush to her aid it was too late. In their rage, they had literally torn Bengta's torturers apart limb from limb, confirming Pam's earlier suggestion that they were quite capable of doing that. She looked forward to mentioning it to the deposed captain in their next meeting. Pam decided that despite her initial misgivings, being blown up had been too good for the ones who had tried to escape.

They were heartless men who sold their own brothers and cousins into slavery back in Africa, chosen by the renegades for duty here because of their ruthless cruelty. Pam vowed vengeance on their evil tribe one day.

Of the crew of the *Muskijl,* only fourteen had survived. Pam had lost five of the *Second Chance Bird*'s men, two sailors and three marines. Their names and faces paraded through her mind, her friends and protectors, smiling and full of life. That's how she wanted to remember them. She would never, ever forget their sacrifice for her cause. *Löjtnant* Lundkvist had lost his leg after all, no fault of the doctor, who truly was a fine physician for his time. The proud, young captain of the enemy warship he had helped capture, would have to walk on a pegleg for the rest of his life. And, finally, there was Pers, who she had brought into her heart as a true son, laying feverish and comatose, somewhere between life and death. Doctor Durand told her there was hope, but she hardly allowed herself to feel it.

Pam stood high on the town's wall, looking out across the harbor. Beside her, Dore's flag flapped in the early dawn breeze, proof of their triumph. She had asked for a little time alone. She needed to stop and absorb all they had gone through. The torches and lanterns of the fleet of ships they had accumulated glowed warmly in the slowly brightening, purple light, casting long, orange reflections across the bay's clear waters. The *Annalise* and *Ide* had been brought into the dock, and the colonists had slept there, back in the relative comfort of their bunks after months sleeping on the ground. The prisoners now occupied the former slave quarters, under guard by grim-faced colonists. There were a few exceptions, five parolees released into Durand's command, men who had been shanghaied into service just as he had. Pam trusted the man and his judgment, but a couple of strong Swedes kept a close eye on them anyway.

Second Chance Bird

As for *Capitaine* Leonce Toulon de Aquitane, that heartless bastard was now in solitary confinement, locked in an outhouse. Pam had told her men to "Put this shit somewhere small and dark," and they had taken her literally. Actually, she thought it was too good for him. She intended to let him spend the entire day there without food and water, enjoying the stench. They would interrogate him the following night, by then he ought to be plenty cooperative.

Pam shook her head in disbelief. How had she come to think such black thoughts as these? How had she come to be a calm, cool, killer of men? Hard times made one harder, if you lived through them. They had been lucky, so lucky to have pulled their crazy operation off without even more loss of life and limb. Pam wasn't much of a Methodist anymore, but she did say a brief prayer of thanks to a God that usually seemed distant and uncaring. All told, she thought maybe He had been on their side for once. She silently prayed He would take their fallen into His arms up in Heaven. They had more than earned their places in Paradise. The thought comforted her despite her modern doubts. She would take all the solace she could get.

The sun came up over the ocean as if in answer to her prayer, a golden beauty of a dawn, complete with radiant beams and towering lavender clouds. Pam couldn't help but smile. She had lost much, but she had won more. This island was *hers*, the dodo would be saved, and maybe there was even hope for a rangy old crow like Pam Miller. Maybe she could make a new and better life for herself now that she had been through all this. *Redemption, la, hallelujah!* She clambered down the bamboo ladder to the trampled path below, and set about looking for her friends.

Walking out onto the dock she was greeted by the bosun, who was bustling his way toward the shore. It was plain to see he hadn't slept much, but his eyes were bright and lively anyway. "Captain Pam! Good morning! I was just coming to fetch you!"

"Good morning! What's happening?"

"You have to come see for yourself, please, follow me!" The bosun, quite uncharacteristically, took Pam by the hand, and practically dragged her behind him down the dock. Pam had to laugh aloud at such behavior from her usually stolid, and somewhat shy around the ladies, friend.

"What is it? What do you want to show me?" she asked, falling into a near jog to keep up with him.

He turned to her with glee on his red-cheeked face.

"It's a miracle, that's what it is!" and he would say no more. They passed by *Second Chance Bird* to board the *Effrayant*. One of her still slightly orange-skinned marines, broad-shouldered Ulf, stood guard. His face was split in a silly grin to match the bosun's. Just what on Earth was going on?

Pam was led onto the deck and told to stand looking out at the water. She heard the bosun whisper something, then there were footsteps. She turned around to see *Kapten* Lagerhjelm and beside him stood . . .

Pam's jaw dropped. She was seeing a ghost. It couldn't be! There, his long, red-and-silver hair a-glow in the morning sunlight like a halo, stood Torbjörn, lost captain of the *Redbird*. Not a ghost, but an angel! He was a lot thinner, and there was a bit more silver in his hair than before, but he was still tall, and a warm smile was spreading across his undeniably handsome face, his icy blue eyes shining. Incredibly, against all hope, he was alive. *Alive!* Pam's heart skipped like a stone across a pond, her palms grew sweaty, and her knees wobbled.

Torbjörn chuckled, that warm, rumbling sound Pam had thought she would never hear again. "Pam! It is so lovely to see you!"

She just stared at him, her mind spinning around on a merry-go-round, unable to find its way off.

He nodded, understanding her startled surprise. "My apologies, Pam. I'm sure it's something of a shock, and you must think me a ghost! I am so sorry for that. The fates cast me off to the north while you went south. I suppose I must call you *Captain* Pam now. You have become quite the hero! I always thought there was more to you than meets the eye! It seems I shall have to find a new job. Perhaps you could use an able first mate?" He gazed at Pam with great admiration on his face, and something more. Something wonderful.

Pam lunged forward, launching herself into an embrace that would have knocked him over if he hadn't been such a large man. She hugged him tightly, unable to form words yet. He hesitated in a gentlemanly way for a moment, then hugged her back with equal strength and affection.

"I am so glad to see you, Pam," he told her softly. "I was so afraid that it was *you* who might have left this world. I thought about you every day, and prayed that—" Torbjörn was unable to finish his sentence because Pam was now kissing him on the lips with a fierce urgency she hadn't felt since she was seventeen. Torbjörn's eyes widened, but the good captain had the presence of mind to kiss her back, and there was no mistaking he was glad to be doing so.

Chapter Forty-Three: A Kiss And Some Coffee

Captured French warship Effrayant, site of up-time Poste de Flacq, Mauritius

The kiss ended delicately, its initial passion consumed and resolved into a lingering sweetness as their lips reluctantly broke contact. Pam blinked at Torbjörn's smiling eyes. She was trembling, excited, ecstatic, and half-frightened out of her wits. *Did I do it right? It's been so long!* Her mind raced, feeling an echo of youthful panic. He held her a moment longer to give her a reassuring squeeze, an unspoken *"Yes, that was good. I wanted it, too."* Pam started a garbled apology for being so forward, but Torbjörn gently shushed her.

"Don't fret, lovely Pam, don't question this moment. We have much to talk about, and there will be time. For now I know we all have a great deal of work to do, much of it sad. Go lead your people, they need you. I will be here with the bosun when you are ready for me." He looked at her, checking to see if she was really going to be all right.

"That reminds me, I have something of yours!" Pam said, suddenly remembering what she carried with her. She gently disengaged from their embrace and reached into her pocket to pull out the up-time made canary-yellow plastic whistle that belonged to Torbjörn, which she had found washed up on the shore after the wreck of the *Redbird*. She handed it to him, and he laughed, delighted and surprised.

"I never thought I would see that again!" he exclaimed.

"I never thought I'd see *you* again," Pam told him, a relieved look on her face.

"Tell you what, you keep it for me, and if you ever should need me, just give a little whistle." He put it back in her hands and gently closed her fingers around it.

"You'll be hearing from me soon," she said, and they laughed.

Pam favored him with a very big smile, a stunner she saved only for special occasions. He returned it in kind.

"I shall be counting the minutes."

The tall Swedish captain of lost *Redbird*, recently resurrected from the roll-call of the dead, bowed, and strode over to the far side of the warship to join the bosun, who, once the kissing had started, had found some critical flaw in the warship's rigging that needed his utmost attention.

Pam grinned as she watched them for a moment, then walked back down the gangplank to the dock, feeling lighter than air. She would have skipped if she hadn't been afraid it would lead to a nasty fall. There were still bloodstains on the rough planks, and she was reminded of the mayhem they had created just the day before. It already seemed as if a century had passed, as if it had all happened to someone else a long time ago, or maybe she had just read it in a book. It wasn't the first time that Pam had felt this way, and she doubted it would be the last. Was that really Pamela Grace Miller, failed housewife, obsessive bird-watcher, and dorky scientist, now out sailing around the Indian Ocean, kissing Swedish sea captains, ordering cannons fired, and sending men (and women, alas!) to their deaths?

She closed her eyes tightly and opened them again. Apparently it was, as she stared at the convincing bulk of the formerly French warship,

Effrayant looming beside her, a powerful enemy ship that she had, she felt quite cleverly, engineered the capture of. If not for her madcap plans there would have been a much greater loss of life, and that comforted her somewhat. Still, too many friends had died. Another part of it was just dumb luck, she had since learned that the *Effrayant* had not been carrying a full complement of soldiers, and she intended to find out why.

She took a long look at the vessel, admiring its majestic size, and predatory grace. It was a killing machine, one of the deadliest this century had. It was by no means the largest type of warship extant in the day, but the light frigate was well-armed, fast, and deadly, more than a match for merchants, and able to give the average enemy warship a good drubbing. Pam had since learned that the name *Effrayant* meant "fearsome," and thought that it certainly did fit the beast. It had downed pretty *Redbird* without breaking a sweat, and had beat poor *Muskijl* nearly to a pulp. She thought the appellation fearsome probably applied to her now, too. It fit her well, in fact.

"All in a bloody day's work for Captain Pam, she-devil of the southern seas," she mumbled, shaking her head in wonder at what strange fortunes had brought her to be at the center of events such as these.

"Time travel," she muttered darkly. "Not recommended. Check your expectations at the portal, and hang on to your sanity."

Pam stalked off down the dock toward the flag ship of her growing fleet, the gaily painted Chinese junk they called *Second Chance Bird*, in search of that sure-fire slice of sanity only a cup of coffee and a good breakfast could provide.

The decks of her ship were quiet, the men still sleeping off their hurts, both physical and mental. Still, there were signs of activity. As could be expected, she found Dore in her galley. Her tireless friend was busy pulling out all the stops as she prepared a particularly mighty breakfast of the kind that could satisfy a hungry band of heroes who had more than earned that pleasure.

She smiled as Pam came in, and silently handed her a cup of coffee. Pam nodded her thanks, and sat down in an out of the way corner on an ornately carved Chinese kitchen stool, painted in crimson lacquer.

Pam took a few sips of the hot, bitter brew, pleased that she herself had harvested the wild, purple-and-yellow beans from the slopes of that mountain in the island's south. It was good coffee, with a rich, bitter flavor that would give any Columbia grown variety a run for its money. She inhaled its dark aroma, oxygen to a Himalayan climber. As she finished the cup, Dore arrived with a refill, her timing impeccable as always. Reality began to come back into focus as Dore's familiar movements, and the delicious cooking smoke of the galley worked with the caffeine to clear her head.

"That sure smells good!" she told Dore, now that she had paused from her fix long enough to have gotten a whiff of the delights breakfast was destined to hold.

"The French ship had bacon, eggs and bread! Real bread, baked only yesterday! Please ask your French doctor to identify their cook. I can make use of his talents if he will behave properly and work for me. I have more mouths to feed now. He would be useful."

"I'll make that happen."

Pam marveled briefly that along her bizarre and convoluted way, she had become someone who could say that, and mean it. Neither of them mentioned that Dore's last assistant cook, quiet, good-natured Mård had been killed in action. It would be a day of funerals, but for now the two friends both needed to simply exist in the comfort and warmth of a civilized kitchen, forgetting for a while that they were on the bottom side of the world, and that it was spinning faster than they might have preferred. If Pam closed her eyes she could picture her little red-and-white tiled kitchen in her little pink house in Grantville, back home in Germany. She laughed aloud at that last thought. *Germany is home now?* Dore looked over to see what was so funny, but Pam just waved her mug and asked for more coffee.

Garrett W. Vance

Chapter Forty-Four: A Private Consultation

Earlier that morning, the remains of the African slavers had been gathered up to be burned without ceremony on the beach, as far down the shore from the settlement as they could get. Around nine in the morning when the tide was right, and with Pam's permission, the French fallen were taken out to the open waters beyond the bay aboard the *Annalise*, to be given a Christian burial at sea. Those proceedings were overseen by Doctor Durand and his small group of French parolees, under the respectful, but careful, watch of Swedish sailors and marines. When he returned, Pam was waiting for him.

"Doctor Durand, I'd like to have a word with you, if you please."

"With pleasure, *Capitaine* Pam," he replied with a polite bow.

"In my quarters if you please. It's cooler there." She turned to the four Swedish marines from the *Muskijl* assigned to accompany the small contingent of French parolees. She would have to learn all their names at some point, for now she smiled, and gestured to them for attention, which they gave with military snap. Choosing the fellow she was pretty sure ranked highest, she gave her orders.

"*Korpral*, is it?"

"Yes, *Kapten* Pam." The man was still thin from his captivity, but well armed, and eager to please. Pam was glad to see confidence returning to the freed captives already.

"Good man. *Korpral*, please take your men down to the galley and ask *Frau* Dore to provide them with lunch for yourselves and the men in your charge. Once you have all eaten, give our guests the liberty of the *Second Chance Bird*'s main deck to stretch out in. I shall be up in my cabin conferring with Doctor Durand."

The *korpral* nodded, but looked concerned. "Would you like one of us to accompany you, and stand guard?"

"Thank you, but that won't be necessary. Doctor Durand has proven himself a gentleman so far, and if he should prove otherwise I will shoot his brains out."

She pointed her chin toward the now notorious Smith and Wesson .38 caliber holstered on her belt. Everyone was well aware that she had killed eight men with it, and were suitably impressed. The doctor gulped and looked a bit pale, but maintained his composure.

"So, don't worry," Pam assured him, "I'll be fine. Have a good lunch and get some rest."

"Yes, ma'am!" The *korpral* saluted her along with his men, and led his group toward the galley.

"Right this way, Doctor."

She motioned toward the ladder to the castle decks. He seemed to hesitate at going ahead of a lady, being a gentlemen through and through, but must have recalled that his situation was still a bit tenuous, and thinking of Pam's pistol, he went first, not making any sudden moves.

The doctor seemed quite impressed by the eastern opulence of Pam's quarters.

"I see the wealth of the Orient is not exaggerated. You say this ship likely belonged to a merchant, but this suite is appointed like that of a prince!"

"It's pretty swanky, yes."

She wasn't sure he knew what "swanky" meant, but the doctor nodded in polite agreement anyway.

"Here, have a seat. You must be as tired as I am."

They both settled into comfortably stuffed chairs at the broad, mahogany table she used as her desk. The doctor was visibly pleased as he settled into the satin cushions.

"*Ahh*, such luxury. Thank you for your kind hospitality."

"It is I who owe you thanks, Doctor Durand. Without your help, a lot more of my people would have died last night. You will be remembered as a hero by this colony, not as an enemy."

"That is good to hear. I hope they will not judge all we French by the gross injustices perpetrated by Leonce Toulon de Aquitane and his bandits. I was as much a slave as the Swedes were, although I didn't suffer nearly so awfully. Still, I am glad to have my freedom again, or at least what freedom you can grant until I completely earn your trust, *Capitaine*."

He smiled at her then, a sincere smile full of understanding and patience.

Pam couldn't help but like the man, and really had to admit that he was kind of sexy. If hunky Torbjörn hadn't made his miraculous appearance when he did, this guy might have been in trouble. . . . The thought made her blush and she laughed softly to cover it.

"I trust you, Durand, but I have to give the Swedes some more time before I let you and your trustees loose. You understand, I hope?"

"Absolutely. Please do as you must; we are quite happy with our treatment."

"Actually, one of the things I'd like to ask you today is if you would like to join my personal staff. We could use a doctor in the colony, as it appears that we neglected to bring one! If you want to leave us, you will be free to, but even if you decide to do that, would you take the position for the time being?"

"I would be delighted to! The truth is I am in no hurry to return to France. I find the weather here suits my tastes, and it would be good to be needed by so many people. How would it be if I promise you at least a year, and perhaps make more permanent arrangements if it should work out?"

"You got it, Doc! Welcome to our misfit band! Let's seal it with a toast—is it too early for a drink for you?"

Pam reached for the bottle of what she thought was some kind of *sake* that she kept on her desk, along with a set of beautiful red-and-gray glazed porcelain cups.

"By no means too early for a Frenchman, but just a little, please. We still have this evening's proceedings ahead of us."

Pam poured them each a cup-full of the nearly clear liquid, and made a toast. "To new comrades!"

"May we enjoy peace and prosperity!" he answered.

They drank their cups dry, and the doctor seemed to like the taste.

Pam poured them each another cupful, which they savored slowly. "It's a rice wine, I think. I tried some at a Japanese restaurant back in my former century. Presumably the Chinese make something similar. It grows on you."

Pam told him, showing him the pale blue ceramic bottle and its gracefully brushed characters. She pointed at the painted label.

"I'm pretty sure these two characters combine to mean 'alcohol,' but that's all I know about it."

"Truly, the Chinese are a civilized folk. Very smooth."

Pam put her elbows on the table and gave her companion a measuring look. The doctor met her gaze calmly.

"All right. Now that we are working together in an atmosphere of mutual trust, I'm afraid I do have some questions about your former employers."

"Captors. Yes, I will tell you anything you want to know, that is, if it is something I myself know. Please understand I was not in that bastard Leonce Toulon de Aquitane's privy counsel, but I saw and heard much."

"Good, that's good. First off, how did they find my expedition? Was it just an accident, or did they know we were coming?"

"I believe it was the latter. It was whispered that the *capitaine* had been contracted by Cardinal Richelieu. A rumor, you understand, but I do believe someone learned of your Emperor Gustav's intention to put a colony on this island, thus beating we French to a territory that would have one day been ours, according to the books of Grantville. As you must surely know, and forgive me for speaking frankly, the arrival of you up-timers has given the ruling heads of Europe fits. They are all studying your future history for ways to get ahead of their rivals, for any advantages such foreknowledge might afford."

"Yeah, I know about that. It's gotten to the point where I take my bodyguard, Gerbald, to the library with me. It's full of creepy dudes who are obviously foreign spies, or worse. I'm sure that most of them are up to no good."

"Well, in France I can say that little good has come of it. I fear for the future of my country, and find it best to stay away for now. And so, after the failure of the League of Ostend, France has been seeking ways to increase its power all across the globe. I'm afraid your native North America is by now dotted with French colonies, and there will be no Louisiana Purchase in this history."

Pam was impressed with Durand's knowledge and insights. This guy had obviously done a lot of reading himself. *Probably best to keep a close eye on my good doctor, no matter how much I like him*, she thought.

The doctor continued, "And it's not just going to be the Atlantic. Some of the leaders, they see far, and will have their hearts set on controlling as much of the world as they can, including this Indian Ocean, and no doubt the Pacific beyond it. And so, they send minions to do their filthy works. I'll wager that all of Leonce Toulon de Aquitane's violence here, and elsewhere, has the secret blessing of someone high up."

"Someone like Richelieu"

The doctor gave a very Gallic shrug.

"Perhaps. There is another thing. I saw for myself that the *capitaine* was quite taken with stories about the bold pirates of the eighteenth century, and am sure he fancies himself to be one. Are you familiar with the subject?"

"Yes, I read up on maritime history in order to prepare myself for what I might face on this voyage. The violence and danger of life on the seven seas was not exaggerated! The whole pirate thing didn't really get into swing until the eighteenth century back up-time, but I can see that won't be the case in this world."

"Indeed, I'm afraid that *Capitaine* Toulon de Aquitane is just the first of many, and already he is not alone here. He was still flying the flag of France at his capture, but I believe he had personal plans beyond serving the crown's interests here in these southern latitudes. When we sailed past the Cape of Good Hope in your pursuit, we rendezvoused with another warship and loaned them around half of *Effrayant*'s soldiers. I overheard much of what was said. Several captains are setting up a base on a small island off the coast of Madagascar called Isle St Marie, which in the up-time history would become a famed pirate haven. The soldiers were needed to subdue a rebellious native population. The island has a strategic location, which is probably how it came to be used for that purpose in the future you come from. From there, they intend to prey upon *all* foreign shipping in the Indian Ocean. I believe the term is 'against all flags.' You have made a great victory here, but more such evil men will come to avenge the capture of *Effrayant* and its *capitaine*, so you must be ready!"

"Indeed. The age of the pirate has come early. Another question: Who were those African slave-masters Toulon had working for him?"

Before the doctor could answer, a worried Dore came rushing in.

"Pam, *Herr* Doctor, Pers is talking in his sleep! I think you had better come!"

They both stood up, putting their drinks down on the table.

"I'm afraid we shall have to finish this conversation another time, Doctor Durand. Will you please come check on Pers?"

"Of course! I am completely at your disposal, *Capitaine*."

"Thank you, Doctor!"

Chapter Forty-Five: Therapy Session

The three of them hurried to Pers' sickroom to find the bosun standing over the poor boy's bed.

"He was talking, but I don't think he knew I was here. It sounded like he might be back in his childhood, speaking to his mother. He was asking about dinner," the bosun said in a voice full of hope and worry.

Pam put her hand gently on Pers' forehead. His skin felt cool, and she thought she could see a bit more color on his cheeks than the day before, but his expression was still slack, the face of one deep in dream.

The doctor took Pers by the wrist to feel his pulse. He allowed a small smile to curl between his fancily mustachioed lip and pointy brown beard. Streaks of gray could be seen in both, as well as in his long sideburns. Pam found him handsome in a weird sort of way, but pushed that thought aside quickly.

"A little better, perhaps, *Capitaine* Pam. You can see his color is returning, and his pulse is a bit stronger. He moved his legs around some earlier today, which is also a good sign. We must simply wait and see."

The French doctor kept his expression positive, but Pam could still see the doubt in the man's gentle, perpetually dark-circled brown eyes.

"I've heard that it helps to talk to a patient in a coma, to tell them to wake up and come back to us," Pam said, tentatively. The doctor only raised his eyebrows but the bosun, whose face was amazingly long for one so round and ruddy, brightened a little.

"Here, let me try," the bosun said, his voice trembling a little. He plainly feared greatly for the boy who had been injured while following orders he himself had issued, a boy he quietly doted on even as he frogmarched him around the deck from one duty to the next.

"Pers! Pers, it's the bosun. I'm sorry you're not feeling good, but you need to wake up now."

There was no sign from Pers' slack face that he had heard. The bosun looked over to Pam pleadingly.

Pam had an idea.

"You're doing it wrong. Talk to him like you would when he's awake. You know, order him around a bit! Give him a good shout!"

The bosun looked somewhat taken aback at the surprising suggestion, but then smiled at what he considered must be his captain's great wisdom. Shouting was one of his strong suits. Doctor Durand had an alarmed look on his face, he was just about to say something when the bosun charged ahead with the new plan.

"Right!" he said and flashed them a dark yellow, but still shiny grin. He bent down over the unconscious youth's dreaming face and let loose in a voice like thunder: "You! Boy! Get your lazy ass out of the sack Pers, and get to work! We haven't got all day, so move it! I want you on deck *now*!"

The resounding shout in the cabin's close quarters made everybody jump, and Pam detected a jerk in Per's lanky frame, a sign that he had at least sensed the bosun's voice on some level.

"Good!" Pam clapped the bosun on the back. "I saw him twitch!"

"As he should, I run a clean deck and everyone does their share!" He looked down at Pers with hope in his eyes. "I hope he heard me, I really hope he did. Wake up, my boy, wake up!" he shouted again.

Doctor Durand stood staring at them as if they were both utterly mad. "Excellent!" he proclaimed abruptly. "What an amazing new therapy! We must write a treatise on its wondrous effects for all the physicians of Europe to share! Now, if you will both *please leave*, I will attend to my patient in restful silence!"

The good doctor's deep voice rang with that special tone that only the best doctors, teachers, and chefs seemed able to produce, a tone that made even the bosun jump quickly at his order.

"Out!" he added, just to be sure he had been understood, but no further urging was necessary.

Pam couldn't help but laugh as she and the bosun got stuck trying to squeeze out of the narrow cabin door at the same time in their effort to remove themselves from the doctor's way as quickly as possible. Once they got themselves sorted out, Pam closed the door on what she was sure was a stream of muttered French curses emanating from the good doctor. They fled to the upper deck, still very worried about their young friend, but also feeling a bit more hopeful for his recovery than they had before.

Garrett W. Vance

Chapter Forty-Six: Twilight and Evening Bell

At five o'clock Pam led the funeral procession from the docks, past the half-finished buildings of the town, and up through the gently sloping fields to a pretty knoll that overlooked the bay. This was the site the people had chosen for their Hero's Cemetery, and Pam thought it a good one. The graves had already been dug, with temporary wooden markers at their heads; these were to be replaced with stone at a later date. Bengta was given pride of place in the cemetery's center. Beside her would lie Asmund, the young man who had been her fiancé, also killed in the revolt. Pam deeply mourned the loss of such young souls, their lives snatched away just as they were beginning a new future together. She began to cry, and made no effort to stop.

To heroic Bengta's left were the final resting places of her fellow colonists, some of whom had died during their enslavement, their remains having been moved here from temporary graves, others who had given their lives in the battle to free the colony. To her right were the graves of the sailors and marines who had guided them here and who had given their lives for the colony's freedom. With its high position, and sweeping view of the town and harbor, Pam felt the location itself was a fitting monument to people so brave as these.

Pam let her tears flow as they wished. She stood between Torbjörn and the bosun, grateful for the comfort of their protective male presences. Nearby, Gerbald and Dore looked on solemnly. The two of them were holding hands, and the sight made Pam feel better. Her men looked touchingly sad and brave, all lined up in their best Chinese finery. She was very, very proud of them all.

The eldest of the handful of Lutheran pastors who had come along to minister to the colony began the ceremony. Pastor Petrus was a serious, but kindly looking fellow, still young in his late thirties. His voice was clear and deep, and full of what Pam thought of as "Godly conviction." Pam's Swedish was good enough now that she could understand everything except for some obscure words in the older hymns.

As she expected, Pam would be called upon to say a few words, as would the bosun and the newly minted Captain Lundkvist. Although he had to be carried up to the grave site by his men, the new captain of their shining prize *Effrayant*, stood firmly against his crutch, bearing the pain of his lost leg with grim pride. Pam went last, after stirring speeches from her friends. Being, however unfortunately, an old hand at funerals, she ignored her usual butterflies and stepped forward.

She kept her own speech short, although it was filled with emotion, praising the courage and selflessness of the fallen and thanking the survivors of these trials for their stalwart support, and continuing dedication to their cause. She ended her part by reciting Tennyson's *Crossing the Bar*, feeling that she had spoken those beautifully appropriate words from another time and place far too often of late. Pam returned to her place of safety between Torbjörn and the bosun, and found herself taking Torbjörn's hand. He smiled warmly at her, and gave it a gentle squeeze. Her mind was a-whirl with emotion this day, but at least some of it was good.

Pam cried hard as each shrouded body was lowered into the ground, shedding just as many tears for the young colonists claimed too early as for her beloved lost comrades from the *Redbird* crew. That afternoon she had found a healthy patch of flowers along the forest's edge that she thought were some kind of hibiscus, wide yellow petals with a blushing pink center and stamen. They weren't roses, but they would do, she solemnly placed one on each filled grave, whispering farewell to each soul as she went.

She was among the last to leave the cemetery, the evening shadows had grown long, and dusk approached.

Torbjörn waited quietly for her, and she was thrilled that he wanted to be her escort. Other thoughts about the handsome captain clamored for attention, but she pushed them back. She was just too tired for that, maybe tomorrow! They walked back down the hill in amiable silence, glad for each other's company. As they walked through town at sunset, various bells began to ring, those on the ships as well as a proper church bell the colonists had brought with them. Pam couldn't help but chuckle as the long, low tones of *Second Chance Bird*'s Chinese gong joined the music. They paused to listen until the last bell stopped, a final salute to lost friends.

When they reached the dock, Pam turned to him and gave him a tired, but appreciative smile.

"Torbjörn, thank you for staying with me during the funeral. You were a great comfort to me."

"The pleasure was mine, Pam." His manly voice was full of sincerity. "Is there anything more I can do for you? I am at your service."

Pam thought there probably was quite a bit more he could do for her, and her body began to tingle in a very pleasant way, but she ignored it. *Not now, you ninny*, she chided herself in her mind. *You would fall asleep about the time things got interesting. There's time!*

"That's very kind, Torbjörn, and I will definitely be taking you up on your offer soon, but today I'm all done. I haven't had any sleep, and I'm about ready to fall down in my tracks." She paused, beginning to feel shy, but made herself press on, "How about you join me for dinner tomorrow night? Dore has come up with some amazing recipes in her new Chinese galley. I'll wager it's the best food on this side of the world."

"Absolutely! I have missed *Frau* Dore's cooking greatly."

He paused, and Pam thought he also looked shy for a moment before he said, "But not nearly as much as I have missed you, Captain Pam."

Pam felt her heart whiz around a few bumpy corners on its roller coaster ride. She took his hands and stretched up on her tippy-toes to plant a kiss on his lips which he accepted with obvious relish. They kept it brief, but it was as sweet as honey.

"I missed you, too, Captain Torbjörn. A lot." She started to tear up again, unable to stop it. "I thought you were gone, you know, but I didn't really believe it, not in my heart."

Suddenly, she threw herself into his arms and they spent a few long minutes in a tight embrace, Torbjörn gently stroking her hair to comfort her.

"I'm here, I'm here with you now. Don't cry, it's all right now, my brave Pam," he said softly in her ear, which made her feel like melting butter.

When she stopped shaking, he gently let her go, and she ran her palm across his chest as if to make sure he was real.

"See you tomorrow," she said, and quickly slipped away up the ramp to her ship's main deck. She turned once more and they each smiled softly at each other, eyes shining as they parted. Pam couldn't help but let a satisfied little smile come to her lips. *Score!* she thought and giggled to herself as she climbed the ladder to her cabin.

Second Chance Bird

Pam fell down on her soft, pillow-strewn bed like a load of lead ingots. She felt so excited about dinner the next day that she was sure she wouldn't be able to sleep. Fifteen seconds later she was out cold.

Garrett W. Vance

Chapter Forty-Seven: A Mysterious Figure

Pam awoke early the next morning. She had slept soundly, and felt completely rested. She lay in her bed for a few minutes while going over the chaotic events of the past few days, and felt a bit better about it all, despite the terrible losses. She had gotten a second chance, and had taken it to victory. It wasn't often she got to indulge herself in some pride, but now was one of those times. *Good job, Pammie!* she thought, *you really kicked ass!* Not only that, but she had a date tonight with a man direct from the young Kris Kristofferson school of hunkiness! The very thought of Torbjörn made her feel like she was falling, but in a very pleasant way.

She got out of bed and opened the window. The sun hadn't risen yet, but she had no doubt Dore would be in the galley already, and there would be coffee! She slipped on a canary-yellow, silk robe, and slid her feet into a pair of slippers woven from some kind of sturdy grass; she had adapted quite well to her Asian wardrobe. The unusual garments were beginning to feel as natural as a pair of jeans.

Down on the main deck, she paused at the rail to gaze at the purple-lit sea beyond the harbor; it would be another glorious sunrise. As she turned to head for the ladder leading below-decks she saw something that made her jump: A ghost was standing at the rail near the prow, white satin sheets flapping in the morning breeze. Squinting her eyes for a better look she saw the apparition was busy polishing the deck rail with a corner of one of the sheets.

"Holy shit." Pam hurried to the prow and paused a few feet from the mysterious figure. She had an idea who it might be, and hoped she was right.

"Pers?" she asked cautiously.

Her "ghost" turned, and she saw that indeed it was Pers, his torso wrapped in one bedsheet with another sheet pulled over his head and loosely tied at his chest. His face was very pale, but he looked alive enough.

"Hey, Pam!" he answered nonchalantly, as if waking from a coma and polishing the rail while dressed up as a phantom were perfectly normal things. "It sure is cold this morning! Do you know where my clothes are?"

Pam realized he was still about half out of it, but that was a huge improvement over comatose! She grinned at him, her heart bursting with relief and joy.

"I'm not sure, Pers, but we will find them." Her voice shook a bit, but she stayed calm. "So, what are you doing?"

"Oh, the bosun was yelling at me to get to work, so I thought I better get to it. Say, where did he go?"

Pers started to look around the deck, his eyes still a bit glazed, but he seemed to be waking up.

"What time is it, anyway?" The young man's face grew perplexed as he began to realize that maybe his situation was just a bit odd.

Pam felt happy tears rolling down her cheeks, warm drops in the cool ocean breeze.

"It's morning, and you were having a dream. Now you are awake!"

She hugged him tightly then, taking care not to dislodge the sheet he had somehow managed to wrap around his tall, thin frame.

"Oh! Good morning!" he said, beginning to sound embarrassed as he fumbled at the sheets to make sure certain private areas remained fully covered.

"Yes, it is indeed a good morning, Pers! Now come on, let's go get you into some proper clothes before you scare the wits out of someone else!"

∞ ∞ ∞

Doctor Durand looked pleased and relieved as he examined a now mostly dressed Pers while Pam, the bosun, and Dore looked anxiously on.

"His pupils are still a bit dilated, but they are returning to normal. His pulse is strong and steady," he told the onlookers. "Pers, how do you feel?" he asked in English, having been informed that Pers could speak the language fairly well, thanks to Pam and Gerbald's tutelage.

The young patient still looked a bit perplexed, but was definitely coming around. "I feel pretty good, still a little light-headed maybe. Umm, excuse me for my rudeness, but who are you?"

Everyone laughed. The doctor had spent much of the last few day's at Per's bedside.

"I am Doctor Durand, and you are a very lucky young man. You have been unconscious for several days. Tell me, what's the last thing you remember?"

Pers' light-blond brows furrowed as he reached for memories damaged by the fall.

"Well, I was climbing up in the rigging and I slipped. I think I fell, and I was very frightened, but then the memory stops."

"You did fall, and you injured your head quite badly."

Pers began to reach up to feel his head but the doctor gently took him by the wrist and stopped him.

"The injury is still bruised and needs more time to heal, so please don't touch it for now. Do you feel any pain there?"

"Just a little, like I would if I bumped my head on a beam below-decks."

"Well, that's good. Do you remember anything else after your fall, and before you woke up this morning?"

"Why, yes. I could hear the bosun was shouting at me to get to work. I wanted to, but I couldn't seem to get up!"

Pam let out a whoop and clapped the bosun on the back. The bosun laughed. and they both chanted, "It worked, it worked!" while dancing a happy little jig together.

Doctor Durand rolled his eyes.

"Yes, it seems that 'shout therapy' might have a place in the care of coma victims, after all. Your friends were trying to reach you to help you wake up, and apparently their efforts succeeded."

Pers nodded, as he watched Pam and the bosun's celebration with wide-eyed fascination.

Once they settled down, the doctor turned to them. "Now, the boy is better, but he is still on the mend. I believe some exercise, both physical and mental, would do him some good, but not too much and not in the heat of the day. Can you find him some light duties, *Monsieur* Bosun?"

"I can indeed, *Herr* Doctor. I'll take good care of him, don't you worry!"

Dore moved over to the bedside to take Pers' hand in hers.

"It is good to have you back with us, young Pers. Now, are you hungry?"

Pers eyes lit up as brightly as they ever had at that question. "Yes! I could eat an elephant!"

Dore patted his hand affectionately, visibly proud that she knew just what their patient needed. "I thought as much. Very good, come with me, then."

She and the doctor helped him to his feet. Pam thought he seemed much steadier than he had during his pre-dawn haunting of the deck.

Durand turned to Dore.

"Madame Dore, I know he must be starving, but please, you mustn't feed him too much, too quickly. I advise you start with a warm broth and barley, or some-such easy to digest food. Once we are sure he can keep that down, you can give him something more, but nothing too heavy, at least for a day or two."

"It shall be as you say, *Herr* Doctor, and thank you for your kind care of our young man."

Dore favored Durand with one of her all too rare radiant smiles; its power actually made the cool and collected gentleman blush.

"Yes, good job, Doc, we really appreciate all your work!"

Pam stuck out her hand to shake his, after a moment's confusion he extended his in return and let her pump it enthusiastically. "Thank you for your kind words, my friends, but really, I was just doing my duties as a physician as best I could. It is my honor to serve."

In a celebratory mood, they all followed Dore to the galley. All that happiness had made everyone hungry.

Garrett W. Vance

Chapter Forty-Eight: A Bit of Exercise

That noon Pam had on her hiking clothes, and was carrying her grandmother's walking stick when she arrived at the galley for lunch. A slightly less orange-colored Gerbald was finishing a sandwich. It looked like the make-up was finally wearing off.

"Hey! Where are you off to?" he asked, starting to get up.

"Sit down. I'm just going to walk along the forest's edge in those upper fields. I want to check out what kind of trees are growing in these hills, and start thinking about some intelligent logging. I hate to cut trees, but the reality is we need to finish the town walls. At least this way I can control the damage."

"I'll come with you," Gerbald said, before hurrying to finish his sandwich.

"No need today, my friend. Take the day off. I'll be fine."

Pam smiled at him reassuringly. The truth was she wanted to be alone, and even Gerbald's quiet when she wanted him to be present was more than she could bear at the moment. Dore handed her a sandwich and a piece of fruit wrapped up in a parcel made of a leaf. Pam shoved it into her rucksack, smiling her thanks.

"Be careful, please, Pam," Dore said, concerned for her safety, as usual.

Gerbald and Dore both looked unhappy at Pam going off by herself, but kept quiet, well aware of how stubborn their friend could be. The three of them had become very tight-knit over the years, and her older "brother and sister" couldn't help being a little over-protective of "their Pam." She flashed them a grin and laughed. "Knock it off, you two. What a couple of worry warts! I'm outta here!"

Pam headed up the dock to shore at a jaunty pace, pausing only to say hello to various sailors and citizens along the way. Several of them, plainly concerned for her safety, asked her if she wanted company on her walk, but she politely declined all offers.

"I'm just going to follow the edge of the upper field around. I won't go into the forest."

The Swedes nodded politely. She had learned they were a people who valued solitude, and could certainly understand that Pam needed some time to herself.

Leaving the growing town behind, Pam was drawing near the cemetery on its knoll off to her left. Beyond it she could see the compound the French prisoners were being held in. *I still need to have my interview with Captain Dick-head, but not today. Let's not think about that stuff just now.* With a physical shake of her head that sent her unruly dishwater-blond locks flying, Pam cleared all thoughts of the death and destruction of the last few days out of her mind. *I need to get ready for the next phase. I need to look to the future.* Somehow managing to grimly hang onto positive thoughts, Pam hurried her step, veering off to the right to avoid the entire area.

Pam reached the bottom of the upper field and kept to the right. It was a broad rectangle of around twelve acres stretching longways uphill from the harbor. Stumps could be seen here and there, but parts of it had been natural meadow before the French decided to have it all clear cut. That made her scowl, but what was done, was done. A small herd of the cows the colonists had brought along watched her with mild brown eyes, complacently chewing the native grass. So far the cows, a flock of sheep, a yard-full of chickens and geese, and some horses were the only domestic animals allowed on the island. Pigs, goats, dogs, and cats were banned due to their penchant for escaping, and becoming destructive feral pests, exactly what this fragile ecosystem did not need.

Maybe someday she would lift the ban on dogs. She knew the people would like to have them. Pam feared the day that some ship would bring rats, or weevils, or worse—it was inevitable. She stopped to look out at the harbor, and decided that extending the dock would be a priority. In fact, she would order a customs house built right out over the water, creating a buffer between ship and shore. It would at least stem the tide of unwanted animal immigrants. That made her smile. She whistled an aimless tune as she continued hiking.

When she reached the tree line, she paused to look back at the town and harbor, a picturesque scene. The houses and buildings that had been completed were now being painted a rich, brownish red. Pam had learned this was called *falun* red, and was a Swedish tradition. The trim was done in white, and Pam thought it all looked pretty great.

"A little bit of the old country," Pam said to herself, "Traditions are good, in moderation."

She knew that there was going to be a difficult time ahead as the colony put the modern farming methods Pam had taught them into practice.

"We'll make some new traditions here, too."

Working her way along the field's edge, Pam admired the lush, tropical vegetation. Behind the various flowering shrubs that had sprung up once more light had become available, tall trees loomed, some of them giants. Pam saw ebony, tambalacoque, and bois dentelle trees among many others. They could all get rich just on the lumber here, and Pam was going to make sensible logging, forest renewal, and habitat preservation one of her top priorities There would be no more clear cutting. In her reading, she had learned that too many places had foolishly used up all their timber within the first fifty years of colonization, which had resulted in poverty, lacking that valuable resource. That would not happen here.

Pam had spent long hours finding every scrap of information she could on the island's flora and fauna, from both up-time and down-time sources. Still, there were many, many species that she couldn't identify. Eventually, they would all have to be documented and named. It would be a daunting task.

"I should have brought along some help for that," she grumbled to herself.

Turning her eyes upward, she jokingly said "Dear Lord, please send me a boat-load of eager graduate students!" Maybe someday. Meanwhile, she was on her own, the lone scientist.

Pushing thoughts of the huge amount of work and enormous responsibilities that were to be hers, she tried to concentrate on enjoying the walk. She wanted to get a feel for the land, figure out how to use it best, with the needs of the colony and the environment both in mind.

About halfway up the gently sloping expanse, Pam decided to cut across to the forest on the far side. There was a place there she wanted to visit. Walking through the grass and meadow flowers was fairly easy going. She surprised a flock of birds with bright orange heads and throats, on an olive green body. They were startlingly beautiful, and Pam gasped in delight. *A nice reminder of why I am here. It's not just the dodos. This entire island is a treasure trove of wildlife.* The flock disappeared into the trees, a cloud of flaming color dissolving into the cool green.

Second Chance Bird

Reaching the tree line on the other side, she began to cast about in the underbrush at the forest's edge, looking for one particular place. After a few minutes she found it. Pam was standing in the exact spot she had first met Bengta. She sat down in a patch of soft grass. A wave of emotion came over her, sadness and loss, but also pride. Pam began to speak softly to her lost ally.

"Oh, Bengta, you were too young to die saving the damn dodos. I know you came here for more than that, for a new life, and I blame myself for what happened to you. I'm responsible. You are the real hero in all this; you are the one who sacrificed everything to free this colony, to make my dream possible. I will never forget you, and I promise you I will do everything I must to make this a success! You are my inspiration. Please, lend me your strength. I need it now more than ever. God bless you, Bengta."

Pam smiled through her tears at the lovely surroundings, thinking that maybe, just maybe she could feel the spirit of the heroic young woman around her, urging her on. Real or not, the feeling was a comfort. Sighing, Pam wiped her face on her sleeve, and pulled herself to her feet with the aid of her grandmother's trusty oak walking stick.

She spent a few more minutes taking in the scene, marking its location carefully with a small cairn of stones to be sure.

"I will make this place a park in your honor, Bengta."

Suddenly, she laughed aloud, a bright sound amongst the hushed chirp and twitter of forest birds. It occurred to her that eventually there would be a historical marker here, the bulky, stone kind found in historical battlefields and around national monuments. Her own name would be inscribed on a copper plate there, along with Bengta's, and the thought of it made her laugh even harder.

"A hillbilly ex-housewife like me, going down in history! I'm going to be part of a future tourist attraction! Holy moly, who'd-a-thunk it?" Still chuckling at the absurdity of it all, she continued up the gently sloping tree line.

Reaching the top of the vast field, Pam looked back down its length. She was a good mile from the town now, and all the boats seemed like toys. She laughed at *Second Chance Bird*, the gaudiest of them all, looking for all the world like a curio picked up at a seaside gift shop. It was three o'clock according to her watch, and the slowly moving air held a golden haze, making the world seem like an idyllic dream.

"Home. This is my home now." Pam decided it for certain, then and there.

She hadn't had much time to think about what would happen after the colonists were rescued, and things were put back in order. She knew damned well what the document the princess had written for her meant to her future. She had drafted it herself, even though she had been afraid of the weight of it back then. It was really an insurance policy, a card to play if she had no other choice. She didn't have to follow its letter if she decided she didn't want to. Now it felt like her destiny. She was ready for the responsibility. She would call a town meeting in a day or two, and everybody would hear the princess' wishes. It wouldn't be much of surprise anyway, at least not to the Swedes.

Dore and Gerbald on the other hand . . . Well, they would probably do whatever they felt was best for "their Pam," and she felt a bit guilty for that crazy kind of loyalty, but they had followed her this far, and it had been their choice. Now they would have to make another such choice. In any case, it was time to start the long process of making this colony a viable economic and self-sufficient entity without wrecking the island's ecology. She had signed up for this, and she would see it through.

Her kin back in Grantville suddenly came to mind, her elderly folks and her son's new family. Damn, she wished she could be there for Crystal and the new baby, but there just wasn't any other way. She did have to go back to Grantville to personally deliver Princess Kristina's dodos as promised, but it wouldn't be until she was sure things were where she needed them to be here. Once there, she would have to break it to her family that her return was just a visit, not forever. She intended this island to be her home, this was where her true calling was.

Heading back into town an idea came to her, and although she tried to resist, she felt herself drawn to the pier. It didn't take long to find Torbjörn, shirtless and sweating deliciously as he worked under the late afternoon sun. Grinning, she pulled out his little yellow whistle and gave it a merry toot.

His gaze turned to her and a bright smile appeared.

"Hey, you!" she called, "Got time to go for a bit of a walk?" she called to him.

"Of course! Lead the way!"

They strolled hand in hand down the beach, headed away from town. They didn't talk much, content to simply enjoy the afternoon and each other's company. Passing around a wooded point, they came to the mouth of small river, so they turned to follow it upstream for a while, walking through soft meadow grass along its low banks. The water was crystal clear and cool, they both paused to take a drink, feeling fairly comfortable that it would be safe in such a pristine environment. Pam turned to the tall Swede, and before she could think much about it she spoke to him in a soft voice.

"So, Torbjörn . . . Do you know how to swim?"

"But of course. Do you?"

"Yeah. What do you say we jump in the river and cool off?"

"An excellent idea." Hand in hand, they strolled along a little farther upstream to a sandy beach at a bow in the river, the water behind it slow and inviting, sunlight dappling its smooth surface.

Pam looked shyly at Torbjörn, who already had his shirt off. He was one hell of a handsome man, a grown-up version of the long-haired 1970s poster boys that posed fetchingly on her bedroom walls back in her teens. She felt shy for a moment, then remembered that the truth was she looked better than she had in years, more like Pam Miller in her twenties than forties. She was physically fit, and possibly even a bit too thin for a change! She had allowed her unruly, dishwater blond hair to grow long, down past her shoulders, the silvery streaks of premature gray arcing through it were actually a blessing, natural highlights! She untied her common sense ponytail, and shook it out, so that it expanded into a feline mane. She felt Torbjörn's eyes upon her, and sensed their approval on some kind of deep, instinctual level.

Oh, what the hell, she thought, her self-consciousness evaporating along with the sweat on her arms in the cool riverside air. *Time to go for it.* She pulled off her clothes, and felt comfortable doing so in front of this lovely man. She paused to give Torbjörn a good, long look, then waded into the sandy shallows, where she made a graceful, shallow dive. She surfaced, and looked back to see that Torbjörn had now lost his trousers, and smiled to see that she had, indeed, made an impression on him. He was a glorious nude. Years of hard work had made him into a muscular Norse god, his long, curly hair a red-gold crown in the bronze, late afternoon light. He laughed, and charged in after her with a great splash, making her squeal with delight.

They didn't touch for a time, content to swim side by side against the slow current, letting the river wash away the aches and pains of their trials. Eventually, they paused beneath the grassy bank, under a curtain of meadow flowers hanging over its edge. They kissed there, softly, barely touching at first, standing with feet lightly anchored in the sandy bottom, their bodies weightless in the gentle press of the river's flow.

They drew each other closer, their kisses growing hungrier, their embrace more powerful.

After a timeless time, Torbjörn gently pulled himself back from their steamy kisses to look into Pam's stormy gray eyes, a sight which always captivated him, mesmerized him with their power. Pam was a strong and graceful tigress, wild and fearless! He had never met anyone else like her, she was a warrior goddess, from the old stories, confident, courageous! He wanted her, and his heart beat fast knowing that she wanted him, too. He smiled then, a question. Pam smiled back, an answer. They embraced again, moving together slowly, then more swiftly, their soft cries a chorus for the river's liquid music. Eternity passed by in ecstasy, and then passed by again.

∞ ∞ ∞

Pam awoke in a grassy nest deep in the meadow, naked, a warm, masculine arm draped over her shoulder. She blinked for a moment or two, trying to remember just how she had ended up here, then laughed as the memory of the tumultuous last few days came, with all its terrors and thrills. It was still early evening, and her friends wouldn't be too worried yet, so she closed her eyes for a few more minutes, soaking in the heat emanating from her Swedish sea captain, a comfort in the cool sea breeze. After a cozy while the shadows had deepened, and it was time to get back. She gently removed the delightful arm, sat up, and began wondering where her clothes were! She found them soon enough, blushing at the thought of the entire town turning out to look for them, and finding them bare as newborns!

She awakened Torbjörn with a gentle kiss. They had all been through hell, but right now, at this moment, she realized she was about the happiest she had ever been.

"Time to go. Dore will have supper on soon."

Torbjörn's bright smile glowed in the evening shade.

Hooray for me! she thought to herself, as she helped her still drowsy man find his clothes. As they walked back to town Pam smiled contentedly, knowing that neither of them were going to get much sleep in the coming night. She fully intended to make up for falling asleep on him the night before.

Chapter Forty-Nine: Looking Glass

"You know, we still don't have a name for the colony." Pers said to Pam as they enjoyed the sunrise on the junk's high castle deck.

Torbjörn was still asleep in her quarters, she had managed to tire the poor fellow out eventually, a memory she would treasure. Gerbald had not yet emerged from his cabin. Dore was up, of course, and the delightful smell of brewing coffee came wafting up from the galley. Pam didn't know why she was up so early. By all accounts she should have slept the entire day away, but instead she felt more invigorated than she had in ages. *Nothing like a good old roll in the hay to melt the years away!* She tried to stop thinking about her wonderful night, and couldn't.

"Hello? Pam?" Pers' young, earnest face leaned in close to hers.

"Oh, I'm sorry, Pers. Just spacing out. A name for our new town? Yeah, it's time for that, isn't it? Do you have any ideas?"

"Not really. I think it should be up to you anyway, and I bet the rest would agree."

Pam moaned a little, realizing that the yoke of responsibility would be settling on her now that the perils has passed. There was a lot of work to do, a whole lot, and she would have to do her part in it. She bit her upper lip in thought, and looked down at the dawn-lit waters. The sea was perfectly still, not a puff of breeze or errant wave to disturb its crystalline perfection. She smiled at her reflection below, a little dark around the eyes, but looking pretty good, in the best shape of her life. She reached up to adjust some of her flyaway dishwater blond hair, the sea a virtual mirror. A mirror . . .

"Pers, I've got it! I have a name! Look down there, what do you see?"

"I see our reflections. The water is very calm today."

"Right! It's often like this around sunrise and sunset. It's just like a mirror! Do you remember the name of that Lewis Carroll book I showed you?"

"The one that inspired the princess to send us to save the dodo? It was *Through the Looking Glass*, wasn't it?"

Pam marveled at how clear her adopted teen's English had become, he certainly had a knack for languages, a real chip off her block..

"Exactly. What's another word for 'looking glass' in English?"

Pers' bright blue eyes looked upward for a moment as he rummaged through his mind. A moment later he smiled, and said "A mirror!"

"Exactly! Let's call this place Port Looking Glass, in honor of Lewis Carroll. Kristina will love that!"

Pers' eyes widened as all the sailors did when they were reminded their captain was on a first-name basis with their princess.

"That sure sounds nice, and fitting, too." Pers nodded his approval. A hearty voice emanated from below-decks, the call for coffee, and both of them hurried down the steep ladders to the galley as fast as they dared.

Chapter Fifty: The Ones That Got Away

Port Looking Glass, December 15th, 1635

"They *what?*" Pam shouted, her voice like sharp metal. Ulf, the Swedish marine who had brought her the bad news flinched, hoping that the American saying about "shooting the messenger" really was just a saying.

"They escaped, Captain Pam, in the night. They all got away, including the officers and their loyal sailors." Ulf's voice was heavy with professional embarrassment. Even though the strapping young soldier had a full foot and a hundred pounds on her, he shrank back as Pam began pacing around her cabin in the grip of rage.

"*How?*"

Pam tried not to shriek at the poor fellow, fighting to keep her voice even. Gerbald, Doctor Durand, and Lundkvist, the newly-minted captain of their captured French warship, looked on, all staying sensibly near the door.

"One of the French trustees did it. We haven't been watching them that closely since the doctor vouched for them."

This made the good doctor wince painfully, his hand moving to his brow in a gesture of pain. Ulf gave him an apologetic shrug before continuing.

"It turns out this one was still loyal to that Toulon bastard. He snuck up to the prison and cut a hole in the back wall. It was only made of bamboo. The civilians on guard duty were all asleep." At least he had managed to get that particular buck passed. *Incompetent farmers trying to do a soldier's work, and failing completely!*

Pam scowled mightily. *Hot, stinking DAMN!* Their real military guys were stretched pretty thin right now, with a harbor full of ships and a town to attend to, so it wasn't that big a surprise. Even seasoned soldiers were known to fall asleep on guard duty, and it wasn't exactly a Sing Sing they had been running. Two more days and that evil bastard would have been hanging high. She had intended to pull the lever herself!

Doctor Durand looked miserable, his long mustache drooping tragically.

"Captain Pam, I am most terribly embarrassed. I hold myself completely responsible. It was I who thought we could trust the man who did this. He appeared to be an honest young sailor to my eyes, pressed into service against his will as I was."

"It isn't your fault, Doc. You're not a mind reader. That snake Toulon must have made the kid an offer he couldn't refuse." She looked at everyone gathered, her expression becoming sad. "I want to make it clear, this is all *my* fault. I should have dealt with Toulon right away, but I got so busy with personal stuff that I blew it off for later. Now he's gone, and I have only myself to blame. Here I am, leading all you people when I really don't have a friggin' idea what I'm doing."

"Let me say that I disagree with that last statement." Lundkvist spoke up. "Your madcap ideas are what brought us to victory. You are a natural leader, and we have faith in you. Do you think a bunch of hardened sea dogs like us would follow you if we didn't?"

This was followed by a murmur of agreement from all gathered. Pam managed a grateful smile.

"Well, you guys must all be nuts, but so be it. Seriously though, if you think I am screwing up along the way, I need you to tell me, I value your experience highly, and couldn't have managed any of this without you."

She turned back to the sweating Marine, who looked somewhat relieved that his captain had grown calmer. "What happened next, Ulf?" she asked him, patting his hand in a comforting manner. He breathed out a nervous breath, and continued.

"They made their way down to the beach where the traitor had a pinnace waiting, one of *Ide*'s tenders. It was big enough to hold them, and seaworthy enough. We figure they're heading to Isle Saint Marie, that's where they say Toulon has his pirate base. They can make it if the good weather holds."

Kapten Lundkvist stepped forward, his new polished wood peg leg giving him a very maritime air.

"The *Effrayant* can be ready to pursue within the hour. We can still catch them!"

Pam shook her head no.

"I appreciate your gumption, but it would be searching for a needle in a hay stack. We need *Effrayant* here to protect us. If Toulon is foolish enough to come back to hassle us, we'll finish him for good. One day, when Swedish power has grown strong enough here, I intend to go burn their little pirate paradise to the ground, and you and your ship will be leading the charge, I promise! All I ask is that you save *Capitaine* Leonce Toulon de Aquitane for me. I intend to kill that motherfucker with my own hands, for Bengta and all the others. His ass is *mine*."

Pam glared so fiercely into the distance that Gerbald was pretty sure the escaped pirate would feel a tingling at the nape of his neck, wherever he was.

After a long, glowering silence, Pam shrugged, shaking off her frustration and anger. "Well, that's that, business for another day. Now, we need to get ready for the town meeting, and before noon or not, I need a drink. Any takers?"

All the men breathed a collective sigh of relief to see the storm had passed. They gathered around the big, red-lacquered table while Pam uncorked a jug of rice wine, pouring it into the small ceramic cups the Chinese used for such occasions.

"Looks like you have your own Captain Hook now, eh?" Gerbald teased Pam.

"The princess has her heart set on calling this Wonderland, but maybe we better go with Never Never Land, instead. All right, 'lost boys,' let's have a toast!"

Pam raised her cup high, as did the rest.

"To our enemies!" May they lose sleep wondering when we will come for them."

Chapter Fifty-One: Welcome to Wonderland

The meeting hall wasn't finished yet, so that balmy afternoon the entire colony gathered in the great meadow above town. A podium had been erected, on which Pam, and various other luminaries of the colony, stood smiling at the people, who smiled encouragingly back. Pam usually got the butterflies when facing a crowd, but today she felt confident; these were friends, and they had all been through much together.

"People of Port Looking Glass, thank you for coming today!" She spoke in Swedish. Her voice came out clear, and was aided in its course over the crowd by a light breeze off the Indian Ocean.

She opened up the small plastic container that she had guarded so carefully through shipwreck and battle, carefully pulling out the rolled-up paper within.

"I have here a proclamation written in Princess Kristina's own hand, and signed by her father, King Gustav Adolph the Second. It reads: 'I, Princess Kristina Augusta, do hereby, and with my father's blessings, claim the islands known up-time as the Mascarenes for the crown of Sweden. They shall henceforth be called the Wonderland Isles. Mauritius, Rodriguez, and Réunion, are renamed, respectively, Dodo,

Jabberwocky, and Bandersnatch, in honor of the works of Lewis Carroll, from whence the inspiration for this colony came.' "

Pam paused, having expected the confused blinks from the crowd. "Folks, I know the names sound strange, but they are from one of the princess' favorite storybooks. As brilliant as she is, she is still a child, so let's humor her, all right?"

Good-natured laughter emanated from the crowd along with murmurs of approval. Pam shared a smile with them and continued on. "I hope this next part won't be too shocking for you! The princess goes on to say 'I also hereby proclaim expedition leader Pamela Grace Miller of Grantville as Royal Governor of the Wonderland Isles for a period of two years, after which you may hold elections in the American style, and choose your own leaders.' "

Pam paused, giving the crowd a long, serious look. "I will not hold you to this, but if you will have me, I will serve," she told them.

The crowd sent up a cheer, hailing their new governor with unmistakable enthusiasm. Pam nodded her thanks, then continued on once the hubbub settled down. "There is a bit more here, and it's important: 'Please be good to the wildlife of these islands, especially the dodo. As a Wonderland citizen it is your duty to preserve and protect nature, including all native plants and creatures. By living in harmony with the good, green Earth I believe you shall become the healthiest, and hopefully, the wealthiest of all people. Good luck to you all, and God bless you. I pray that you are successful in this great endeavor, and wish you all the best.' "

Pam looked back at the crowd, who applauded with vigor. She spoke again, moving on to the brief speech she herself had prepared. "My fellow Wonderlanders!"

The crowd clapped enthusiastically at this, and more cheers went up.

"My first act as governor is to ask you to select a deputy governor from amongst yourselves to join me."

This was met with more applause.

"You have suffered much, and weathered great hardship! You are the bravest of the brave! The scoundrels who held us hostage have forced us to change our plans somewhat, but we are adapting. We have sugar cane and potatoes in abundance already, and that is just the beginning! By this time next year we will be the 'Spice Basket of Europe,' which will make us all very rich indeed! We are a free people, we work for ourselves, and each other! Together, we will build the most successful colony the world has ever seen! Thank you all!"

Pam bowed, smiled, and waved at the exuberant crowd in what she hoped was proper public official style, hoping that their pleasure would last when it came time to enforce certain laws protecting the island's unique natural heritage. Hopefully, her plans for relatively non-invasive agriculture and forest management would indeed be as lucrative as she thought they would. She sighed and thought, *We will just have to cross that bridge when we come to it.*

Chapter Fifty-Two: The Ships Come In

One Year Later, December 1636

Pam came out of her office/laboratory, a very functional, peaked roofed, rectangular building on the edge of the forest, painted the same deep *falun* red as nearly everything else in Port Looking Glass. Gerbald had soon dubbed it "Pam's Bird Barn." The moniker had stuck to the point where she had given in, and neatly painted it over the door.

Pam was on her way to check on the new rice paddies, part of the agricultural bounty they had traded for with a group of Japanese refugees on their way to Grantville. The very unexpected visitors had stopped for supplies four months before, fleeing an unfriendly situation in Cambodia. She shook her head in amazement at the memory. This really was a Wonderland. There she had been, pow-wowing with real live samurai straight out of Clavell! That unexpected visit was quite a story, but one for another day. There was no time to reminisce at the moment, she was just too damn busy. She often wished that there were two of her, one to play the governor, the other to be the scientist.

The rice paddies were terraced along a stream that ran out into the placid waters of Looking Glass Bay. A few of the Japanese families had elected to stay at Pam's own invitation. She had been concerned about whether the Lutheran Swedes would accept a group of largely Catholic Asians, but it hadn't been a problem, they understood that the newcomers had unique skills that would help their colony's further success.

In addition to the Japanese, shortly after their victory over the rogue French the year before they had rescued a group of shipwrecked Dutch colonists bound for Ambon, in the Molucca Isles. The Dutch vessel was too badly damaged to go on, but the gracious Swedes invited them to remain permanently in Port Looking Glass, a generous offer which the beleaguered refugees accepted gratefully.

Pam was tremendously pleased that the colony was becoming truly multicultural. The "American Way" Grantville had brought back through the centuries was alive and well here in the Indian Ocean, of all places. Pam was damn proud, her plans were literally bearing fruit, far more than she had even hoped for.

As she walked, a Japanese gentleman named Hironaka, their chief rice expert, hailed her from the low, earthen wall that held the paddy's water in. Pam waved at him, then realized he was pointing emphatically, motioning for her to look to the harbor. Just then, the town alarm bells sounded. Pam turned to see *Effrayant* leaving her moorage, hurrying out to meet the small fleet of unknown sailing vessels heading their way. *Muskijl* and *Second Chance Bird* followed, entering into a defensive formation with *Effrayant*, implementing their oft-practiced plan for an unexpected sea invasion. Pam gave Hironaka a quick bow, it was impossible not to pick up the habit from her congenial new Japanese friends. She headed up the beach toward the pier in a full on run.

There were at least nine ships, the one in the lead looked to be a warship large enough to give even fearsome *Effrayant* trouble. Pam paused to catch her breath, breaking out the small birding scope she kept on a leather thong around her neck. Forcing herself to breathe slowly and deeply, she focused on the big ship. Yes, banks of guns, but no sign

Second Chance Bird

of firing crews making ready. She caught a glimpse of gold and blue, biting her lip, she scanned the rigging.

There! Pam laughed aloud with delight. The ship was flying the Swedish colors! She began running again, her nerves buzzing with excitement. They had been visited by merchant ships from several nations over the last year, but this was the first time a ship from home had come!

The waterfront was filling up with interested colonists. They made way for her, and as she hurried out onto the pier, Pers came running to meet her.

"They're friendly, right?" she called out. One never could be too sure.

"Pam! They are from Sweden!" Pers replied, a gleeful expression on his youthful face. He would turn nineteen soon.

To further reassure her, the "all's well" bell rang on *Effrayant*.

"Not all of them. Recognize that flag?" Pam pointed at one of the five ships making their way carefully into the harbor under escort from their defenders.

Pers studied it with his youthful sharp eyes.

"She is flying what looks to be a naval ensign, red with a black saltire cross bearing gold stars. . . . That's a ship from the United States of Europe!"

"Well, howdy doody. I wondered when someone from my new old country might come to check on us." She took Pers by the arm and said, "Shall we go say hello?"

"Yes, ma'am, t'would be a pleasure!" Pers answered in his best West Virginia drawl; he was almost as good as Gerbald now, who surpassed even most hillbillies in his mastery of the accent.

The commander of the port shore guard, Lieutenant Järv, one of the *Muskij*'s Marines, was waiting at the end of the pier with his men. They took up a protective position around Pam, who was embarrassed at the fuss, but thanked them politely. She mentally put on her 'governor's hat', wondering for the thousandth time just how the hell *that* had happened.

The USE ship came in to the dock first, a three-masted caravel. It was quite well-armed, and even boasted the same kind of carronade that perched menacingly on *Second Chance Bird*'s deck. Anyone trying to board her might not live long enough to regret it.

Dore had been left ashore when the big, comfortable junk that served as their home headed out to meet the newcomers, under the command of Captain Torbjörn. Dore joined Pam, eyes squinting in the tropical sunlight. She spent most of her time cooking for the sailors in the domain that she ruled with an iron fist, the junk's galley.

"All this fuss! I was about to bake potato flour biscuits!" Dore was always certain to be put out at being separated from her work, which she treated with a profound sense of duty and dignity, as if it were a holy calling.

"Visitors from the old country," Pam said, without as much enthusiasm as she might have expected.

Now that the initial excitement had worn off, she dreaded the official hoopla to come. It would be a shame having to deal with a bunch of nosy officials on such a nice day; she was behind in organizing her field notes on the dodos and their island's unique eco-system, and resented an unannounced distraction. Even so, she put on her best official smile, and waved to the ships now tying up to the pier.

Aboard the caravel, which she could now see bore the name *Linnaeus*, a crowd of around twelve eager-looking young people in their late teens gathered at the rail, their faces bright and excited. A pert young woman with a magnificent head of curly brown hair, and an air of confidence, organized them all into a line. She then marched them down the gangway to stand before Pam and her guard. Out of the corner of her eye, Pam noticed that her adopted son Pers was staring at the attractive leader of these visitors as if she were Helena of Troy come to life before his very eyes. *Oh, brother, I know that look, and they call it puppy love!*

"Welcome to Port Looking Glass and the Wonderland Colony," Pam said in English to the young lady, most certainly a down-timer, but wearing up-time style clothes. She might be as old as twenty, and was obviously the one in charge of this gang. "I'm Governor Pam Miller."

The young woman's large, hazel eyes widened as if she was meeting a movie star. "*The Bird Lady of Grantville*! I've been looking so forward to meeting you. You are our inspiration!" The girl's English was slightly accented, but otherwise quite clear.

"That's me, I guess." Pam rolled her eyes at that damned "bird lady" moniker as she always did. Apparently she wasn't ever going to be able to shake it, no matter what her current title and station.

The young woman, now looking a bit embarrassed at her initial starstruck reaction, straightened up and stuck her hand out in the American style, which Pam took. They shook vigorously, the kid had a good, strong grip, and Pam felt herself beginning to like her already, despite her secret wish that they would all haul anchor and go back to where they had come from.

"I am very honored to meet you, Governor Pam! I am Dorothea Weise, a student from the Katharina von Bora College in Quedlinburg. My companions come from various higher learning institutions around Europe, and we represent a variety of subjects we thought might be useful to your efforts—botany, geology, animal husbandry, biology, just to name a few! We have all come to assist you in your work here!"

It was Pam's turn to look goggle-eyed. *Assistants? Someone to help with the mountain of scientific work? Even so, they're all so young!* It was too good to be true. *Be careful what you wish for* . . .

"Pardon me for saying so, but don't you have a teacher, or someone older with you?"

"Oh, of course! We are led by Professor Horst Altmann of the University of Jena."

"Well, where is he?"

"Unfortunately, the sea voyage did not agree with him. He is quite ill, and abed in his cabin. We are very worried about him."

"I'll send our doctor to check on him right away."

Pam felt a bit flummoxed by this unexpected development. *A helpful boon? A potential huge pain in the ass?* Taking a deep breath, she regained her composure, and managed to ask, "Who sent you?"

"Princess Kristina! She is our main sponsor!"

Pam looked northwest-ward in roughly the direction the USE might lie, and muttered under her breath, "Thanks, Princess! Just what I need is a bunch of kids to look after!"

The students, none a day over twenty-one, blinked at her like a pack of confused puppies, unsure, and eager to please. She turned back to them, regarding them skeptically for a moment, but then her stern expression softened to a smile.

"Oh well, you may just prove to be useful. Ms. Weise, you and your group are now the Wonderland Colonial Natural Resource and Wildlife Service."

She handed the stack of field notes she had been carrying to the erstwhile brunette.

"You are obviously a natural leader, so I'm making you the assistant director of said service. You shall report directly to me."

The young woman looked stunned, then a bit embarrassed. "Shouldn't such a high office go to Professor Altman? That would surely be the proper thing."

"On this island, I'm the one who decides what's proper. First, I have to see if I like him or not. Don't worry, I'll give him a fancy title too, and hope he proves useful. But, since he's sick, and you are very plainly bright-eyed and bushy-tailed, I'll start with you. Your offices and laboratories are up there." She pointed to her labs on the hillside behind town, the very sensible-looking building backed by tall, graceful native trees.

"We will have to build some expansions. We can get started on that tomorrow. Read those notes, it's a good place to start." All the students and their newly-designated assistant director nodded enthusiastically, murmuring their thanks.

Pam realized that Pers was still standing beside her with eyes only for the fetching Dorothea Weise, and gave him a quick elbow before he started drooling. A really wonderful idea occurred to her then.

"*Assistant Director* Weise, this is my adopted son and personal assistant, Second Mate Pers of the Royal Swedish Navy, serving in Wonderland's defensive squadron."

Pers turned to her, stunned at his own sudden promotion. Pam gave him a quick grin and whispered in Swedish "You earned it, sweetie."

Turning back to her new helpers, she continued in English, "I am now assigning Pers to be my liaison to your department. To start with, he can escort you to temporary quarters. If you don't speak Swedish, you will need to learn it. Pers will see to your instruction, he speaks fluent English, Thuringian-style German, and a bit of French."

Dorothea was visibly impressed by this, which made Pers look as if he might faint. He stood frozen in place until Pam gave him a gentle shove. Blushing uncontrollably, he stepped forward and bowed dashingly to the pretty new assistant director. The young woman shook his hand while favoring him with a warm smile, which made him turn an even brighter shade of scarlet. The smitten lad managed to find his voice, telling them in English, "Follow me, please," before turning on his heels and marching up the pier toward shore at a considerable speed.

Despite her natural confidence, Dorothea was looking a bit overcome by all this. She paused to thank Pam breathlessly for her kind welcome before leading her group in pursuit of Pers lengthy stride. Pam watched them as they went, grinning like a fool. *Well, this may turn out to be a good thing after all.*

Lieutenant Järv and his men were all chuckling amongst themselves, making bets on how long it would take the newly minted second mate to raise his flag on that piece of lovely German territory he had discovered. Pam couldn't help but chuckle herself, then saw *Kapten* Lundkvist leading a group from the Swedish warship toward her.

"Straighten up, you degenerates," she growled good-naturedly at her guard, "Here comes the official delegation. Pretend you still have some proper military discipline."

"Yes, ma'am!"

Pam laughed as they all stood up ramrod straight, and saluted her in the snappy American naval style they had adopted.

"Governor Pam!" *Kapten* Lundkvist called out to her, his voice full of excitement, his peg leg tapping a jaunty beat as he came rushing ahead of the rest of the contingent. "These people have come from Sweden to re-supply us, and more!"

Pam nodded, and raised her arms wide in a gesture of welcome to all the newcomers as Lundkvist saluted her and fell into place at her side opposite Järv.

"It is lovely to have you all here!" she greeted them in her now fluent Swedish. "Let's get out of the sun before we make our introductions. It will melt you like wax if you let it! Right this way!"

She turned and marched for shore, head held high in what she hoped was suitable gubernatorial bearing.

"To the meeting hall, Governor Pam?" Lundkvist asked her.

She was excited now, her mind racing with thoughts of how to make the best of these new developments. She wanted to hurry, but was careful to match the top speed her chief military officer could manage on his prosthesis.

"No, I have a better idea, gentlemen," she replied with a wide grin.

Reaching shore, she turned left, and led them down the freshly-constructed boardwalk toward the *Dodo's Nest*. This was a spacious seaside saloon that had sprung up on the waterfront like a volunteer potato in a backyard garden, an inevitable feature of an environment like this. It was definitely time for a mug of cool beer, and a shot of that lovely herb-flavored Swedish *akvavit* her people were producing, most likely followed by a few more rounds of the same.

"Official business is thirsty work, gentlemen. Here we do things the Wonderland way."

They all shared a conspiratorial grin, knowing full well that good old Captain Pam could hold her liquor with the best of them. These muckity-mucks from back home wouldn't stand a chance.

∞ ∞ ∞

The leader of the fleet from home was the esteemed *Flotilj-amiral* Gunvald Engstrom, an accomplished, and highly-decorated career military man in his late fifties and, as a "flotilla admiral," currently the highest-ranking Swedish officer in the Indian Ocean. He had been as frosty as a Scandinavian winter wind until Pam had gotten some of her private reserve of Chinese rice wine down him. Now he was just "Gun," and was laughing at her jokes as if he were a favorite uncle doting over a clever niece. Torbjörn, Gerbald, the bosun, and the rest of her men present were all biting back their laughter as they watched Pam work the stern old sea salt, playing him like a hooked salmon ready to jump right into the net.

One of *Dear Gun's* orders was to determine if the colony was being adequately governed by "That American woman," and it was the first to be crossed off the list. He and Pam were already thick as thieves, and he clapped and cheered as the men who had followed her through various dangers regaled him with tales of her courage and prowess in battle.

"Pam, you are like a warrior-woman from the old times, you have a heart of steel!" he proclaimed as she handed him another stein of beer, his ninth or tenth. "I can see that Wonderland is in good hands!"

Pam put on a modest look, and patted her new best friend amiably on the back of his wind-burned hand.

"Oh, Gun, you flatterer! I just do what I have to do for our people, and for the glory of the crown. Remember, as a citizen of the United States of Europe, your king is my emperor, long may he live! *Skål!*" She raised her glass in toast. Mugs clacked noisily around the room. "Now, Gun, tell me more about what you have brought us!"

As it turned out, it was a lot more than she had expected. The emperor had apparently listened to her ideas regarding Sweden missing out entirely on becoming an Asian power in the up-time world. Engstrom's fleet included six fluyts full of colonists and their necessities, three for each of the remaining Wonderland Islands. Looking Glass Bay currently resembled a crowded parking lot. It had been decided that if they meant to make their claims to the Mascarenes stick, they had better have boots on the ground, possession being nine tenths of the law.

Pam was reassured that she would be in charge of the operation, governor to all the Wonderland Isles, just as the princess had requested, and that the new colonies would follow the same eco-friendly farming methods as Port Looking Glass, which made her breathe a big sigh of relief. Three more fluyts carried supplies for Port Looking Glass, including ammunition (*Praise the Lord!*), new varieties of tropical seeds and starts gathered from the Americas that had been donated by several interested botanical societies, more scientific apparatus, and a small library of useful books. Pam was practically beside herself with joy at all the new toys.

The flotilla admiral's personal vessel was a refurbished warship, the *Vaksamhet*, or *Vigilance*, employing a variety of up-time inspired improvements. It was big, fast and deadly, and would help patrol the seas around the colonies along with *Effrayant* and *Muskijl*. Wonderland would be well guarded. Even better, all the ships and towns would be provided with radios, giving them a huge advantage over any would-be threat to their safety. Pam grinned like the Cheshire Cat. It was almost Christmas, and for once she was getting everything she wanted. Pam was on top of the world until Gun said something that let all the air out of her elation.

"Pam, our dear sponsor, Princess Kristina, has personally requested that I ask you when you intend to bring dodos back to Europe? She knows you have a great deal of work to do here, but she is hoping perhaps next year? We will help you accomplish this in any way we can, she stressed that it's very important to her. She is having some kind of a special dodo building made of glass constructed near the University of Jena, I'm sure Professor Altman and his students can give you the details. . . ."

Pam smiled, and nodded politely. The truth was, she hadn't really intended to go back to Europe any time soon, although she knew she must at some point see her family, which now included a new grandson.

"Yes, Gun, another year at best. It will take that long to start the new colonies, and make ready for the voyage." Pam hid her frown by emptying her freshly-poured mug, and motioned to the barman for another. *Back to Grantville. Bah humbug!*

Garrett W. Vance

Chapter Fifty-Three: Time Flies

Port Looking Glass, Wonderland Isles, October 1637

It wouldn't be quite a full year before Pam would make the dreaded journey back to Europe. It was decided they should leave before the end of October for the best weather. *Second Chance Bird*, *Annalise*, and three of the second wave's cargo fluyts laden with goods grown on the islands and some traded for with visiting foreign merchants, would convoy along the coast of Africa, hoping to arrive in the northern spring or summer. Pam's junk was already well-armed, and all the fluyts were fitted with guns, so there wasn't need of a warship escort. *Effrayant*, *Muskijl* and *Vaksamhet* had tangled with pirates of various ilk several times in the last year, and needed to stay to watch over the young colonies. Pam assured Engstrom that her ship and crew could handle just about anything, and if they couldn't, they still had the benefit of speed.

The good-byes were the hardest part. Gerbald and Dore would go with her, of course, as would Torbjörn, Nils the bosun, and most of their original crew. Not too surprisingly, Pers had elected to stay. As it turned out, the lovely and energetic Dorothea turned out to be just as interested in the tall young Swede as he was in her, and wedding bells would likely ring at some point. She hoped she would be back in time for her adopted son's special day.

The arrival of the students had been a great boon after all. Professor Altman, upon recovering from the voyage, turned out to be a pretty nice old guy, not too stuffy for a down-timer scholar. He was a horticulturist, so Pam put him in charge of their experimental agriculture projects. The colonies were now growing around fifty percent of the spices and fruits she had planned for, with more to come.

They were still having trouble figuring out how to get the vanilla pollinated without bees, but it had been done in the 1800s up-time, in that world's version of the Wonderland Islands as it happened, so at some point they would solve the mystery. The native coffee now grew in abundance on the mountainsides, and cinnamon trees from Ceylon were thriving in the island's gentle climate.

Her generosity to the Dutch merchants carrying the Japanese Ayutthaya refugees to Europe had ensured Wonderland a place on all the latest trade maps. Now it wasn't unusual to see more than one junk in Port Looking Glass' harbor.

Their understanding of the island's unique ecologies grew daily, and Pam now had a variety of medicinal plants to bring back to the Grantville Research Center's associate laboratories. She also had half of an encyclopedia's worth of information on the climate, ecologies and cultures of the Indian Ocean. Without feeling quite like Charles Darwin, she was proud of her scientific achievements, and it made her feel a lot better about the center continuing to pay her a small salary while she was gone. She had earned her keep, after all. Money would not be a problem in her future, even without her share of the junk's treasure. Pam had now joined the Grantville rich. And so, resigned to the fact that she really must make the trip, she went about putting her life in Wonderland on hold, vowing to all that she would be back again as soon as she could manage it.

Inevitably the day to leave came. The entire town turned out, lining the shore, the soldiers had to keep them off the pier for fear it would collapse beneath their weight. Pam made a point of walking slowly down the boardwalk, shaking every hand offered. Swedish, Dutch, German,

French, Japanese—they had come from many lands, but now they were all Wonderlanders, just like her. Pam was having a hard time maintaining her composure, the out-flowing of love from her people was overwhelming, like too much of a fine wine; she felt dizzy. At last, she stepped onto the pier and was escorted by the town guard, wearing spiffy new blue uniforms with red and gold trim, out to her waiting ship. Pers and Dorothea waited there, Pam hugged them both and gave them her blessings. They were as much her children as those she had left in Grantville.

"Come back, Momma Pam, okay?" Pers said to her softly, embracing her in his strong arms without any of his former shyness.

"I will, Pers, I promise. I love you, son, and I will think of you every day. I expect you and Dorothea to take good care of things for me while I'm gone, right?"

"You got it." Pers wanted to say more, but the words were tangled in his throat. Pam shushed him, and pulled him down to a level where she could kiss him on the cheek, then gently pushed him back into the waiting arms of his lover.

Doctor Durand stepped up to her, his face as long as a bloodhound's, fancy mustachio at half-mast.

"So, have you decided, Doctor? Are you staying or coming with me back to Europe?"

"Yes, Pam. I intend to stay. These people need me."

"I'm glad. I'll feel better knowing you are here with them. I really do consider you one of my best friends, you know."

"And I you, dear Pam." the doctor bowed deeply, perhaps hoping to hide his tears behind the wide brim of his fancy French hat. Pam grabbed him by the arms and hugged him, an embrace which he returned shyly, patting her gingerly on the back.

Next came the sailors and marines who had been under her command, but intended to remain on duty in Wonderland, lined up at attention. Pam thanked them one by one by name, shaking their hands, and telling them how lucky she was to have had such brave men at her side. For a bunch of tough seamen, there was quite a bit of moisture around the eyes. At the end of the line she came to Captain Lundkvist and Flotilla Admiral Engstrom. They both saluted her, their faces stony as they tried to hide their feelings with military pride.

"You know, you guys don't have to salute me. I'm not governor any more, just crazy old Captain Pam," she told them.

"It doesn't matter," Lundkvist said. "I would follow you to the ends of the Earth if you asked it."

"I know you would, my dear, dear friend. If I were truly going to the ends of the Earth, I wouldn't go without you."

She took his hands, and held them tightly for a long moment, not wanting to embarrass her chief officer with a hug.

"As would I," Engstrom added, his voice freighted with emotion. "You have done great things here, Pam Miller, great things. The crown owes you more than it can ever repay."

"You saying so is payment enough, Gun," she said, taking his hands next. They were strong, and rough, yet trembled slightly. "I am so proud to have served with you, with you all. It has been the greatest experience of my life. I thank you."

She saluted them both, and turned to the gangway before her own tears let loose, making it hard to see where she was going. Gerbald and Dore waited for her at the rail, each taking an arm as they helped guide her up to the castle deck where the bosun and Torbjörn waited.

"Ready to go, Captain?" Torbjörn asked her, taking her hand in loving support.

Second Chance Bird

"Aye, Co-Captain, let's blow this town." She wiped her eyes on a sleeve of her favorite blue-and-gold Chinese coat, and turned to her waiting crew. In her best captain's voice, she bawled out, "Make sail, men, time's-a-wasting! Get the lead out!"

The bosun gave her a wide, yellow-toothed grin, and began barking orders, while the men of the *Second Chance Bird* bent to their tasks, happy to be going to sea again. Pam turned and waved at the crowd as they followed *Muskijl* out of the harbor—she would escort them as far as the southern tip of the island. The sound of cheering faded into the distance as Pam took one last look at Port Looking Glass, reflected perfectly in the mirror bright waters of her harbor.

"I'll be back again my friends, count on me." she whispered, then turned her face into the stiff ocean breeze that blew beyond the bay, inhaling the salt air deeply, as if it were the scent of roses on the bloom.

Garrett W. Vance

Chapter Fifty-Four: Precious Cargo

Castaway Cove, Dodo Island, Wonderland Isles

Pam and her crew grew somber as they sailed around the rocky headland where the *Redbird* had gone down. They all doffed their hats, standing in a moment of silence for First Mate Janvik, who been lost that terrible day. Pam had brought along a bouquet of beautiful native blooms. She threw it into the aquamarine sea when she thought they might be over the final resting place of her sunken ship, while all the men saluted their fallen comrade.

Pam didn't know whether to cry, or whoop with joy as they pulled into the cove that had been their castaway home for so many months. They would stop here to take on the last of their cargo, the most important export of all: live dodos.

Most of their convoy would simply wait at anchor while Pam went ashore with a group of her sailors and marines. The bosun remained on board with a skeleton crew to mind the ship. Dore stayed behind, too, having no interest in revisiting their former refuge.

"I have seen enough of that God-forsaken beach to last a lifetime!" she told them, arms crossed in disgust at the very sight of it.

"We will bring you back some coconuts, my dear!" Gerbald told her, which made Pam let out a very un-ladylike snorting laugh. None of the formerly marooned would ever relish that fruit again! Dore just rolled her eyes, with her trademark disdain.

"You two go enjoy your foolishness. Just be careful, and come back soon!" She gave them both a quick peck on the cheek before descending back to her galley kingdom, head held high with pride.

When the longboat skidded onto the familiar white sands, Pam was the first to jump ashore. Torbjörn followed her, and she took his hand.

"You've never been here before, Lover. You missed out on the whole castaway experience. Come on, I have to show you something." As they walked down the strand Pam picked a few wildflowers along the way.

After a while, they came to the small hill that served as their cemetery. Pam put the flowers on the graves while Torbjörn recited a sailor's prayer in Swedish. They bowed their heads for a few minutes, remembering their missing friends, then Pam led him over to have a closer look at one of the wooden grave markers, weathered by the elements, but still readable. She silently vowed to put up a permanent stone monument here as soon as it could be done. With a spooky grin, she pointed dramatically at the marker in grand Ghost-of-Christmas-Future-style.

"The reports of your death were somewhat exaggerated," she said with a strong drawl. "You are a regular Mark Twain."

"I'm not sure who that was, but that's *my* name on there! I didn't even know I was sick!" he said, bending down to marvel at the sight. They shared a short, bittersweet laugh, and embraced.

"You did a nice job, Pam. It's a lovely bit of painting."

"I missed you a lot, you big oaf. I had already fallen for you even back then. I can't tell you how glad I am to have you here, alive and well."

"I can very much say, *me too*! Thank you, my Pam." He pulled her gently into a passionate kiss.

After a long, blissful while they parted. Pam cocked her head at him with a sly look on her face.

"Want to see my bungalow? We could take a little rest there, if you like."

"Oh, definitely, but I have a feeling we won't be getting much rest."

"No, we'll be busy. Come on." Pam felt giddy, it was like being back at a favorite summer camp, and this time she had a hunky boyfriend, to boot!

∞ ∞ ∞

The camp had weathered its abandonment quite well. The stranded sailors, with nothing else to do, had built to last. Now they were busy sprucing it all up again. Pers and Dorothea intended to make the place a permanent research station, and would be coming to stay in the next few weeks. While the sailors worked on that project, Gerbald and Pam went looking for their old friends, the dodos. The trails were a bit overgrown, but Gerbald's *katzbalger* shortsword made a fine machete, and soon they were making the gentle climb up forested slopes into the mountainous interior.

Finding the dodos was, of course, key to the mission, and they would take as long as they needed. Pam had been adamant on not capturing any of the birds living near Port Looking Glass. An effort had been made to keep those populations wild, despite their lack of natural fear, but the flock here had grown used to humans, and were accustomed to getting handouts, something Pam was counting on. She carried a hefty sack-full of treats for them, enough to lure them back to the beach and the waiting travel cages. She hated to do it, but had no choice. Besides, it was undoubtedly for the best to not keep all her dodo eggs in one basket. A population in far-away Europe would ensure the species' ongoing survival, even if the Wonderlanders somehow failed in their stewardship.

After an hour or so, they were rewarded with the sound of deep, throaty coos. Coming into a clearing, they found a small group of the birds, several mothers and their half-grown chicks. The older birds stared at Pam with their disconcerting yellow eyes. Could that be recognition? She was certain she had seen them before. There were small variations in each individual, and she knew these hens had been amongst her pets back at the beach camp.

"Hey girls, remember me? I got goodies!"

She held out a handful of choice nuts. The dodos let out squawks of pleasure, and rushed over to her, nearly knocking her down with their enthusiasm. They were *big* birds! Gerbald rescued her, carefully pushing them back.

"They haven't forgotten their favorite food source!" he said, laughing.

Pam scattered the nuts on the ground and laughed along as the hens gobbled them up, soon joined by their ungainly, but undeniably cute chicks.

They spent the rest of the afternoon playing Pied Piper, moving through the forest until they had a flock of some thirty dodos following them, including enough males to ensure a breeding population.

"Come along kiddies, it's time to go down to the beach! You get to go on a boat ride!" Pam called out gaily, making Gerbald grin happily at seeing his friend acting silly for a change; it had been too long. The demands of her office had been great, now Pam was free to just be "The Bird Lady" again.

Capturing the dodos for transport was ridiculously easy, just a matter of leaving a trail of breadcrumbs up gangways into temporary travel cages made of bamboo aboard the longboats parked on the beach, from which they would be transferred to the special travel pen Pam had designed and the men had constructed in the main cargo hold of the junk.

The very last dodo, a rather cantankerous older male, decided suddenly that he didn't want to go along with the rest, and began making a fuss, clucking his displeasure and trying to back out of the cage. Pam grimaced at him. With as much gentleness as she could, she firmly placed her leather boot in his rump just below his fluffy tail, and shoved him back in. Gerbald closed the door, and gave her a wry arching of his brow.

"Thank God, nobody's got a camera," Pam said. "Pam Miller kicking an endangered species in the ass would be just the thing for the front page of the newspaper."

The *Second Chance Bird*'s dodo pen lay directly beneath the large hatch doors of the spacious hold, where the birds, and the many potted trees and plants accompanying them, would have fresh air and sunlight for at least part of the day. By midnight, the dodos were safely tucked away, and everyone caught a bit of sleep. They sailed at dawn, Pam keeping vigil on the castle deck, watching the island that had been her home for so long recede into the distance until it disappeared over the azure horizon.

"I'll see to it you get back here, if you wish it," Torbjörn told her from his place at the wheel.

"I wish that, very much," Pam replied, giving him a smile and a kiss on the cheek before going down to her cabin to catch up on lost sleep. It would be a long voyage, without much to do.

∞ ∞ ∞

The days passed by, one slipping into the next as they headed west, Antarctica to their south, Africa to their north. They would sail as the crow flies if the winds allowed, taking the most direct route possible. No one seemed much worried about attack from the famed Barbary pirates or potentially hostile European forces, anyone taking on the *Second Chance Bird* would find themselves regretting it.

Pam often sat on the deck with her feet hanging down into the hold so she could watch her charges, listening to the throaty coos and clacking beaks of the dodos emanating from below. The birds had adjusted well enough to shipboard life, and seemed content to eat as many fruits and nuts as she could give them, to the point where they were actually gaining weight and beginning to resemble the fat and spoiled captive dodo that must have been the model for John Tenniel's illustrations.

The thought of taking these creatures out of their natural habitat and dragging them all the way back to Europe didn't sit well with her now that she was actually doing it. But, she had promised the princess, and there was no way around that. It was better she did it herself than trust it to anyone else, if something went wrong it would be on her conscience. So, she was making the long trip "home," when she would much rather be back in Wonderland. Pam simply chocked it all up to fate, and resigned herself to it, instead of fretting the way the old Pam would have. Her actions mattered to a lot more people than she ever could have conceived of back up-time, here was a job that only she could do, a need only she could fill. Captain Pam smiled contentedly into the fading daylight over the South Atlantic as the *Second Chance Bird* and its precious cargo plowed on toward Europe.

Chapter Fifty-Five: Mission Accomplished

Hamburg, United States of Europe, February 1637

It was on a bright, unseasonably warm, winter day that the *Second Chance Bird* came to the end of its long voyage around Africa. There were a great many stares from the shore as the fancifully-painted junk headed toward Hamburg harbor, flying a bright, new copy of the dodo flag of the Wonderland Colonies that Dore had designed, crewed by darkly-tanned Swedes, some with their blonde hair bleached nearly white by the tropical sun. They had accumulated a large fleet of various craft following behind them, curiosity seekers anxious to see what such an odd-looking foreign vessel was doing plying the cold waters of the North Sea.

Pam, knowing in advance from the radio that there would be some kind of an official welcome wagon waiting, put on her favorite black Chinese dress, a sexy, side-slitted affair, silk with a filigree of gold flowers. She nodded to herself approvingly, knowing that she looked pretty damn good in the racy little thing. Her necklace of precious "pirate pearls" went on next, and with a wry smile she strapped on her pistol belt, enjoying the feeling of being a bona fide bad ass. The final touch was letting her long, flyaway hair free of its pony tail, a wild mane for the lioness. She felt very pleased to be making herself part of the spectacle. The shy Pam of old was long gone.

There was a festive gathering on the dock they were headed for, including a brightly-painted banner proclaiming "Welcome Back, Bird Lady!" which made Pam laugh aloud. The moniker didn't rankle her any more. *If you can't beat them join them. The Bird Lady I shall be.*

As they tied up, a USE Naval band started playing. It took her a moment to realize the song was "Country Road." Pam smiled at the choice. At this point it would be kind of nice to see their little circle of West Virginia again. She chuckled happily to see that Princess Kristina was jumping up and down waving crazily, backed by a mob of Grantville students from the old Summer Nature Program. Pam thought the girl looked quite a bit taller, and maybe a little more careworn than before, but she was definitely still a goofy kid. Suddenly, Pam realized who was standing behind her—it was her son Walt and his wife Crystal, and she was holding . . . the baby! Pam really had become a grandma, and while she was thrilled, she had to quell an inner voice that shrieked, *But I'm much too young!*

The next few minutes passed in a blur as she was engulfed in hugs from Crystal, and kissed her new grandson, who pulled her hair and laughed, which made Pam love him all the more.

"Boy oh boy, has your ole' granny got some stories to tell *you*, my lad!" she told him as she looked into his bright eyes—they were the Miller stormy gray, which was good, but thank God he had his mother's lush red hair!

Walt was quiet, as usual, but they smiled and embraced. Hopefully, she could make things right with him this time. Eventually, the initial fervor died down, and Kristina approached her, a shy smile on her face.

"I'm glad you made it home, Pam. I was worried," Kristina told her in her perfect, yet quaintly-accented, English.

Second Chance Bird

Pam smiled, and replied in her perfect yet—according to her boyfriend—quaintly-accented Swedish. "It was touch and go for a while. I'll tell you the whole story when we get a chance."

Kristina raised her eyebrows, impressed with Pam's mastery of her own native tongue, and continued in the same, "I should like very much to hear it!'

Pam's face took on a somber cast. "Some good people died making this happen, and I need you to hear their tales. We owe them a lot."

Kristina bowed her head, her face also grown somber. "I knew that would probably happen from the start, and I'm very sorry to hear it. Even so, I still feel that the cause was worth it. . . . Do you, Pam?"

Pam marveled at how someone so young could seem like such a wise old adult at times. "Yes, I do, Kristina, I do. It was all worth it." Pam made her face brighten and took on a cheerier tone. "Sorry for being a downer, there will be time to mourn lost friends later. Today is for celebration, so let's cheer up!"

Kristina brightened as well, but Pam could still see pain in her eyes. She had heard the news about the death of her mother, the queen, and knew Kristina had suffered much in the years since they first met at Cair Paravel back in Grantville. Pam reached into her trusty old rucksack, which a madly grinning Torbjörn held for her, ecstatic at meeting his beloved princess in person. Pam pulled out a finely-carved Chinese box made of teak. With a bow and a flourish, she gave it to the princess.

"I have some additions to your crown jewels for you, a gift from the crew of the *Second Chance Bird*. It's *real* pirate treasure, which we captured from *real* pirates!"

Kristina's eyes took on a happy sparkle, bright enough to match the jewelry and gems that waited within. "Really? Pirate treasure? How grand, thank you! I wish to thank them all myself as soon as I have the chance," she exclaimed with delight, hugging the box to her chest.

"They would like that, very much. You are one popular kid!"

"I have something for you, too, Pam," she said, switching into English. She carefully handed the precious box to one of her guards, then raised her hand to get everyone's attention.

"The race to save the dodo is over, and just like the 'caucus race' in Lewis Carroll's wonderful book, everybody wins." With a grin that nearly split her perpetually pale face, Kristina reached into her pocket, and pulled out a silver thimble.

" '*We beg your acceptance of this elegant thimble.*' " Kristina quoted the Dodo as she placed it in Pam's hand. It had the Tenniel version of the bird etched on it, along with an inscription in English that read *Thank you for saving us—The Dodos.*

"You did it, Pam. Only you could. We are all very proud of you."

Pam laughed, her sharp gray eyes growing misty with emotion. "Yeah, I guess I really did. And I couldn't have done it without you pushing me out the door. You are the hero here just as much as me, kiddo."

Pam felt the weight of all she had been through, all she had worked so hard for, lifting off her shoulders. It seemed like a dream already. Her hand shook, as she gazed down at the pretty thimble, shining brightly under the northern spring sun, blurring as her eyes filled with joyful tears.

Kristina saw that her friend was feeling a bit overwhelmed, so she stepped forward and embraced her in a hug that would do any bear proud. The gawky young girl was stronger than she looked. Pam hugged her back, just as she would her own children, her heart full of pride at their accomplishment. They had changed the world for the better, a small change, perhaps, but one that would reverberate through the new centuries ahead, a second chance for a funny-looking bird that was no longer doomed to extinction, not in Pam Miller's world, anyway.

"Everybody wins," Pam whispered.

Second Chance Bird

In the hold of the *Second Chance Bird*, a dodo squawked, wondering what was holding up feeding time.

THE END

Printed in Poland
by Amazon Fulfillment
Poland Sp. z o.o., Wrocław